When I get to the last page of a good book, I want to continue being part of the story. I don't want it to be over. That is how I felt with Kathleen's book, *A Gift of Love*.

The story is gripping, the heroine is a delightful friend, and the way her faith in God carries her through is miraculous. This book is well worth reading, especially to those who have been in abusive marriages. To those who have not, it brings an understanding of what some people experience.

The fact that Alison survives a tragic accident and all that happens to her, and comes out the other side with her faith in tact is due to her abiding trust in a loving God. You too can be acquainted with God's peace by reading this book.

Sharon Fraser, author and teacher

From danger to suspense; from love encounters to God encounters, Kathleen Reichert's book, *A Gift of Love*, has it all. Don't tell me this is just a "Chick Book!" There's intrigue in every chapter. You must read this book with all its twists and turns.

Honestly, the best part for me was the portrayal of a life filled with infectious prayer, and I mean infectious. I found myself reading every prayer out-loud to receive direction and hearing each loving answer that came from God. It's about how Alison was able to walk out of her own personal HELL. Get this book into the hands of any wounded soul and watch what will happen.

Jim Paul - pastor, author and Conference Speaker.

I so enjoyed reading A Gift of Love, an epic story, which is, in some ways, too true to life. It's a tale about a woman, very much like many women today, who look at life differently. Even when things looked their worst, Alison continues to believe in a promise of something better. Through difficult situations, betrayal, deception, criticism, and circumstances out of her control, she continues to press into God, continually believing in the power of "real love."

I was delighted by the way my dear sister in the Lord, Kathleen, set the stage in Hamilton and wove the life of Phoebe Palmer in the 1857 revival in Hamilton as part of the intrigue of this story. The truth stated about "that day" and a "new day" to come for Hamilton brought a great sense of reality to the tale of a battered woman who overcomes by the grace of God.

Through out this book, you will find a scarlet thread woven of faith, hope and a trust in God. As you share the twists and turns of Alison's life, may her prayers become yours as you receive answers and comfort while praying along with her. You may even find that trusting in God while in the face of adversity, abuse and what seems like destruction, will bring your destiny.

Coming from a broken home and marriage myself, I identified with Alison as I read every chapter. If you are in a difficult situation, I pray for an impartation of faith to overcome be upon your life as you share this story of tests and triumphs. I pray that you will realize, in the reading of this fiction, that as truth resounds within its pages, you will apply God's truth in your own life as Alison did and that you will be set free.

Pastor Mave Moyer
Governing Official to the Network
Eagle Worldwide Ministries

A GIFT OF love

For Jean

Pay special attention to chapter 16.

K Reichert

KATHLEEN REICHERT

A GIFT OF LOVE
Copyright © 2012 by Kathleen Reichert

All rights reserved. Neither this publication nor any part of this publication may be reproduced or transmitted in any form or by any means, electronic or mechanical, including photocopying, recording or any information storage and retrieval system, without permission in writing from the author.

This is a work of fiction. Names, characters, places and incidents either are the product of the author's imagination or are used fictitiously, and any resemblance to actual persons, living or dead, businesses, companies, events, or locales is entirely coincidental.

ISBN: 978-1-77069-737-9

Printed in Canada

Word Alive Press
131 Cordite Road, Winnipeg, MB R3W 1S1
www.wordalivepress.ca

WORD ALIVE PRESS
Just Write!

FSC — MIX — Paper from responsible sources — FSC® C016245

Library and Archives Canada Cataloguing in Publication

Reichert, Kathleen, 1951-
    A gift of love / Kathleen Reichert.

ISBN 978-1-77069-737-9

    I. Title.

PS8635.E3958G54 2012   C813'.6   C2012-905990-0

table of contents

Acknowledgements	vii		Twenty-one	145
Introduction	ix		Twenty-two	151
One	1		Twenty-three	159
Two	9		Twenty-four	167
Three	15		Twenty-five	175
Four	23		Twenty-six	185
Five	29		Twenty-seven	191
Six	37		Twenty-eight	197
Seven	43		Twenty-nine	205
Eight	51		Thirty	211
Nine	59		Thirty-one	221
Ten	65		Thirty-two	229
Eleven	73		Thirty-three	235
Twelve	81		Thirty-four	247
Thirteen	89		Thirty-five	255
Fourteen	95		Thirty-six	267
Fifteen	101		Thirty-seven	275
Sixteen	107		Thirty-eight	283
Seventeen	115		Thirty-nine	289
Eighteen	119		Forty	295
Nineteen	129		Forty-one	301
Twenty	137		Forty-two	309

acknowledgements

My first thanks always go to my God and Father. I believe He initiated this story and encouraged me to complete it. Sometimes I thank God by blowing Him a kiss. I put my hand on my lips, then I fling my hand heavenward as a silent thank you in sign language.

My husband, Lynn, deserves more thanks than I can express. He has been patient to listen to my ideas and has encouraged me to pursue my dream. He has given me space and time that could have been his. Lynn has listened to me read chapters, given advice for changes, and read the whole novel out loud to me. When I lost enthusiasm, he encouraged me to carry on.

Stan Kirkham encouraged me to pursue art, so he has to be given thanks for a portion of this book as well. Some day I'll be able to thank him in person when I see him in heaven.

Monique Berry first edited this novel. At the end of the first draft, she embellished the last page with stickers, including a bow, roses, and Proverbs 16:3: "Commit thy works unto the Lord, and thy thoughts shall be established." These were her written comments: "Wow! What a pleasure it has been to sit in the passenger seat of this novel with you at the wheel! A great beginning and a great ending. I looked forward to this day for a long time. I look forward—even more—to seeing your dream printed, published, and held by many."

Jennifer Kruis, my massage therapist, critiqued this story without expecting any rewards or acknowledgement. Thank you, Jennifer, for all the time and unselfish effort you contributed to encourage this story to survive.

Thank you Donna Durek for critiquing the final revisions, not expecting to receive any rewards.

The excerpt from the book *Hinds Feet in High Places*, by Hannah Hurnard, was useful to express the premise of this book better than any of my own words ever could.

Betty Maltz, author of *Prayers That Are Answered*, was an encouragement to me when I started to keep a journal, and I used some of her words in this novel.

Thanks goes to Emily Matthews, author of the poem "A Gift of Love," for the use of her poem and for confirmation of the title I had already chosen.

Thank you Janette Oke for your encouraging words:

"I have completed reading your manuscript, and you certainly have tackled some serious and contemporary issues. I have no problem with the way you have dealt with them and trust that your book, when published, will be a source of help for people who are going through like situations.

"I do wish you the every success in your writing carrer.

"God bless!"

I send many thanks to the three main people who gave their time to read the whole manuscript, and then gave their encouraging endorsements: Sharron Fraser, Mave Moyer, and Pastor Jim Paul.

I would like to thank Audrey Dorsch for her efficient editing, and for making this a learning experience as well as an enjoyable one.

introduction

Before you begin reading, I wish to express why this book is important for married people and for those who are marriageable. God created the matrimonial union so that two people would be one and never be divided.

This paraphrased scripture from *The Message* (Mark 10: 5–9) says that marriage is an art of God's design:

> *Moses wrote this command [allowing divorce] only as a concession to your hardhearted ways. In the original creation, God made male and female to be together. Because of this, a man leaves father and mother, and in marriage he becomes one flesh with a woman—no longer two individuals, but forming a new unity. Because God created this organic unity of the two sexes, no one should desecrate his art by cutting them apart.*

As an artist, I can truly say that I wouldn't want one of my works of art to be desecrated by being cut in half.

If your marriage is in trouble, or you are contemplating divorce, please seek God's counsel. There still may be hope.

The passages that Alison writes about listening for the Lord's voice are taken from my own personal journals, which I have kept since 1994. When I wanted to insert a journal passage, I sought the Lord concerning which journal to use and then opened the book at random, except for one birthday message, the message after the proposal, and the one titled, *Believe and be Satisfied*. The first passage my eyes fell upon was the one I felt God wanted me to use. The message seemed to always fit the story line. None of the passages have been altered, except for punctuation and when Rolph was substituted in place of Lynn, my husband.

I hope you not only enjoy this novel but that you can learn something from it for your life. If you think there maybe a potential story within you that's waiting to be written, I encourage you to take the challenge of creating your own masterpiece.

chapter one

"I've been living with Reb." It was a husky female voice on the phone.

"What?" Alison yelled into the receiver. Her hand instinctively flew to her abdomen as if to guard her little one from the shock.

"Reb Steele. Ya know, your husband?"

"Who are you, and what do you want?"

"My name is Christine. I want Reb and I'm going to get him. And if I hear that you make things rough for him in leaving your marriage, I'll get ya back."

Alison felt desperation crowd around her. Dizzy, she slumped against the side of the seven-foot antique bookcase.

She roused herself when she heard Christine chuckle then say, "We made a little girl together. She's two and looks just like her daddy." Christine's amusement stopped. Alison heard a soft blowing sound as if the caller was puffing on a cigarette. "Now I'm pregnant with his second child."

Losing strength, Alison let the phone fall onto the lime-coloured sofa cushion. Reality slapped her. *Our baby is not Reb's first child— maybe his third?* Her stomach pulled tight.

Betrayal.

Rejection.

Regret.

Alison's ears buzzed, so she dropped her head between her slender thighs, her auburn curls brushing her ankles.

The line stayed open; Alison continued to hear the woman's amusement. She straightened up again, using all her inner strength to pick up the phone. "You can have him!" The receiver clanked into place.

"So, Reb, once 'Rebel for the Lord,' how you've changed." Alison's voice sounded strained to her ears.

Oh God, I feel so stupid for letting Reb deceive me. Every time he was absent from our bed, why did I believe him when he vowed that no woman was involved?

Her mind jumped to one incident involving a woman, more than three years ago. She replayed the scene of Reb flinging his sandy mane as if he had won some bizarre medal. He had told his story, ignoring the candlelit table.

"I went into a variety store. A handsome broad said, 'Hey there, good lookin', I haven't seen you before.' When I asked if she greeted all the men that way, she said, 'No. Only ones with bedroom eyes like yours.' Then she asked if I wanted to see her black lace undies." He laughed with his head bobbing up and down like a seagull guarding its find. His chest rose as Alison's head drooped. "I can't help if women are attracted to me," he added.

"Why are you telling …?" Alison remembered stopping mid-sentence when she had considered the possible repercussions.

"Jealous, Allie? It makes me laugh seein' your eyes turn from blue to green." He had tweaked her cheek roughly then dug into the meal.

Alison suspected now that being upfront was his tactic to hide the whole story and that he had been physically involved with this woman. She paused to calculate. A two-and-a-half-year-old child could be the result, if conceived around the time of his boasting. Deep sobs shook her chest and belly.

Alison regained her composure. *No more! I won't let him back into my life again. I'll change the locks!*

Alison forced her thoughts to change. She focused on her twenty-sixth birthday coming up tomorrow, Sunday. Despite her grief over Reb's confirmed departure from their marriage, she felt the grip in her chest lessen as she contemplated being in church with her brothers and sisters in the Lord.

She smiled at the ticklish kick of the little person growing inside her. A son or daughter would arrive in about four and a half or five months. She planned to love and raise this child the best that she could in the ways of the Lord.

***

Alison drove into the church's ploughed parking lot after the late-March snowstorm. The dark western sky predicted another heavy drop before the day's end. Alison pushed aside the thought of broken vows and decided to be as upbeat as possible. Because her coat hid her expanding abdomen, she believed no one had guessed she was pregnant. *No one will know of my inner turmoil, either. I will smile, talk pleasantly to everyone, listen to the sermon, and take notes as usual.*

The serene, comforting warmth of the sanctuary welcomed Alison as she slipped into her usual pew just before the first lively song. After the welcome from the pulpit, joyful music, announcements, and offering, Pastor Ed McAlester began his sermon. His enthusiastic message told of an end-time revival coming to Hamilton, to Canada, and then to other nations.

"This will be a last great revival, where many will be saved and will witness healings. Since almost everyone has some ailment, either a serious condition or a small irritating ailment, acts of healing would be the best way to get people's attention, don't you think?"

Alison pondered this last statement. She nodded as she envisioned herself sitting in a crammed auditorium with people in line to give testimony, carrying crutches or braces or pushing empty wheelchairs.

Her pastor's voice registered again. "A revival, or should I say, an awakening, happened in Hamilton one hundred and twenty years ago in 1857. In our modern day of 1977, it is difficult to picture what our city would have been like as the steel industry started. The streets were not jammed with cars, but horse drawn carriages clattered along the roads and women's hoop skirts brushed against wooden sidewalks.

"The revival was significant, yet an unfinished work. Although the Holy Spirit was obviously present, no physical healings were recorded.

"A married couple named Walter and Phoebe Palmer, who were living in New York state, conducted meetings in Ontario."

Alison's ears perked at the mention of the name Palmer. That was her maiden name.

"They preached in Georgetown and Oakville, and then on their way back to New York City, they stopped in Hamilton, a city of twenty-three thousand at that time. It certainly is larger today with approximately three hundred and ten thousand.

"They stayed with some friends overnight. While they were here, two Methodist ministers asked them to speak in their churches, sharing their conviction of a needed revival. On the first night, sixty-five people attended, and twenty-one of them became believers. Those two engagements turned into six weeks of meetings.

"As Phoebe Palmer spoke, the fire of the Holy Spirit came upon the people."

Maybe she's my great-great grandmother. I remember my father telling stories of his grandparents. They were from New York State, but I'm not sure which part. I know my ancestry includes preachers, musicians, and artists. Wouldn't it be a surprise if I were related to these Palmers? She returned her attention to the sermon.

"By the first Monday evening, October nineteenth, over one hundred people were converted. In less than two weeks, nearly four hundred people accepted salvation. People of every rank, both labourers and professionals, attended. Young and old, rich and poor, all prayed together.

"Mayor John Moore was present and gave his testimony. Then the meetings became the talk of the town. They generally started at seven in the morning and ended at ten in the evening with hundreds in attendance. Even factory workers came during the noon hour."

Pastor Ed used this moment to drive a point home to the congregation: "After twenty minutes into a sermon, I've seen some of you looking at your watches. I'm wondering how many of you would sit through one of those meetings. Will you be ready when revival comes to our city again?"

Alison looked at a friend in the same pew as they raised their eyebrows; they knew they were guilty.

The pastor continued. "Usual church meetings with formal sermons were replaced by inspired testimonies. The Palmers knew that God had sent them to Hamilton.

"The prayers of those saints, I believe, laid the groundwork for a harvest of repentant souls in the coming last, great revival. Wouldn't it be wonderful if we were all chosen to be part of this experience?"

Alison's spirit called out YES!

***

On the way to her parents' home, Alison pondered how to tell them that her marriage was definitely over. Janette and Bill didn't even know that Reb had been gone for the past three months. She could only guess how concerned they might be about her news.

Although preoccupied over how to relay her story, Alison approached their home for her birthday lunch relatively calm. *I shouldn't feel ashamed that my marriage is over. At least I'll be able to tell Mom that I have biblical grounds for ending my marriage—adultery.*

Although there was a nip in the air, her father was waiting on the porch when Alison stepped out of her car. An inquisitive look crossed his face as he hugged her and gave the usual birthday greeting then asked, "Are you alone?"

"Yes, Dad. I'll explain everything to you and Mom together."

As Alison entered, her mother sang out her birthday wish. Janette looked past her daughter and saw that she was alone. Alison looked at the shiny hardwood floor and said in a barely audible voice, "Reb won't be coming."

"Has there been a fly in the ointment?" her father asked.

She could see that her mother had the table set for four, adorned with her special dishes decorated with pink and blue roses. A tantalizing aroma filled the air.

"I was going to tell you everything after we'd eaten, but I suppose now would be best." Just then Alison had an idea of how to break the news. "Mom, Dad, I have two things to tell you. One will make you happy; the other will probably cause you concern."

Alison's dad took her coat. "Doesn't she have a sense of the dramatic, Mother?"

Janette's gaze concentrated on her daughter's beautiful face with high cheek bones like her own mother's. "I want to hear the happy news first, honey."

Looking from her mother to her dad and back, she announced, "You are going to have another grandchild this-summer. August twentieth is the due date."

Her parents laughed together. Janette clapped her hands, and then left them clasped on her chest as if she cuddled the baby already. Her attractive face, with straight nose and full lips, turned sombre.

"Is the bad news that Reb is not happy with thoughts of providing for a child?" Janette asked. It was well known that he kept jobs for a short time only.

"He doesn't know we're expecting. He's been gone for months."

Her mother gasped as she shook her head. "But it's your birthday!"

Alison could not see her mother's face clearly any longer, for her tears started in earnest. "Mom, this isn't the only birthday he's been away." She remembered three years ago when he had said he was going on a motorcycle trip by himself to Virginia. *He could have been with Christine then, or someone else.*

"I didn't know," Janette said.

Alison fought to get the words past her aching throat. "Mom, Dad, my marriage has been very strained; now it's over. Reb has been staying with another woman, and she believes she's pregnant with his second child."

"His *second* child with her?" asked Bill.

Alison nodded.

Her dad stepped back. "But now that you're pregnant, won't he care when you tell him about his legitimate child?"

"I'm not sure, Dad." Alison's tears coursed down her flushed cheeks.

"What will you do?" To know the action she would take was her dad's usual way.

"I'm packing his belongings today, and tomorrow I'm continuing to teach."

Bill's head dipped as he raised his eyebrows. "Tell me what's been happening, Alison. Why would Reb need to find another woman? Weren't you meeting all his needs?"

"That sounds accusatory," Alison blurted out. "You're siding with Reb!"

Janette's mascara ran in black streaks down her cheeks, mingled with tears for her youngest child. "Forgive your father. It's just that it's such a shock, and seems so impossible. You had one or two times of trouble, or at least we didn't hear about more." Her mother usually tried to fix the rough spots in her family's lives.

Alison's words came out in starts and stops. "I didn't want to tell you all my troubles. There've been so many. I didn't want to worry you." Hoping that would be enough detail, she let her eyes drift to the food, even though she didn't feel like eating.

They did manage to eat, after much-needed prayer. Alison asked them not to sing happy birthday this time. None of them were interested in trivial talk, either.

Her mother's face twisted into a look of worry. "You'll need extra rest now. If you're anything like me, you'll feel tired and nauseated on and off throughout your pregnancy. Let's get you home. Actually, your father and I can help you pack Reb's belongings." Janette turned to Bill, and Alison saw her mother give her dad "the look," which may have compelled him to agree.

"Thanks, Mom, for your concern and help. I knew you would understand and support my decision." She ignored her father as she stuffed down the hurtful thing he had said.

When they arrived at the apartment, there was no indication that Reb had been there. It didn't take long for the three of them to pack his clothes and so-called toys, race-car trophies, and eight-track tapes into an old suitcase and garbage bags. Her mom and dad left with wrinkled brows.

After watching their car diminish as they drove down the street, a familiar sinking feeling of abandonment hit, causing Alison to stand motionless.

chapter two

Alison could clearly hear the steady ticking of the black walnut clock that Reb had made with her dad. It could have been as comforting as hearing the grandfather clock at Grandma and Grandpa's house when she was a contented youngster. She looked at the blue-and-red cross-stitched motto on the wall opposite the clock. For the millionth time, it begged to be read. "Love isn't love until you give it away."

Although the needlework colours were fading and the linen background yellowed, she cherished this wedding present from her grandmother. When Grandma Palmer handed her the treasure, she said, "This was given to me on my wedding day, and its truth guided me through forty-five fulfilling years of marriage. I want to give it to you so you will be reminded to give love regardless of the cost. If love is given in return, you'll know that it's a love that will last for eternity."

Kathleen Reichert

One genuine gift I've received from Reb is my baby. I'm truly thankful for this child. She massaged her abdomen. *Life isn't a picnic, that's for sure. It's more like a full-course meal: some food benefits and some becomes refuse. Yeah, just like the trauma at Lake Moses five years ago.*

***

The holiday that Reb had promised materialized. It was to be a belated honeymoon. They left from Hamilton for their motor trip through the U.S. to British Columbia and spent many enjoyable days camping, driving, and stopping at points of interest. Alison's favourite stop was at Yellowstone Park. They watched Old Faithful blow right on time, saw wildlife up close, stood just a few feet away from a huge moose, and viewed at least a million stars in the Milky Way while lying on the grass, side by side.

They reached their destination, and trouble started to brew when they looked out to sea and Alison didn't express enough enthusiasm over the magnificent Pacific Ocean. She had imagined huge waves crashing onto immense boulders as the tide rolled in. Instead, a calm, wide beach surprised her with one-foot waves lapping onto drab grey sand. Reb glared at her. When she asked, "Is anything wrong?" he replied with a "humph." The look on his face made her refrain from making another attempt; she bowed inwardly to his dark mood. Now her task was to guess what had caused his hostile silence this time.

A couple of days later, their journey home took them through the state of Washington. Deep crevices divided the dry mesa into brown buttes, making the whole scenery desert-like, especially since the temperature hovered near 105 degrees. Her skin felt irritated as the furnace-like air blasted through the open window of the '61 van, making her torso prickle with sticky sweat. She leaned her head back and closed her eyes.

Reb's angry voice made her jump. "Is that all you can do is sleep? After all I paid for this trip, you could at least try to stay awake!"

Forcing her eyes wide open, she looked out the side window, away from his glowering face.

A few moments later he ordered, "Look on the map and find the nearest lake. It's getting hotter than hell in here."

She scanned the map retrieved from the glove compartment. "Here's one, and it's close by."

"Let's go then." He allowed her to give directions.

They approached Lake Moses, saw the crowded beach and the cement-block change house. He backed into one of the last available parking spots.

"Well, what are you waiting for?" Reb barked in his usual controlling way.

With a towel draped over her shoulder, Alison hurried to change into her one-piece suit with the bright sunflowers that ran from shoulder strap to hip. In just a few minutes she stepped out of the dark change room into the glaring sun. At first she was blinded by its white light as high noon approached. When she was able to focus on the parking lot, the van was not in its parking spot. *Why didn't Reb tell me he was going to leave? Oh, maybe he just decided to get something to eat and drink.*

Putting her irritation aside, she splashed into the lake and forced her mind off of the troubling situation. Every five to ten minutes she looked in the direction of the parking lot. Failing to see the faded red Volkswagen, her uneasiness mounted. She asked a sun bather for the time and found that an hour had passed. The temperature stayed in the 100s and the strong sun's rays made Alison squint at the children playing in the shallow water.

The lake itself was a tranquil scene of greenish blue ripples with the opposite shore just a short distance away. Inside her mind a war raged. *Oh, God, what is happening? Has Reb abandoned me? Hold on, Miss Panic; he could have had car trouble. How long should I wait before contacting the police, or sheriff, or whatever they call the officers in this state?*

She sat on the beach for hours, dipping into the lake from time to time to cool off. Her fair skin was becoming red. The burning sensation was secondary to the ache in her chest. She swallowed repeatedly, hoping this would stop the tears from pooling in her eyes and sliding down her cheeks. *What will the other bathers think? I have to get my mind on something else to curb these terrible thoughts. Think; think of something other than being left behind. And if I draw attention, and Reb sees people gathering around me, I'll be in even worse trouble.* Involuntarily, her breath was coming in short pants. Dizziness and a buzzing headache nauseated her. *I wonder if these are symptoms of sunstroke.* Panic consumed her.

She trudged from the beach, making slow progress as the dry sand gave way under her feet. The need to avoid illness urgently took over the fear that gnawed at her mind.

She cried out to God: *Help me, Father. I know that You would never leave me. Please help me to make it through this ordeal. I believe You would've chosen a better life for me, but I didn't even seek Your wisdom when I said yes to Reb's proposal. Please give me guidance on how to survive today, as I surrender everything into Your hands. Amen.*

Alison yearned for this calamity to end and longed to be home again, but her immediate need was to quench her intense thirst. As she neared the change house, the refreshment stand on the other side wakened her hunger. The tormenting aroma of grilled hotdogs made her empty stomach growl. She had no money. All she possessed was a bathing suit, a towel, and the clothes she'd been wearing.

Anxious to see how God was going to see her through, she hurried to the snack bar. "Could I have a cup of water, please?"

The young man behind the counter replied abruptly. "Water's only free for customers who order food."

Alison looked down at her feet. It took courage to tell even a small part of what was happening. "My husband dropped me off at the beach and then left. That was several hours ago. He didn't leave me any money."

A nice girl behind the counter intervened and offered Alison a cup of water. She downed it, and the girl poured another. "I'm sure you'd like a salad and a hotdog, too."

"Yes, please. Thank you for your generosity." She believed God was working through this intuitive teenager. "You're an answer to prayer."

After gulping three cups of water, Alison began to feel revived. She raised her head to the heavens to offer a silent thanks. Standing at the counter, eating the precious hotdog and salad slowly, she believed she'd survive this latest cruelty.

Further expressing her concern, the kind girl asked, "Would you like to use the phone in the park office to call someone?"

"If I need to use the phone, I'll be back. Thanks again for your kindness; the food sure hit the spot."

The girl smiled and winked her reply.

Alison turned to look for a place to rest and think. *He did have a strange look on his face before I left to change. Did I say something to upset him? I can't remember anything out of the ordinary.*

The sun, now sending rose-coloured rays in every direction, signalled the time for bathers to leave. Grey storm clouds gathered while thunder sounded in the distance like the rumbling of an old man's belly. The wind started to blow fiercely, followed by pelting rain. Alison returned to the shelter of the change house. Every ten minutes or so she stuck her head out to look at the parking lot. Large droplets pounded the concrete and sand. *From now on, the smell of wet, hot pavement may trigger the memory of this agonizing time.*

After the thunder and rain ceased, the Volkswagen recklessly entered the gravel parking lot. Relief mixed with fear. Her inner anger threatened to expose itself, but she dare not express it if she wanted to see Ontario. Although Alison had been praying on and off these last nine hours, dread filled her soul.

"Why did you leave me, Reb? And without a word or money?" She wanted to add: This is the cruellest thing you've ever done.

"You're such a b----," he roared. The last stragglers turned their heads in their direction.

Alison knew from experience that she must end the questions. Silence reigned again, which was fine with her because she didn't care to talk to him, either. The wound had gone deep, and she feared that it would never heal. Tears flowed for two hours as she held her sobs inside. The ache in her throat was unbearable. Alison kept her face turned to the window to hide her watery eyes. For the next two days Reb drove constantly, stopping only for gas, washroom breaks, coffee, and snacks. No apology or conversation followed.

***

Her musing ended as an urgent thought burst to the forefront as if commanded—barricade the door! Alison secured a kitchen chair under the doorknob, then piled Reb's luggage and stuffed garbage bags, filling the space from door to opposite wall.

Soon after she finished the chore, a key rattled in the lock. Alison's heart flipped over with panic, but Reb wasn't able to open the door, not even a crack.

With a phoney sweet tone, his muffled words penetrated the closed door, "Alison, what's keeping the door from opening?"

Unable to keep her voice from shaking, she said, "I don't want you to come in, Reb, so I blocked it."

"But, Alison, I've a birthday present for ya. I want to give ya a birthday kiss and make up. I've missed you so much."

The previous quiver disappeared as her anger rose. "I won't accept anything from you. I'm finished with this marriage because of you and Christine."

"I don't know how you found out about Christine, but it's over and I wanna new start with you, babe."

Her voice became even stronger. "Not this time! Leave or I'll call the police."

"Open this door or I'll break it down!"

"I'm calling the police now!" She headed for the phone in the living room.

Before she could finish dialling, she heard a crash of splintering wood. The chair fell to pieces. Reb burst through the opening then kicked aside the suitcases. He looked like a deranged man, bulging eyes glaring at her out of a scarlet face. The Christ-like nature that had been evident in many of his previous ways now switched to that of a demon.

He charged at Alison with a fury that she had never seen. His fist connected with her jaw with a resounding snap, causing her to fly back against the bookcase. She bounced forward onto her face, rigid as falling timber. A second later, the bookcase crashed down on her. A searing pain pierced through her mid-section. It first zapped down her spine to her feet, then an instant later shot to her head. Light faded to black.

chapter three

Janette, startled from her sleep by the phone's shrill ring, saw that it was just past midnight.

"Hello."

"Mom, it's Reb. There's been an accident. Alison is on her way to Hamilton General's emerg. Our bookcase fell on her and she's unconscious."

"Oh no! How did it happen?"

Bill rolled over. "What is it?"

"Alison's on her way to the hospital. We've got to go right away." She told Reb they would meet him at the hospital and hung up the phone.

They quickly dressed, pulled on their winter coats and boots, and navigated through snow drifts. The hazardous roads had caused many cars to careen into other vehicles, and the usual ten-minute drive to the hospital took forty. Bill let Janette out and left to park the car.

Pungent smells assailed Janette's nose as she ran to the triage window. Not waiting for the nurse to look up, she blurted, "You have Alison Steele here; she was brought by ambulance less than an hour ago. Where is she now? And do you know where her husband might be, Reuben Steele?"

The nurse replied, "A young woman by that name was sent to surgery over two hours ago. I didn't see anyone with her besides the paramedics."

"That's impossible. Her husband phoned me when the accident happened just over an hour ago."

"Why don't you wait in here and I'll send someone to talk to you." The nurse ushered her into a small area in the emergency department that was partitioned off only by a curtain, like the other cubicles. Janette wrung her hands as she waited for Bill and the promised employee. She tried to pray, but worried thoughts kept nagging her. Her head jerked up when a moaned prayer filtered through the thin barrier.

A male voice said, "Oh, Lord, what should I do?" Then silence, except for muffled hospital noises, a clang from a kidney basin perhaps, urgent voices from emergency personnel giving orders in the hall. The man's voice continued. "I don't want to let her go. Give me wisdom. She may even be in heaven now and I'd be dragging her back into a disabled existence. Lord, do you want me to pull the plug?"

Janette felt compassion for this man who called out to God. *That poor man. I wonder if I could help?*

The man was asked to go with an attendant.

After some minutes he returned, and then a female voice asked, "Mr. Vonderland, have you made a decision?"

"Yes. I want to stop the artificial life support."

"I have orders to do that now, if that's what you wish."

A shaky "yes" was all that the man managed.

At that moment, Bill came to sit beside Janette and took her hand. "The nurse just told me that Alison is having surgery on her back and that they expect it to be quite a while before she's in recovery."

"Her back was injured?"

"Yes. That's all I know."

"Thank goodness you're here." Janette leaned over, resting her head in the crook of his neck, and wept.

***

Mr. Vonderland let out a wail that tortured Janette's ears. She understood that he needed to let out his emotions. His wife must have taken her final breath.

A short while later, Bill and Janette looked toward the opening in the curtain as a gurney rolled past. They caught a glimpse of a young, still woman with an extended abdomen.

"Do you think she's dead?" Bill asked.

"From all that I've heard, I believe so."

"I wonder why they didn't cover her face."

"I think they do that these days for compassionate reasons."

Bill nodded. "We should concentrate on our own problems. What do you think will happen to Alison and the baby?"

"I don't know. I've been praying ever since I heard the news."

"Let's pray together. God knows I blew it badly with Alison yesterday. I've asked God for forgiveness. Let's pray for her now."

They both bowed their heads as they held hands. After moments of silence, Bill began, "Father, I ask you to forgive me for what I said to my daughter. I haven't been able to ask Alison to forgive me; please give me the chance. Please save her and the baby's life and bring them both safely through the surgery. And give the surgeon wisdom and steady hands. Will You turn this tragedy into a double miracle?" Bill straightened as he released a jerky sigh, squeezing his wife's hand gently.

Janette prayed. "We're supposed to thank You in all things, so I want to say thank you for seeing our daughter and grandchild through the anaesthesia and the surgery. We're anxious but I know you understand human nature. Hear our plea for everything to turn out for everyone's good. Yet, not our will but Yours be done.

"And about this man next to us. I pray for strength for him in the tragedy that he's going through, and if You want me to speak to him, make an opportunity come about. Amen."

Janette looked up after her prayer and there stood a tall, handsome police officer with a tawny complexion.

"Sorry for interrupting, but I've been asked to speak with you and answer some of your questions. Are you Alison Steele's parents?"

"Yes." Janette thought his deep voice resonated like a tympanic drum.

"I'm Corporal Ron Mackenzie, but you may call me Mac. The hospital informed me that there's no private room available. Is it alright to discuss your daughter's matters here?"

"Yes. We need to hear them now," said Bill.

"I was called in on this case because of a report from a paramedic. Any injury of this kind must be reported."

"Officer Mac, we know very little about what has happened to our daughter. Will you please tell us what you know?" asked Bill.

"Last night around eight p.m., we received a report of a disturbance from a neighbour in your daughter's apartment building. Neighbours heard a man's angry voice in the hall, and then sounds of someone kicking in a door. Soon after this call, the paramedics reported an alleged incident of domestic violence."

Janette gasped. Bill squeezed her hand again.

"The written report stated that when they arrived they found your daughter face down on the floor with books strewn around her and a man sitting beside her. When they examined her, they found an ugly mark on her jaw as well as a swollen, bleeding nose. She was unconscious the whole time. I assume the man is your son-in-law?"

Bill nodded.

"It was a good thing that he didn't move her."

Janette looked at Bill's pained face as he started to cry.

"Mr. Steele told the paramedics that no violence had happened. They reported that he'd been very congenial and was going to follow them in his car, but he never showed up." Mac took out a writing pad. "Do you know of any marital problems between them?"

Bill answered. "Yesterday afternoon, Alison told us that Reb—Reuben Steele—had been gone from their home for several months and that he was having an affair."

"Do you know of any previous physical abuse?

This time Janette spoke haltingly through her tears. "I know of an incident not too long after their wedding. Alison called me after Reb had punched her in the face."

"What measures were taken?"

"None that I know of."

Bill remembered Janette telling him about it.

The officer promised to return when Alison was able to answer questions.

They remained seated, waiting for the promised hospital personnel. Several minutes later, a man in a lab coat entered.

"Hello, my name is Dr. Jameson. I'm here to answer some of your questions; that is, the ones I know the answers to."

"We're Janette and Bill Palmer," Bill said. They shook hands.

"What information can you give us?" Janette asked. "All we know is that our daughter is having surgery on her back after a bookcase fell on her."

"Your daughter was admitted late last night. The paramedics reported that there were bruises on her jaw as if she had been struck."

Bill hung his head as Janette's tears continued.

The doctor continued. "Apparently, a bookcase fell on her, and she broke her nose when she fell to the floor on her face."

"Do you know anything about the surgery?" asked Bill with a husky voice.

"Yes. The X-rays showed that her back was fractured and splinters needed to be removed. Because she didn't regain consciousness there may be damage to her brain, also. We don't know if there has been permanent damage to her spinal cord. The tests showed significant swelling. She was also bleeding vaginally."

"Oh, no!" sobbed Janette.

"Let's not jump to conclusions, Mother." Turning to the doctor Bill asked, "What harm has the fall done to our daughter and grandchild?"

"It's too soon to know about your daughter. Let's wait until she gets out of surgery. I'm sorry to tell you, though, that she lost the baby."

Janette wailed and Bill took her in his arms and mourned in his own way.

Janette raised her head and asked, "Where's the baby's body?"

"It's wrapped in a blanket and lying in the morgue. Don't worry about the arrangements. You need to concentrate on your daughter now."

The doctor patted their shoulders and said that the surgeon would see them soon, and left the cubicle.

***

They went to the lounge, where they could get a cup of coffee from a vending machine and then possibly go to mourn in a more private area. A dark-blond young man sat at a table alone. His head was resting on his folded arms, his shoulders shuddering. Janette suspected that he might be the man she had asked God for an opportunity to encourage.

With tears still on her cheeks, she walked over to him and put a hand on his shoulder. "Excuse me, sir. Were you the man in emergency who was asking God for help?"

His words were forced out one at a time as if he were a robot. "Yes, I guess you overheard. My wife has just passed away, along with our unborn child."

Janette knew that she was to press on. "I asked God if I could speak to you."

"You did?" He allowed a small lopsided smile in response.

"Yes. My name is Janette Palmer, and this is my husband, Bill."

"My name is Rolph Vonderland." He didn't offer his hand in greeting.

"Rolph, I heard you call out to God. We are Christians, and I'm guessing you are one, too?"

"Yes, I'm a Christian."

Janette continued with more confidence. "I asked God to give me a chance to bring you a 'word' of comfort."

"Thank you, I'd appreciate that. Did you want to do that now?"

Without knowing what she would say she trusted that the right words would come. "Yes, I would." She took his hand and bowed her head and so did Bill. "Dear Heavenly Father, Mr. Vonderland is one of your children and I ask You to help me pray the right words."

After a pause, she continued. "The Lord would like you to know that you made a wise decision and that your wife and little son are with the Father. There will be a time of mourning that you will need to go through, and not too long after the mourning period, love will surround you again.

"Father God, comfort your son and show him the way through the valley of the shadow of death. Cause his heart to know that it's only a shadow for those who are in Christ Jesus. Meet all his needs according to Your riches in Glory. In Jesus' name, I pray. Amen."

"Amen. Thank you very much. How kind of you to take time for me when you are going through a struggle yourself." He paused and then looked up at them. "How did you know my wife was carrying a son?"

"God gave me the words to say to you; I hope they helped."

"Thank you. Yes, most definitely. Now tell me about your dilemma."

"Our daughter, Alison, was injured in an accident last night and is in surgery right now, and she has also lost an unborn child," responded Bill.

"I'm sorry for your loss, as well."

Then Janette asked, "Would you like to talk about what happened, Rolph?"

"You go first. Tell me about your daughter."

"We know very little, Rolph," said Janette. "She is having back surgery right now because a large bookcase fell on her last evening."

"I'm sorry."

"We have hope that she will recover fully. As for you, there's a lonely road ahead of you for a while." Janette paused, and then continued, "May I tell you a story?"

"Sure."

"A father took his little son to the big city. The five-year-old grasped his father's big hand as they stood at the corner to cross the street. Just then a huge, noisy truck barrelled by, causing the pre-schooler to jump behind his dad in fright. The little boy said, 'That truck hit me.'

21

The father responded, 'No, the truck didn't hit you; it was only the shadow.'

"You see, Rolph, you have only been hit by the shadow of death. Your wife and son are in that wonderful place called heaven, and you will get to see them some day to spend eternity with them. That's why Psalm twenty-three says, 'Though I walk through the valley of the shadow of death, I will fear no evil.'"

"Thank you, Mrs. Palmer, I'll remember your story. I feel strong enough to go home now. I hope you don't mind that I can't talk about my wife's accident right now."

"We don't mind at all. Goodbye, Rolph."

chapter four

With extreme willpower, Alison pried her eyes open and saw a blurry tiled floor some distance below her. How she could possibly be in this position was unclear. *Where am I? Was I in danger? I can't move. Why do my legs feel like dead weight? I can only breathe through my mouth. My back hurts!* Slowly, she realized that she must be in the hospital and lying in a bed for those who have had back injuries. A mirror below her gave only a view of the bottom half of the door. She wanted to see if the damages to her face were as bad as they felt, but the mirror didn't lend itself to that. Then an accumulation of pain fully aroused her—continuous sharp stabs followed by drawn-out eruptions of agony, like Morse code. Her fear intensified when she grasped the significance of what might have happened. An unintelligible sob burst from a deep place within. "Aaaaugh!"

Her mother, who had stayed the night in the hospital room, was beside her immediately. "Alison, I'm here. Are you in pain, honey? Should I call the nurse?"

A moan escaped through barely parted lips. "Yeah."

After informing the nurse of Alison's pain, Janette returned. "I've been here the whole time, Alison. Your dad was here for many hours last night, and he's outside taking a break right now." She had an idea. "I'll get on the floor so we can see each other face to face." She folded a blanket to serve as a pad

A pained expression mixed with horror on Janette's face. Alison could only imagine how her own face looked. After only a few silent moments, Janette returned to the chair when the nurse entered with a syringe.

Alison didn't feel the injection, although she saw a pair of white Oxfords come near the bed, pause, and then leave. In a short while, the medication started to take effect. Her mother's voice reached her through the induced fog. "Honey, it's eight in the morning. You arrived at the hospital last night and came out of the recovery room just two hours ago. The doctor who performed the surgery told me that he would visit this afternoon to answer your questions."

Through Alison's semi-dream consciousness, a nagging question surfaced. "Mom—is the baby okay?"

Janette returned to the floor. Alison saw her mother swallow hard and direct her watering eyes to look at her. "I wish I wasn't the one to have to tell you this. I've prayed so hard for the right words, but the sad truth is the baby didn't survive. I'm so sorry, sweetheart."

Tears burned in Alison's eyes, and then splashed to the floor next to her mother's head. Janette pulled some tissues from a box beside her and reached up and placed some into her daughter's hand.

Alison sobbed, "Why would God … allow this … to happen, Mom?" Then she thought of the one who was truly responsible. "All I have done is pray for Reb. How will I be able to forgive him for this?"

Mounting grief bombarded her with two negative thoughts one after another with no time for recovery: dead baby, dead marriage, dead baby, dead marriage. Despair threatened to take over as her breath quickened.

A Gift of Love

The accusatory feeling toward God left as quickly as it had come. *Help me, Father, I'm hurting so badly.* Then she gave in to the tears altogether to allow them to wash away some of the emotional pain.

Janette got up gingerly, being careful not to bump the bed, and knelt on a pillow. She smoothed Alison's hair and prayed, "Let Your love come upon her, oh Lord, and transform these tragedies into precious jewels that will be in her crown of righteousness. I want to thank You for preserving her life. I ask that You heal her injuries quickly and that she will be able to cope with this tragedy. In Jesus' name. Amen.

"Oh, honey, I wish I could take your place instead of seeing you suffer. I feel so helpless."

"Mom," said Alison between deep sobs, "your prayer helped—but I want to see my baby."

"I'll see if that's possible. I'm not sure who I should ask, give me some time to check it out." Janette encouraged Alison to call out to the Lord often, and left the room to allow her to mourn in privacy.

Come take me in your arms as You have done in the past, Lord, for I am more in need now than ever before.

***

Alison recalled a time when she had actually felt God holding her. During the first month of her marriage, her pastor had called and said he wished to visit. Alison agreed, not thinking to consult Reb first. He returned from work, his bulky frame in soiled coveralls seeming to fill the small kitchen. She told him, "Our pastor is coming over this evening."

In an instant, Reb grabbed her by the throat and cut off her air supply, refusing to let go even though Alison looked at him with pleading eyes. The room started to dim as she went limp. Reb let go after she passed out. She awoke on the floor with a severe headache, then tried to think of what had just happened. Reb was gone.

As she slowly rose to her feet, feeling dizzy, the doorbell rang. She smoothed her hair and welcomed the pastor and his wife as best she could. Knowing her face showed that something had gone on, she said, "Newlyweds do have different personalities to work on, don't they?"

Karen, the pastor's wife, approached her, obviously seeing the red marks on her neck, and asked permission to prepare an ice pack. She had Alison sit at the kitchen table and applied the pack.

They gave Alison time to tell what had happened, and they took turns praying with her. They shared some scriptures to encourage her not to give up praying for Reb and reminded her that God loved him despite his actions.

Karen encouraged Alison to release her frustration and hurt. "Tell us anything else about your husband that you would like us to know, Alison."

Husband. It's strange that the first time someone uses this title, I'm feeling like calling it quits.

"I can't predict when he is going to become angry and strike out at me."

Karen leaned forward and put a comforting hand on Alison's shoulder. The pastor gave some advice. "Spend some time in prayer and read these scriptures. Feel free to call me tomorrow. Here, read this. It may help." He handed her a book that he gave to every newlywed couple in his congregation.

After they left, Alison prayed for Reb with more fervency than she'd ever remembered doing. She knew that Reb had to be willing to respond to the beckoning of the Holy Spirit. No one could change him but himself.

He didn't return that night. She slept alone, lying diagonally across the queen-size bed between cool sheets. During the night, she awoke to the sound of her voice talking to the Lord. The presence of the Holy Spirit surrounded her, and she felt as if she were receiving a deep satisfying hug. Every inch of her body felt a strange embrace, which far surpassed any human hug. As she rested in His presence, the feeling gradually lifted, making Alison cry out, "Oh, Lord, don't leave me yet!" His hug returned, even stronger the second time. Eventually she fell asleep, feeling as though she was in her heavenly Father's arms. After a night of being submersed in God's love, she felt some emotional healing.

Reb called from a motel room the next morning to find out if Alison had recovered from his latest outrage. His voice was dripping sweet.

"Alison, I'm so sorry. How will you ever forgive me? Before you say anything, please listen to what happened. I think I've just had a miracle. As I sat on the bed, light filled the room as if someone turned a beacon on. It must have been light from an angel. I want to serve the Lord now.

"Alison, you must have been praying. I don't deserve to have a wife like you. I wouldn't blame you if you never let me come home again."

Alison remembered saying, "Reb I want to believe you, but give me a good reason why I should."

"If I go for counselling and start going to church again and treat you like I did when we were dating, will you take me back?"

"It depends on how the counselling sessions go."

After several weeks, it seemed as if complete reconciliation had taken place as they made a commitment to work on having a successful marriage. Alison forgave him with a sincere heart, having hope for a new life.

***

Now here she was on a motorized, rotating bed in the trauma unit at the Hamilton General Hospital because of him. Alison felt something indescribable in the pit of her stomach. It felt like despair, but she wasn't sure because she had nothing to compare with these feelings. A verse from the first chapter of James came to mind: "Consider it pure joy whenever you face trials of many kinds." More than anything else, she wanted to succeed in passing this test gracefully, but the panic kept rising. *This test is more severe than anything I've experienced, but maybe I'm making too much out of my legs feeling numb.*

A few moments later, Alison's whole body began to shake. Her mother reported this to her nurse and then tried to distract her by brushing her auburn hair then braid it into a thick cord. The nurse brought in the next sedative. Once the medication had had a chance to take effect, the nurse turned Alison on her back.

A few minutes later Alison tumbled into a strange dream where she was a magician's assistant on a large, dark stage in a black box, ready to be sawn in half for the grand finale. The magician's face had transformed from a handsome stranger into Reb's menacing face. Anxiety grew along with her quickening breath. She struggled to free herself, but her legs seized up. The saw started ripping into her middle. She felt it mangle her organs as it severed her body. Her lower half was being separated from her upper body. Wanting desperately to get out of the box, she found that she couldn't move.

As she struggled in her dream, a sharp pain jolted her awake. Alison let out a shriek like one might hear in a horror film. Just before the sleep totally lifted, she sensed someone standing close, then heard the door close. *If that was Mother who just left, she would have come back when she heard me scream.* Seconds later, a nurse rushed into the room.

The nurse made a quick assessment and looked at a trickle of blood from the IV insertion site. She looked under the bed. After cleaning and drying Alison's arm and washing the perspiration from her face and neck, she left with something in her hand.

The nurse returned and bent down again, and Alison heard the rattle of a paper bag. Then the nurse left the room.

When she re-entered several minutes later, she asked, "What caused you to scream like you did?"

"I was having a nightmare. A sharp pain in my arm woke me."

"Bad dreams are a common side effect of narcotic drugs. Unfortunately, these sedatives are necessary to control the pain so that you can get *some* rest. It's five p.m. and you are due for another dose. It's important to reduce your discomfort when I rotate the bed."

Could that be right? It seems like only a short time since she turned me.

Janette returned to the hospital room as Alison was positioned to face the brown tiles again. Janette lay on the floor.

The nurse stood beside the bed to speak to both of them. "The doctor came while Alison was sleeping. He'll return at his next opportunity.

"There is someone who would like to visit you, Mrs. Steele, and he's just outside." Janette hastily got up from the floor.

chapter five

Alison heard the nurse explain to the man, "She has just been turned to face the floor, and the bed has to remain that way for several hours. Plus, she has just received a sedative, making her groggy, so make your visit brief."

Alison heard him take a few steps. Janette said, "You're the officer who asked us some questions last night, aren't you?"

"That's right. I'd like to speak with your daughter. The nurse said she'd be capable of answering a few questions."

His voice is very deep, thought Alison.

"I've forgotten your name," Janette said,

"Ron Mackenzie, Mac to you," he said as he approached the bed.

Directing his attention to Alison, he said, "Mrs. Steele, are you able to answer a few questions?"

"Yes," came the muffled voice.

"Do you know what day of the week it is?"

"Monday, I think."

"That's correct. Can you give me today's date?"

"March twenty-third, 1977."

"Correct again."

Mac continued. "I'm sorry, Mrs. Steele, for the trauma you've experienced."

The toes of his leather boots are worn. They look old.

"Thank you, officer," said Alison.

"Will you please call me Mac?"

She hesitated, thinking that he was a different type of policeman than she expected. "Alright."

"I must tell you that anything you say may be used in a court of law. I have a recording device." He paused, "Do you understand?"

"Yes."

"Now that I'm satisfied that you are mentally alert and able to answer my questions, what is your recollection of last night?"

"Reb, my husband, broke the apartment door, forced his way in, then punched me. I fell backwards against a bookcase. My mother told me that the bookcase fell on me."

"Why did he have to force his way in?"

"I found out about his affair. I didn't want him to return, especially on my birthday. I barricaded the door."

"Yesterday was your birthday?"

"Yes."

"What a shame. Did you have a particular reason for being afraid?" Mac asked.

"I was worried about my response. I didn't want him to convince me to forgive him and take him back. I want the marriage over."

"Have incidents of physical abuse occurred before?"

"About every other week I'd get a slap or shove."

Mac's voice became quieter. "Are you aware of Reb's police record?"

She gasped. "No! I didn't know."

"In 1969, he was charged with breaking and entering with an intent of a felony, use of a deadly weapon, and fraud from NSF cheques. With assault added to his record, he's going to prison for some time."

"He must have been on probation when we married. That must have been why he went out often without telling me where he was going. How could he have withheld this information from me for so many years?"

"That doesn't sound out of character to me," Mac interjected. "Had Reb been drinking, or did he appear to be on drugs at the time of the incident?"

It took some moments to think of yesterday's details. "I don't know; it all happened so fast. I didn't smell his breath."

"Did he drink or take drugs in the past?"

"He was drunk a few times. I don't know if he was on drugs, but I smelled marijuana on his clothes."

"I guess that's all for now. Do you have any questions?"

"Where is Reb now?"

"We had him in for questioning, then let him leave. You're the only one who can lay a charge, and I'm here today to encourage you to do so."

"What do I have to do?"

"I'll record your information in a formal report, I'll need you to sign it; and then I'll verify your signature."

"What will happen after that?"

"The police will go to Reb's last address, and if he's there, he'll be arrested."

"Will he be released again after questioning?"

"Don't worry, Mrs. Steele, no harm will come to you. He'll be behind bars until a bail hearing can be set."

Not liking the sound of her married name, Alison said, "Call me Alison, please."

"Sure thing, Alison."

"You won't allow him to come here if someone posts bail, will you?"

"No. There will be a restraining order so that he'll not be allowed to come within a mile of you."

Alison let out a slow breath.

"Are those all the questions you have for now?"

"If I think of any, how can I reach you?"

"I'll leave you my card." He placed his business card on the bedside table, nodded to her father who had come in during the questioning. Then Mac left with a "So long."

Alison lifted a weak hand to wave.

Bill entered, bent to kiss Janette, who sat at the side of the room, then walked to his daughter's ultramodern bed. He gingerly positioned himself cross-legged on the floor, rested on one palm, then offered a half smile as he tilted his head.

"Hello, my sweetheart." He stretched to brush a kiss on her cheek then returned to his former position. "Alison," he paused for emphasis then continued, "I wanted to tuck my tail and run because of what I said about you not being enough for Reb. Will you please forgive me, sweetheart?" He hung his head and waited for a response.

Alison took a few seconds to get the drift of what her father was talking about. The memory came back. "Yes, Dad. I forgive you." The atmosphere of the room seemed to feel lighter; actually, she felt a release.

Bill turned to look up at Janette. "Was that the policeman we met last night, Mother? Was he here to ask about Reb's whereabouts?"

"Yes, that's him. And no, he asked Alison some of the same questions he did me. The only way they'll arrest Reb is for Alison to lay charges. And she's the only one who can do that. It may be difficult for her."

"Yes, we'll have to give you time, sweetheart. But it seems the right thing to do." Not expecting a response, her father asked about his daughter's condition. "Has the doctor been here to explain?"

Janette said no.

"How much has your mother told you?"

Alison forced the words out through a tight sore throat. "I'm tired, Dad. Could Mom tell you?"

***

Her parents went into a sitting room to talk while Alison slept.

"She knows about the baby, Bill."

"My poor girl."

"She wants to see her baby's body."

"I didn't even think about that. I'll go to the desk and ask some questions."

"Thanks. And Bill, we can't leave the news of her paralysis to the doctor; it's better if it comes from us." Janette added, "We may never find the right time, and the longer we leave it, the harder it'll be. I don't think I can be the one to do this, honey."

"I hear what you're saying. Let's pray. I'll need God's help for the right words. Goodness knows I've made mistakes already in what I said to Alison yesterday."

"Yes. Well, that's behind us now, dear. I'll meet you in the chapel, and we can pray together."

***

Bill stood at the desk and cleared his throat. When the clerk lifted her head, he said, "Who do I speak to concerning my daughter's baby? She lost a premature baby during yesterday's surgery."

"Oh. I've never had to deal with something like this before. Will you please give some time before returning? It's getting late. Tomorrow would be the best."

"Okay." Bill nodded and left for the chapel.

In the silent, dimly lit chapel, he took a seat and bowed from the waist. He squeezed his eyes shut, hoping to keep back the tears. He prayed, "Father God, this will be difficult to break the news to Alison that her legs are permanently paralyzed. You know the doctors told us that there's no chance of her walking again. But Jesus, You dealt with impossibilities every time You performed miracles. Please help me to communicate hope to Alison and that she has a full life to live even if she never walks again. Amen."

The prayer wasn't long, yet it succeeded in relieving Bill's tension. He smiled at Janette.

After many minutes of praying together, Janette and Bill felt spiritually renewed as they left the chapel. They walked hand in hand down the corridor. Pausing at Alison's door, they encouraged one another with a loving squeeze.

Stepping in, they saw Alison lying on her back. They released their hand clasp and stood on opposite sides of the bed looking at their youngest. Her eyes were open and filled with tears.

"Mom, Dad, I'm scared about not knowing what's happened to me. Why can't I move my legs or even wiggle my toes?"

She noticed her parents' red-rimmed eyes and heard an audible sigh from her mother. Her father delayed in speaking. Alison thought, *He's probably shocked by my appearance.*

"The weight of the bookcase fractured two vertebrae and crushed your spinal cord," Bill explained. "The X-rays showed bone splinters."

He paused to allow her time to digest this new information, but Alison rushed ahead. "What happens now? When will I be able to get out of bed? I mean, once the bones heal and the spinal cord returns to normal?"

Bill's struggled to keep his voice calm. "Alison, the surgeon will explain further, but he has told us that he doesn't expect you to be able to walk."

With a wide-eyed, frightened look and puckered brow, she opened her mouth to speak but no sound came out. Her lips trembled then she asked, "For how long?"

"I believe the surgeon implied that this is a permanent condition."

"Oh, Dad, surely you misunderstood the doctor!"

"Honey, what we need to do right now, before anything else, is pray."

Bill and Janette joined hands across the bed, placed their free hands on Alison's shoulders, and prayed without closing their eyes. "Father God, we need your help right now because we don't know what to do. Alison is hurting physically and emotionally. Will You please ease the pain? Help us accept what we need to accept, and let us fight the good fight against the enemy of our souls. Please relieve Alison of this agonizing struggle, and bring her Your peace."

Alison's mother, crying freely now, came around the bed to join her husband, who was blinking rapidly, trying to hold back the tears.

Her mother managed to ask, "Alison would you like us to stay with you, or give you some time alone?"

"I think I would like to be alone, please."

"It'll probably be an hour before we get back. Will that be alright?" asked her father.

"An hour is fine."

Alone now, as tears made minute rivulets into her hair, she envisioned herself in a wheelchair, her legs withered, shapeless, with nothing for her to do. Like a haphazard hopscotch game, her mind jumped from one topic to the next. The only common denominator was wondering how her life would be affected by paralysis: *My teaching days are over. Who will ever want me? I may never have another child.*

After almost an hour of crying, she determined to make the best of this catastrophe. *Mom and Dad aren't to blame; they're just repeating the surgeon's words. And the doctors may be wrong. God heals. Anything is possible with Him. I'm going to believe that I'll be able to walk again. It may take time, but I'm going to do it.*

"Lord Jesus, please heal my back—the fractured bones and the crushed spinal cord." She purposely didn't want to think about the loss of her baby, so she concentrated on her healing.

chapter six

The next morning, Alison felt the weight of her troubles: the loss of her baby, health, independence, and marriage. Surely no one would hold it against her for feeling miserable. Her face awash with tears, she didn't even try to hold back the audible sobs.

At the pitiful sound, a nurse entered her room with purpose in her walk, tissues in her hand, and an agenda on her mind. "Hi. I'm Nancy, and I'll be your nurse whenever I'm on shift. I can identify with part of your loss; I miscarried my first child. Would it be alright if I tell my story?"

Alison nodded.

"I experienced the same great loss, and with it came an unfounded fear that I would *never* be able to carry a baby to full term.

"It took me eight years to become pregnant in the first place. We became pregnant after my friend's husband said a powerful prayer.

According to hospital policy I'm not allowed to say more unless a patient asks for prayer. I'll just say that God granted me the privilege of having a child. I became pregnant the next month."

Alison thought, *Oh, Nancy must be a sister in the Lord. God must have picked her out just for me.* "I'd call that a miracle."

"I thought so, initially. In less than a week after I received the lab results, I was in considerable abdominal discomfort. My mother said some pain could be expected, so I didn't complain until a few days later the pain became excruciating. I was rushed to the hospital with an ectopic pregnancy."

Nancy had Alison's total attention. "What's that?"

"It's where the egg travels only as far as the fallopian tube and becomes fertilized there, causing the tube to expand and sometimes rupture, like mine did. Thankfully, I knew better than to wait any longer before going to the hospital. I could have bled to death internally."

"So, what eventually happened?"

"I knew that I had even less of a chance of becoming pregnant, half the chance actually, but I chose to keep on believing."

"Does this story have a happy ending?"

"Yes. My first daughter's name is Abby and she's six years old. But that's enough about me. Tell me, how are you doing?"

"The only way I can explain it is that—I feel so low." Alison wondered if she'd ever feel truly happy again.

"That is a very normal response. You probably don't wish to talk about your troubles right now, but we can speak about what may be adding to your emotional upset. Just know, there're always hormonal imbalances after a birth of a child—full-term or not. There are also emotional responses to physical pain. Talking about your baby can help to sort out some of your feelings."

"I'd like to see my baby. Is that possible?"

"Oh, my—I thought that was all taken care of. I'm not sure how to respond. Let me do some checking."

Nancy had turned to leave when Alison asked, "Just to clarify, you're a Christian, right?"

"It takes one to know one, right?"

Alison nodded and asked Nancy to pray for her. Her nurse didn't hesitate. "Father, You know all things, and I'm asking you for wisdom to pray the prayer that needs to be voiced. Help Alison, in her own time, to be able to express her hurt concerning her child, who we believe is in heaven with You. Give Alison Your comfort and guidance now and in days to come when her thoughts might drift to the loss of her child and the different things her baby would have accomplished. At each milestone, help her to turn to You. Thank you for hearing our prayers and giving Alison extra strength. We pray in Jesus' name. Amen."

***

Mac returned with Reb's charges typed. Alison was lying on her back with her eyes closed. As he approached the bed, he paused and sucked in an involuntary breath. He took in the scene: her thick auburn braid with a curl at the end, her high cheek bones and full lips. Her beauty wasn't even marred by the discoloured jaw or swollen nose. His body responded with a pleasurable, yet strange, tingly ache at the base of his skull. As he stared at her, she must have sensed his gaze. She slowly opened her eyes.

Being careful not to stutter, he took a deep breath. "Hello, Alison. I hope I didn't wake you."

"Hello, officer. You didn't; I was only resting my eyes. I just now became aware that someone was in the room."

"Call me Mac, please. How are you feeling this morning? Have you received medication, recently?" he asked in a quiet tone.

Alison wondered at his apparent nervousness. He had seemed to be so forthright yesterday—not likely the type to be shy. "I'm as well as can be expected. And to answer your second question, no, I haven't had any medication recently. So, my mind is clear."

"Uh, yes. Then you are able to sign the report after I read it to you?"

"Yes. Go ahead." Her voice was steady, while his sounded a bit shaky.

It only took a few minutes for him to finish reading. He seemed to be searching for a reason to linger.

"Are you feeling alright about this report, Alison?"

Alison noted that he spoke her name with warmth; she remembered a more business-like manner yesterday. "I think so. My mind is a little jumbled this morning."

"I do understand. You've had the great loss of your baby as well as this tragedy."

"Oh. You know about my baby?" *That's the reason for his soft tone.*

"I got a full report from the nurse. It's the investigative part of my job. I'm sorry for your loss."

"Thank you, officer." She voiced her thoughts about him. "You're different from what I thought policemen were like."

"I'll take that as a compliment. Thank you. But please, call me Mac."

"Alright … Mac."

"You have a musical tone to your voice. Do you sing?"

"Yes, I do." She couldn't hide her blush or even look down.

Mac was back to business. "Your husband will be officially arrested today, if everything goes well. I'll keep you informed. Goodbye." He left without his military gait.

***

Mac was waiting at the elevator when Nancy approached him hastily. "Are you the officer in charge of the investigation concerning Alison Steele?"

"Yes, I am."

"I have an incident to report, and a piece of evidence that may indicate concern regarding Alison's safety."

"Is there a private place where we could discuss this?" asked Mac.

Once they were seated in the plush seats along the highly varnished table in the conference room, Nancy took a printout form from her pocket. "This is the lab report from some fluid spilled in Alison's room yesterday. It was morphine."

"What medication is Alison receiving for pain?" Mac wouldn't jump to conclusions until gathering more details.

"She is getting Demerol every four hours."

"Tell me what happened yesterday that has you concerned."

Nancy told him as much detail as possible. "Yesterday evening, just after five p.m., Alison screamed with a bad dream but also from pain. Someone had tampered with the IV system; there was a considerable amount of blood on her arm and sheet. But the main mystery was that Alison sensed that there was a stranger in the room and saw the door closing."

"Did you see anyone leave her room just after the scream?"

"I saw a housekeeping staff member walking slowly down the hall with a mop. Why do you ask?"

"Anyone is a suspect in our business."

"Oh. I didn't think anything of this because we see them going in and out of rooms and down the halls all the time."

"Could you describe this person?"

"Yes. She was tall, about five foot nine, had a husky build, and had thick, shiny, blond hair. I need to tell you the rest of the facts."

"Sure. Go ahead."

"When I entered Alison's room, I noticed a puddle of clear fluid, about two and a half inches in diameter, just under the bed with the cover of a syringe beside it. I recovered most of the fluid with a clean syringe, and sent it to the lab to be analyzed."

"Quick, thinking," said Mac.

"Thanks."

"Did you happen to keep the syringe cover?"

"It's in a bag at the desk."

Mac left with the paper bag and lab report. He told Nancy he was heading to the housekeeping department to find out how easy it was to steal a housekeeper's uniform.

chapter seven

Alison's first day in the hospital had been spent waking and sleeping, drifting like a dinghy without direction, blurring the memories of the previous day except for the lucid discussion with Nancy. She remembered an indescribable hush descending on the room as Nancy ministered to her.

This second post-op day started with Alison trying to deal with her overwhelming emotions. Her sanguine personality had gone into hibernation. It wasn't like her to complain or to have two negative thoughts in a row.

That surgeon is neglecting me! Why hasn't he talked to me? What's going on? Why hasn't anyone told me about my baby's body? Then her conscience pricked her, so she quickly turned her thinking around.

Oh, God, You don't want me to be angry, and You know my mind would be more at rest if I knew more about my surgery or how long the doctor thinks I'll be in hospital. I know I've been impatient, but now I'm trying to acknowledge that You will look after everything. Thank you, Father. Amen.

Not even five minutes passed before Dr. Shapiro walked into the room. Instead of thinking this was a coincidence, she believed that God heard and answered her prayer. A scripture came to mind: "Your Father knows what you need before you ask Him" (Matthew 6:8).

"Hello, Mrs. Steele. I'm Dr. Shapiro. I performed the surgery on your back. I'm sorry for the delay in coming to see you."

Alison was able to give a weak smile. The doctor's voice sounded just like her brother's. He had the same grey eyes. "I accept your apology. I don't know the details of what has happened or will happen to me. Please tell me everything straight out, and remember, I only understand layman's terms."

"I see you are a direct woman and understand some physicians' downfall.

"Your nose was broken and was easily realigned. The swelling will recede soon and you'll be able to breathe normally. You experienced a concussion that was benign. Two of your backbones have been broken, the eleventh and twelfth thoracic vertebrae—these bones." The doctor turned and indicated a spot half way down his back. "This is where most of the damage occurred. Splinters were removed, and this is the location where your spinal cord was crushed, causing your legs to be paralyzed. Do you understand everything I've said so far?"

After a few moments of attempting an interpretation of what he had just said, Alison asked, "What does benign mean?"

"Oh, yes. I guess I forgot my promise already. Benign means that there is no abnormality or disease present."

"Okay, I understand that now, but when you say the blow caused my legs to be paralyzed, for how long do you mean?"

"To my knowledge, there has never been a recovery of movement of the extremities in any patient with spinal damage similar to yours."

Stunned, her only response was tears spilling onto her cheeks. A silence followed Dr. Shapiro's explanation. Alison felt abandoned in a world of antiseptic smells and sterile surroundings.

Shoving aside the prediction of unending paralysis, her thoughts jumped to the next sorrow. Sniffing, she managed to ask, "What happened to my baby? I want to hear everything."

"You were bleeding vaginally, and by the time we got you prepared for surgery, the fetus was expelled." The doctor forgot his promise again and went back to the harshness of medical terms.

She resented the term fetus but decided to ignore this offence. "You mean I gave birth while under anaesthesia?"

"Yes. She appeared to be between four and five months gestation. Would that be correct?"

With sobs erupting, Alison asked, "I had a girl?"

"Yes. A girl."

"Oooh!" It was a lament, rather than a remark. Silence, except for her sobs, filled the room. The doctor sympathetically handed her some tissues. "I want to see my baby." *I will state my request to everyone until I get some answers.*

Dr. Shapiro continued. "I'll see what I can do. In the mean time a counsellor has been selected to help with your case. I've asked her to arrange a session. Before I go, do you have any questions concerning your medical treatment?"

She wiped away her tears then blew her tender nose, gently. "How long before I can be up in a chair?"

"About six weeks."

"That seems like a very long time."

"Yes, I know. But that's how long it takes for bones to heal. Are you experiencing much pain? Is the analgesic I ordered sufficient?"

There he goes again with his medical terms, but at least I know what he's talking about. The conversation was over for her anyway. Alison only nodded a response to his last question. The doctor bowed then left.

The startling facts of a lost baby girl, as well as her damaged body and the doctor's belief that she wouldn't walk again, created a shock that kept bouncing from one dreadful prediction to another like a horrible pinball game. Still she was able to call out to God.

She felt God's presence surround her like a protective garment and experienced His heavenly peace. It reminded her of the experience she'd had when God gave her that intimate hug after Reb's strangling hold. She let the tears flow because she believed it would bring a measure of release. Despite the disturbing prognosis, she had a determination to survive and succeed. She dared to believe that she would, indeed, walk again.

She needed someone to talk to. Right then pastor Ed walked in.

When she saw her pastor, Alison decided to keep the facts of the loss of her daughter for later. *One crisis at a time.* "I'm so glad to see you, Rev," she said as she dried her cheeks.

"Alison, I was so sad to hear of your injury and surgery. I felt guided by the Lord to see you this morning. The last time I was here, you were asleep."

"It's remarkable that I just finished asking God to speak to me, and then you showed up."

"Oh, that's why I felt an urgency to come now. Is there something I can do for you?"

"Yes. Could you please hand me my Bible? I know it's in this room. It's rather small, bound in red leather."

His eyes quickly scanned the ledges. Spotting it immediately, he picked it up and gently placed it in her hands.

She held the precious pages on her chest. "Thank you."

"I met your doctor in the hall. When I said I'm your pastor, he told me he didn't expect you to walk again."

"And I'm thinking it's only a matter of time before I do walk again. Does that make me rebellious?"

Carefully Rev responded with compassion. "It's not wrong to want to walk again. But it isn't wise to rush ahead of God. He still needs to make His plan known, and He may have a greater purpose than we perceive. Let's pray."

"Yes. Please pray."

"Bless the Lord, oh my soul, and all that is within me; I will bless Your holy name. Alison and I come to You for help in this situation. She's feeling hurt and confused because she's been told that she may not be able to walk, and it is so distressing. Father, put Your strong arms around her and let her sense Your presence.

A Gift of Love

"Direct my words concerning the scriptures that You have given me to bring insight, and ultimately, peace. In Jesus' name, I pray."

"Amen," Alison chimed in. "Thank you, but it's hard for me to imagine how God could use me as a cripple."

"God knows all things and has allowed this injury. I don't pretend to know why. He knows everything that is going to happen to you and He allowed this situation." He looked at her to see how she responded to that concept. Some people would blame God for not intervening. "You may look back on these days and understand the reason for this trying time. Until your understanding is clear, all you can do is trust Him and His word. This is the scripture that I believe God gave me for you to hear today. I'll read it to you if I may?"

"Yes, go ahead. I believe God leads you."

"'Anyone who does not take his cross and follow me is not worthy of me. Whoever finds his life will lose it, and whoever loses his life for my sake will find it.' Matthew ten, thirty-eight and thirty-nine.

"You might think these are unsympathetic verses to give you. As I'm reading it again, I'm beginning to comprehend why God brought it to my attention. When Jesus was speaking these words, He knew of the cross that He would carry. He also knew it would become the symbol of His death. He was willing to die to pay for everyone's sin and to sacrifice His own life, so that we could have eternal life.

"I believe God wanted you to hear these verses because you have a choice to make. You can try to avoid thinking of this injury as part of His plan, or you can use this time for His glory. Start looking for ways He could use you and your story as a witness for Him."

She sighed and dried her tears. *God, help me to understand.*

"Please don't take anything I say as words without compassion. I realize you have pain and losses to deal with. The good that will come from this injury may take time to be revealed. Live one day at a time rather than focus on the healing that you may eventually receive. It could be that a wheelchair will attract others as you speak about Christ. I believe you will recognize His plan and find this new life exciting."

Silent for several moments, Alison tried to take in the full meaning

47

of what Pastor Ed had said. She compared herself to a sunflower that slowly turns its face toward the warmth.

From the moment my mother and father told me what the doctor had said, I rejected the prognosis of being in a wheelchair for the rest of my life. Knowing that God is a healing God, He may heal me. But for today, am I willing to accept this bed? And, as time progresses, will I be able to accept living my life from a wheelchair?

Swallowing hard as salty tears welled up again, she was able to say, "Thank you, Rev, for caring enough to lay it out straight. I've had to suffer in the past, but this is more than I ever considered I would have to bear."

"These verses come to mind," said Rev. "Romans five, three to five: 'We also rejoice in our sufferings, because we know that suffering produces perseverance; perseverance, character; and character, hope. And hope does not disappoint us, because God has poured out his love into our hearts by the Holy Spirit, whom he has given us.'

"You are a mature Christian, Alison. I believe you are spiritually advanced beyond your chronological years.

"I envision you ministering from a platform to many people, although only a few of them are in wheelchairs. Your talent will take on a different perspective, and you will explain spiritual ideas in a way that people will be able to receive the most understanding. I also see you writing a book that only someone in your position could write. God seems to have given you the time to devote to some of these activities, which will soon take place. They may not occur in the same order I've said them, but I believe they will start to happen. I believe that this was spoken as an unction from the Holy Spirit."

When her mind fully perceived that these words were from God, a smile stretched out to accept them. "Was that a word of prophecy then?"

He smiled back. "Yes."

"Could you write that out for me?"

"Yes. I'll do that now." His memory was fresh, so in a short time he had it ready for her to read. "Would you like me to write some key scriptures about prophecy I think will help?"

"Yes. Write them in the back cover of my Bible, please."

"That's a great idea."

He handed her the written prophecy.

She accepted it and read it, wondering when these things would happen. "Thank you. After you leave, I will think about what you have said."

"Good." He looked at his watch. "It's time for me to go."

"Thank you for coming. I do feel I need to rest now."

Alone with her thoughts, her mind turned back to a time when Pastor Ed had talked about his past.

He had been a 'druggy' who became a 'Jesus freak'. Many of the hippies in the late '60s held to the slogan 'Make love, not war.' In the early part of that decade, some equated the Jesus People with hippies. Rather, their slogan might have been, 'Love Jesus, love people.'

The Jesus People did not stay within the walls of churches; rather they chose to announce the reality of Jesus' forgiveness on the streets. A man in his thirties took the opportunity to tell Ed about Jesus Christ's death on the cross for the forgiveness of sins. Ed was strung out on drugs at the time but was still able to comprehend this simple message.

The remarkable change Ed experienced didn't involve a haircut or a different style of clothes. The driving force was that God wanted to transform the inner man. He was twenty-three years old when he was changed for eternity. After his conversion, he joined the Jesus People movement that gathered in Toronto in a large mainline church on Bloor Street, close to Spadina Avenue. The leaders, Merv and Merla Watson, named these meetings The Catacombs.

Ed had recalled that drums and dancing were part of their regular expression of worship. Drums were certainly not normal instruments in church services in the early '70s, and dance was thought to be sacrilegious. The leaders of The Catacombs instructed the young people how to "sing in the Spirit." These practices were very different from those of other charismatic churches.

***

The nurse returned to administer the next injection, and Alison's thoughts returned to the present. She decided to pray before the sedative caused a deep sleep.

Kathleen Reichert

Father, I feel excited at the prophetic word Pastor Ed gave me, and at the same time, I'm feeling so sad. I lost my daughter, my marriage, and my independence all in one day. I know You'll take wonderful care of my little one, but I feel lost. Still I want You to use me and my talents. Thank you, God. I love You. And I trust You.

chapter eight

Alison awoke the next morning with new hope. Miraculously, she had slept uninterrupted for six hours, even sleeping through the rotation of the bed.

The past few mornings, fresh and mild, promised a pleasant spring to those who could be outside enjoying it. This year Alison would not see the crocuses bursting out of the snow, yet she tried to thank God for each new day and to stop feeling sorry for herself. She asked for an attitude change to be part of one of God's miracles for today. Then she decided to think that if He had allowed this tragedy to happen, He could also help her to use this day to bring glory to His name. And until He let her know differently, she wouldn't ask to be in another's shoes. To grab hold of the day with a positive manner became her daily goal. She refused to waste a moment of the sunlight hours in regret or worry.

Alison's parents would be visiting today, after taking a well-deserved one-day break. *Will they be happy if I tell them how Rev ministered to me? I'm sure Mom knows about the gift of prophecy, but has Dad ever experienced a prophecy for himself? I hadn't until yesterday.*

After praying for her parents she opened her eyes and saw that Nancy had come to give her the usual morning care. After everything was put away, Nancy handed her the Bible. Alison found the verses that Rev had marked:

"Follow the way of love and eagerly desire spiritual gifts, especially the gift of prophecy.... Everyone who prophesies speaks to men for their strengthening, encouragement and comfort. He ... who prophesies edifies the church. I would like every one of you to speak in tongues, but I would rather have you prophesy." (1 Corinthians 14: 1–5)

The Bible says to desire this gift, so that's what I will aim to do.

Father, will you please give me the gift of prophecy so that I'm obedient to Your word? Thank you. I receive it by faith. I pray in Jesus' name. Amen.

Someday I want to encourage someone as Rev's words have encouraged me.

She had never considered ministering from a platform or writing a book. She decided to start with journalling her days in the hospital, then changed her mind and started from the beginning of her relationship with Reb.

She asked Nancy for some writing materials.

***

Alison pushed away the tray that held cold and hot beverages, a thick, overly sweet pudding, and the forever-solid gelatine. *I should be grateful that I'm able to eat after the days of just ice chips, but this menu is exactly the same as yesterday's. I hesitate to complain out loud, yet I know You hear everything, even my thoughts.*

All she did these days were sleep, force Jell-o down, and then sleep again.

After a nap, her family doctor, Helen Whiting, arrived. Alison interpreted the doctor's wide-eyed frown as surprise at Alison's appearance—her nose still swollen and her face bruised.

Checking Alison's chart, the doctor said, "I see that you're progressing well according to the nurses' notes. I'm sorry to hear of your trauma. You never even hinted that your husband was physically abusive. Renew my memory—what's his name?"

"Reb."

Alison felt she had to explain. "I know I should have confided in you, but just speaking about the facts would have forced you to report him, and I feared something worse could happen. My secret hope was that he'd eventually change. I didn't think I was in danger, because he'd left our apartment. I assumed that he was out of my life for good. Now the worst has happened."

"I saw in your chart that you lost your baby as well. I'm so sorry. It must have been a terrible shock."

"Thank you for your concern. I imagine it will take time to grieve for my baby, and I know her spirit is in the hands of my heavenly Father. I would really like to see her face, though. I don't care if she's cold when I hold her. I want to see what she looked like."

"I'll see what I can do. I'll get in touch with the OR people to see who was in charge of the baby's body." After a pause the doctor asked, "Is there anything else you would like to talk about?"

"Could you have the IV removed? And could you give me more information? The surgeon told me that my spinal cord was crushed beyond repair but has not been severed. In your opinion, is there any hope that I may walk again? How long will I be in this bed? And when will I start physiotherapy?"

The doctor chuckled and noted that the concussion had not affected her speech. "It seems that I have opened up the question box."

Alison gave a little laugh at the mental picture of a box with question marks popping out. "I guess I do sound very inquisitive."

Helen smiled. "You have a right to ask questions." She looked at the fluid-flow chart and nodded. "I will discontinue the intravenous therapy. Now, to answer some of your questions ..." After pausing to weigh her words, she continued. "No one can determine, for sure, the amount of damage you have sustained. The surgeon has given you an educated evaluation based on what he has previously seen.

"Let's prepare you for the worst while expecting the best. If, indeed, you are paralyzed, I believe you have the determination to live a productive life. If there's a chance that you will have some sensation in your legs, I know you will have the courage to put all your strength into being mobile again. I'll arrange for the resident doctor to get the physiotherapy department to plan your treatment and speak to you soon. We'll let him decide when you should begin."

"When will I be able to sit in a lounge chair? I would like to see more of my surroundings, and I wish to write a journal."

"There has to be some evidence of bone repair first. Usually there is a six-week period before X-rays will be taken again. Until then, try to relax and have someone write for you."

"With God's help I can try to be patient. Thank you for the suggestion."

"You have a great attitude, yet I feel it will be a benefit for you to see the hospital's counsellor."

Alison trusted her doctor's judgment. "I'll give it a try."

"I'll see you next week to keep tabs on you. Goodbye for now."

"Thanks for everything. Goodbye."

***

Immediately after Dr. Whiting left, Bill and Janette came. They reassured her that their thoughts had been with her and were thankful to have caught up on some rest. "Is there anything from home that you would like us to bring next time?" Janette asked.

"Before we talk about that, did you get some information about my baby's body?"

"Yes, I did," Bill replied, "and I'd like to talk about the unfortunate event later. Will you trust me in this matter?"

"Just tell me, Dad. I need to know!"

"I'm sorry, sweetheart; the hospital personnel in charge of labelling the body neglected to do so. Our granddaughter's body was mistaken for an aborted baby and handled as one." Bill and Janette cried as they thought of the sorrow it was bound to arouse in Alison.

"That's criminal! I won't get to see her in this life. Oh, no!" The three cried together; their mourning lasted some time. After they talked everything through, Alison purposed to move on. *Another hurdle to hand to the Lord.*

At first her dad wanted to look into legal matters, but they decided to leave everything alone. They had enough to deal with.

Janette finally asked again if she would like anything from home.

"Yes. I've been thinking I'd like the cross-stitched motto from Grandma. It'll remind me of the mission the Lord has for me to give love. It has been so easy to be caught up in everything being done for me that I forget about others."

Her dad spoke with thoughtfulness. "I think you have an unselfish spirit."

Janette agreed. "That's so true. You tried to encourage us yesterday on the phone. It sounds as if we're going to have a preaching daughter."

"Thanks, Mom and Dad, for your encouragement." Alison paused. "This is a change in subject, but I've a question I was going to ask you when I was at your house for my birthday, and I totally forgot until just last night. Our pastor was talking about Walter and Phoebe Palmer, who were credited with starting a revival in Hamilton in 1857."

"Well, I'll be. We have the same last name. Tell us about the sermon," said Bill.

"The Palmers lived in New York and happened to preach in Hamilton. A revival started in the Methodist churches. Have you heard anything about it before? Could they possibly be our relatives?"

"I've never heard about a revival in Hamilton," Bill said. "I don't know if we're related or not, honey, but I can check it out. It sounds like it means a lot to you."

"I think it would be neat if we had relatives that were well-known evangelists."

They continued their conversation with family happenings. Her grandfather was doing well despite his diabetes and enlarged heart. Alison's brother and his wife were planning a visit soon.

Her parents left, saying they'd return soon with some information about the famous Palmers.

"Hello, Alison. How are you?"

Surprised to see Mac towering over her in street clothes, she said, "You startled me. I didn't hear you come in."

"I'm sorry. I'll clear my throat next time." He made a ridiculous face with two fingers touching his cheek and the other three extended at the side of his mouth as he cleared his throat loudly, 'Ahem.' He hadn't shown a humorous side until now.

Alison chuckled. "It looks like you came to cheer me up."

"Actually, I wanted to let you know that I heard Reb's statement. I believe it's untrue. Reb told me that you had provoked him verbally and that he didn't strike you but that you ran into his extended arm. He also refuted the fact that you were pregnant; he claimed you were lying just to increase the seriousness of the charges."

"Instead of being shocked about my pregnancy or remorseful that I'm paralyzed, he thinks only of himself?" *Typical*. Alison knew that Reb was a self-absorbed person. Still, she wished he felt remorse for what he had done.

"Let me tell you, I've seen plenty of angry men in my line of duty, but Reb takes the cake. He lost control very quickly. I saw his true nature when he heard the charges against him. There wasn't a sign of remorse for what he did to you. The blood vessels bulged on his neck. He lashed out at me, which earned him solitary time in a four-by-six-foot room."

After a pause, she said, "I didn't really expect too much sympathy from Reb, but I did think he'd make some comment about our baby."

"No, he didn't say anything more than what I told you, although the ambulance attendants reported that Reb had removed the bookcase and books off your back. He checked your breathing before he called the ambulance, but he didn't move you. He said that he remained beside you until the paramedics arrived."

Alison's chest had a strange stirring. She managed to say, "He was always regretful when he saw the damage he caused."

Alison lost concentration on what Mac was saying. She appeared to be looking at the officer, but in reality she was gazing right through him. Her face was a study in solemnity, not revealing any feelings. She thought only about her baby. As Mac began to speak again after a pause, she returned her attention to him when he cleared his throat for real this time. Then she saw his rosy cheeks. *Was he blushing?*

"I'm curious as to why you continued in a marriage with such a rough character. I've investigated a lot of women, but you don't seem to be the usual type of victim I see."

Alison saw an even deeper colour creep up Mac's neck.

"I can't answer why I stayed with him, except that at one time I truly loved him."

"Do you know why I visit more often than is really necessary?"

"No. Why?"

"Because, actually, you're the one who cheers me."

"Really? Is your job so terrible?"

"It can be."

His short answer puzzled Alison, and she wondered how her drab, pale presence could cheer anybody. *Each time he comes, he seems so nervous. It's like he wants to smile but doesn't. He's quite handsome, maybe too handsome. Too young to be a corporal like it says on his badge.*

Mac brought her out of her musing with a question. "Why don't you seem as despondent as most victims?"

Alison's spirit livened with this chance to witness. "I'm able to go to Jesus for help with my dark questions. I have a certainty from the Bible that God answers them. I feel He's a friend that I can call on any time."

He nodded. "I used to go to church." A small crease on his brow showed that her words had affected him. "Like you, I'm a believer and attended church for almost a year, but I stopped going.

"Let me tell you why I started to go to church in the first place. I got my first scare when a bullet went through my hat but, thank God, not through my skull. Unfortunately, my pursuit of God diminished as time faded the memory of my close call. Now I want to seek God because of your attitude toward Reb. You appear to have an absence of bitterness toward him, and you want him in jail because you don't want him to come after you, not because you want him punished."

Oh, I've been misreading his feelings. He's a Christian. That would explain his soft voice and kind manner. She returned her concentration on the conversation. "I want Reb to be restored to God, but I also want him to take responsibility for his actions."

"Yes, that's exactly what I mean; you seem to want the best for him." Mac paused. "After seeing your attitude, I'm thinking about what I would have done if I were you. I seem to be a Christian in name only, but I want the real thing—a deep relationship that you seem to have. And I want to know there's a place in heaven for me should the next stray bullet enter my brain."

"You may want to try my church."

"Is it close by? And do you think I'd like your pastor?"

"Yeah. He used to be part of the Jesus People. He comes complete with his own backup group—drums, and electric guitar. And the church is not too far from here—six to eight blocks."

"You sold me. I think I'll give it a try. What's the address?"

He took another business card to write the name and address of her church on the back. After repeating it to make sure it was correct, he gave her a broad smile and said, "Goodbye for now, Alison."

Their developing friendship pleased, and at the same time surprised, Alison. *Here I lie in a faded hospital gown with a messy braid and no makeup. Am I imagining that he might be attracted to me?*

chapter nine

Janette brought string to display Alison's precious wall hanging in the window. Alison watched with trepidation, while her mother stood on a chair to reach a hook.

"When you're on your back you'll be able to see it," said her mom cheerfully, now safely on the floor. "Why is this saying so important to you?"

Alison paused. "It's a precious reminder of the love Grandma and Grandpa showed each other. Someday I want to have a partner to love, and maybe another child or two. I've been hurt by Reb, but that won't stop me from loving again."

***

Bible in hand and looking comfortable in faded jeans and sweatshirt, Pastor Ed visited Alison for the third time.

"How is one of my favourite people?"

"Progressing, Rev."

He took a supine position on the bare floor, where he could look at her face to face. "Everyone misses your passionate soprano voice on the worship team. Many of them wanted me to tell you that they are praying for you and would like to come visit when you're up to it."

"I'm looking forward to visitors now, so please spread the word."

"I'll do that. Tell me, Alison, what specific prayer requests do you have other than the obvious?"

"I didn't tell you the last time you were here, because I was coping with the fresh news of my paralysis, but I also lost a baby girl. With my overwhelming loss, the tears are always just below the surface. Now, I'm wondering if the Bible says anything concerning the spirit of one who hasn't even been born. Are they automatically accepted into heaven?"

"Oh, Alison. I'm very sorry to hear of your loss. I didn't know you were pregnant. This whole trial must be so difficult. Let's read what the Bible says about unborn babies. You may know this Psalm of David—chapter one-thirty-nine, verses thirteen to sixteen: 'For you created my inmost being. You knit me together in my mother's womb. I praise you because I am fearfully and wonderfully made; your works are wonderful, I know that full well. My frame was not hidden from you when I was made in the secret place. When I was woven together in the depths of the earth, your eyes saw my unformed body. All the days ordained for me were written in your book before one of them came to be.'"

Pastor Ed saw the tears forming and reached for a tissue. Tears had washed her face many times since the injury.

He continued. "Although every human being is said to be conceived in sin after the fall of Adam and Eve, an unborn baby is the most innocent. I believe that your baby is in heaven right now in Jesus' arms. He knew your baby girl before you even realized that you were pregnant. Since your baby didn't have a chance to know about Jesus, she also didn't have an opportunity to reject Him either."

Alison hung onto every encouraging word her pastor said, like someone reaching for a handhold to avoid plummeting over a cliff. After hearing the comforting passage, Alison believed with her whole heart that she would see her baby in heaven. "Thank you, Rev. Is there anything you could suggest to bring further healing to my emotions?"

"I have dealt with other mothers who miscarried, and even those who chose to abort their babies. These women were helped by naming their baby and saying a goodbye prayer."

"Oh, Rev, I would like to give her a name." Alison sighed, then her genuine smile brightened her face. "I need some time to think about a name. Then we can have a service here in this room. I know my mom and dad would like to join us. Do you think Karen would come?"

"I'll ask her; I believe she'd be honoured. I could do a service next Monday, if that gives you enough time to contact everyone you want here?"

"I'll phone you to confirm the date and time, Rev."

"Yes, that would be fine. Before I go, let's pray together and ask for God's comfort and continued relief from the physical and emotional pain you're experiencing."

Having expressed that God heard their requests, they bid one another goodbye.

***

"Hello, my name is Skeeter Johnson, and I am the head of the hospital's physiotherapy department. And this is Rachelle, your personal therapist." Skeeter winked at Rachelle, possibly thinking Alison didn't see.

Rachelle was a well-developed young woman with straight blond hair and fair skin.

"Hello," said Alison as she stuck out her hand. Rachelle did the same.

Alison turned her attention back to Skeeter Johnson. He wore jeans and a paisley-patterned shirt opened to mid-chest, exposing a gold medallion. She would have expected him to wear a lab coat, but she figured that as a department head he must be able to wear whatever he wanted. His clean-shaven chin showed a "Kirk Douglas" cleft. And all that identified him as a professional was his clip-on badge.

"Mrs. Steele, I believe?"

"Call me Alison, will you please?"

"Well, Alison, it looks like we have our work cut out for us. First, I want to ask, What do you understand about your injury?"

"Dr. Shapiro told me that my spinal cord has been compressed at the halfway level, and two vertebrae were splintered. He believes I'll be paralyzed in both my legs for the rest of my life." She successfully quelled her emotions.

"How did you take this news?"

"I'm not sure. I'm doing all I can to keep my head above water."

"You poor girl. I understand your dilemma. I grew up with a brother who was a quadriplegic." He frowned. "I can tell you this much, it's going to be weeks before you're able to sit. In the meantime, we'll get you started with exercises that you can do here in bed."

Skeeter handed the rest of the session over to Rachelle, who was holding two-pound handgrip weights.

"Rachelle is especially knowledgeable about paraplegia. I think she enjoys the challenge. I'll leave the rest up to her. Good luck to you, Alison."

"Thanks."

Rachelle put down the weights and took a measuring tape out of her pocket. She measured the circumference of Alison's biceps and forearms. In a sing-song voice she said, "These measurements will increase as your muscles develop; they'll be a good indicator of your progress. My plan is to teach you how to be as independent as possible. There are others on the team to encourage you and give support. We all want feedback from you. My job will be to set reasonable goals, let you know what to expect, and then we'll celebrate your progress."

"Sounds great."

Alison's exercises started with a series of bicep curls. She lifted the weights above her head and back down as instructed, repeating the exercise several times with each arm.

Rachelle was pleased with Alison's first efforts and gave her thigh an affirming pat.

All of a sudden the covers shifted. "Did you see that?" said Alison a little louder than she intended. "My leg just moved!"

"Yes, I did see it, but that was an involuntary movement."

"If my leg can move like that, maybe it will move when I want it to."

"Alison, let me explain about spasms. Spontaneous movements, or spasms, are common with paraplegics, especially when they are fatigued. And a spasm can happen when there is pressure from a touch, as was the case today. Just ordinary tension in your body, or any infection, will cause a spasm. These uncontrollable movements happen because the connection from the brain to the muscle has been damaged."

Alison's voice dropped. "Oh, I think I understand."

"Don't let this brief false hope cloud over all that you've accomplished today."

Alison made an effort to sound brave. "Alright. When is our next session?"

"I'll be back next week to see how you are coming along with what I've given you so far."

"I'm going to put my utmost into developing my arm muscles," said Alison with a lilt in her voice.

"Good. I wish all my clients were as enthusiastic as you."

"I have an advantage."

"Oh? What's that?"

"I'm a Christian, and God is looking after me."

Rachelle raised her eyebrows. "Time will tell. Goodbye for now."

"Bye, Rachelle. I'm glad you are my therapist." Alison smiled.

Rachelle responded with a wave as she left.

***

With a lightness in his voice, Bill greeted his daughter. "How's my girly, today?"

Alison was surprised to see a change in her father. *At least this forced smile was better than his grim expression.* "Hi, Dad. It's been a long time since you called me that."

"Yes, too long." He paused, took a deep breath and said, "Seeing my daughter confined to this monster bed seemed to make me tongue-tied. But enough about my feelings. Have there been any new developments with you?"

Although she felt like complaining about the sleep-interrupted nights, Alison grinned instead. "I'm developing more muscle." She held up her right arm in a flexed bicep pose, and chuckled. "Well, what do you think? Are my muscles growing?"

"Let's have a feel." He lifted his hairy hand to squeeze Alison's arm. "Well, that's impressive for less than a week's work. I do believe your arm feels a little firmer."

"Thanks. I've been working hard. Dad, there's something else that's very important to me. I want to honour my baby girl with a memorial service, even though I didn't get to see her."

With a sad expression, remembering their loss anew, he nodded.

"I'd like to have a small ceremony here in my room. I want a few people to come—family, a few close friends, and my nurse, Nancy. I told Mom about it and asked if she could make arrangements with Pastor Ed."

"To tell you the truth, I believe that would be very healing ceremony for all of us. I'll let you know as soon as things are arranged."

"Oh, thanks, Dad. See if next coming Monday would be good for everybody." She hoped that he would remember the day. "And Dad, did you look into my request about Phoebe Palmer?"

"I'm sorry, honey, I forgot all about it. I'll go to the library, today." He planted a kiss on her forehead and left.

chapter ten

Although Alison's faith had sustained her during the difficult years of marital abuse, the past few weeks seemed to be the ultimate test. Late in the evening someone dropped a metallic object in the hall just outside Alison's door, which caused her to awaken from needed sleep. Not having full presence of mind, she blurted out loud, "Do you have to be so clumsy?"

A high-pitched, barely audible voice said, "Sorry."

Immediately, Alison regretted this outburst. *Why is it that sometimes I feel that I'm accepting this tragedy and other times I'm so swift to lash out?*

She prayed in the dark. *Lord, help me to believe that good will come from all I've lost. I'm feeling sorry for myself and I drag the past into the present so many times. I don't want to waste precious time being miserable. Take away these resentful thoughts. I need courage to keep pressing on. And would You please ease this pain?*

Tomorrow, I'd like to be alert. The medication makes me drowsy, so help me to need less. Thank you Jesus, Father, and Holy Spirit. Amen."

Alison slept well after that prayer. The next morning, she had a new mindset. She knew it was her decision to transform her downcast state of mind into one of purpose. To scale the steep mountain of physical limitations and to reach the land of recovery would take every ounce of fortitude that she could muster.

This was the day she would meet a hospital's counsellor. After breakfast and morning care, an attractive woman entered the room. She introduced herself with her head tilted, giving her large hazel eyes a certain appeal. "Hi. My name is Sharon Taylor. I've been selected to help you express your concerns and to effectively find an avenue for you to be productive in your future."

Alison smiled a warm greeting, wondering if all counsellors used this type of vocabulary and if she had memorized that introductory statement. "Hi. I guess you already know my name, Alison Steele."

"Yes. May I call you Alison?"

"Please do. Thank you in advance for your help. I'll need all I can get."

"Good. I'll do my best. I'm aware of the facts of your injury and the loss of your child because of it. If you feel you are able to talk about it, I'm here to listen and to be your ally."

She's making it sound like I'm in a war. Maybe I am.

Sharon continued. "I'm aware that your husband is responsible. Do you want to talk about that night?"

"I know I have to deal with the events at some point, but I feel I don't want to start our conversation there. Actually, I don't know where to start."

"Perhaps you could begin by recalling your negative emotions, and then try naming them."

Alison nodded her consent. When she was ready, she spoke the first words that came to mind. "Shock. Disbelief. Fear. Anger. What did I do to deserve this?"

Sharon sent Alison a compassionate look. "That's a very descriptive list for your first attempt at something like this. Those emotions are totally understandable, but I want to make you aware that the last one could cause a less-than-healthy attitude toward yourself, although it is quite common for victims to transfer some of the responsibility of the abuser onto themselves. You may even question whether you could have done something to prevent it."

Alison shrugged. *I know I didn't always have my eyes wide open. I did love Reb. And love is blind at times.*

Sharon continued. "Paralysis is difficult enough when it is due to an accident. Even more so when someone you care about has put you in danger."

Alison was starting to understand her own emotions. "I never thought about it that way."

Sharon observed Alison's brow wrinkle, and ended the conversation by saying, "I'm thinking that you are in pain and that I should end the session."

"Alright." Alison had anticipated a longer consultation; she wondered if these sessions were of any value, or if they were even necessary. After all, she was expecting her emotions to heal as well as her legs. She rang her call bell and asked for medication.

***

In the dark of early morning, hushed chatter and occasional laughter from the nurses' station invaded Alison's room. *I need more rest to be able to handle this morning's service. I don't know why I'm feeling so irritated, almost to the boiling point. If I don't fight to control this annoyance, I won't be in the right frame of mind for the flow of the Holy Spirit.* To lower the temperature of her thoughts, she considered what she would say at her baby's memorial.

She conjured up a beautiful vision of her daughter in heaven. She prayed to the source of all wisdom. *Jesus, is it possible to speak to my daughter through You?* Alison couldn't think of a verse in the Bible that supported one view or another. Keeping her mind quiet, she sensed that it was fine with God.

"This service is for you, my little one, resting in our Father's care. I suppose you are happy and have adjusted to your new home. I'm about to give you a name that will be not so much for your sake as for mine.

"Some of our relatives will see this ceremony as a type of birth announcement. For others, it's your naming party. The rest may see this gathering as a funeral.

"My dear baby, before I announce your name to others, I want to tell you the names I've chosen. In teachers' college I had two friends that were more like sisters—Kathryn and Lynndale. I want your first name to be a combination of these lovely names—Kathlynn. Your second name is Shannon, named after an unforgotten friend from Grade two. And your last name is Palmer."

***

Alison tugged again on the violet satin nightgown that her mother had purchased. The bandage on her nose had been removed, and the bruises were no longer noticeable as she looked at her reflection in a mirror from her over-bed table. While she waited patiently for everyone to arrive, she stared at her grandmother's motto. Then she occupied herself by counting those who would attend: her mother and father, Pastor Ed and Karen, Nancy, Kathryn, Lynndale, and Alison's sister, Daneen. Her thoughtful brother, William, had sent a card, and a letter had come from her grandfather.

The hour arrived and everyone stood in place.

***

As Nancy turned to shut the door for privacy, she saw Mac approach in the hallway, dressed in his crisply pressed uniform. She boldly asked, "What is the nature of your visit?"

"I'm not on official business. I'm just visiting as a friend."

Mac hadn't seen Alison for days. She had been on his mind constantly, and he wanted to see her beautiful face again. He had planned to tell her his impression of her church and pastor since attending last Sunday's service.

"A memorial service for Alison's baby is about to begin," Nancy informed him.

"Alison has become a friend of mine. She'd allow me to attend."

"These people have come by personal invitation."

Mac persisted. "Could you ask her?"

"She has invited all the friends she wants to be here; besides, there's not enough room for more."

Mac frowned, lowered his head, turned on his heel, and left.

***

Eight people solemnly gathered around her cold, steel bed, each adding warmth to the medical feel of the room.

While songbirds warbled in cheery unison outside her window, Alison began to speak, "Thank you for coming this morning, everyone." Alison looked from one face to another lining the sides of her bed. "Some of you had not even heard of my pregnancy or about the loss of my baby until you received your invitation to this memorial service." She took a deep breath and then wiped her eyes and blew her nose. "Forgive me, I'm very emotional today. But please don't feel sorry for me; God knows what's best. I know my baby is alive in heaven. She's residing in the best home anyone could imagine.

"I've named her Kathlynn Shannon Palmer. Giving her a name has helped me to picture her alive and well. This memorial service also helps me to deal with saying goodbye, even though I was unable to say hello." The tears continued to flow, making it difficult for her words to be clear.

After taking a shallow breath through her clogged nose, she introduced her pastor. "I'll hand the service over to Pastor Ed McAlester."

Pastor Ed admitted that this was the first time he had conducted this type of service and that he had taken hours to decide what scriptures to use. He had prepared a brief sermon on the importance of relinquishing one's sorrows in life without holding resentment. Those present needed comforting words and wisdom as to how to handle possible unforgiving thoughts they might have about Reb.

"Alison, your little one has just begun to live without the hindrances of earth's troubles. And there's no way of knowing if Kathlynn will age, as we perceive aging. This we do know—the Bible says in the gospel of

John that we are to comfort one another with this passage of scripture: John fourteen, one to three: 'Let not your heart be troubled: ye believe in God; believe also in me. In my Father's house are many mansions: if it were not so, I would have told you. I go to prepare a place for you. And if I go and prepare a place for you, I will come again, and receive you unto myself; that where I am, there ye may be also.'

"If we were all living with Jesus in the atmosphere of paradise, how could we be anything less than overjoyed?

"God bless you, Alison." The service concluded.

Nancy left first to continue with her routine. Daneen bent to kiss her younger sister, then left with a thoughtful expression on her face. Ed and Karen patted her shoulder, kissed her cheek, and said goodbye. Janette and Bill remained at the side of the room with their backs toward the younger women. Kathryn and Lynndale stayed to talk and to express their pleasure in having Alison name her baby after them.

A general-duty nurse brought in Alison's lunch on a well-used, beige tray. It had the usual fare of an over-cooked mixture and a small side salad. When the young women left, Alison's father and mother approached her bed. Her mother asked if she could help her with her lunch. "I can imagine how difficult it is to eat while flat on your back."

"I'm not very hungry, but I'll try a little. Thanks for your help, Mom." Alison took a mouthful of casserole after they said grace.

"Mother and I went to *The Hamilton Spectator* and asked to see their archives. We got some help from a nice young lady," Bill said. "She found an ancient newspaper from microfilm with Walter and Phoebe Palmer's names. The revival was apparently big news and she came up with quite a lot of information."

Between bites Alison said, "That's great, Dad. I'm listening."

"I made notes of the highlights. Phoebe was born on December eighteenth, 1807, died on November second, 1874.

"She didn't live very long, only sixty-sixty years." Bill continued to read. "She committed her life to Christ at an early age and at the age of eleven wrote a poem that even adults enjoyed. She lived in Brooklyn, New York, where she married Walter, a physician.

"In the first ten years of marriage, she and Walter suffered the deaths of three of their four children. In 1828, their firstborn son, Alexander, died at nine months of age. In 1830, their second son, died at seven weeks—no name was mentioned. Three years later, Phoebe gave birth to their first girl, Phoebe Sarah Palmer. She was the only child to reach adulthood."

Bill stopped reading to emphasize a crucial point. "You see, they didn't have any surviving sons, so our Palmer name didn't come from them. There's no way we can be their direct descendants."

Terribly let down, a small tear appeared on Alison's cheek. She didn't usually cry this easily, but her emotions were still in a tender state.

Bill glanced at his daughter, not seeing her tear, and continued to read.

"In 1835, their second daughter died when the curtains surrounding her cradle caught fire."

Alison gasped.

"Phoebe wrote concerning her daughter's death: 'Time I would have devoted to her shall be spent in work for Jesus.'

"She was described as a well-polished public speaker, and had published four hymns."

After a pause, Bill added, "There was very little information given about the revival in Hamilton. It said that 1857 was the zenith of Phoebe's career as a revivalist. The revival progressed from Hamilton to New York state. Apparently, the short revival in Hamilton affected only one denomination." Bill looked up from the paper. "Doesn't it seem to you that God had more in mind for our city?"

Although crestfallen, Alison was able to respond, "Yes, Dad. I've a deep belief that I'll get to see more of what God wanted. My hope isn't conditional on being her direct descendant. I only wished I was."

"Yes, I understand, daughter. I do have some other news for you though. The woman at the *Spectator* found information about our ancestors. I found out that my grandfather, Ray Palmer, who lived in New Jersey, was a congregational minister. He may not be as famous as Phoebe and Walter, but I'm glad to know his deeds were not forgotten."

"Well, isn't that something!" exclaimed Janette as she squeezed Alison's hand. She picked up the tray from the over-bed table and put it in the hall. When she returned, Bill turned in her direction and said, "I wouldn't have known this information about my family if Alison hadn't asked me to do this research."

"If you're comfortable, sweetheart, we should be going," said her mother.

"I'm good. See you soon."

chapter eleven

Alison tried to objectively assess her feelings for Mac. *It's been only a short time since I've actually seen him as a friend. What's nice is that we can talk about almost anything. I know I'll see him often at church after I'm discharged—that's if he actually decides to make it his home church.*

Here I'm thinking about my discharge, and I haven't even been out of this bed. It could be months before I'm released from the hospital.

I don't know where these thoughts about Mac will take me, but I'm tired of pushing them away.

Mac, the epitome of manhood in Alison's estimation, stood at least six feet tall, with a full head of chestnut hair and the darkest brown eyes she'd ever seen. It was impossible to distinguish between the iris and the pupil; they reminded her of chocolate Smarties. And who could compete with the cutest cleft chin she had ever seen?

Alison prayed, *God, are You in this friendship? Romantic feelings could spoil the free and easy way Mac and I relate to one another. Since Mac is athletic. I believe he'll eventually be drawn to a physically capable woman, like I used to be.*

Thanks for listening and always being there. Amen.

***

Less than an hour later, Mac entered her room during afternoon visiting hours. It was his day off and he wore a stylish, matching outfit of the Arnold Palmer line. Its light tan colour set off his dark eyes, hair, and complexion.

"Spring has finally arrived and so have I," he announced.

Mac's overconfident air usually annoyed her, but she had come to enjoy his light-hearted company.

"Did Nancy tell you that I was annoyed at not being allowed to go to the memorial for your daughter? I think that you would have let me attend. Right?"

"Nancy told me what she said to you, and I understand her reasoning. But since you are a Christian friend, it would have been okay. It's just that you are such a new friend that I didn't think of inviting you. I hope your feelings weren't hurt."

"Not exactly, but I did want to see you before I began my shift that day. This time I waited for a day off."

"It's kind of you to spend part of your day off here in this oppressive place." Just then a moan reached their ears from the hallway, reminding them of the suffering around them.

"I see what you mean, but I don't find it oppressive, because you're here." He winked and smiled that gigantic grin of his that might have charmed many ladies. *I don't want to encourage him, so I'll change the subject.*

"How did you like my church?" She really was interested.

"It was great. I especially liked the music."

Her first thought was to test him to see if he had truly listened to the message. "Did the sermon speak to you in any way?"

"Yes, the text was, 'He that finds a wife, finds a good thing.' It was very timely for me because I am looking for that special someone." He gave her a smile, with one eyebrow raised.

She swallowed hard, and then stared at him. She couldn't even return the slightest smile. "I'm sure the right girl will come along in time. You're quite young yet." *He looks several years younger than me, but couldn't have reached the rank of corporal that soon.*

"I have my eye on one particular one." He smiled at her again.

Alison, not able to return the smile, searched for a question on a more general subject. She asked how he liked the sanctuary.

"It's just like any other church I've seen—you know, shiny pews, coloured windows, and the usual red carpet."

"Mac, I'm very tired today. Would you mind if we keep this visit short?" She could see his disappointment, but he agreed to return the next day.

***

That night Alison was feeling exceptionally warm, which must have triggered a dream of her being a moulded clay pot, baking in a kiln. In her dream she examined the other pots on the shelf, each having a different colour and shape. Some were beautifully designed, and some had nothing special about them. Several were smashed on the floor, while others were imperfectly glued together. To her surprise, a few were in miniature wheelchairs. She saw her likeness portrayed on one marred vessel, but this pot was not in a wheelchair.

On waking and remembering every detail of the dream, she instantly knew its interpretation. When a newly moulded piece of pottery is put into a kiln, it is made stronger by the heat. The heating process changes the painted glaze from a neutral brown into various bright colours. She saw herself as a recently formed, yet flawed, vessel that must be put into the fire—her disability—to be made spiritually stronger. She determined that when it came time to emerge from the high temperature, she'd be like a beautifully coloured piece of art. And possibly, one day, maybe not even in a wheelchair.

I believe that someday I'll walk again, but for now I must accept that in the near future, a wheelchair may be a part of my life. At least it will partially get me to where I want to go. Someday, when Rev's prophetic word becomes reality, I believe that I'll use an empty wheelchair, sitting beside me, to draw interest. As Rev said, I'm obligated to accept this hardship so that I may reach out to other sufferers—some disabled, some not.

***

Later that morning, as the day shift started, Alison developed a full-blown fever. When Karen entered after being off for five days, she noticed Alison's lips, bright red with fever blisters, contrasting with the pallor that circled her mouth, showing that she was breathing shallowly and wasn't getting enough oxygen. She took Alison's temperature immediately: 103 degrees. The previous shift had not reported any abnormalities. The nurses' notes for the past five days didn't give any clues as to what caused this decline. Karen took a urine sample to check for a bladder infection. Next, she would look at Alison's incision site.

She administered pain medication but felt it urgent to rotate the bed immediately. Alison moaned as the bed started to move. As soon as Alison rested on her stomach, Karen saw the blood stains and smelled a sickening, sweet odour. The cause of Alison's fever became obvious as Karen lifted the nightgown. The incision wasn't infected, as she had first thought; rather Alison's tailbone area had an angry pressure ulcer.

Alison's voice interrupted Karen's shock. "My lips feel funny—as if they're puffy."

"You have some fever blisters, Alison."

Now Alison knew why she had dreamed about being in a kiln.

"Are you worried about your condition?" Karen asked.

"Some, but I trust you'll tell me anything I need to know. But I don't trust the nurses from the agency that have been on duty the last few days."

"Can you tell me their names and why you don't trust them?"

"The one working the day shift, named Rhoda, had a badge that said 'Care Watch Agency.' For the last three nights I don't remember my bed being turned or seeing the nurse on duty for the next shift. When I mentioned it to Rhoda, she told me that the night nurse reported that

I had slept through the turning. I believed her because I slept through the turning once before, but when it happened three nights in a row I wondered if someone was lying. She ignored many of my questions. I never did get a straight answer."

"Will you describe Rhoda, please."

"She's tall and resembles someone I may have met before or it could be just her voice, but I can't think from where. She has shiny, short blond hair, seems to be in her thirties, has large eyes, and is overweight."

"I see," said Karen. "The reason I asked is because you have a bedsore that wasn't there five days ago when I was last on shift. I'll be checking into this whole matter."

"Will I still be seeing the hospital's counsellor this morning?"

"That will have to be postponed because I'll get orders to start treatment right away and rearrange your counselling meeting for this afternoon, when you can be on your back again."

Nancy left to speak to the head nurse.

***

Nancy returned in thirty minutes to inform Alison, "We don't have a record of a Rhoda. But the other nurses remember one who was lazy and didn't even seem capable in turning the patients."

"That's strange." Alison made a decision not to panic.

"I'm sorry you received such treatment that caused you this setback, but I expect a full recuperation."

"That's good to hear. When am I to have my session with Sharon?"

"She'll visit your room the first chance she has following lunch."

***

After the clearing of the lunch tray, a letter arrived in a yellow envelope with a flowery scent. Alison's name and the hospital address were typed. Alison ripped it open and began to read, "My dear wife." The paper rattled as her hands began to shake. *It's from Reb! He must have been trying to disguise the sender by perfuming the envelope and choosing feminine stationary. The restraining order stipulates that he's not to contact me. If I read the rest of it, will I be breaking the law too?*

77

Images of his hate-filled face breaking through the barricaded apartment door flashed through her mind. She shuddered.

What if there's information that will help my divorce proceedings? There may be information that backs up my story of abuse and adultery. She gave into this impulse and started to read.

> My dear wife Alison,
> I shouldn't even be in prison for hitting you this once. If you drop the charge, my lawyer could get me out of here tomorrow. The other prisoners treat me awful. They're all perverts.
> Didn't I do something right? I bought you a diamond ring and a silver heart necklace on Valentine's Day last year. I called the ambulance, sat beside you, and didn't move you. I tried to help the attendants get you into the ambulance.
> If you don't do this, you'll pay.
> I'll definitely find a way,
> Tomorrow or even today.
> —Reb

I'll pay? I'm already paying because of his violence. He hit me "this once"—yeah, right. What about all the other times? This letter doesn't even sound like it's from Reb. He never wrote a riddle in his life. And what does it mean "tomorrow or today?"

She managed to rip herself away from the letter and prayed. *Please help me, Lord. My thoughts are all mixed up. I need to talk to You about my anger and the fear that is surfacing. Living in dread of seeing him again, or wondering what else he might do, is a terrible way to live.*

Lord Jesus, rescue me from my own fears. Your Word says that perfect love casts out fear, and I know that You love me perfectly. Show me what I should do to be peaceful and courageous. Amen.

Sharon walked into the room, and Alison hurriedly stuffed the letter into the drawer on her over-bed table.

"Hi. Is my timing okay?"

Alison didn't look up. "Well, I was expecting you." Her mind was still on the letter. *He didn't even say anything about the baby.*

"Are you able to share what was in the letter that seems to have shaken you?"

Alison made a quick decision to confide in Sharon. "It's from my husband. I'm wondering how he was able to send a letter from prison while there's a restraining order in effect. Do you have any ideas?"

"I don't know all the details of our penal system. My guess would be as good as yours."

"I just hope he isn't going to send any more."

"You could just leave them unopened, and give this one to someone you trust. Can you think of someone?"

"Yes. But I'm afraid of how my friend would react. He'd probably think less of me for reading this letter."

"Let's not talk about the letter for now. Okay?" Sharon waited until Alison finally looked her way. "My goal today is to help you see your true self, rather than the way Reb saw you."

With a higher-pitched, strained voice Alison said, "I really don't care what Reb thought, or does, right now." Alison thought better of taking her anger out on Sharon. "I'm sorry. I shouldn't have said it like that."

"It's better to let your emotions out rather than bottle them up. Don't you agree?"

Alison nodded.

"Tell me of a time when you felt controlled, stifled, or totally demeaned by Reb. I don't want you to hold anything back. Cry. Scream. All is permissible. You need to release the tension by expressing yourself."

After a quick prayer for the precise memory, and thankful that an incident came clearly to the forefront, Alison began. "On one extremely hot summer day two years ago, I wanted to get out of our small, stifling apartment. It was on a second floor of an old house without air-conditioning. I'd had several sleepless nights and felt totally spent. Reb announced that he was going to the beach. And I thought he told me so that I could get some things together. As I followed him down the stairs, where his sister was waiting at the bottom, he turned around and said, 'Where do you think you're going, b-----? You're not going anywhere with the house that f-----n' messy.' I was humiliated in front of my sister-in-law." Alison held tears back as she reached the end.

"What was your response to his commands and dirty words?"

"I didn't dare say anything in front of his sister because she always sided with him. They left. After I cleaned up the house, I went for a long walk."

"Did you cry?"

"No. I just swallowed my pride and did the 'good-wife' thing."

"How do you think you would respond today?"

When Alison didn't answer, Sharon prompted. "Let me hear what you would have liked to say to Reb."

In a voice louder than even Alison expected, words came spewing out like an uncapped geyser. "Reb, I don't need you to give me a break. I can take one any time because I deserve it. I work hard at my job and at home. You chose to humiliate me in front of your sister and that is the last time. I deserve an apology right now while your sister is still here!"

Sharon, wide-eyed, rested back in her portable chair that was high enough to make her level with the high hospital bed and said, "That's the way, Alison. Do you feel better?"

"Yes. I believe I do."

"I'm proud of you. I had a meeting with your head nurse, family doctor, and physiotherapist. We're all working together to help you recover physically and emotionally. You have been holding back for a long time, and it's time for you to be set free. If there is anything you need to get off your chest, I want you to vent all these feelings to us."

Alison was able to look Sharon in the eye. "Yes, I will. And thanks." *She's a very gifted, caring person. I think I like her now. She's less formal than she was at our introduction.*

"I believe that's enough for today, Alison." Sharon left with a smile.

chapter twelve

Lying on her back, Alison stared at her cross-stitch, moving with the room's air currents. *Teach me, Father, Jesus, Holy Spirit, what You really want me to know about giving love.* She made her mind quiet, shutting out other thoughts, and concentrated on what the Lord might say.

"You are correct in seeing love as a gift, but it doesn't have to be received to be called love. This kind of love is a true, unconditional love. I loved you before you came into existence, before you were able to show love in return. When unconditional love operates, you leave the results with Me. Lean on Me and I will make everything right in due time."

I think I just heard from God. Love is an action word, and it is to be given unselfishly, expecting nothing in return. When I'm up and able to write, I'm going to record these insights in a book.

Mac strode happily into Alison's hospital room, wearing his uniform. His good looks took her breath away for a second. She wondered if she would get over the effect his presence had on her. Licking her blistered lips, she asked her pressing question before she lost her nerve. "Mac, what will happen when Reb is released from prison?"

"Don't I even get a greeting first?"

"I'm sorry. Hello, and thank you for visiting. I need to confess; I think I've made a mistake. I received a letter from Reb. I'm afraid I read it, even when I guessed it might be wrong." She took a quick breath and continued before Mac could say anything. "He told me he wants me to drop the charges, and he ended with a weird riddle that implies he'll retaliate if I don't."

"Don't apologize. You didn't do anything wrong." Mac paused then looked at her face intently. "Alison, are you feeling okay? You look flushed."

"I've had a little setback, but the nurses are looking after me now."

"I'm sorry to hear about your illness." Sensing that she didn't want to go into details, Mac turned his attention to the letter. "Could I read Reb's letter please?"

She took it out of the drawer and handed it to him. She studied Mac's expression. He sniffed the letter and raised an eyebrow in a questioning look, then read the whole page. "About you reading the letter—anyone would be curious. Reb isn't much of a poet, but he does sound like a typical abuser. He's not remorseful that you're paralyzed but angry that he was incarcerated.

"It'll be my duty to make sure this letter is authentic. If it's from Reb, he's the kind of guy who may commit a more serious violation if he's not held accountable."

"Do you really think there's doubt that he wrote it? It mentions things that only he'd know."

"Reb could have told those details to someone," said Mac.

Alison nodded.

"Coming back to your original question about what will happen once Reb is released—by law, he must attend an abuser help group for several weeks. It's a new requirement as a part of his probation. But that won't start until almost a year from now, and the order concerning your personal protection will continue after that."

"Do you think he'll get a year in prison?"

"Yes, because of the seriousness of his actions, although I feel it should be more."

"Do you know if there is such a thing as being rehabilitated from spousal abuse?"

"I've no statistics about that, but I'd think not without God's help."

Alison pressed. "Do you think he'll get out before the whole sentence is finished?"

"I'm sure that he won't get off early for good behaviour, because of his violent temper. Also, he seems to have no regard for anyone in authority."

"You're right about his temper. I guess I shouldn't worry about him being released early." She swallowed. "I'm ready to hear about this abuser group."

"It's a relatively new program in which the abuser is shown how to look at his or her actions and learns different ways to respond instead of acting out in anger. Several newly released inmates discuss their stories, get feedback from the other members, and a counsellor acts as a mediator and teacher." Mac paused. "Before Reb's release, I suggest you meet with his probation officer."

"Why would that be important?"

"In previous cases I've seen the perpetrator describe a distorted view of his abused wife. He usually tries to make a good impression on the probation officer with a type of male bonding technique that he learned behind bars. He may even have learned some personal information about his probation officer's family. This way he can show concern over some problem that each family is bound to have. Reb may give the impression that he's the nicest guy in the world. He may tell lies about you that could be very believable, such as that he acted in self-defence because he believed you were trying to kill him."

"Oh, really?"

"I heard of one abuser who obtained counterfeit receipts from a drug store. He convincingly alleged that his wife was attempting to poison him. My advice is to visit the probation officer, when Reb's release is near, to make it harder for Reb to portray a distorted view of your personality. Reb already told me that you charged at him as he tried to get out of the apartment. The judge didn't buy his story, but that doesn't mean everyone will see through his attempts to shift his blame. He's quite a performer. The ambulance attendants reported that when they arrived Reb was very calm and showed great concern for you. He already admitted that he doesn't see himself as a 'real abuser' and said that the courts should go after men that are more violent than him."

Would he really lie like that just to save his own skin? "This is a lot to think about." Alison could feel her voice become shaky.

"I hope I haven't upset you."

"It's quite unsettling, but I'd rather know what could happen than to be left in the dark."

"That's my girl." He winked at her.

This last statement made her blush. *Oh, no! I'm afraid he's gone beyond the boundaries of professionalism. If he would only look for a girl who would suit him; someone who could jog with him and make pretty babies.*

***

After Mac left, Alison needed a sleep. When she finally opened her eyes, she focused on a red, white, and sliver striped package with a red crinoline bow, sitting on her over-bed table.

I wonder when this was delivered.

Alison reached for the package and searched for a card. There wasn't any. She gently tore the paper away to reveal a white, five-by-eight inch, confectionary box. The colourful foil elastic slid off easily to reveal uniform mounds of dark chocolate—each encircled with a lace doily. They looked as if they had come from a bakery rather than a factory. *I'll save them for when I have company. Sharing them will be fun.*

***

Daneen came for a visit while her husband, Mark, stayed home to watch their children. Daneen tried to smile at her sister, but it lasted only a few seconds. The creases on her forehead showed emotional pain, and made her look older than her thirty-eight years.

"I feel like declaring war against God for allowing this to happen to you," Daneen spit out. "And Reb is where he belongs—in jail."

Lord, give me what to say that will help her. "I'm okay, sis. I'll get through this. And how would you declare war against the Creator of the universe, anyway?" Alison chuckled.

Daneen smiled as she dipped her head. "Allie, it hurts to see half of you unable to move and the other half the same as I've always known you to be. Why are you smiling?"

"You know about my relationship with Jesus. My beliefs have remained the same." Patting her own legs she said, "This doesn't change anything. I believe God has a special plan for me, even if I have to do everything from a wheelchair."

Daneen shook her head and had a very thoughtful look. "I'll think about what you've said. In the meantime, what can I do to help?"

"You can help me by listening to my latest news and share a secret, like old times when I would come to your house to sleep over."

"That sounds neat. I like secrets, but tell me the news first."

"I've decided to write my autobiography to help other women with similar problems."

"I could have used some help myself years ago. It was just last fall, when you stayed with me over night while Mark was away on business, that I told anyone for the first time that I'd been abused in my first marriage."

Alison nodded.

"I told you about the time Daren dragged me by the hair down the street when I was pregnant with Victoria. I guess I experienced a different kind of pain than you because I didn't lean on God like you do. Daren never left a bruise, so no one ever guessed what I suffered.

"Remember the morning after our talk—you mentioned that your nipples were tender?" Thinking it was insensitive to talk about Alison's baby, Daneen said, "I'm sorry, I shouldn't bring that painful memory up."

"It's okay, Dannie. I have to grieve my daughter's loss. Don't try to save me pain by avoiding talking about memories."

Daneen sighed. "Okay. Remember the rest of the conversation?"

"Yes. You asked me when I had my last period."

"And you told me it was two weeks late but you assumed it was due to all the stress of Reb being gone without a word of explanation."

"I felt nauseated, and my whole body was upset. Food had no appeal for me, and then your words took me by surprise—'I think you're pregnant,'" said Alison.

"Yeah, and you suspected that I was right, but you still had mixed thoughts. I remember your exact words. You said that God wouldn't allow you to become pregnant now!"

"Well, I know that God allows all kinds of trials, but several months ago I didn't know how I could tolerate a pregnancy, having such emotional turmoil."

"How did you really feel about the pregnancy?"

"When the doctor confirmed your suspicion, I was overcome with worry. Feeling nauseated didn't help. I also questioned God's timing. Week after week, as I started to feel better, I looked forward to loving this little child I carried. I thought finally I'd have someone to love unreservedly and some day receive love in return. And the longer Reb stayed away, the more I gradually started to accept a life of single parenthood and look forward to it."

"Well, I can tell you it's not so great. Then Mark came into my life."

"Yes, he's a good father to Daren's daughter."

"Yes, he is."

"Can we talking about my writing? You were very good in English in college."

"Sure. That's great you want to write a book, but I can't wait any longer to hear your secret."

"Oh, okay. I think Mac, the police officer, is interested in me."

"What's been happening?"

"He's been winking at me and making excuses to visit. Yesterday chocolates just appeared in my room. But it's not just what he says and does, it's his whole demeanour."

"How do you feel about this?" asked Daneen.

"I'm keeping a tight rein on my feelings. I don't know what to say to him. What would you do?"

"I'd give it time. You aren't divorced yet, and you have been through a lot of trauma. There's no rush in deciding if you want a man in your life. Allow time for healing."

Her sister was wise.

Alison thought that this was a perfect time to share the chocolates. "Can I offer you a chocolate?"

"No thank you. I've been trying to watch what I'm eating lately."

"Good for you."

"I don't like to call it dieting. That always seems to set me up for failure. Sorry to end this conversation, but I must be on my way, Allie."

"Thanks for coming, sis."

Thank you, Lord, for letting Daneen see the difference You make in my life. Draw her to Yourself and bring her to the place of repentance.

They kissed each other's cheeks. Daneen returned a big smile.

***

Mac returned to give a report about his investigation of the letter from Reb.

"Hello, Mac. Thanks for the beautifully wrapped box of chocolates. Would you like one?"

"I didn't send you chocolates." As Mac peered into the opened box that was still full of a homemade-type candy, a warning bell rang in his head. "Who else could have given you these?"

"It's a mystery, because there's no card. I just assumed it was from you."

His brow wrinkled. "I certainly would have put a card with it. Let's be careful. I'd like to take them with me."

Alison raised questioning eyebrows. "Sure. What do you think is going on?"

Mac pulled a pair of latex gloves from an inner pocket of his uniform, and put them on before picking up the box to put in a paper bag taken from her over-bed table. "I'd like to find out who your secret admirer

87

is," he joked. "Seriously though, it's too early to speculate. Don't worry; I won't leave you in the dark when it comes to information about your safety."

After a pause, Mac said, "I have some news. I visited Reb, and he told me he didn't know anything about a letter, and that his girlfriend, Christine, visits him weekly to listen to all his complaints. He also answered some of my questions about her. Her last name is Thornily, and she works at the Money Save convenience store on Woodward Avenue and also sells used vehicles."

"My instincts were right. Christine is the lady with the black lace underwear."

Mac snickered. "What has black lace underwear have to do with anything?"

"I'll explain sometime."

"Okay. I like mysteries." He smiled and returned to business. "Tomorrow, I plan to visit the used car sales lot in my street clothes and pretend I'm interested in buying a car."

"By the way, did I mention that Christine's pregnant? She could be anywhere between five to eight months. Did Reb say anything about that?"

"No. But she can't be eight months because she wouldn't be working two jobs."

"You're right."

"I'll get some more answers today, if everything works out." He left, saying he would see her in a few days to give her a report.

chapter thirteen

Mac contemplated the information nurse Nancy had given him concerning the effects a significant dose of morphine could have on a patient of Alison's size and condition. The amount of fluid recovered from the spilled morphine was considerable.

"Morphine is effective in handling pain for many patients," Nancy had said, "but it's not recommended for those who are on total bed rest because they naturally breath slower and shallower, and could develop lung problems. This narcotic decreases the number of respirations a person breathes per minute, predisposing the patient to develop pneumonia and possibly death. Alison has started on respiratory exercises for that very reason, making sure she fills her lungs with each breath."

Mac considered this incident as an attempt on Alison's life. His heart wrenched to think someone might be trying to kill her. The candies looked homemade, making him suspect a woman. Wasting no time, he arranged to have the chocolates analyzed.

No fingerprints had been recovered from the grooved surface of the syringe needle cover, and there were no prints, other than Alison's, on the box of chocolates. He would have to discover another way to find this deranged person.

***

Days later, Mac received a call from Hamilton's forensic lab.

"Corporal Mackenzie?"

"Yes."

"This is Dr. Clark, from the forensic lab, I've the results you've been waiting for."

"Good. Go ahead."

"The reports showed a significant amount of lysergic acid, known as LSD, in the chocolates we tested. All the other components are normal household ingredients, except for the shiny wax coating. It contained warfarin, a blood-thinning medication or a poison for rodent extermination. It is a small amount, yet more physically harmful than the lysergic acid. Either the culprit is lacking in knowledge or is just trying to cause suffering."

"Can you isolate the source of the warfarin?"

"It possibly could be determined with extensive testing. We didn't do a detailed study to determine if it came from common rat poison or the therapeutic source, Coumadin."

"I'll give you clearance to start that testing now."

"I'll start today and have you sign the papers when you pick up the report. I'll have it for you tomorrow."

"Thanks."

***

The next morning, Mac visited Alison. "I have more news for you. I told you I would keep you informed if my investigation divulged any questions about your safety. Are you up to it?"

Alison felt her heart beat faster. "Is it about the chocolates?"

Mac nodded.

Attempting some humour, she added, "I guess no one has been tempted to eat them then."

Mac chuckled then said seriously, "There's more. It also has to do with the letter. We've had some time to investigate the letter and the chocolates. I feel there may be a correlation."

"How does that letter have anything to do with a box of chocolates showing up in my room?"

"I think the same person may be responsible."

There was a lull in the conversation, then Alison said, "Probably now is the time to tell you the story of the lady with black lace underwear."

Mac gave her a questioning look.

"Almost three years ago, Reb told me about a woman who seduced him at a store, inviting him to view her black lace bra and panties. I received a call from the 'other woman,' Christine, just a few weeks ago, on March twenty-first, and had a suspicion that she was the same lady. She told me that she has a two-year-old girl, and claimed that Reb is the father and that she's expecting his second child. Christine told me that if I made things rough on Reuben, she'd retaliate. If Christine did indeed write the letter, that would fit with her previous threat. The letter said, 'If you don't do this for me you'll pay. I will definitely find a way, tomorrow or even today.'"

"You have it memorized?" questioned Mac.

"I guess I memorized the rhyming part without knowing it." Alison stopped and exclaimed, "Oh! I just had an idea. I think I know who one of the agency nurses might be—Christine! That's why I thought I recalled her voice."

Mac didn't follow her line of thinking. "Help me out here. What are we talking about now?"

"I developed a bedsore recently and it was caused by an agency nurse not turning the bed a few nights in a row. Nancy said that no one knew her and she didn't show up on the agency records. And it has just come to me that the agency nurse's voice was Christine's. Oh yes, I meant to tell you that she seemed to know the other nurse too."

"Someone should have reported these agency nurses to me. I'll go to the used car sales lot to interview Christine today."

***

The next day Mac returned to tell Alison what happened.

"Christine Thornily is quite personable. She's very well-versed in different makes of cars and answered all my questions about their mechanics. Her attitude was very friendly. Actually you could say overly friendly. She seems to be quite intelligent and knows about the workings of a hospital. Her sister worked in the hospital in the housekeeping department."

Alison was surprised Mac had gotten around to talking about medical things. "How did you work in that subject?"

"She offered all the information. She's quite a chatterbox. "

"What does she look like?"

"She's plump, but didn't look pregnant to me. She's about five foot nine, has dark hair, and a fairly attractive face."

Alison and Mac talked about how the facts seemed to point to Christine's possible involvement with the spilled morphine and tampered chocolates.

"What will you do next?" asked Alison.

"Keep cool; don't worry. No further harm can come to you here. I've set up a guard by your door starting this evening. He's one of the hospital's security." Mac bid her goodbye.

She lifted a wilted hand to wave.

***

The end of the seemingly interminable six weeks of the bone healing process had arrived. Dr. Whiting gave the order for Alison to be transferred to a regular hospital bed fitted with a trapeze. With great pleasure, Alison bid the monster bed goodbye. Comfortably dressed in a loose track suit, she lay flat on top of the covers of her new hospital bed.

Dr. Whiting entered the comparatively spacious hospital room. "You are one of those patients I rarely saw in the office; now I see you every week. I remember how you looked the first day after the injury.

You had a swollen, discoloured jaw, a nose almost double its normal width, and eyes with dark circles that changed in colour with each visit. Now you look quite pretty in your track suit."

"Thank you. But did I look that bad, Dr. Whiting?"

"Call me Helen. I think we should be on a first-name basis. To answer your question, yes, you looked bad but not worse than I expected. Tomorrow is the day you graduate from lying flat to being upright, and then the next day you may sit for sixty minutes."

Alison's eyes lit up with excitement and she slapped the mattress on both sides of her body. "Finally the day has come. Hallelujah!" She paused to process what her doctor had just said. "But why can I sit for only an hour? Why can't I stay up all day?"

Chuckling at Alison's child-like expression of enthusiasm, the doctor replied, "Because you can't just sit for long periods after being flat for so many weeks. You'll have to sit upright gradually so you're circulatory system will be able to handle the change in blood pressure. Otherwise the blood would drain from your head suddenly."

"You mean I'd pass out?"

"Exactly."

***

The next day, the ordeal of returning to a sitting position became an act of heroism. After describing the procedure briefly, the day shift nurse abruptly left the room. Alison thought, *This sounds as if it's going to take no more than a few minutes, twenty at the most.*

When the young, stout nurse returned along with an orderly after breakfast, Alison was transferred onto a tilt table. She was strapped to it with leather bands buckled at the shoulders, waist, hips, and above the knees. Alison didn't realize why they were necessary. The unbending, thinly padded surface started to tilt two inches at a time, stop for fifteen minutes, and then resume. When it reached the first level, it didn't seem to be a problem. That soon changed.

Alison, who could never handle amusement park rides, rated this tilt table as the worst ride ever. In her imagination, this slab of a mattress turned into a torture rack as it inched up. The dizziness caused her to be nauseated and feel faint. She took shallow breaths as she moaned, unable to muffle the sound. When the nurse heard her, she gave her Gravol and instructed her to take deep breaths and numerous swallows. Alison called out to God minute by minute until the procedure was completed. The ordeal, which seemed as if it took the whole day, actually lasted five hours. For the first time in many weeks, she would be able to sit at eye level with everyone.

chapter fourteen

Rolph Vonderland leaned back in his chair at his desk. He took a deep breath and sniffed the familiar pungent ink at *The Hamilton Spectator*. He finally forced himself to focus on the pile of papers before him. A pink slip caught his attention; this would be a major assignment, his first one after returning from compassionate leave. The note directed him to meet an officer Mackenzie in the hospital foyer at noon today.

Rolph spent the morning planning how to spend his time productively for the coming week, and then left for the hospital. He arrived on time, entered the large foyer, and spotted the tall, muscular police officer immediately. "Officer Mackenzie?"

"Yes."

Rolph slung his camera over his shoulder, and they shook hands.

"I'll get right to the point," Mac said. "In my visits to the trauma unit, questionable things have been happening: IV equipment was tampered with, and recently a gift of chocolates sent to a patient contained drugs. We've done all we can to trace these acts to a specific individual. I think it's time for the media to get involved. Perhaps the perpetrator isn't aware that his or her actions could cause severe harm, even death. Maybe they've been following someone's instructions. There's hope they will read about this crime in the paper, give themselves up to the police, or at least end further attempts."

"Why did you want to meet me here at the hospital?" asked Rolph.

"To take some photos of the trauma unit and build a story around this helpless victim to create sympathy, but without revealing her true identity."

"Have you arranged a substitute for the real victim to give the story greater personal interest?"

"I guess we think alike. Yes. We have another young woman who has also had a similar accident, but less severe."

"Great. Let's go to her room."

A young woman, confined to the same type of bed Alison had graduated from just recently, had agreed to be the substitute after Mac told her a portion of the story. She understood that her picture would appear in the newspaper without her name, and a disclaimer would state that she was a substitute for the real person portrayed in the article.

Mac and Rolph were walking along the corridor toward the nurses' station when Janette approached from the opposite direction after leaving Alison's room. Janette recognized Rolph.

Not knowing of Janette's and Rolph's previous meeting, Mac said to Rolph, "Isn't this good timing? I can introduce you to the mother of the woman in your story. It may help to write the article."

Mac was about to introduce them when Janette said, "Rolph Vonderland isn't it?"

"Yes. You have a good memory for names, but I don't remember yours, although I do remember your prayer for me and the story of the little boy."

Janette gave her name and said she was pleased that he had remembered her prayer and the story. He confirmed the comfort he received when God had revealed to her about his unborn son.

"I remember. Your daughter had an accident the same night as my wife, Nora." He released a heavy sigh then handed Janette his business card. "Maybe we can meet and talk about the newspaper article that this officer thinks will help your daughter."

Janette took the card and gave Mac a questioning look.

"I'll phone you this evening," Mac said to Janette, "and explain what I believe is happening concerning your daughter's case."

Janette nodded and proceeded to the elevator, shaking her head.

***

That afternoon held another adventure for Alison. After lunch, Nancy was by Alison's side to assist her to sit on the edge of the bed to dangle her legs. "Hello, mighty woman of valour," was the nurse's greeting.

With a lopsided grin, Alison responded, "Hi, yourself. You had a day off when I needed you the most. Can't you just live here?"

Nancy chuckled. "I prefer my queen-size bed to those cots. How about giving your favourite nurse some slack?"

"Okay. Tell me the plan so I can be more prepared than yesterday."

"I'm sorry you had such a hard time with the tilt table. I've asked Rachelle to come today, and she'll arrive any time now. So this is how you'll start today. The IV pole is for you to hold after you are in a sitting position at the side of the bed. You'll need to hold it continually to keep yourself from toppling over. I'll be beside you to help."

Rachelle, the physiotherapist, came into the room while Nancy was speaking. "Your legs are not able to stabilize your upper body, she explained. "The centre of balance of your body has changed due to the muscle atrophy of your legs and hips. It will take at least two weeks of exercises before you'll be able to alter your position from lying to sitting all by yourself."

They pulled her to an upright position then pivoted her until her legs hung limply over the edge of the bed like a china doll's. An orderly stepped in the room as Nancy had prearranged, and they lifted her into a padded lounge chair and would reverse the process in an hour. Alison was thankful for the change in scenery. Although a little dizzy, she could look all around and even look out the door.

Nancy set a lap board in front of her with all she would need to write. Alison had made some sketchy notes of the story she'd already planned in her mind on those sleep-interrupted nights. *Now for the real thing. Ha, ha!*

She examined the scribbled notes she'd painstakingly written while on her back and began deciphering them.

Title: Down But Not Out. That sounds more like a fighter's biography, Alison thought. *In a way it's true. I am a fighter.*

She began her outline.

THEMES:
1. How to know when to leave a marriage you thought was blessed by God, or the big question for some Christians—should I seek divorce?
2. Being courageous while enduring pain.
3. Help for the reader to get out of an abusive marriage.

SIGNIFICANT EVENTS:
1. My first meeting with Reb in church.
2. Honeymoon—'I gotcha.' The significance of that statement as it relates to being made to feel as a possession rather than a partner.
3. The first hit.
4. The choking incident.
5. Being locked out of the apartment. Not being allowed to have a key and how it related to recognizing controlling characteristics of an abusive husband.
6. Abandonment at Lake Moses.
7. The whipping from an electrical cord incident.
8. The phone call from Christine.
9. March 22, 1977: birthday at my parents' house.
10. The fateful blow.
11. Finding out about paralysis and the loss of Kathlynn.
12. The memorial service.

She could see that the point-form information in front of her was disconnected and needed much reorganization.

Alison started to write her fist draft on every other line.

Before describing my present state of affairs, I would like to introduce myself. Alison Elaine Palmer was my given name, and I have decided to take that name again. It seems like a long journey from being known as Alison Steele.

What does a twenty-six-year-old paraplegic hope to gain by writing an autobiography? Perhaps when all the facts are exhausted I'll come up with answers for myself. A wheelchair would never have been the platform I'd choose to conduct my life, but here I am, destined to face life's challenges.

I used to start my day with a long run and then bike to work. Like almost everyone, I took my independence and ability to go wherever I pleased for granted.

Although dwelling on the past can be entirely useless, I would like to tell you of the events leading up to being hospitalized and becoming Alison Palmer once again.

Being a high school physical education teacher brought my life fulfillment. I dedicated many hours to overseeing track and field competitions. My favourite was the hurdle event. Today my hurdles come in different forms.

University did not prepare me for my present status as a patient in the trauma unit of Hamilton General Hospital. There are those who give advice about many positive venues to channel my restlessness, yet questions remain: Where will my life progress from here? Who would ever want me for a marriage partner? Resentment threatens to consume my thinking, but my Christian values say to choose peace rather than bitterness.

Here is a defining statement I just read this morning in the wee hours when sleep eluded me. In the chapter called "In the Mist" of her book *Hinds' Feet on High Places,* Hannah Hurnard states, "Something in her … responded with a surge of excitement to the tests and difficulties of the way, better than to easier and duller circumstances." My life is far from dull and my excitement is contemplating what the future may hold in this unconventional journey with the Lord.

The doctors tell me that my status will cause me a lifelong struggle, but God may reveal a different plan. Until then, I am determined to be thankful for this new chapter of my life.

These verses convey my meaning in the best fashion: "Do not be anxious about anything, but in everything, by prayer and petition, with thanksgiving, present your requests to God. And the peace of God, which transcends all understanding, will guard your hearts and your minds in Christ Jesus." (Phil. 4: 6, 7)

My goal is to write about the lessons that arise as I endeavour to be fully free of the memory of the pain, which at times threatens to take control of my thoughts. But it is for the sake of my friends in the world, other suffering women, that I am compelled to tell my story.

She reread it and, after making several changes, declared it a very good start. Alison put away her writing materials and got out her Bible.

chapter fifteen

When Mac entered Alison's room, she wasn't there. He checked at the nurses' station and found that she had been transferred to a rehabilitation ward.

He stepped into Alison's new room. "Alison, you're sitting up!" Mac's face lit up with wonder.

"Yes, I am. I want to tell you the tilt-table story before I head for my first wheelchair lesson."

"Okay. But what's a tilt table?"

Alison told all the unpleasant details of that experience and Mac truly sympathized. Then he said he was heading to see Reb.

"Well, keep me informed."

"Sure thing, beautiful."

"Beautiful? Do you say that to all the girls?"

"You are beautiful. I've thought so since the first day I saw your face."

"I heard I looked pretty rough."

"Pretty and exotic with those colourful eyes." Trying to continue the light mood, he said, "So what do you want me to say when I enter your room—'Hi, homely'?"

Alison laughed. She enjoyed having Mac around and adored his jovial nature. *Now for some serious stuff.* "Mac, I've been dying with anticipation. What progress have you made with the letter and chocolates?"

"Hang on to your pants." Mac looked down at her peach-coloured sweat suit admiringly. "I guess it's applicable today. When I heard of the change of your room, Nancy told me that you were about to have your inaugural trip in a wheelchair."

I can try to match his humour. "Are you saying that as soon as I get my wheels I'm going to act like the president of this new ward?"

"If the wheelchair fits, ride it."

"Ha, ha. Okay, you win the funny award."

"So when is this big event?" asked Mac.

"In just a few minutes. Rachelle should be here soon. I'm a little nervous. I don't know if my arms are strong enough."

"You have plenty of strength, but maybe Rachelle would let me help this once."

Rachelle overheard as she entered the room with Alison's shiny wheelchair fitted outfitted with blue leatherette armrests and seat. After introductions, Rachelle said, "It would be fine for you to help, Mac. But let me demonstrate an exercise that Alison must do.

"It's arm push-ups for the purpose of relieving pressure on your buttocks. I'll demonstrate." Rachelle sat in the chair, placed her hands on the armrests and lifted her torso. "It looks easier than it is. You must do at least five repetitions every thirty minutes at the beginning. Today, you'll only be in the wheelchair for a total of sixty minutes, which will be long enough. They're not padded like lounge chairs. This wheelchair was ordered from our department and paid for by your father. It reclines, so once you're discharged you can take short naps and be in a position to attend to your personal needs."

This caused Alison's cheeks to heat; she hoped that Mac didn't know everything about her catheter.

Mac asked, "May I place her in the wheelchair now?" His voice sounded soft, as if he were asking to lift a precious jewel.

Rachelle nodded.

He swooped under Alison in one fluid movement and gently positioned her in the wheelchair. "I must be going. I'll tell you about the interrogation with Reb tomorrow. I can tell you this much, there has been a positive change. Take care."

"Ah, thanks for dropping by and for your help."

He waved as he left the room.

***

While Alison was in the gym, Skeeter Johnson stuck his head in the door. "Oh. Hello, Alison." Trying to make his visit sound unplanned, he said, "Since I'm here, I'll give you a display of my wheelchair prowess. You'll need to be able to do wheelies to climb curbs if there aren't any ramps. And you may also need to know how to break a fall and then get into the wheelchair from a lying position."

He hasn't taken his eyes off of Rachelle more than a moment. I'm getting the impression that he came to visit my therapist more than to demonstrate his skills for me.

After he made sure the brakes were firmly engaged, he mounted the wheelchair from behind with bravado. First he took a spin around the room, including several wheelies. The show ended with a convincing fall. A stuntman couldn't have done better. He ended the performance by saying, "Before you leave here, you'll be able to accomplish most of these moves I've just demonstrated." Alison's eyebrows raised in doubt. Skeeter tried to hide a laugh then departed as quickly as he had come.

Alison exclaimed to Rachelle, "Wow! That was quite a show. Does he do this for everyone?"

"Not exactly." To avoid further questions, Rachelle returned to her instructions. "You need to know the basics in manoeuvring your chair. I want you to try to do what I say, as I say it. First, know where your brakes are." Alison put both one hand over each brake lever. "That's right. Now put the brakes on as tight as you can, then try to move the wheels."

Alison thought this would certainly be the easiest part.

"Now try to move forward or backward."

Alison had pushed the levers forward but not firmly enough.

"You can still move the wheels. Reapply the brake. That's better."

Rachelle set up an obstacle course of strategically placed chairs. "Weave through the chairs, first one to the right, and then the next to the left." It was difficult, but Alison was successful. Then Rachelle sat in another wheelchair and showed Alison how to turn around in a limited space. "Pull back on one wheel as you push forward with the opposite wheel. You must think carefully about how to make the wheelchair respond to where you want it to go, but one day it will become second nature."

Alison thought her rebuttal. *I'll do my best, but I plan to walk again someday.*

Rachelle ended the session with stretches and passive range-of-motion exercises for Alison's legs. "The next workout will be fun. We'll be playing catch with various sizes of balls to build upper body strength and stability."

"I'll do my best," Alison said with a forced smile.

On returning to her private room, Alison discovered that she was thoroughly exhausted, yet satisfied in what she had accomplished. She felt hot and sticky, as though she had just run a race. *The following months will show how well I'm able to cope—a disabled person in an able-bodied world.*

Rachelle assisted Alison onto her bed. She put up the side rail with its familiar clang. It always felt as if her freedom were being locked away. *It's much like the sound of a prison door closing.* She couldn't help thinking about Reb. *How was he managing in that rough environment?*

Alison told Rachelle, "I want to take a short rest, and then work on my writing."

Rachelle located the writing materials and handed them to Alison. Alone with her thoughts, before she drifted into an afternoon nap, Alison wondered if she would have a soulmate in the future. She knew Mac was showing interest in her with his witty words and more-than-friends smile. She saw signs of it every time he visited. *Does he care for me, or is he just being Mac?*

With many questions unanswered, she drifted off to sleep.

Alison dreamed she was walking then tripped on the hard ground. A stranger's hands reached to help her to stand. As she straightened, her head raised to meet aqua-coloured eyes whose gaze seemed to interpret her thoughts. *Are you going to have an important part in my future?* A tingling sensation passed through her body. This young man's compassionate look made a connection with her soul; she felt the thrill. Linking arms, they walked side by side down a lane canopied with breeze-blown autumn leaves like multi-coloured acrobats performing a show. With the gentle crunching of leaves under her feet, she felt a wild beating in her chest.

When she awoke, her heart was thumping at the same tempo as in the dream. *I wonder what this dream means. I remember the scene, the man's eyes, and every emotion. It's strange. I don't remember seeing eyes like that before. It's been said that women don't dream about strangers.* Most of her dreams were forgotten or became fuzzy in a short period of time; this memory she reviewed several times.

She raised the head of her bed with a push of a button, picked up the pencil and wrote the day's date on the top of the page, May 6, 1977.

She looked at her scrawled notes: "describe Reb, first glance, plan to introduce myself." She wrote:

> The first time I saw Reuben Steele, I thought I would like to get to know this nice-looking man with the light-coloured eyes and light brown hair. He sat two pews behind my parents, Bill and Janette Palmer, and me. Glancing back, and trying not to be obvious that I noticed him, I decided to introduce myself after the sermon.
>
> As soon as he came into my line of vision, I lost my nerve. My eyes riveted on the glowing warm tone of his face and muscular broad neck. I became completely tongue-tied.

The next thing she'd jotted down was, "first words—stuck-up or what?" *That should have told me something about his personality. And my reaction showed my immaturity.*

Weeks passed and I failed to gather enough courage to initiate a one-on-one conversation with Reuben. In mid-March, at the conclusion of the church service, the congregation gathered in the foyer. A din of various topics arose as I descended the stairs. From behind, a male voice startled me. "Are you stuck-up or what?"

As I whipped around, I stammered back an inane reply. "I don't think so."

I didn't think I was a snob, so why didn't I stand up for myself?

"April '71, phone call, Youth for Christ"

At the end of April, after we'd spoken several times in a friendly yet superficial way, Reb asked a mutual friend for my phone number. When he phoned to ask if I would go with him to a Youth For Christ rally, I turned him down because I planned to do homework for several Grade thirteen courses. He kept me on the phone until I agreed. I hung up and rushed to get ready.

"His testimony, hitchhiking, how got name—Reb"

That night I learned that he'd recently accepted Jesus Christ as his Saviour. After reading, *The Cross and the Switchblade*, by David Wilkerson, he put God to a test while hitchhiking: "If you're real, God, allow the next car to give me a ride without sticking out my thumb," prayed Reb. And so it happened.

He seemed to have a simple, genuine faith. His desire was to help others leave the drug scene, because drug abuse had been his failing. It was on the streets of downtown Hamilton where these converted gang kids nicknamed him "Reb," a rebel for Jesus.

We were married on Easter weekend, April 10, 1972, at the end of my first year of university. It had been less than a year since our first date.

chapter sixteen

Sharon pondered how to get to the bottom of Alison's trouble. Alison avoided participating in any discussion that attempted to deal with her future as a paraplegic. Sharon had been meeting with Alison every week and discussed many situations where Reb had made her feel small and under his control, but Alison became evasive when conversation turned toward her paralysis. *This could be the day that a missing piece of the puzzle of understanding Alison's psyche may be revealed.*

"I know this isn't an original way to start, but how are you, Alison?"

"Everything seems to be progressing. I took my first spin in a wheelchair this morning."

"I heard it was to be soon. Well, tell me what you thought about the experience and how you feel now."

"I thought it was very good to be moving about. It takes more muscle strength than I have right now, so I'm quite spent, physically."

"I'm sure you gave your best effort, and I'm proud of your enthusiasm. Now, are you willing to carry on with our discussion from last week? You were telling me that there was another incident that you wanted to talk about."

"Yes, I remember. Reb showed signs of having a controlling nature as early as during our honeymoon, but I misinterpreted it until recently."

"Yes, tell me about it."

"He kept repeating a phrase, 'I gotcha.' It's strange, I thought it was cute at the time, but now I believe that he thought he finally possessed me—like a kind of prize.

"You know about most of the severe abusive events, but what was most difficult was when he gave me the silent treatment. I left little notes here and there in the apartment and in his lunch pail, but he never responded. And he would never say he was sorry after an incident. He'd lead me to the bed and assume that it was the same thing. After each episode, we'd patch up the broken pieces and carry on. I was afraid to mention his previous bad behaviour."

Sharon was beginning to understand this woman more and more.

"Soon after the first punch, his dirty language started. He seemed to have dropped all his Christian values. Then he didn't even want to go to church any more. I continued to go, and he didn't like that at all. One very cold Sunday, he said he was going to lock me out of the apartment if I went to church. "

Sharon nodded; she was getting the picture.

"I'd tell him that I felt closer to God when I sang and listened to the pastor's encouraging sermons. He knew that I had gone to church every Sunday before we married. I'd tell him that the Bible said that we are not to leave out going to church. His classic reply was, 'How about, love, honour, and *obey* your husband?' Then he commanded me not to go to church, and said if I went out the door, he wasn't going to let me come back.

"I wondered what I should do. If I stopped going to church, what other demands would he make? I prayed for help in what to reply."

"Did you get some insight?"

"I thought I did because I became courageous enough to ask Reb to come with me. I reminded him that he did like the minister, and we needed to thank the Lord for his new job. I suggested that he come and give thanks.

"Anger was his answer to everything. He bellowed, 'Get out of here, if you love your church so much. I think you love God more than me. Go to church and see what happens!'" Alison's voice became shaky as she related the story.

Sharon didn't interrupt because Alison had good momentum. Sharon's eyes never left Alison's. She leaned forward to take her hand, hoping her body language conveyed interest.

"I felt that I should go to church anyway. I told Reb that I'd be back in an hour and a half, and said that we could do something together. I left believing he wouldn't carry out his threat.

"I wondered why he never allowed me to cut another key so that I could have access to our apartment. It seemed that he wanted to control my every move. Our whole courtship must have been only a personal challenge for him."

"Men like your husband have controlling natures," Sharon responded. "Basically, he probably didn't know how to channel his passions in a productive way; nor had he learned how to express his feelings or understand how new situations affected him. Have you ever heard this saying: 'Hurting people hurt people'?"

"No. But it makes sense. They don't know anything else, right?"

"Exactly." Sharon perceived that Alison's voice had finally lost its emotional wobble. Would you like to continue with what happened when you returned from church?"

"Alright. Reb had put the security chain on the apartment door, locking me out like he'd threatened. No amount of knocking and coaxing made him let me in. I wondered if I should go back to the church, but I reasoned that it didn't make sense. Besides it was very cold. So I stayed in the hall and prayed that Reb would open the door soon.

"I fell asleep on the carpeted floor outside our apartment door with my purse as a pillow. I jumped up quickly when I heard the rattle of the chain. My head was spinning and I had a crick in my neck. The door was left slightly ajar.

"Nothing was said between us when I went in. I just got ready for bed. I slept intermittently the remainder of the night, with no physical contact with Reb. He clung to the edge of the bed, like he had on many other nights in the previous few months.

"He didn't speak to me for several days—his usual punishment. I continued to carry on a one-sided conversation, still trying to do as my mother suggested."

"What was her suggestion?"

"She said to behave as if nothing had happened, because that was how she handled her marital tiffs."

"Did you really think this was the best way to handle the abuse?"

"I didn't have any other practical advice, so I did follow it, yes. I was also afraid of my dad rubbing it in that I had made a mistake in marrying Reb."

"So, you never confronted Reb with his deplorable behaviour?"

"No. I was too afraid of what he would do and that it would make matters worse."

Now Sharon felt she understood Alison's reasoning and how her situation had gotten out of hand. "I might have done the same thing if I were you."

Alison allowed herself a slight smile.

"Did you consider getting your own place or look into getting a divorce?"

"You see, Reb had kept his word and hadn't hit me since the first few weeks of marriage. I thought in order for him to turn back to the Lord, I just needed to pray harder. So, for many days and nights I called out for the Lord to intervene on Reb's behalf."

"When did he break his promise to never hit you again?"

"A few months after our first anniversary he whipped me with an electrical cord. He accused me of wanting to listen to the television instead of him. I didn't stop praying. I believe prayer changes things."

Sharon shifted in her chair as if suddenly uncomfortable. "Maybe it's time for a break. I'll see you next week."

A Gift of Love
***

Three days later, as Alison was sitting in her wheelchair with her back to the door, Mac tiptoed into Alison's room. She caught the movement in her peripheral vision and looked up quickly to see an elaborate bouquet of lilies in hues of mauve and pink.

"Oh. Are they for me?"

"Yes, of course the flowers are for you. Doesn't one bring flowers to friends when they're in hospital?"

"They're lovely. Thank you."

"They aren't as lovely as you," Mac said, smiling.

A flush rushed to her cheeks. She felt that Mac's compliment was inappropriate for their type of friendship. *What if he's thinking I'm his girlfriend? It wouldn't work. Someone like me could never hold his interest. Or keep up to his fast pace.*

"Your blush tells me I need to set the record straight. I decided you needed flowers to bring colour to your surroundings, and besides I'm here on business. I did some investigating concerning Reb's letter. There were no detectable fingerprints on the envelope or the letter, but Barton Street jail assured me that a letter could never have escaped their detection. Another clue that it may not have been written by Reb is that it's out of character for him to write in rhyme. Since the envelope had a distinct sweet smell, I'm thinking it may have come from a woman, one who knows about your life with Reb. If you should get a similar letter, I want you to hand it directly to me without opening it."

"I'll do that, Mac."

"I also went to the jail to ask Reb more questions about Christine."

"What happened?"

"He greeted me with such a glare that I said, 'That look could make an RCMP fall off his horse.'"

Alison let out a good laugh.

"I thought it was pretty funny too, but Reb kept scowling."

"Did you learn anything?"

"He wouldn't answer my questions, even when I told him that his cooperation would look good on his report. Instead, he ended up in solitary confinement again because of his foul words."

"Will you try again?"

"Yes, after he's done his solitary time."

***

Rolph Vonderland had the majority of the newspaper piece written but needed more information. The story demanded all the details he could get.

He found Janette's address and knocked on the door. "Hello, Mrs. Palmer, do you have time to answers some questions for *The Hamilton Spectator* about your daughter's stay in hospital?"

"Oh, *The Spectator*? I didn't guess your job was so prestigious. Yes, Rolph, please come in. I'm wondering why the public would want to know about Alison."

"A number of people will be interested in her story."

"I guess you know about these things. Please come in."

"May we sit in your kitchen?"

After Janette removed the tablecloth, he set his briefcase down.

"A story like this is what people like to read."

Janette looked intently at Rolph's sea-blue eyes and the lines that showed a sorrow that still lingered. "Before we start on the article, I want to ask how you've been managing these past weeks."

"It's been rough. There was an insane time when a woman resembling Nora walked down the street ahead of me and I'd try to catch up to her before giving myself a mental shake."

"That's natural, Rolph. May I pray for you again?"

"Yes, please, Mrs. Palmer."

"Dear Heavenly Father, I come in Jesus' name to ask something special of You for Rolph. He has been having a troubling time since Nora has gone to be with You. Help him to remember Nora with joy and not try to push her memory away, but to embrace everything they experienced together. And when someone reminds him of her, put the right thoughts in his mind that will take him through the grief. Allow him to hear Your voice and continue his life in peace. Please send someone special into his life in Your good timing. Amen.

"Now where would you like me to start about Alison's story?"

"Give me a rundown on her first twenty-four hours in hospital."

After about an hour of deep conversation and intense questioning, Rolph had a good idea of the indignities of being a captive on a trauma unit: the sleepless nights, the extra treatments for ulcers, the stiff, painful upper body muscles, and the confined feeling of being unable to get out of bed or walk to the bathroom.

They made tentative plans to speak to each other again after the article was published.

chapter seventeen

Sharon coordinated a seminar for May 30, inviting Dr. Karr, author of *Life After Paralysis,* as the main speaker. His specialty dealt with the romantic, emotional, and marital needs of the disabled. The topics for discussion included intimacy, sex, and babies. The posters for the event drew a lot of attention. Local radio and television stations and *The Hamilton Spectator* spread the word to surrounding communities. It would be held in the large auditorium of the hospital.

Sharon thought this would be good for Alison, and since she was able to sit in her wheelchair for lengthy periods now, there shouldn't be any problem for her to attend.

***

Tension grew in Alison several hours before the early evening meeting. She thought about how to prepare her question, and then decided to write it out: If an able-bodied person seemed to need a disabled person to be more than friends, how could you discover whether it was a developing relationship or something abnormal? She sighed with relief that she was able to express it partially on paper. Now it was time to be escorted to the auditorium.

Dr. Karr, a middle-aged man who was sitting in a wheelchair, started by addressing the fact that negative feelings concerning sexuality pervade the thoughts of people who are paraplegic, quadriplegic, or hemiplegic.

"Just because the sexual organs may not function as they did before the paralysis doesn't discount that all humans are sexual beings." His basic advice was, "Don't fear intercourse. Caring and touching is what truly satisfies." He was evidently speaking from experience, because he was a married man and the father of three children.

"Relationships, in general, must seek interdependence. Each partner must have contributions to offer to the relationship. Everything that involves the physical aspects of sex must not be expected to come from the able-bodied partner alone. And if you start out as good friends, it is highly possible to become wonderful lovers. A healthy relationship is always based on love, trust, commitment, and shared values."

Dr. Karr's lecture seemed to be "the happening" for many in the city that night. Every seat was occupied.

Mac attended the meeting in street clothes. He soon gave up his seat to a lady who came late. He stood, leaning against the back wall.

"If one has a good body image before the paralysis, it is less of a problem when one becomes less than perfect. The able-bodied partner may be initially uncomfortable in seeing atrophied legs, but the important thing to remember is that love can overlook many faults."

Alison ran her fingers down both thighs.

"Before entering such a union, able-bodied partners must ask themselves if their commitment is based on reality. Have they thought through questions such as, Is there any resistance from family or friends? What would their reaction be to the disability? Might the relationship limit the able-bodied partner's freedom? And finally, what will be the outcome of the union later in life, when the able-bodied partner also becomes dependent?"

Alison paid special attention because she hadn't considered all these factors. She thought she wouldn't have to worry about most of these topics because she was going to walk again. But it was time to rethink her immediate future.

"Some able-bodied people have such a strong desire to be needed that having a dependent partner is what they want."

Alison paid special attention because this statement started to answer her written question.

Dr. Karr continued. "But I caution—everything has to be talked out extensively before entering a lifetime commitment. And the commitment must be one that lasts a lifetime, not just a passing fancy."

Next was the question-and-answer period. Members of the audience were to write questions then deposit them in a box. The participants would be anonymous.

When Alison turned around to put her question in the box, she made eye contact with Mac. Sweat started to bead on her face and she could feel her heartbeat in her ears. She wondered if he noticed that it shook her to have him there. He smiled and gave a low wave as she returned to her place. She nodded with a forced smile and was thankful that he remained leaning against the back wall.

Rolph Vonderland rushed into the auditorium with his camera. He started snapping pictures, after nodding at Mac. No one else seemed to pay attention.

The first question read was Alison's.

"What an interesting question," Dr. Karr commented. "Since most of the population is able-bodied, it is not unusual for an able-bodied person to be interested in someone who is disabled.

"I have a rhetorical question for whoever asked this question. Does it matter that the able-bodied person feels a desire to be needed? If his or her conversation shows an abnormal desire to be needed, love can still exist. It can be a successful relationship if both parties are equally in love. Or if this weren't a suitable situation for either one, then one would tell the other plainly that they do not wish to carry on. It's simple and effective.

"I would like to add that I have some information with me about dating agencies that deal with the disabled. I have caution, however, if both partners are disabled. Although it can be a means of camaraderie, it can also create a double burden physically and financially. Relationships in all *walks* of life …" He paused. There was a titter throughout the audience. The doctor continued. "Forgive my pun. Relationships in all walks of life head either for success or failure. The questions you should ask are, Do you communicate well? Do you have complementary skills? Do you maintain individual friendships? There are many more situations to consider, of course, but these are the ones that come to mind at the moment."

The question-and-answer period ended after several other questions were answered. Many people left, including Rolph. All the information was significant for Alison, especially the answer to her question.

Now she had to face Mac. She decided she would let him initiate the conversation. On turning the wheelchair around, she discovered that he'd left. A sigh of relief escaped her. Or was it?

chapter eighteen

Alison was becoming expert in handling her wheelchair. It truly had become second nature to make it go exactly where she wanted it to go, as Rachelle had promised. She could even do a wheelie. Today she was going to take a solo excursion to her counselling session in Sharon's office. She felt like a calf let out of the pen for the first time to kick up its hooves.

"There's an extraordinary glow to your cheeks today," said Sharon.

"I do feel good."

Sharon didn't want to dampen Alison's positive outlook, but now was the best time to deal with the next matter. "I'd like us to discuss what may arise after Reb reaches the end of his prison sentence. To be forewarned is the best preparation I could give you."

"Why would I need a warning? I thought dealing with Reb was all behind me now. I heard from Mac that his sentence was one year and one day. It seemed strange. I never asked why the extra day. Now I'm wondering what that means."

"I've heard that it means that there is little chance that he will get out before a whole year is up."

"Then we know when he will be freed—around March twenty-third, next year," Alison's voice trembled slightly. "That is, if they count all the time he was under arrest."

"That gives us time to prepare. Have you considered seeking a divorce?"

"Yes. I made a decision to hire a lawyer when I found out that Reb was unfaithful. This happened the next day." She looked down and patted her thinning thighs.

"Yes. Well, good. We're both on the same page then. Try to make time soon to contact your lawyer, and I'll gather information that I have in my files."

They talked about future sessions with Rachelle and preparations needed for Alison's discharge in less than three months. Short-range goals and long-range goals had to be discussed, no matter how tedious.

Rachelle was Alison's friend, and one fact had become clear in the recent weeks: Sharon was more than a counsellor now, Alison considered her a friend also.

***

That evening Mac visited Alison to talk specifically about her thoughts on Dr. Karr's lecture. He thought that many of the doctor's comments supported his own convictions and that this was the time to express his love.

Mac hunkered down in front of her and greeted her with "How's my girl?" Then without waiting for a reply, he pressed ahead, "What did you think about Dr. Karr's statement that friendship are good starting points for romances?"

Alison took in a quick breath. "You are my friend, Mac, but so is Rev. Every friendship I have with a man doesn't mean I want a romance."

"Did I say that?"

"Okay, tell me what you want me to understand."

"I'm hoping that you feel the same way as I do, that our friendship is special enough to call it the beginning of a relationship." He raised his eyebrows in an adorable way as he hoped for an affirmative reply. "I have feelings for you, Alison." Mac knew that he had expressed this very thing in many ways, but she still seemed to be stunned by his declaration.

"Reb—I mean, Mac, thank you for such a compliment. I really don't know what to say except that I don't share your feelings. I'm a paraplegic bound to a wheelchair, and you are so robust and energetic. I can't imagine us sharing a romantic kind of relationship."

"I'm not just going to give up because of that one statement. I'm going to convince you that we can be together—if you'll give me a chance."

"I'll always be your friend and always be thankful for your involvement in my life."

Mac let out a long sigh. "I guess I'll have to be content with our friendship for now." He plastered a smile on his face as he tilted his head. "But I'm going to have fun convincing you to my way of thinking."

"Oh, Mac. Let's talk about something else, like, did you find out anything more about the Warfarin?"

"Yes. It was the medicinal form, Coumadin. Whoever had this drug available was probably acquainted with someone who was being treated for a circulatory condition."

"Does that change any of your conclusions?"

"The morphine incident happened almost immediately after your surgery. It tells us that we are looking for someone who had morphine and possibly Coumadin on hand. It adds another reason for me to think that the same person is involved with both incidents. I plan on getting answers that will confirm my suspicions."

***

A few days later, Mac entered her room with eyes twinkling as he balanced a box of chocolates on his large hand. "This is for my dear friend. Chocolates without poison." He chuckled as he held out a shocking-pink, heart-shaped box of expensive truffles.

"Thank you, Mac, but this gift seems more than just a gift for a friend."

"I'm celebrating because I was able to talk to Reb. The last solitary confinement made him more cooperative."

"Good. Tell me what you learned."

"He told me a few details about Christine's life. Her mother died at home last February, of cancer. When I asked if Christine expressed anything about getting revenge, he said he wanted his lawyer present before he answered any more question."

"Why is that such good news?"

"Don't you see? Because her mother needed drugs, she might have had access to the medications in question."

"So, what is the holdup from taking her in for questioning?"

"If I can get an admission from Reb that he heard her talk about revenge, we could arrest her. I'm going to try to make arrangements for Reb's lawyer to be there next time."

"How soon? I know I'd feel safer if she was in custody."

"Just be patient and open that box of candy. I want a taste."

***

Janette picked up the newspaper from the driveway and showed it to Bill. "The article by Rolph made it to the front page, with a colour picture. Here, read it out loud, would you?"

Bill cleared his throat. "This is a great photo, but I don't understand why Alison's picture couldn't be used. She's much prettier."

"That's not the point, Bill. We wouldn't want Alison's trouble known by all."

Bill paused a moment. "Yes. I guess you're right."

***

Another week passed and Alison's counselling with Sharon took a more direct approach. "You never did tell me about the first time Reb hit you."

"Why would that be important now?"

"Because when Reb is released from prison, I want you to remember how it all started, so that he'll never get back into your life. Please tell me everything you can remember."

"Okay. Three weeks after our wedding, Reb didn't return from work at the usual time. I remember making an especially good supper, and it dried out in the oven. I finally decided to put the meal in the fridge, and I went to bed, leaving the light on in the hall. When the apartment door opened, I heard Reb stumble in the hallway.

"His hair was dishevelled and his shirttail was sticking out. He blocked the light from the doorway so I couldn't read his expression.

"I asked, 'Where have you been?' He answered with a slur. 'It's none of your businesh.'

"All I said was, 'Oh! You're drunk.'

"He took one flying lunge toward me. A punch snapped my head to the side. A shrilling sound exploded in my ear, and my cheek burned like a torch had been lit beside it. The pain blocked out what he shouted as he stomped out of the room.

"I just spoke the truth. I remember questioning how he could hurt me like that if he loved me."

"People do uncontrollable things when they are intoxicated. What happened next?" Sharon responded.

"I didn't know who to talk to about what happened. My dad was out of the question; he had done everything he could to discourage us from marrying in the first place. I remember wondering if I should confide in my mom.

"I heard Reb fumble in the fridge. That's when I stumbled to the relative safety of our small bathroom with my throbbing head. Fearing his intrusion, I locked the door and muffled my sobs in a bath towel. I examined my face in the medicine cabinet mirror and saw a flaming mark on my cheek.

"When my tears subsided, I decided not to stay in the bathroom. I thought he'd probably be asleep. The bedroom door was locked, so I caught snatches of sleep on the sofa. In the morning I was counting on my mother to have a sympathetic ear.

"When I finally called, my words came tumbling out. I told Mom what had happened. I remember telling her that Reb was a totally different man than I thought I'd married. And that he must have been play-acting when he said he loved God first, and then me. I wanted the marriage to be annulled.

"My mom said she was sorry, but she also reminded me of my wedding vows and said that God hates divorce. Her advice was to carry on as if this incident hadn't happened. That's the way she handled her marital difficulties and so should I.

"I told her that I could cover the bruise with makeup, but how could I cover the pain in my heart? I never confided in her again about Reb's abuse."

Sharon took her shaky hand.

"Two evenings later, Reb explained why he was late that ill-fated night. He'd been fired and didn't want to admit it to me because I still needed financial support while studying at university. He said he regretted drinking, and then driving home under the influence, but he didn't say that he was sorry for hitting me. But he did promise to never strike me again. And I believed it."

"This is the general chain of events: the remorse, the apology, and then the promise; it's classic. After the honeymoon period, it starts over again with more abuse."

"I've got the picture. I'm a much wiser person now."

"I believe that's true, Alison. Let's go to a happier topic. In a few months' time, you'll be living on your own. Remember, your half-year goal is to live independently. I thought it was a good goal but too optimistic. You're proving me wrong. Your estimate will be closer than what I was thinking."

"I remember setting that goal, and lately it has been going through my mind. Do you think it's really going to happen soon?" said Alison.

"Yes. You're probably looking at three to four more months instead of six."

"Will I need help when I'm on my own?"

"You'll need bi-weekly nursing care until you're able to give the proper attention to your needs."

"So when do you think I'll be discharged?" said Alison, leaning forward in her wheelchair.

"It looks like you'll be on your own in the fall. On the day of your discharge I'm planning to throw you a party, so be prepared to invite your friends."

"Oh, you don't have to do that. To live on my own will be exciting enough."

"Don't get too enthused yet. There are still months of hard work ahead. Tell me, do you have a family member or friend who could help secure an apartment for you?"

"My friend, Mac, offered to help a while ago."

"Great. Just give me his full name and phone number and I'll send him a list of available apartments that have ample room in the kitchen and bathroom, wheelchair access to laundry facilities, and ramps instead of stairs."

Sharon's unexpressed agenda for Alison was for her to fully accept her disability by giving up hope of ever walking again. "Alison, before you head back to your room, I want to express again the importance of accepting your lot as a paraplegic and moving on to accomplishing a career from your wheelchair."

Every time Alison had an inkling that this line of thinking was about to arise, she would resist with words of hope. This time she decided to change her tactics. Instead of trying to support her point of view, she agreed, at least with her body language. She privately held onto her belief that she would be healed of paralysis. "Thank you, Sharon. I hear the care in your voice. I'll make a success of it. Bye."

***

Daneen visited in the early afternoon, after Alison had phoned to ask her to think about some advice of what to expect with divorce proceedings. "And don't forget to bring your comments about my writing, too."

Daneen started the conversation. "I like your beginning chapter, but I don't know if it's a good idea to put so much scripture in it. It's your autobiography and you get to say anything you want, but I'm just not sure how much 'God-stuff' you should include."

"I understand where you're coming from, Dannie. We think differently because I'm a born-again Christian."

Daneen shot back with a laugh, "Is there any other kind?"

Alison laughed heartily, surprised by her sister's response. "I didn't know you had the Palmer humour."

"Apparently I do."

"Now, to switch to a serious matter—divorce. I remember when you wanted me to divorce Reb before I had proof that he was unfaithful. You said you were afraid for me. How right you were; but hindsight is twenty-twenty."

"I'm glad to hear you are moving forward with getting a divorce. I can give you the name of my lawyer. She does legal aid work. I'm sure you're eligible."

"How do I go about getting it?"

"Ms. Jerome will give you papers to fill out and she'll submit the application to legal aid. I'm sure she'll visit at the hospital."

"Okay, great. I'd also like to legally change my name back to Palmer."

"I don't think that's a problem. Many women take their maiden name again after being divorced."

"I didn't think it could be that simple."

"I'm only guessing."

"Can I switch topics?" Alison asked.

"I bet I know what it's about—Mac, right?"

"No. I'm thinking more about my writing. I don't want you to spare my feelings, just give it to me straight."

"Okay. You could improve in your descriptions." Pulling out a sheet of paper, Daneen pointed. "Here in this passage, describing your first impression of Reb's looks, it reads, 'The glowing warm tone of his face and muscular broad neck riveted my eyes.' You could write, 'Seeing his well-formed body in a new light was like seeing him for the first time. His muscular sinews rippling under his tanned skin, with veins resembling a country road map, caused my eyes to rivet there. A pair of pale blue eyes with romantic drooping lids, made me wish for that first luscious kiss.' Something like that—what do you think?"

"That sure is more descriptive." It was all Alison could do not to snicker.

"Thanks. I made some grammatical corrections in red ink.'"

"I appreciate the time it took you to do this. Thanks."

"You're welcome. Now I'm changing the subject. Allie, how is it that you haven't become despondent or vengeful after all that Reb's done? Has your faith something to do with it?"

Thank you, God. This is what I've been waiting for. "Yes. I have the assurance that God has a special plan for my life, and that everything that happens to me has an ultimate positive purpose."

Forgetting about her curiosity about Mac, Daneen left Alison's side, shaking her head. "See you soon."

***

In the quiet moments after Daneen left, Alison began to think about the next day. *Mac is due to come tomorrow and I'll give him the good news that I'll be discharged soon and ask him to help with the apartment search. He may even have more interesting news after seeing Reb.*

chapter nineteen

Mac entered Alison's hospital room dressed in his uniform, indicating that he was either on his way to work or on a break.

"Hi, Mac. I've got great news. I can start planning my discharge. You said you would help me find a place, right?"

"That's right, beautiful. I've got all day tomorrow to look for the perfect place. Sharon called and dictated a list of buildings to consider. Being eager for you, I didn't want to wait for a letter."

"And here I'm talking like an impatient child."

"Yeah. And you're so cute when you're excited."

Trying to ignore another endearment, she tilted her head and shrugged. "Thank you for your willingness to help. You're the only one who offered, so when Sharon asked if there was anyone in my family who could do the leg work, I thought of you first."

"Thank you. I guess I'm family if you call me your 'brother in the Lord.' Anyway, I'm at your service, fair lady." He bowed, swinging his arm across his chest, hat in hand.

Next he whipped out a map. "When I located the first building on the list, I decided to go there this morning and look at the outside. I'll show you." He pointed to a street on the east side of Hamilton.

Alison knew the street very well. "Oh, Maplewood Avenue. That's a beautiful part of the city with big trees and large homes."

"As soon as I've viewed the whole apartment and a few of the others on the list, I'll come and present the details."

"This hospital room is not my home any longer. I'm anxious to leave."

Mac reminded her, "Your counsellor said that you have a few more months."

"That won't seem so long because I'll be busy planning. You never know—the date of discharge may be moved ahead." Mac raised a questioning eyebrow. Alison said, "I purpose to be hopeful."

"It's true that there's power in positive thinking." He pulled up a chair and looked into her eyes. "I have more information after my last visit with Reb."

"Don't look so grim. I can take it."

"His lawyer didn't come, but I wasn't going to waste the time. Reb started by wanting to make a deal. For his cooperation, he wants his sentence reduced. Then he'll give additional information about Christine. He wants the sentence to be shortened to six months instead of a year."

"That's criminal."

"I believe that description fits. The fact is that prisoners don't have bargaining rights. By the way, she might not even be the one who tried to harm you."

"I'm wondering what would happen to her and her children if she's truly guilty."

"Okay. I must be going Miss Caring Heart. Phone me."

"I will. Bye."

***

A Gift of Love

Alison had been making progress in writing her story, even with all the disturbances in her days. She had a special bag where she kept her pages. *Where did I leave off? It's been too long since I wrote last. My mind's been too busy. Oh, yes. After leaving Lake Moses.* She read the last sentences: For the next two days Reb drove constantly, stopping only for gas, washroom breaks, coffee, and snacks. No apology or any conversation followed.

Then she picked up the narrative again, telling about the return home.

Near the end of our vacation, as we approached Ontario, Reb broke the silence by informing me that there was only enough money for gas to get home. So we didn't eat.

We finally arrived in Sudbury, Ontario, where my brother, William, and his wife, Judy, lived. It is a six-hour drive from Hamilton. In their company Reb pretended everything was fine and spoke normally to me. They fed us and lent Reb some money.

The next morning, after we packed everything into the van and I climbed in, Reb said, "Get out. I'm not taking you. I've had enough of you." He threw my suitcase onto the driveway. I stumbled out of the van and he left, squealing the tires.

This second desertion was traumatic, but at least I was with family. William invited me to stay with them for awhile. Three days later I developed a fever. I didn't want to go to a doctor I didn't know, so William gave me money for a bus ticket home. I figured I'd feel better in familiar surroundings.

Neither our compact car nor the van was in the underground parking lot. This, plus returning to an empty apartment with no groceries, threw me into another panic. I didn't want to depend on my parents for help, but I called my mother to take me to the doctor and to pay for the medicine. It turned out I had an uncomfortable, but not serious, bladder infection.

My life seemed a total mess. In my apartment I was free to cry on my pillow, letting out my stress as I petitioned the Lord.

My reaction to the second abandonment and wanting to be free of Reb's abuse was to pack all of his belongings and set them in our parking space.

I didn't have money to change the locks on the apartment door, so I couldn't stop Reb from coming back. Instead of ending the marriage, I forgave him when he apologized with all the right words, which included Christian phrases such as, "forgive seventy times seven." He said he wanted to come back to church but attend a different congregation in a small village nearby. I took him back, thinking that, as a Christian, this was my only alternative once someone asked to be forgiven. It didn't take long for Reb's church attendance to cease and for the abuse to resume.

After months of the same rough treatment, I finally made an appointment to see the pastor who had tried to discourage us from marrying. Talking about the abuse in my marriage was distasteful to me, but it was time to reveal the whole story. Reb had failed to come home several nights. I had suspicions he was with another woman, but I didn't have proof. He told me he was with his buddies. He hit me and abandoned me. I needed answers. Did I have to stay in a marriage like this? Did the Bible say anything about divorce being a lawful way out of an abusive marriage? My pastor stated very clearly that divorce was allowed if one or both of the partners were unfaithful. He read the verse Matthew 5:32 from his King James Version of the Bible. Jesus said, "But I say unto you, That whosoever shall put away his wife, saving for the cause of fornication causeth her to commit adultery: and whosoever shall marry her that is divorced committeth adultery." The pastor concluded by saying, "If you divorce, you will never be married again as God intended." I could only nod in response.

I left the pastor's office feeling hopeless because, in his opinion, there seemed no way out of this marriage.

A Gift of Love

That's enough writing for now. Alison's nerves were on edge after intensely reviewing her disturbing past; once in bed, she fell asleep quickly.

***

Tuesday morning sped by with exercises and an introduction to occupational therapy.

"Today, you'll start learning how to handle meal preparation," Rachelle said. They headed down the hall. "I hear that you have a friend looking for an apartment for you."

"Yes. My friend, Mac. He said he'd let me know when the mission was accomplished."

"Mission, eh? Well, there's still time before you'll be completely ready to leave the nest—each chick must eventually learn how to fly. We're going to the hospital's disability-adapted teaching kitchen. We've a simple menu for you to cook today, including some cookies to top it off."

"Great. Sounds like fun."

They continued to the elevator, with Alison propelling her wheelchair with the speed of her former gait.

"It will be, as long as you treat the knives with respect." Rachelle laughed as if the short bursts were coming from her belly.

Alison couldn't help but laugh. "I'll try. How hard can it be?"

"Nothing will be the same as your past experience in the kitchen. You'll have to cook from an altered height, making everything seem challenging because of the change in your perspective. And you'll need to accomplish these tasks by yourself, unless you're independently wealthy." She laughed again. Alison felt their kindred connection deepening.

In the occupational therapy room, a tidy miniature kitchen waited for her. It had a pedestal style sink, so a wheelchair could fit under it. The counters, an easy reach from a sitting position, held cooking tools. A gadget that looked as if it might be used for picking up objects leaned against a cabinet.

Rachelle handed her the device. "Have you seen one of these before?"

"No, but I've guessed its use."

"Good for you. We simply call it a 'reach.' Take it in your hand—like this—pick up these jars, and put them in the cupboard above." Rachelle handed her the tool.

"Okay. Like this?"

"That's right. Be sure to get a firm grip." With a soft laugh, barely audible, she said, "If you drop it, don't worry. You'll just get to practice another chore, sweeping." She pointed to a broom and a long-handled dustpan in the corner. Alison had seen that kind of dustpan used by a janitor; she knew its lid closed when lifted.

The large jar was easier than the smaller one because Alison didn't have to squeeze as firmly. She wondered why they didn't use unbreakable objects. Rachelle answered the unspoken question. "We could use plastic jars for this exercise, but have you ever seen pickles in plastic?"

"No."

"Your hand grip is very strong for a woman, and you have advanced in all the assigned exercises with great enthusiasm. So, go ahead."

Everything went well, from cutting vegetables and grating cheese to cooking macaroni and mixing cookie batter, placing the neat mounds on a sheet, and then into the oven. Alison felt a great sense of accomplishment and could imagine herself handling her own kitchen.

***

For several days Alison thought about Reb's possible early release. She reasoned that she should gladly tolerate the guard at the door. *If Reb stayed in jail, I'd feel safe for months longer, and what would happen to Christine if she went to jail with a baby on the way and a pre-schooler? By this September, I could be established in my own apartment anyway.*

She hadn't seen or heard from Mac since last Tuesday. *He said he'd continue the hunt for the perfect apartment. It must be taking all his extra time.*

***

Sharon had personal goals for Alison to accomplish in the next few months before leaving the hospital. She wanted Alison to fully express her negative feelings about Reb. Sharon felt that Alison should clear the air of painful memories and move on with her life instead of living in a fantasy world of regenerated limbs.

Alison's usual answer every time Sharon wanted to talk about her past was, "I let go of the past and let God take care of the future. That's why it's called the past. I allow it to pass." Alison hoped for a time when her memories of Reb would focus on the previous positive aspects of his character and that her mind would refuse all dark thoughts about him. Until then, she would keep leaving her heartache with Jesus.

Sharon said, "Alison, I've admired your beliefs, yet I wish you would look at reality. Reb has harmed you emotionally as well as physically. You avoid talking about his release from prison. I'm not sure that you will resist him, should he try to regain your confidence. What would you say to him if he should try to see you once you are living by yourself?"

"I don't know really."

"What if he breaks his parole agreement and tries to soft talk you?" Sharon paused, her brow wrinkled with concern. "Oh, I have an idea. Let's do a role-play to prepare you for such a situation."

"Okay. It couldn't hurt. Go ahead."

Sharon walked out of the counselling room and shut the door behind her. Alison heard a knock.

"Hello, who is it?"

Sharon put on her best mixture of a Humphrey Bogart/Marlon Brando voice. "Shweetheart, it's Reb. I have a present fo' ya."

Alison laughed. This humorous side of Sharon was new to her.

"Alison, baby, do ya remember our honeymoon? Well, I really want to do it right this time when we remarry."

Stifling her last snickers, she took in what Sharon was trying to do. "Reb, we're never going to remarry. You're not welcome here. Leave before I call the police."

"Alison, what about forgive anyone that asks t' be forgiven? I'm askin' now. Will ya forgive me?"

"I have forgiven you, Reb, but that doesn't mean I must take you back into my life. I'm moving toward the phone now!"

As Sharon opened the door, her huge smile showed her approval. "That was perfect. I think you're going to be alright."

chapter twenty

August ended with temperatures in the high seventies. *It's a perfect day for an outing,* thought Mac. As he entered the hospital elevator, he pictured how Alison's face blossomed when her beautiful bow-shaped mouth curved into a smile. *Her violet eyes always sparkle when she smiles. She'll certainly be glad to leave the hospital and see the apartment. This will be her first time outside since the accident. Let's see—that would be over five months ago.*

***

"Hi, beautiful. Are you ready for an adventure?"

Alison, used to Mac's endearments now, just asked, "What are we doing?"

"We're going to look at an apartment."

She bounced in the wheelchair with the help of her muscular arms. "Show me the way to the exit!" Her six-month goal of living by herself soon would become reality, and right on schedule.

Since childhood Alison had done some painting and sculpting as a hobby, and lately she had been daydreaming of getting back to creating masterpieces while sitting at a large window.

"I hope this apartment has a great big window," she said as Mac wheeled her down the hall. "Eventually, I want to earn my own income rather than receive a disability cheque."

***

Before long, they pulled up in front of a majestic, four-storey stone building that she guessed to be approximately sixty to seventy years old.

"This is it." Mac walked around his gleaming extended-cab pickup. He placed the wheelchair on the sidewalk, then picked her up from the front seat. Squeezing her close before placing her in the wheelchair, he said, "You're as light as a child, but you have all the curves of a woman."

"Mac!"

"I'm sorry I embarrassed you. Forgive me?"

"Sure." When Alison looked at the ornate entrance she exclaimed, "I'm overwhelmed. It's so beautiful, with its columns and granite steps. I can barely wait to see the inside. It must have been an upper-class dwelling in its day." They proceeded around the back to the wheelchair entrance.

The garden, obviously planned by a professional, grew plants of every colour: black-eyed Susans, daisies, asters, and chrysanthemums.

"This part looks as if it has been built recently," commented Alison.

"Yes, that's true. The entrance and elevator are new. There used to be stairs here. It was early this year when they designed some of the suites for the disabled."

"It looks wonderful, Mac. I can hardly wait to see the apartment. Is it on the first floor?"

"No. Those were all rented shortly after the renovations were completed, but there is one on the second floor that hasn't been rented. Let's go see what you think."

The elevator ran smoothly. The width of the halls and the door openings was adequate for wheelchairs.

Alison said, "I guess when it was constructed, buildings were made quite spacious."

"I think you're right. And that makes it perfect for the disabled."

"I wonder if I'll ever get used to that term—disabled."

"I believe the Lord's going to heal you, so you won't need to."

She jerked her head upward to look at his face. "Do you really believe that?" She wondered why he had never spoken of this before, or even hinted at this belief.

"Of course I do."

At that moment, she gazed at Mac with wonderment. *He's been my sounding board, but now I know that he believes the same as I do.*

Mac continued the tour. "The superintendent gave me a key, so we can go ahead and see the apartment without him. He said I didn't need to contact him until after you've decided." He went through the door and held it open. "Entrée, madam."

"Oh, Mac, it's beautiful. With a few feminine touches it will be charming."

"I think it's charming now." He feigned a hurt look.

"Don't get me wrong. I like it. It just inspires me to think of decorating." She changed the subject. "Do you think this room was a study?"

"Yes, it seems to have been, with all these shelves and that built-in desk. This looks like a good place to write," said Mac.

She felt a spark of excitement, as if his statement was a confirmation of what she felt God had already revealed to her. *Maybe I'll be doing more writing in an earnest way. I wonder if my autobiography will be interesting to others.*

They continued their journey down a hall of striped wallpaper in browns and rusts. These hues added darkness to the dimly lit corridor. Alison made a mental note to have the wallpaper replaced. *For now, I could hang some of the paintings from my university days and have brighter light fixtures installed.*

A small kitchen was set back from the straight line that the hall created. The fridge was a half-size cottage-type that sat on an extended counter with space underneath for her legs. The stovetop was level with the counters, and the oven was above, within her reach.

On the opposite side of the kitchen were two fair-sized windows, with enough space between them for her four-place-setting table. While dining, one could look into the courtyard with its trees, a birdbath, and a feeder hanging from a higher branch. "Perfect."

After the kitchen, the hallway took a jog. The bathroom—rather the shower room—was the next in line on the left. There was a pedestal sink, a large shower that she could wheel into and transfer to a shower chair, and a toilet with all the needed grab bars.

The bedroom was on the same side as the bathroom. It seemed to have plenty of space. There were shelves instead of a dresser. The only piece of furniture that remained from previous dwellers was an ornate wardrobe occupying one corner. It had wheels so that it could be moved to wherever she decided was best.

"Oh!" A sharp breath escaped as she gazed just beyond the living room at a window that took up two sides of an alcove. Alison entered and found it had room for her wheelchair to turn freely, plus space for an easel to fit across one corner. The windows started two feet above the floor, rising almost to the ceiling. They were separated only by the framework. The other wall was mirrored, so it looked as if the third side were a window as well. With enthusiasm raising her voice louder than usual, Alison said, "I'll do my art in here!" The 'here' echoed as it escaped into the unfurnished living room.

"I hear some excitement."

"Come see this beautiful tree."

Mac was quick to oblige. Outside the huge window stood a spreading crimson king maple tree that extended across the width of the front of the building. Its deep maroon leaves provided dense shade.

Mac agreed. "Yeah, it's a great tree. There're a lot of them. I guess that is why they call this street Maplewood."

Alison smiled. Tearing herself away from this special spot, she looked more closely at the living room. The highly polished hardwood floor reflected the wood-burning fireplace with its reddish mantel. "That mantel might be made from rosewood or mahogany," guessed Alison.

"I think you're right about the mahogany," said Mac.

"This is more wonderful than I imagined."

"I'm glad you like it. The first month's rent has been taken care of and you only need to pay last month's rent before moving in. I took the liberty, knowing that you would love it."

"Mac! You did that for me?"

"Yes. And I can afford it. Besides I wanted to demonstrate what a wonderful friend you've become to me. This was the only sure way of securing it before someone else snatched it. It felt good to do this for you."

"Thank you so very much, Mac. As soon as I'm settled I want you to come over for dinner as my thank you."

A big smile made his eyes more energetic than ever. "You've got a date."

***

The next morning, Alison awoke again to the mundane décor of her hospital room. The only personal touch was her cross-stitch, with its message of love, that reminded her of her grandmother. She felt down but wasn't exactly sure why. She guessed it could be that she longed to be in her apartment, which was like a palace compared to this room. The calendar was to the left of her, and she noted the date: August 20. *Oh, this is the date my Kathlynn was to be born. I'll celebrate instead of dwelling on sad feelings.* She thanked God for looking after her little one, and then decided to phone her mother.

"Mom, this is the day that Kathlynn was to arrive, and I want to rejoice instead of being blue. Do you have any time to visit today?"

"Yes, I do after I rearrange some details. I want to be with you on this important day. I'll call when I leave the house."

"That's a good idea. Can you give me an approximate time?"

"Probably within two hours. Is that okay?"

"Sure. See you soon. Bye."

***

Janette tried to think what she could do to make this day special and could only think of a birthday cake. *That's good, but I'd like to bring a gift. Heavenly Father, please give me an idea.* The first thought that came to mind was to go to the Bible Book Store and see what publication might interest her daughter. At the store she found a book that looked appropriate—*Seven Ways to Beat the Blues God's Way*. As she read the cover, introduction, and chapter headings, she was convinced that God had directed her.

***

As Alison waited for her mother, she had time to reflect on the past five months and decided to mentally count her blessings:

1. I survived when other patients around me died with complications.
2. Life will be different in the future. I just know that new, productive adventures lay ahead.
3. Mac is involved in my life, and only God knows what could develop.
4. A new apartment is waiting to be decorated.
5. Pastor Ed said that speaking engagements were part of my future and that I'll write a book.
6. A massive revival is on its way to Hamilton—my city.

This last thought gave her spirit a push to pray for this future awesome event. Before she realized it, two hours had passed and her mother arrived with the book. They spent a pleasant time together, chatting and perusing the chapter titles. Alison felt much lighter after her mother visited.

As soon as her mother left, a "candy striper" handed her a letter. Alison took it and smiled at the girl. "Thank you." It was a white envelope with a typed address but without a scent this time. Like the other letter, it had no return address. She phoned the police station for the first time, and was put through to Mac.

"Hello, Mac, this is Alison. I received another letter."
"I'll be right over."
"Thanks."

***

When Mac arrived, he looked serious. "Did the letter just arrive?"

"Yes." She handed him the letter and watched his facial expressions.

He opened it and began to read it silently.

> My dear Alison:
>
> I can't believe you refused to drop the charges and then requested a favour from me to give information about my friend, Christine. She has no desire to be involved in your life whatsoever, and that's all the information you'll get. She has a right to her privacy.
>
> I'm glad you didn't give in to my request of getting me out of here. I'm actually enjoying jail now. The guys respect me and have appointed me as their leader. I get to work out every day and one guard seems to like me and is working to get me some privileges.
>
> I just want to let you know I may be out of here sooner than everyone thinks. I may even show up on your apartment doorstep.
>
> —Reb

"Alison, I don't want you to read this letter. Will you trust me on this?"

"Yes, Mac, I trust you."

"I'll tell you this much: I think it's from the same person. I'm sorry I can't stay and visit, but I'll see you tonight with an update about your apartment."

"Sure, Mac. See you."

chapter twenty-one

Sharon introduced the session with two questions: "Do you find yourself reliving past hurts? Do you bristle when you hear Reb's name? Take time to think before you answer."

"Yes. At times negative incidents push in without warning." It had happened just that morning before she was fully awake.

"You may be harbouring resentments. Thinking about grievances can cause your mind to stay on alert mode so that wounds caused by bad experiences can't be healed. Having resentment is like taking a poison and expecting the other person to die."

With a little chuckle, Alison said, "That sounds like a great beginning to a sermon."

"Ahem. You don't have to go to church to know the benefits of forgiving those who hurt you." It seemed as if Sharon didn't want to talk about anything related to church. "I believe that forgiveness is about having inner strength to release bitterness. It's never about the offender deserving it. When you forgive, you're not condoning the offence, rather choosing to release negative feelings concerning it. And forgiveness can be given without reconciling your marriage. You understand that point already, right?"

"I sure hope so, but at times my feelings take over my logical thinking. You've given me a lot to think about. I admit that I do relive the past, but I thought that there was nothing I could do about that. The troublesome thoughts seem more like flashbacks I've no control over. Though I've taken them to God, they reoccur."

"I'm not saying it isn't difficult, and certainly seeking divine assistance is commendable." Sharon added, "You may have another kind of resentment that may be present without your awareness."

Alison was curious.

"You may need to deal with submerged anger toward God because He failed to prevent the injury."

Alison wondered how this woman could be so intuitive about some of her own private thoughts. "There was a time when I had questioned God, but now I don't."

"Oh? What caused the change?" asked Sharon.

"My pastor gave me a prophecy of how God may use my disability for His glory, and that made all the difference in the world."

It was apparent to Alison that Sharon didn't want to hear about "church stuff."

"Enough said on that subject. Let's deal with how you feel about Reb. You may need to express out loud that you forgive him. The first step is a mental consent to release anxiety should it follow."

Alison took a few minutes to mull over this information. It dawned on her that God was using Sharon's words to help her. "Okay. I'm willing to do that."

Sharon saw that Alison was struggling. She instructed, "Just tell Reb out loud that you forgive him even though he's not here."

"I can do that." Alison enunciated slowly, haltingly, but deliberately, "I … forgive you … Reb."

"That's the way." Sharon added, "I have one last question. Do you hold yourself responsible for triggering the offence? I'm wondering if you need to forgive yourself."

"At times I'm down because I let the abuse carry on. I should've seen the danger signs when he began the abuse again. If I'd seen the warning signs, I wouldn't have lost a baby." Alison couldn't carry on because she began to cry.

Sharon put a comforting arm around her and handed her some tissues. "You need to forgive yourself so that you can concentrate on maintaining your health. 'Should-haves' only cause one to reflect on what can never change."

"Oh, Sharon, you have reached the root of these bad thoughts. I understand now that each time I'm tempted to blame myself I must begin with forgiving myself. I'm not quite sure how to do that."

"By recognizing your lack of ability, the battle is already won. Meditate on that for a while this week and tell me anything else that you come up with.

"Well, I think we have accomplished a lot today." Sharon sighed with a self-satisfied smile.

"I agree." Alison believed that God had used Sharon without her knowing it.

***

Mac arrived just before lunch. "I had a call from *The Spectator;* the paper received an anonymous call concerning the article about your case."

"You didn't tell me about an article!"

"Oh. Didn't I?"

"No!"

"Oops. Sorry—I forgot." Mac explained about the article and the other patient's photo. "I thought an article about your case would stop further attempts to harm you. And it worked. So will you forgive me?"

"Okay. I forgive you. Now tell me about the phone call."

"Well, yesterday there was a call with a disguised voice that said he or she was sorry and wouldn't do any more harm."

"How come you don't know if it was male or female?"

"The reporter said the voice was distorted. I pressured him to hazard a guess, and he said if he had to, he'd guess female." Mac observed her screwed-up face and felt a hurt in his gut for her. "I've got good news."

"Oh? What is it?"

"The apartment is finalized, my lady, and I feel like celebrating." Alison's face transformed back into the beauty he knew her to be.

"It sounds like you're the one getting out of confinement," Alison said. "Personally, I can't remember what it feels like to be free to come and go whenever I please."

"It's been hard on you, but I never hear you complain."

"That's because I don't like complaining when people can hear me."

Alison continued. "I want to thank you again. I'm very grateful for all you've done, Mac."

Mac was still chuckling about Alison's previous statement. "You're very welcome. Now, let's go celebrate."

"What do you mean—go?"

"I've arranged to take you out of here for a couple of hours, okay?"

"Where are you taking me?"

"That's my secret. I'm here to pick you up for a date, and I'm not giving you a chance to say no." He put her sweater on, wheeled her out into the parking lot, picked her up and seated her in his truck, and then hoisted the collapsed wheelchair behind.

He had reserved a table at a restaurant called Little Budapest, where the waiters dressed in traditional European costumes and a violinist played "The Hungarian Rhapsody" as he roamed among the tables. Alison laughed at Mac's antics, mimicking the violinist and such. They ordered chicken paprikash and a walnut torte for dessert.

Mac thought, *I've brought flowers, cards, and candy. Alison has only responded with "You shouldn't have" or "Thank you." Now's the time to change the temperature of our relationships.* Mac had been waiting since the seminar, but the timing never seemed to be right, until now. They were basically alone.

Mac's thoughts were going a mile a minute. He prayed during a pause in the conversation. *I want to say the right thing, in the right way, except I don't know how to start. She has turned away every affectionate advance I've made. Father, how can I express the way I feel about her? Please help. Amen.*

First wiping his palm on his pants, Mac reached over with his clammy hand, hoping she wasn't aware of his nervousness. He took her hand and looked directly into her eyes. He tried to smile. "Alison, Dr. Karr said that it's not unusual for an able-bodied person to be interested in a disabled person." He paused and swallowed. "And I'm very interested."

Mac saw Alison look down at his hand on hers. Then she spoke slowly. "Mac, I like you. You have been so kind and giving, but all I have to offer you is friendship. I don't know anything about your family and friends, or if they would have trouble with our friendship, never mind more than that. And I know my limited lifestyle would curb your freedom." She kept her eyes averted from his.

He tipped her chin up. "Will you let me worry about those things? I'm in love with you, with who you are and all that you believe. I want to be near you every moment. Just give me a chance before you write us off before we've even started."

"Can't we just keep everything the way it is? I'm so glad you are involved in my life, and you support my belief that God is going to heal me. I want to remain your friend. You have so many abilities. The right girl will come across your path. She'll be able to jog with you and give you babies and be the lover that you need."

Swallowing hard, he said, "Thank you for those kind words, but you can't know I need all those things."

"Every normal man does."

"Who said I'm normal?" Mac crossed his eyes as he pulled up his eyebrow and stretched his mouth into a "Laurel and Hardy" grin.

He had her laughing so hard she fell to the side in his direction. Alison blurted out while still in the throes of laughter, "So, can we still be good friends?"

Mac's face suddenly took on a very serious look. "Yes. I'm your friend, now and forever." He kissed her cheek very close to her mouth, then left to get the truck.

Alison guessed that he was taking her to the apartment. She took this brief time during the ride to seek God. *There must be a way to discourage Mac without hurting him too deeply, Lord. I feel guilty in accepting his help when I don't intend to marry him. What should be my next step?*

An inner voice said, "*Trust Me. Relax and let Me take care of you.*"

Alison took a few deep breaths. She hadn't realized that she had been holding her breath. Believing that God had spoken to her heart, she determined to leave everything with Him and allowed her muscles to relax.

As Mac lifted her from the cab of his truck and lowered her into the wheelchair, he spoke softly in her ear. "Hey, beautiful, you'll love the apartment with the old wallpaper gone and fresh paint in its place."

Alison ignored the ticklish shiver that his closeness brought and forced herself to ask normally, "What colour did they paint it?"

"It's called Quiet Sunrise. It actually makes the hall look sunny."

"Did they do anything else?"

"Some brighter, modern light fixtures; the rest of the apartment looks fine the way it is. To change the subject, I have a little news about the latest letter. It has been confirmed that it was typed with the same typewriter, but the stationary is different. We can safely assume it was not from Reb. And I doubt that he's getting out of jail earlier than the first of April. I'll still need to do another thorough check on this letter tomorrow."

"Let's forget about everything that could spoil this experience," Alison said, and they entered the apartment.

chapter twenty-two

Weeks had passed since Daneen had visited, and Alison was concerned. She decided to intercede for her older sister. Her eyes were closed in prayer when Daneen walked quietly into the hospital room.

Daneen cleared her throat. "Allie, are you sleeping?"

A little startled, Alison responded, "Hi, Dannie! No, I was praying."

"I could have guessed that. Listen, I have to tell you, a strange thing has been happening. Something you said weeks ago has been haunting me."

"Really? What was it?"

"You said that everything that happens has an ultimate purpose, even if the plan is carried out from a wheelchair."

"Yes, I remember something to that effect."

"I've recently started to think again about the terrible things that happened to me in my first marriage, and I wondered if God has a plan for me too."

"I believe that the Holy Spirit is calling you to Himself. You may be ready to pray and surrender to Jesus."

"I think you're right, but I don't know how to pray. Will you help me?"

"Yes, of course. Do you want to pray after me?"

"Yes, I'd like that. Please go ahead."

"Dear Heavenly Father." Alison prayed in phrases, pausing to let Daneen repeat after her. "I come to you in the name of Your Son, Jesus. I have come to realize that You died on the cross for me. Please forgive me of my sins. I'm looking forward to a changed life and an eternal home in heaven when I die. Thank you for hearing my prayer. Amen."

After the prayer, Daneen's face relaxed, erasing the fine lines that can come with worry, and then smiled. "So, am I a born-again Christian?"

"Is there any other kind?" Alison laughed.

Daneen laughed along with her, acknowledging her own repeated quip.

***

"Are you getting excited about the party? It's only a few days away," said Sharon.

"I'm ready to celebrate all that I've learned here. Practically everyone I know will be at the party. Thank you, Sharon, for making it possible."

"You're welcome. It's what I do best."

"You are the best."

"Oh, and how many counsellors have you had to compare me with?"

Alison laughed. "I see what you mean. You've been my only counsellor, but I still think you're still the best."

"Thank you, Alison. This is my last chance to get on my soapbox and reiterate my concerns for you. The abusive type of men—like the one you married—believe that women are here to serve men. And they can be overly protective of their spouses. It's known as the 'controlling factor' of their nature. Alison, you have to be strong if Reb tries to come back into your life. I see you as a rose without thorns. You need to keep yourself protected."

"That's sweet of you to say, but you worry too much."

"Before you dismiss my concern, there's more I'd like to tell you. It's about how repetitive thoughts from your bad experiences may disturb your future. They can lead to harmful physical effects. That's why they are called 'toxic thoughts.' When you replay negative experiences, they produce harmful chemicals in your body. One way to alleviate these harmful effects is to practice 'stress breathing.' When you relive the same thoughts, the severe hurt is felt again, causing your breath to become shallow. The best thing to do in times of remembering adverse memories is to deep breathe. Take a full breath in to a slow count of four, while relaxing your abdominal muscles, and then exhale, tightening the same muscles with a count of four. It's an effective remedy. People also breathe shallowly when sitting. So this is a compound problem for you. I want you to remember this information and rectify your breathing with these exercises so you can have a long, healthy life."

"I didn't know about this. Thanks for this information."

"You're welcome." Sharon took a deep breath herself. "And, you know my most rehearsed topic ..."

"Setting goals," said Alison and Sharon in unison.

"They're important! Without them, it's like going on a trip having no destination. So, what is your short-term goal once you leave the hospital?"

"After I have my apartment in order, I want to develop an art business."

"How so?"

"I can do portraits at home and also build up an inventory of watercolour paintings and pastels. I'm going to look into advertising and into different ways of becoming known in the art community."

"It sounds like you have done quite a bit of thinking. My lectures have not been in vain." They both laughed this time. "Now, for your long-term goals."

"That's more difficult. Do you think I'll ever be married again?"

"That definitely is a long-term goal. There's no reason why you couldn't have a mate. You're young and you have a lot to offer a man. Many men aren't put off by women in wheelchairs."

"That sounds encouraging. But what about intimacy? How could I ever satisfy a man?"

"Sex happens naturally when two people love each other. I know of a female specialist who could help."

"I would be more comfortable with a woman, but wouldn't a future husband feel self-conscious talking to a female doctor? I assume both of us would need counselling."

"I believe it would be good for a future husband to hear a woman's point of view. He may feel uncomfortable with either a male or female therapist, but a woman knows more about how another woman feels. I believe he'd agree to talk to her because he'd want to please you. And if the plain facts were told to him, I'm sure he'd feel at ease.

"Alison, I understand that this is a natural concern for you, but let me tell you that the best part of sex is what goes on in your mind, not what happens to your body. The feelings can be imagined as you see your partner's actions. The pleasure can be similar to feeling them physically."

"So I'll have to keep my eyes open?"

Sharon hooted. "Alison, you're a character."

"To change the subject, do you want to hear another long-range goal?"

Sharon was still chuckling. "Sure."

"I want to learn how to drive a hand-controlled vehicle—probably a van."

"I think that's very possible. There's just one more thing I need to inform you about. You'll need some help with activities of daily living at the start. We've picked out a caregiver for you, a young woman named Sandy who comes highly recommended. She's a twenty-three-year-old who was at the top of her class. I know you'll like her. I also heard from your father that your bi-weekly care is covered, financially."

"Great! Thank you, Sharon. Thank you for everything."

***

Daneen phoned. "Oh, Allie, I love being a Christian. I have so much peace, now. I was afraid of driving or even walking out the door. Now my days are filled with lightness and calm."

"I'm so glad to hear this, Dannie."

"This is off topic, but I believe that God's prompting me to encourage you to make an appointment with Pastor Ed to talk about divorce. By the way, what happened when my lawyer visited?"

"I never heard from her and I didn't pursue it, thinking it must have been the wrong timing. But you may be right. It may be time to go ahead with this, and I'd like to discuss it with Pastor Ed."

After saying she would see Daneen the following night at the party, Alison phoned her pastor. They caught up on church news, and then embarked on the subject of divorce. "You know that God hates divorce but has made provision for it. Our denomination believes that divorce must be avoided except when infidelity is a factor." He added with conviction in his voice, "Enough is enough. Reb made his choice when he sought this other relationship. It's time for you to move on."

"There is something holding me back. My previous pastor said that if I divorced, I wouldn't be able to marry again as God intended. What do you think?"

"Unfortunately, many believe this way. I do not. Our God is a God of second chances or He wouldn't have said in the scriptures that divorce was allowed when there is infidelity. So, erase all the other voices and go with what the Lord's leading you to do."

After speaking with Pastor Ed, Alison contacted the lawyer. The business card that Daneen gave her was still in her over-bed table. She phoned the law office and made an appointment for mid-September with Ms. Jerome to come to her apartment.

***

"Now that I know how to get permission for you to leave the hospital, I thought you might like to go to church," said Mac.

Alison was speechless for several seconds, watching him study his hands and twist his police academy ring. "You couldn't do anything nicer. I'll let my nurse know so they can have me ready in the morning."

His head came up quickly, wearing a giant smile. "Great. I'll be here at ten. That should be enough time to get you up the stairs and into the sanctuary."

"You can't imagine what a treat one of Rev's sermons will be to me."

"They've started to grow on me, too. Have you noticed me sprouting lately?"

Alison laughed at his word picture. It was true that he had matured noticeably in the past five months. He was still her humorous friend with whom she liked to spend time.

***

It was like a dream to be sitting in the back of the church. Her mind wandered. *I hope that in the future there'll be wheelchair access, because not everyone can whisk me up in their arms like Mac. And he has to work every other Sunday. I just hope that I won't need to use the washroom while I'm here. Good thing my parents started to attend again. Mom won't mind helping me with emptying the leg catheter bag if any trouble should arise with it, but I don't think that she has the strength to support my weight if I should need to sit on the toilet.*

After Mac returned from placing the wheelchair in the foyer, Alison saw an unusual expression on his face as he looked down on her, and then sat next to her at the end of the pew.

The music prelude started. Alison couldn't wait to see her parents' faces when they spotted her. She wasn't worried that they were not there yet; they usually arrived late to most functions. During the first hymn, they came up behind her and gave her a big hug.

Ed McAlester stated that the sermon's focus would be on listening to God. They sang two more hymns, heard the announcements, and took up the offering.

The pastor began the sermon. "The Greek word *logos* means the written word of God. The word *rhema* means the spoken word of God. God is constantly speaking to us, and it is our privilege to listen to Him.

"Some well-known writers in Christian circles record what they believe God is saying to them. One who practises this is Betty Maltz. She had a near-death experience, which she told about in her first book *My Glimpse of Eternity*. She was pronounced dead after her appendix ruptured, but she came back to life when her father prayed just one word, 'Jesus!'"

If God can bring a woman back to life, He certainly can make another one walk again, thought Alison.

"Betty encourages a Christian to wait on the Lord after quieting one's mind from distractions, and then write something he or she believes God is saying. In fact, she has said she would like to be blind for a period of time so that her attentions would be less distracted, and then she could more effectively hear the Lord.

"In the chapter, 'Dialogue with God,' in her book, *Prayers That Are Answered*, she teaches that praying is discourse, which is described as being a two-way conversation. Both listening and talking are required aspects of communicating. It's the same with God. Betty states that her only source of wisdom is God. Because of this, she has a daily routine of seeking God's input the moment she awakes. She says her God is quiet-spoken, gentle, and considerate; yet there is a steel-like quality to His words because sometimes He has corrections to give. But the most important fact is that if we seek God's voice, we must obey His instructions.

"Another Christian writer, Joni Eareckson, who is a quadriplegic, is spending her time creating art, writing, and public speaking."

Mac tapped Alison on the shoulder and raised an eyebrow. She smiled back, remembering that she had told him about the prophecy from Pastor Ed many months ago that she would do the same.

"Joni has a special device that is controlled by an instrument in her mouth. This is how she composed her autobiography, *Joni*, which has been published just recently. Joni's story encourages paralytics by expounding that God has a purpose for them in being wheelchair bound."

This sermon renewed Alison's fervour to complete her autobiography. She wanted to warn other abused wives of the possible dangers that could result from a husband's uncontrolled anger.

The congregation was dismissed with a benediction. Alison felt that God had this sermon arranged just for her. Pastor Ed had had no idea that she would be in the service today.

Bill and Janette came to stand by their pew. Alison caught their inquisitive expressions. "Mom, Dad, this is Mac. You met him at the hospital. You probably don't recognize him out of uniform."

"I thought you looked familiar," said Janette. "I was wondering if you would like to join us for lunch at our favourite restaurant."

Mac responded, "Thank you for the offer, Mrs. Palmer, but I'm working the afternoon shift and there isn't really enough time today. I'll take a rain cheque though."

"That's a deal. We can plan it soon, now that Alison will be discharged from the hospital soon."

***

Leaving the church, Mac was distracted as he wondered how the writer of the second mysterious letter had obtained the information about Alison's discharge. *I bet I can get some information. I need to visit Christine again at the used car dealership.*

chapter twenty-three

Sharon decorated the conference room with a banner in purple, outlined in gold that read, "Farewell Alison." Streamers and balloons of the same colours hung from the ceiling. It looked ready for an elaborate party. The kitchen staff took special effort to make fancy sandwiches and squares. Someone from every department involved with Alison's care attended: Nancy, Skeeter, Rachelle, Dr. Whiting, Dr. Shapiro, as well as her immediate family, except for William and Judy. Many friends sent their best wishes.

Sharon had prepared a little speech: "I want to congratulate Alison and to give her a positive picture of her future and of her soon-to-be re-established independence. Knowing Alison, she will be looking forward to each new day."

Turning to Alison, she said, "I wish you prosperity and happiness. You have been a positive example of an enthusiastic learner for everyone on the team. You faced each day with cheerfulness and with tremendous calm. We all have been taught an important lesson: to take what life hands us, and use what we learn as a positive basis to influence others. There are many challenges ahead of you yet, Alison, but I know you will conquer them all. Congratulations."

In two hours the party ended and Alison gladly retired to her bed because she knew that she would awaken early in excitement for the move. *The party was successful in saying goodbye to all my therapists, but what about Mac? Will he be content to see me only in church? After all he can't just come to visit any time he pleases anymore. He'll need to phone ahead to see if it suits.*

As if Mac had heard her thoughts, he came to her room one last time. "Alison, I plan to be available whenever you need me. I've taken tomorrow off to help with the move."

"Thanks, Mac. My father always says, 'Many hands make light work.'"

"Your apartment isn't far from the station. If you ever need me, I can be there in minutes. I'll give you a special number."

"That's kind of you, but I don't think police assistance is what I'll need. I'm safe. Reb is in prison for at least five more months and the restraining order will continue after that."

"I can take you to church every other Sunday."

"My dad bought a car especially to carry me and my wheelchair. He'll be taking me each week."

Mac laid his hand gently on her shoulder. She looked up at him. He hung his head and simply said goodnight after kissing her cheek.

A nurse came in to make sure Alison was settled for the night. Usually the checks during the night didn't awaken Alison any more, but tonight was similar to the start of her hospitalization. She heard every noise. She slept for only a few hours. The night nurse had offered her a sleeping pill, but she had long ago decided to eliminate them. She didn't like the way they left her groggy and unable to think clearly the following day.

Five o'clock finally came. Though it was still pitch black outside, the night nurse consented to bathe and dress her for the big day and reminded her of the pressure-relief exercise she needed to do often. Alison settled in the wheelchair that would be her dwelling for many hours today, and got out her writing materials.

Looking back in one of her diaries, she reviewed an entry from three years ago:

> Sept. 1, 1974
> I finally finished my last year of teachers' college with honours, graduating fourth highest in the class. Reb and I celebrated with my parents and my pregnant sister, Daneen. After the presentation of the awards, a sit-down dinner followed, and then a dance. Reb, not being the dancing kind, let my father do the honours. Both my parents were awed over my award for best marks in field placement, but Reb didn't offer a word of praise. Being thankful that my schooling was over, I start working in a Christian high school in Ancaster. I will teach phys ed for the girls from Grades 9 to 13, which includes gymnastics, and track and field. The school needed an art teacher as well, so I will become the sole art teacher of the academy. God is so good! I suspected that this was His appointment all along.

With the overhead light beaming down on her, she continued to write her manuscript:

> Reb became even more critical of me once I started teaching. A high school teacher earns a good wage but nothing to brag about. I believe that Reb felt less significant than me because his salary was lower than mine. I didn't understand this at the time.
> I believe he felt better about himself when he put me down. His words made me feel that I was the source of all his trouble. He'd say that the house was not clean enough. We both worked full time, and I was responsible for the cooking, cleaning, and laundry. The meals I prepared included desserts to appeal to his sweet tooth, but none of these efforts seemed to make a

difference in our ability to get along. Nothing seemed to appease the beast within.

The moment I was feeling fairly safe in our relationship, the abusive incidents started up again. Objects flew through the air. He had built a coffee table with my dad; one night he threw it across the room, making a hole in the wall. If I didn't put the ironing board away immediately after using it, he would throw that. If I left the dishes unwashed for a time, he'd smash them to the floor. If I left my Bible in his sight, he'd throw it too. Eventually the cover became loose, and my precious guide looked abused also. I believe I now understand why Reb did this to my Bible—he was running from God, and the sight of His Word reminded him of his straying path.

Every time the words "Praise the Lord" slipped from my mouth, Reb would go into a rage, as if some evil force were responsible for his actions.

***

Alison's writing was interrupted by a breakfast tray. *Is it that time already?* She really enjoyed writing, although the content was disturbing. She wanted to return to it after breakfast, but Mac arrived earlier than expected to take her to supervise the arranging of the furniture in her new apartment.

Her father had the crew, which included her mother, sister, and volunteers from the church, already in action by seven. Yesterday afternoon before the party, the rented truck had been loaded with all her belongings that had been stored for the past six months.

Mac took Alison up to her apartment and situated her in what would become her favourite place, the alcove, where she could see the placement of the inherited bookcase, which her father made sure to anchor to the wall, and an old chair. A new sofa, two end tables and lamps were a generous gift from her father. Mac left with a list of food to buy for the volunteers' coffee break and lunch.

William came in the door shortly afterward with two dining room chairs. Alison didn't know that William was in Hamilton; he wanted it to be a surprise. Before she saw him, he quietly placed the chairs in the dining room, and then walked up behind her as she was surveying her new neighbourhood from the window. He covered her eyes. In a falsetto voice he said, "What a lovely apartment you have here, miss. Guess who?"

"The milkman with laryngitis."

Laughter erupted. "Oh, sis, you're the craziest."

"You didn't come just to help me move did you?"

"I was going to go to the party last night but I had car problems—the transmission again. I thought I'd stay to help you move and visit with mom and dad, and of course you."

"I really appreciate this. How's Judy?"

"She's fine. She has to work tomorrow. I'm glad I came, although I did a lot of complaining, waiting for a tow truck."

"Your support means a lot to me. Thanks."

"Good thing the bad weather's going to hold off until tomorrow. The reports say a tremendous thunderstorm is coming."

"I love to watch lightning," said Alison.

"I better keep working; Dad wants to finish this morning," said William.

Everything happened so fast that Alison felt her surroundings were surreal. Her father and brother kept returning with boxes as if moving at warp speed. They carried the table with two chairs on top.

Mac returned with the food. Daneen brought out cold drinks and put the Tim Hortons coffee and doughnuts on the table.

"Mac, I'd like to introduce you to my brother, William, and my sister, Daneen." Daneen took a long look at the man her sister had been talking about for the past months then turned to face Alison and winked.

After the coffee break, everyone seemed to put even more effort into carrying boxes, paintings, her precious electronic piano, and dresser. Janette carried the framed cross-stitched motto. "It must have a special place in your lovely apartment."

"Put it on the mantel, Mom. Dad can hang it later."

A hospital-type bed arrived next, so her new caregiver could raise and lower her position. But its main purpose was so she could use the trapeze to manoeuvre in and out without assistance.

Alison had a grand time giving orders and seeing her apartment shape up in just a few hours. She tried to unpack the boxes marked "kitchen" that was put on chairs, but her mother and sister wouldn't let her. Some women and one man from the church came to assist shortly after the bed arrived. It was assembled within an hour. The whole move took just under four hours. They rejoiced in accomplishing a job well done as they ate lunch.

When everything from lunch was cleared, Alison's father came in the door with a huge grin on his face and a large box in his arms.

"I have a housewarming present for you, my sweetheart."

"Oh, Dad, you've done so much already."

His face continued to beam while he ripped into the box, revealing a tiltable art table. It had an adjustable arm that held a lamp and magnifying glass. Drawers on each side would hold her supplies. There were compartments for paints and brushes—almost everything she'd need to start her fine-art business. She was totally thrilled with the gift. Waiting to open the box marked art supplies from her old apartment would be a challenge. Alison dearly wanted to start her first piece as soon as possible.

It was time for everybody to wish Alison their best and let her be alone for an hour before her caregiver arrived. Mac kissed the top of her head and wished her a pleasant afternoon.

The art table had been assembled and situated on an angle in the alcove to give her a view of the front lawn and street. Alone now, she wheeled herself into a position, with the table over her lap. *Ah.* A sigh of relief and relaxation drifted through her whole body. Well almost—her bottom was sore. *I forgot to do my exercises, with all the excitement!* She did a few repetitions; something was wrong. *I won't worry about that now.*

She had waited for this day of being on her own since she heard that a new type of life was necessary. Now it seemed that her life had been moving on its pre-planned course. Until today she had felt as though she navigated her life on uncharted waters; now she sailed in an intended direction.

Alison was looking over her prized new possession from her daddy, opening each drawer, when the door buzzer rang. *Ah, my caregiver is right on schedule.*

"Hello, my name is Sandy Dailey," said a very pretty woman with strawberry blond hair pulled into a long ponytail and cheeks lightly sprinkled with freckles. She stepped in confidently, shutting the door behind her. Alison's wide, deep blue eyes and smile greeted her, as if to say, "I like you already."

They said simultaneously, "Hi. I'm glad to meet you." The giggles gradually diminished as they shook hands.

"That statement is probably the extent of our seriousness," predicted Sandy.

"That's good. I need a friend more than another professional."

"Great. First, may I look through your apartment before starting the preliminaries?"

"Sure."

After Sandy walked through the kitchen, bathroom, and bedroom, making note of the bed and trapeze, she returned to the alcove. "This is a unique apartment." Taking a stance in front of the wheelchair, Sandy said, "I can see that you're going to be spending quite a bit of time in this bright area." Recognizing this would be Alison's delightful hideaway gave them an immediate bond.

Next, Sandy found a cabinet in the bathroom to place her equipment, ready for her next visit. Returning to Alison's side, Sandy asked if she could go shopping for her.

"No, thank you. My mother and sister filled the fridge and cupboards. They bought everything imaginable."

"Is there something in particular that you would like me to fix for your supper?"

"Oh. I thought I would be responsible for my meals."

"That's commendable. How about I stand by should you need any help?"

"Great."

A few hours later, Sandy readied her for bed. "I'll help you for several days until I feel confident that you're able to take care of these tasks alone."

Alison noticed a concerned look on Sandy's face as she exited, but there was no time to question her.

So ended Alison's first day of freedom.

chapter twenty-four

Good morning Father, Jesus, Holy Spirit. Thank you for the joy of being alive and for having a home of my own. Hallelujah! Then Alison's memory replayed the special parts of Sunday's sermon about the steps in listening for God's voice. She attempted to practise the pastor's suggestions, but an underlying doubt remained—*will God really speak to me?* She knew that the problem for many seekers, including her, is that hearing from God takes a great deal of patience. The King James translation for patience is "long-suffering," which to Alison's thinking was a more descriptive word.

Although she truly wanted to hear from God, her eyes kept drifting toward the windows of the alcove, to the gathering dark clouds and increasing wind. *Broken branches and loose shingles will be the results,* she thought. She wheeled over to the bookcase and turned on the radio. A warning broadcast from CHML told everyone in the area to take shelter from a severe thunderstorm expected that afternoon that would last several hours. As a child, she had loved to run outside during warm showers and catch raindrops on her tongue. The impossibility of repeating this childhood play reminded her abruptly of her limitations.

Returning to her previous thoughts, she quieted her mind to receive from the Lord, but she had difficulty concentrating because of a nagging pain in her backside. She wasn't sure what was causing the pain. *Maybe it's from sitting for so many hours in the wheelchair yesterday.* She changed from trying to listen to the Lord to urgently requesting Him to relieve the pain.

Alison remembered her past experience with ulcers. Suddenly a wave of excitement, hit her. *I can feel pain!* This was the first time since the accident that she had had any sensation below her waist. Gratefulness to the Lord bubbled up from the depths of her being; along with it flowed hope of regaining normal feeling in her legs.

Alison prayed aloud and heard her words echoing encouragement.

"Thanks, Lord, for this opportunity to be alone, having no one to hear except You. Up until now, I have done all the talking and haven't thought to listen, but this changes today. If it is true that You continually want to talk to Your children, then I want to hear what You're saying. I come now and ask you to cleanse me from the sin of negativity. My first thought was that the pain was bad news. Now I know it's the best news. I praise You, Lord! And I thank you for my new apartment and being able to live on my own.

"Now, I wish to hear from You. Amen."

As her mind kept wandering, she wondered how long it would take to keep her thoughts focused. Thirty minutes then thirty-eight minutes passed. She scolded herself for looking at the clock again. After repeating the same prayer for forgiveness, she felt a peace drift over her as an inexplicable quiet seeped into her being. *It must be the Holy Spirit's presence.*

She wrote the fresh, living words that began to form in her mind.

"You are like an olive branch that gives its fruit to be crushed, so that pure oil may flow out. Each fruit you bear must be squeezed until others benefit from the essence of your fruit.

"Keep your thoughts pure by bringing Me your concerns. As you let Me handle everything, burdens will lift. Continue to pray often and leave every worry with Me."

As she wrote one word, the next word was waiting to be written; she perceived that the Holy Spirit was dictating to her. An exhilarating feeling came over her. She believed that God had made personal contact with her.

Thank you, Lord. How wonderful You are. Still, I'm unsettled because of this pain and what might be causing it. I had pressure sores before. Because they took so long to clear up, I'm thinking this time will be the same. You have told me to keep bringing my requests, so I'll repeat it again—Lord, please heal me and allow me to walk again.

I desire for You to have full use of my life. I know good will come from this experience. And as I write my story, I believe that's part of Your plan to bring emotional healing.

Jesus, I believe You are giving me more feeling in my body and I choose to believe that feeling the pain is evidence that You are healing me. Therefore, I'm even glad for the pain. Thank you!

As I return to write about my past, no matter how emotionally disturbing, I know You want me to continue. I may cry, but I know releasing these emotions will continue to be good for me. Amen.

Before doing anything else, Alison phoned Sandy to report her suspicion of a pressure sore.

"Are you in your wheelchair right now?" Sandy asked.

"Yes. Since seven this morning. I've been writing my biography and having morning devotions."

"My, you are an early riser. I knew about your art, but no one told me that you were a writer."

"I'm just starting out."

"Good for you. So, you've been up long enough already. I want you to make yourself a lunch of mainly protein and then remain in bed on your side until I get there, okay?"

"Okay."

"I'll bring equipment and dressings to get ahead of the situation. Don't worry."

I've heard to not worry for the second time today.

"I'm not hungry yet, but I'll make a tuna sandwich to take to the bedroom and a glass of milk. Is that enough protein?"

"That's good. Don't forget some vegetables."

"Right. See you in a couple of hours. I'll leave the door unlocked."

"Good. Bye."

***

After eating, Alison positioned her writing pad and reread the last portion of her autobiography. She tried to edit what she had written so far. Writing, while lying on her side, reminded her of earlier days.

> Loneliness didn't have such a hold on me as before the awesome experience of feeling God's supernatural hug the night of the choking scare. I no longer asked Reb to change; instead I relinquished him into the Lord's hands. It was time to just rest in His arms and renew my trust.
>
> When Reb didn't return, I poured out my distress to the Lord. The first day went by without a word from him. None of the hospitals in the city had his name listed as being admitted. Calling his work was not a choice because I imagined the rumours it could cause. The only other avenue was to phone the police and report a missing person. I was not comfortable with that either, so I decided to leave everything in God's hands.

Alison began to add to what she had written.

> I visited my older sister, Daneen, who listened to my dilemma and offered comfort. She could identify with me because she had experienced marital abuse. That night, we had a frank conversation. She advised me to seek a divorce. I responded with reluctance because I had no proof that Reb was

unfaithful. Daneen said she was afraid for my safety. I told her that I'd be all right, and she asked me to stay overnight.

The next morning I said, "Boy, my nipples are tender."

Alison stopped writing because the tears welled up, making it impossible for her to see her writing. She tried not to think about her horrendous past. *Holy Spirit, please come with your comfort again.* Relaxing her head on the pillow, she drifted into a brief dreamless sleep until a knock on the door woke her. She reminded herself to give Sandy a key, and then called out, "Who is it?"

"It's Mac."

I didn't even give him my phone number. She immediately regretted neglecting this after all he had done for her. She shouted, "Come in."

"Hi, beautiful. You always leave your door unlocked?"

"I'm expecting my caregiver. I forgot to give her a key," Alison hollered.

Mac ventured down the hall and found her in bed, fully dressed, facing away from the door. "It's raining cats and dogs. And they're making quite a racket."

With a chuckle, she said, "I guessed the lightning is becoming more frequent, because the radio keeps sizzling." From her bedroom window she could see only the brick wall of the house next door; it had a wet sheen. It was quite dark for mid-afternoon.

After a brief pause, Mac asked, "I hope I'm not intruding."

"I was taking a nap, but I'll forgive you for waking me."

Mac walked around the other side of the bed and saw her smirk. "You'd better or I'll return this housewarming present."

"You shouldn't have. After all you have done to find this apartment and paying a month's rent."

"I told you I could afford it for my dearest friend."

"Thank you, Mac. Would you please roll up the head of the bed so I can open it?" She rolled over on her back, trying not to grimace.

"There's nothing to open. Just take them out of the bag. I didn't have time to wrap them up."

Alison removed the art supplies: brushes of all sizes, a tablet of watercolour paper, graphite pencils, a kneaded eraser, assorted hues of watercolour paint, and even an electric pencil sharpener. "This is wonderful. You must have received expert help."

"I just asked the sales lady what she would buy if she didn't have any supplies."

"Thank you, Mac."

"I wanted to include a bouquet of flowers, but I'll leave that for next time."

Alison didn't know how to respond. She didn't want to confront the issue again today.

He searched for some candles and a flashlight. After making sure the flashlight worked and lighting two tall candles, he said, "You'll need light if the power goes out. Romantic, eh?" Before he went out into the heavy rain, she made sure he had her phone number so he could call before dropping in the next time. He patted her arm, winked, and then left. Alison rolled onto her other side.

The thunder turned into a continuous rumble punctuated with louder bursts. Large droplets pinged on the window. Alison estimated the closeness of the storm by counting the number of seconds between the flash and the boom. Crackle … one thousand, two thousand … crash. Crackle … one thousand … BANG. With the next belch from the invisible dragon, the lights went out. The radio was silent, and the bedroom glowed with the candles lit less than a half-hour ago.

When Sandy arrived, the rain was still steady and the power was still out. She used the flashlight to assess Alison's bedsore. She cleansed and dressed it. The rest of the treatment would have to wait until the electricity returned.

"The open area isn't as severe as I thought. Once we can use the heat lamp, it will dry and toughen the skin. I've cleansed the open area, applied an antibiotic, then dressed it with a porous pad."

"How long do you think it will take to heal? Last time it took so long."

"Every sore heals at a different rate, but I'm hoping two weeks should do the job."

"Do I have to remain in bed?"

A Gift of Love

Sandy stood in front of her. "My goodness, no. You'll have to be in bed about twenty-five minutes, twice daily, morning and afternoon with the heat lamp. I'll come to do the treatments twice a day and divide the amount of time I would usually stay in half."

"What's your opinion? How is it that I can feel pain?"

Sandy looked up thoughtful. "I don't know. I'll ask your doctor. I'll help you up for supper."

"Thanks."

Sandy left after situating Alison in the alcove to watch the lightning display. Tonight was especially dark because of the cloud cover. As Alison looked down on the sidewalk, a teenager swung her purse as she strode down the street; then a tall person descended from a bus. She could see only brief glimpses when the lightning flashed, much like watching a fast-forward flick. In one frame the tall man was stepping off the bus, and in the next he was limping along the sidewalk beside her window.

This tall, light-haired man, who didn't have completely healthy legs, seemed entirely content. Even with the rain drenching him, he swung his arms freely and appeared to be whistling. His hobble seemed to be due to a deformity of his right foot. It appeared to be pointing in the opposite direction to the path he was taking. *His happy disposition makes me want to smile. I wonder if he's a Christian.*

chapter twenty-five

Mac phoned after his shift finished. "Alison, does your radio still have battery power?"

"Hi, Mac. No, the batteries must have died."

"I'll come right over with some."

"What's the urgency?"

"The forecasters have issued a tornado watch. They have sighted mesocyclones that often precede tornadoes."

"What's a mesocyclone?"

"Basically, they are rolling clouds that run horizontally in a counter-clockwise direction and can send a funnel down at any time. And if the barometric pressure drops drastically, we're in trouble."

"I didn't know you were such a weather expert."

"I guess you could say it's my hobby."

"I'd like to let you know that you've done a good job in scaring me."

"Good; you need to be."

"I'll leave the door unlocked."

"Be careful who you invite to come in."

A few seconds after Alison hung up, the phone rang again. "Did you forget to tell me something, Mac?"

"Mac is it?" said a masculine voice.

"Who is this?"

"Have you forgotten my voice so soon?"

Oh no! "Reb! How did you get my number?" Her heart beat so wildly that it felt as though it were going to crack her ribs.

His voice sounded rough, like a character from a gangster movie. "Hello, Alison. I guess you weren't expecting me to call today or maybe ever. And to answer your question, I can get any number I want."

"This is the first time you've talked to me since … since my birthday."

"So, did you get my letter?"

She decided to play innocent. "What letter?" *I thought he wrote two letters.*

"I made special arrangements to send you a letter to ask you to drop the charges. Besides, I didn't even know you were pregnant until my lawyer told me. I thought you had just put on some weight."

"Not knowing doesn't change the fact that our baby is dead."

"Maybe it wasn't *our* baby," he shouted.

Alison held the phone away from her ear. *How many more ways will he try to hurt me? Dear God, what should I say next, or should I just hang up?*

God's guiding voice came from within her. *"Give it to him straight, and then end the call."*

"It seems as if you want to stir up trouble, Reb, so I think we should say goodbye."

"Yeah, goodbye forever. Give me a divorce, Alison."

After placing the phone on the cradle with a shaking hand, she talked to her heavenly Father. *That wasn't pleasant, Father. Be with me right now and help me to stop shaking. I need Your comfort.*

A Gift of Love
✱✱✱

The wind continued to howl as Mac arrived, dripping wet. He placed two bags on the counter then looked at Alison's pale, stricken face and red-rimmed eyes. "What's happened?"

"Reb phoned me right after I hung up with you. He asked me why I didn't drop the charges as he asked in the letter. He said he didn't know I was pregnant, and then implied that the baby wasn't his. He ended with a demand for a divorce."

"Oh, my darling. No wonder you've been crying. He does the hurting and then tries to make you feel that you are in the wrong, but don't let him." Mac got down on his haunches and hugged her tightly. "It's okay to cry to let it out. I'm here now."

Alison was feeling more relaxed. "Thanks for your encouragement." She sniffed and dabbed her eyes then let out a deep sigh. "What's in the bags besides batteries? It seems a long time since I had that sandwich for lunch."

"Lady, you read my mind so well. Two submarine sandwiches."

"Oh, good. Thank you."

After he put the batteries in the radio and they finished eating, Alison told Mac that Reb had admitted to writing a letter, but not two.

After a few more rumbles and flashes, Mac continued on the same topic. "It's important information that could have taken me a long time to figure out. You were very clever to bring out this fact about the letters without him catching on."

"Thanks."

"You're welcome. So we have two different people writing letters. But I don't want you to worry about any of this."

"I'll try not to," she said with a forced smile.

"Why don't I go downstairs for your mail to see if there's anything to distract you from your troubles."

"Thank you. That would be nice."

Mac returned and handed her a forwarded letter plus some advertisings. Alison ripped open the envelope immediately and read while Mac looked about her apartment for leaks and checked the news again.

Kathleen Reichert

The letter was from Lynndale, Alison's friend from school. After the usual preliminaries of a letter, Lynndale had written that she felt she had a message from God sent to her by another friend and that she should forward it to Alison.

Everyone longs to give himself/herself completely to someone, to have a deep soul relationship with another, and to be loved thoroughly and exclusively. Nevertheless, God says to a Christian, "No. Not until you are satisfied, fulfilled, and content with Me alone. I love you my child, and until you discover that your satisfaction is to be found in Me only, you will not be capable of the perfect human relationship that I have already planned for you. You will never be united with another until you are united with Me—exclusive of anyone, of anything, of any desire or longing. I want you to stop planning, stop wishing, and then allow Me to give you the most thrilling plan in existence. It is one you cannot even imagine. I want you to have the best! Please allow Me to bring it to you.

"Keep experiencing a deep satisfaction of knowing that I AM. Keep learning and listening to the things I tell you. For now, you must wait! Do not be anxious. Do not worry. Do not look around for the things you want. Just keep looking up to Me, or you will miss what I want to show you. And when you are ready, I will surprise you with a love far more wonderful than you could ever dream of having.

"Understand that not until you are ready will the one I have for you be complete. Not until both of you are satisfied exclusively with a perfect love for Me will you be ready for each other. And, dear one, I want you to have this most wonderful love. I want you to see in the flesh, a picture of your relationship with Me. I want you to enjoy, substantially and permanently, the everlasting union of the most beautiful, perfect love that I alone can offer you. Know that I love you dearly. I am God almighty. Believe and be satisfied."

Alison reread it, pondering its deep meaning. Her next thoughts were of Mac, knowing his desire to have someone, too. She wondered if she might be falling in love with him, or was it appreciation for his kind words and the ways he showed that he cared. *I'm wondering if I'm falling in love, or falling for love. I'd better be sure before I stumble into trouble again.*

***

The effects of the storm were apparent the next morning. Branches from the trees that lined her street littered the ground, including some from her favourite maple. The news reported homes damaged by trees crashing into roofs along the route of the mighty wind. This kind of weather, seldom seen in Hamilton, must have shocked many residents and business owners. Fortunately, Alison's only trouble was that her electricity had been out for a few hours.

Before Alison did anything that morning, she determined to spend time with the Lord. *Speak to me, Holy Spirit, as I read the Bible.* Alison turned to the gospel of Luke, Chapter 15, and read about the lost sheep, the lost coin and the lost son.

In the last story, she noticed that the father ran to the son, but the son did not run to the father, possibly due to weakness from hunger or from being ashamed of his filthiness. She noticed a difference in the verbs the son used when he demanded to be *given* his share of the money compared to his humble request to be *made* a servant.

Lord, I've asked you to return the use of my legs and to remove the pain from the ulcer, but I've not asked you to make me into the person who enables others to accept You as their Saviour. I would like to start doing that.

Speaking her next prayer aloud seemed to make it binding: "Father God, make me a spokesperson of the gospel while I am still in the wheelchair. Make me an effective speaker sitting or standing before one or many. Make me a writer who represents the gospel in a pleasing way. Make me an ambassador of love. Amen."

She reread the first message that God had given her in her journal. It did not take as long now to keep her distracting thoughts at bay. It was as if she felt the words of the Lord pour into her spirit:

"Let the energy I give well up into every part of you. My Spirit will pour out as you recognize His presence inside your being.

"My children lack many benefits because they do not put My Word to use. Some think it will just come to them without any effort, but I am saying, 'Be a good student.' Let the living waters flow—the river that connects the throne to your heart. When you have an inclination to find a scripture that will impart wisdom in a situation, ask it to be shown to you. Be confident that the Holy Spirit will bring it to your memory.

"My Word is for your use. If you made some food that would bring health to your family and they did not eat it or use up every part of it, you would stop trying. I do not feel the same. I will never give up, although I have similar emotions. I can hurt as you hurt. Consider this the next time you hear Me call, and you are tempted not to follow the instructions you are hearing. If you are not sure of My exact meaning, act on your inclinations. I will do more through one who is not sure of their capabilities than one who does not try at all. My power is in you to do what My Word has commanded you today."

***

Mac donned dressy casual clothes to visit the used-car sales lot. His first trip there had given him a general idea of Christine's personality, but there was little information he could use in a court of law. Today he wanted to uncover some concrete evidence. He contemplated every angle of how to start the conversation, and then decided to involve her in the topic of effective drug use for the terminally ill who die at home, as her mother did.

As he got out of his truck, a woman came out of the office. *Is it Christine?* Her face had a striking resemblance, but this woman seemed much thinner. As she approached, Mac realized it was indeed Christine. *This woman is definitely not pregnant.*

Christine called out, "Hello. You're back. Are you still interested in a sports car?"

"I've had time to do some thinking on it, but it's more of a dream than a need."

"That's my middle name—dream-maker." The words rolled off her tongue in a seductive murmur.

They strolled to the first sports car. After some small talk, Mac said, "You were very knowledgeable about hospital affairs the last time we spoke; I'm wondering if you know about the drugs that are given to terminally ill patients. I'm asking for a friend. Since you told me that your mother died at home of cancer, I've been thinking that you would know something about the subject."

She raised her eyebrows. "That's funny. It's one of my pet peeves. A doctor knows that a patient is dying, yet he limits the amount of drugs as if he's worried the patient will become addicted. For example, morphine is given in such small quantities, how could it do any good in stopping pain?"

"You know about morphine?

"As I told you, I've had some experience with it. It doesn't make me an expert or anything."

"You don't have to be an expert to have deep convictions about something."

She took a step closer as she spoke quietly. "It's the best way to go, if you ask me."

"Oh? How do you see it?"

"Did you know that if you get enough of that drug, you just stop breathing?"

"No I didn't. You sound more like a nurse than a car salesperson."

Christine blushed and smiled as if she received the best compliment.

Mac thought he'd better look interested in a car to eliminate suspicion. He played his part well and implied that he would seriously think about the last car he looked at. He stretched out his arm for a handshake before leaving.

***

Every weekday at five-thirty in the evening, Alison watched the passengers getting off the bus at the corner. Watching these people from her window made her feel as if she were in a different world, where not every aspect of the day revolved around her disability. Soon that tall man with the blond, wavy locks would come by. Watching for him became a highlight of her day. *God, if you are trying to show me something, You sure have an unusual way of doing things. I haven't met this man, nor have we had eye contact, yet I feel I know something about his character. I do pray for him, that You will bless his work and make him a blessing to others.*

He must have suffered with his malformed foot. He may have been through surgery, pain, and possibly ridicule as a child. Whatever he has suffered, I ask that you will help him deal with any remaining hurt. Amen.

Her eyes followed him. *He must live nearby. Oh, there's a camera around his neck. Maybe I'm wrong about him living in the city; yet Hamilton isn't exactly a tourist attraction.* She was intrigued.

At that moment, he glanced up at the window as if she had willed him to look. He smiled. *Oh, he sees me. No use hiding now.* Naturally, Alison returned the smile.

Father God, I'm wondering why this man has caught my interest. Perhaps it's his disability, or that he seems happy as he walks. I'd like to meet him someday and ask why he's so joyful.

I'm feeling lonely right now. I realize Mom, Dad, and Daneen will come to visit, but I feel they'll be coming out of obligation. Please forgive me; I sound like a grumbler.

Lord, I'm not questioning Your wisdom in allowing me to experience this segment of my life from a wheelchair, but I'm lonely. I'd like a special person in my life.

Your word says that grace is made perfect in weakness. I'm very weak for sure.

***

Every day, Sandy left her parents' home at seven-thirty in the morning to start her rounds. She put Alison first on the list.

Sandy greeted Alison cheerfully. "Thanks for the key. I feel so much better that your apartment door is locked. You can't be too careful these days."

"Yes. And I'm feeling much better; my bottom must be healing."

Sandy set up her equipment, "I'm glad to hear it, but it doesn't happen that fast." She took off the dressing. "Oh, Alison, it looks much better; more than I've seen before. It's baffling. I've never observed someone heal this quickly. The perimeter of the wound is extremely red, which means that new tissue is developing, and the centre is light pink—another good indication of the healing process."

Sandy entered her observations in the progress chart, wearing a slight smile.

"Did you know you have a cute smile when you write?" Alison asked.

"Thanks. I like to see my patients respond so quickly, and I enjoy writing. I know it seems strange when it's just a chart."

"I started writing a journal while I was in the hospital, and now it's turning into an autobiography."

"Good for you. I see we have writing in common. I took a course in college called Creative Writing: Editing to Publication.

"In school I tried to get out of doing compositions," Alison said, "and here I am choosing to write and having fun doing it. Have you had anything published?"

"Just a little article in the school newspaper about why journalling is important."

"I'd like to read it, if I could."

"I'll see if I can locate it, but it's probably been thrown out long ago."

"That's too bad. Would you like to read what I've done so far on my autobiography and maybe give me a critique?"

"Yes. I'd like to do that." Sandy collected her supplies and the start of Alison's autobiography.

"Before you go, did you hear from Dr. Shapiro about why I could be feeling pain?"

"No, I didn't. I wasn't expecting him to reply quickly. I hope you have some patience, patient." They laughed. Sandy left and locked the door.

Alison went immediately to her alcove to put the last touches on a painting. It depicted five eagles showered with golden rain. She chose to title it *Latter Rain Anointing*. The five white eagles symbolized the fivefold ministry: apostles, prophets, evangelists, pastors, and teachers. All of the eagles were in different stages of flight. The dark clouds portrayed

183

evil, parting and allowing the sunshine of God's love to reach the Earth. Through the parted clouds, a golden rain fell. The rain represented the anointing oil of the Holy Spirit that landed only on the eagles, which were not flapping their wings but soaring into the heavens. Beneath them was a boiling sea of blue and reflective gold. Alison was always amazed at the beauty she produced with the Lord's guidance.

chapter twenty-six

Alison left her Bible open to 1 Corinthians 7. She reread verse 15: "But if the unbeliever leaves, let him do so. A believing man or woman is not bound in such circumstances; God has called us to live in peace."

Oh, Lord, I believe You're telling me to be mentally and emotionally free of Reb. I'm going to relax and picture myself sitting on Your lap, listening to Your words of wisdom, and then write them in this special book. I want to tell You how much I love You. Speak, Lord; I want to hear Your voice.

Thoughts of Reb's phone call upset Alison intermittently, but now calmness descended as she turned her thoughts heavenward. God directed her to take the baton—her pen—and run with it as if she were a competitor in a race:

"*Walk in My way where challenges wait, and supernatural power will come. It is always easy to follow the world's way, where one imitates everyone* on the same path. While on God's quest, each one has a personal unique mission revealed when He chooses to disclose it. Don't be afraid to approach Me, rather seek Me with all your strength.

"As you continue on your journey, you will become stronger and be able to climb greater heights. The world will be left behind in the valley where its glamour no longer distracts.

"The interesting trails in front of you are all correct, but only one is perfect for you. Look closely because your trail is marked with different signs that will peak your interest. You will not question, 'Is this my path to travel?'

"You will find great joy and a contentment that you have never known. I will take your hand and we will have an intimate conversation as lovers do. Only you and I will be able to understand its nuances.

"This sweet communion and union are planned for each one of My loved ones. Not all respond with intimacy, but I am confident that you will. May I have this dance, My beloved?"

Looking up to God became her aspiration, rather than looking down at her useless legs. *I can walk, run a race, climb and dance without using my physical legs. Lord, I will rejoice in what you have given me: active hands, artistic ability, and eyes to see the beauty around me. Our endless dance begins today.*

***

Alison received a phone call from Ms. Jerome, the lawyer who had been working on her case since the beginning of the month.

"Your divorce has been granted," she announced, "and legal aid has paid all the expenses. The one-year waiting requirement was waived because of your special case."

Alison would have danced a jig if it were possible. "Really and truly?"

"Yes, truly. Some housewarming present, right?"

"Thank you so much. I'm tongue-tied at present."

"You don't have to say anything. And you're welcome."

Alison felt relief flood over her, although in the secret place of her soul regret remained. She could do nothing about these wayward feelings of loss, so she decided to pray for Reb's return to the Lord. *Jesus, my emotions are so mixed up. I don't want Reb back in my life; nor do I want reconciliation, but could You make him a rebel for You again? Only You know if that is possible, so I'll leave him in Your hands. Amen.*

***

It was starting to get quite dark already; she turned on her lights and then went to fix a simple meal. She put the plate on a tray on her lap and reached to play a tape of classical music. A soft glow filled the alcove. As she looked up from her plate, the handsome man with the disabled foot waved and smiled at her from the sidewalk. *It's only polite to wave back.* She gave a royalty-style wave accompanied by a hesitant smile.

***

Reb had been released from prison. The lawyer with whom Reb had connections had bargained to reduce Reb's twelve-month sentence to five and a half months. If Reb had been violent toward a stranger instead of his wife, the sentence would have been more severe, with no parole allowed.

Reb's scheme was to interfere with Alison's life in any way he could devise. He'd find a way to get around the parole stipulations, even if it meant convincing his parole officer that he just happened to go to the same church she attended. In Reb's mind, he had suffered unusual punishment in prison at the hand of the other inmates because of the charges. Only some of the prisoners condoned knocking around a prissy wife. Now he had a plot to teach her how it really feels to suffer.

***

Rolph Vonderland walked by the church on Ellis Avenue again on his way home from shopping on this pleasant Saturday. He felt a strange pulling to attend this church tomorrow, instead of his family's congregation. This same drawing had happened several times in the past months, but he dismissed it. *God, are you trying to redirect me? Am I supposed to leave my family's church and attend here? I'll try it tomorrow.*

With the ulcer pretty well healed, Alison sat on the pew, with her wheelchair out of sight. Mac returned from parking her chair and then sat beside her. He smiled as she sang the familiar hymns and the more bouncy choruses. Then their attention was on the pastor as he stood behind the pulpit.

Pastor Ed started his sermon. "Little becomes much when placed in the Master's hands. A little boy put his lunch in the Master's hands. Five thousand men, perhaps five thousand women, and as many as ten thousand children came to hear Jesus speak. That totals twenty thousand people. Can you grasp the enormity of this feat? We don't know for certain how many, because only men were considered. I see the astonished looks on the women's faces. Don't worry, ladies, that wouldn't happen today."

Pastor Ed noticed two newcomers, one who had arrived on time and another who entered now to sit in the back pew.

"Turn to the book of John, Chapter six; we'll start reading at verse three. This miracle occurred near the time of the Jewish Passover, possibly a Thursday sometime in April one year before Jesus' death. From passages in the other gospels—Matthew, Mark, and Luke—we understand that it was late afternoon or early evening. It's the only miracle recorded in all four gospels.

"The crowd had been there for an extended period, and they must have been hungry. The disciples' dispassionate solution was to send the people away to get their own food. Jesus told His disciples to feed the people instead. Andrew, Peter's brother, said that it would take eight months' wages to pay for the food.

"Surprisingly enough, the disciples must have already searched to see what food was available because they had already located a boy who now stood near them with his lunch. This could be the first of two miracles that day—the first being a boy who didn't eat the lunch his mother packed." Alison and Mac turned to each other and laughed.

To recap the story, Pastor Ed said, "We have one young boy, two little fish, and five small barley loaves. You see, all Jesus needs is a little amount surrendered to Him to perform a huge miracle.

A Gift of Love

"Jesus instructed the disciples to seat the people on the grass. He blessed the food, broke the bread, and then placed it in baskets. The food kept multiplying until there was enough. Possibly those sitting close by could see that when Jesus broke a piece off, more bread appeared.

"There was only barley loaves left over. Fish do not keep very long, and besides, the disciples forgot to bring the cooler." Pastor Ed paused for effect as the audience chuckled.

"This event ends with the disciples gathering twelve full baskets of bread fragments. *Nothing was to be wasted!*" Pastor emphasized the central theme. "And God can still use fragmented people, too.

"All who witnessed this miracle wanted Jesus to be made king, but Jesus' kingdom was of another world. In the next verses, it is recorded that they sought Jesus because they had their fill of food. People, in general, seek for things that satisfy their flesh. But on the cross, Jesus gave of His flesh. He is the bread of life that can satisfy our spirits.

"At the last supper, the day before His crucifixion, Jesus said, 'This is My body, broken for you, eat *all* of it.' Could this be why the bread was gathered, so that all would be eaten? Was it meant to be a symbol of what would happen the next year on the cross?

"Jesus received something as simple as bread and fish, and He multiplied it. Could He not receive the little you give Him and multiply it? You may have only a little time to devote to God. If you give Him your time, He can multiply those minutes. You may receive a blessing of having extra time to do something else you have desired to do. If you give Him your little treasure, He will multiply what is left to meet your needs and more. If you give Him your little talent, He's able to multiply it, making it into a great talent. If you put your insignificant life in His hands, His nail-scared hands, He will make your life worth much, but you must be willing to give Him your *all*."

Mac squeezed Alison's hand. They were both appreciating the message, and it challenged them to dedicate their possessions and talents to Him.

"If you will do this today, your life will never be boring; you will have a full, abundant life. Do you feel broken? He will not waste one fragment. Your entire life has not been spoiled by your past wrongs, even though it may seem that way. There is forgiveness at the cross. You can become much in His hands."

Pastor Ed extended an invitation. "Those who would like to place their little time, their little treasure, their little talent, and their insignificant lives in Jesus' hands, come forward and receive prayer." Many came.

One newcomer, however, remained in the back pew with his head down; the teardrops falling on faded blue jeans were Reb's. He felt the closing words stab his chest like little daggers—"There is forgiveness at the cross. You can become much in His hands."

***

Reuben, whose name means "to see," thought he had not been seen. He had come to church to have an encounter with his ex-wife, unaware that he would re-encounter the God of his past.

He repented, seeing himself as the cause of Alison's paralysis. It tugged at Reuben's emotions to see Alison with her thin legs flopped to one side. He thought, *In spite of everything, she looks good.* And there was a man sitting beside her. Reb used to notice how beautiful she was to him and other men. It used to make him crazy with jealousy. Today, the attention of this man did not affect him the same way, and he wondered what had changed in him.

Overcome by his emotions, Reuben quickly retreated from the church. However, he was not retreating from God. He left with a quiet, thoughtful disposition, filled with an unfamiliar hope.

Reuben prayed as he walked to the bus stop, *"My God, I haven't talked to you for so long that I'm not sure You can even hear me. I feel a strange pull toward You. I want to repent of my sins and beg You to change the life I've been living. If You don't waste fragments, and You do care for the broken, I'm one of them. I do not want to be called Reb anymore. I want to put away my rebellious ways. Make me feel like a son. Oh, God, forgive me!"*

Reuben felt brand new, just like the first time he accepted Jesus Christ into his life but better. He was going to make something out of his life. It would start by having a positive view of the abuser support group he had been attending.

chapter twenty-seven

When Mac and Alison reached the foyer of the church, he whispered in her ear and smelled the sweet, flowery scent of her perfume. He invited her to a restaurant to share what he had learned about Christine since his last visit to the used car lot. Before getting an answer, he straightened when he sensed someone standing behind him.

Mr. Hardin, one of the church ushers, said, "Sorry to interrupt, but I need to tell you that a young man, who sat in the back of the church, looked at you two intently many times during the sermon. I've never seen him before, but I have an inkling he might be someone you're acquainted with. However, he did seem to focus on the sermon when Pastor got into the meaty part. I saw tears in this fellow's eyes after the invitation. I was about to slide over to talk to him when he got up and squeezed in front of me and left."

Mac responded. "That's strange. Can you describe him? Maybe that will give me a clue as to who he might be."

"He had a muscular build. I especially noticed his thick neck. Women might find him attractive, I guess. He had a tattoo of a skull and crossbones on his left hand." Then Mr. Hardin excused himself.

Mac looked at Alison to see her reaction; her face had lost its usual colour. Recalling Reb's tattoo, Mac said. "That sounds like Reb."

Alison took in a breath. "It couldn't be him; he's in prison. Isn't he?"

Mac had an idea. "Didn't you say he phoned you a few days ago?"

"That's right, but I thought he must have found a way to phone while in prison."

Mac took Alison's hand and squeezed. "Now we know differently."

After telling her father that she had a ride, Alison left with Mac in his truck.

***

Alone in his room at the halfway house, Reuben knew what to do. He went down on his knees to repent of every sin that he could remember, even the death of his baby. He knew that the Bible said that Jesus forgave him, but he wondered how it was possible after what he had done.

Knowing he could not reverse the harm he had caused, he wanted to make amends in some way. He called out to God. *What can I do? I can't approach Alison, and I can't write her a letter. How can I let her know that I am deeply sorry?* Reuben bowed his head and rose to a new level of surrender.

He determined to go to his group session with anticipation, to participate in community service with joy, and to look for a church of his own. *I believe I've made the first step toward change. I wonder if my parole officer will sense the difference.* Even if he didn't, Reuben felt the transformation—he felt deep relief.

***

Mac chose a nearby coffee shop rather than a busy restaurant to converse with Alison in relative privacy. They entered and gave their order. Once seated, Mac took her hand and looked into her eyes. "Are you okay? I've never seen you this agitated."

"I wonder what will happen. Will Reb try to find me at my home? He knows the phone number. Can he find my address?"

"I'll notify the station of your situation. They'll keep watch. I don't want you to worry your pretty little head about it."

With her head down, she mumbled, "Are you sure?"

Mac put his arm around her shoulders. "God is watching over you, and so am I. And so will the police."

"Yes, you're right. God knows and cares about what happened today." She took a deep breath and looked up at Mac's sincere face.

The server delivered their order.

Alison calmed herself and said, "Now, tell me about your last visit with Christine."

Mac explained how he had gotten her to talk about morphine and her knowledge about how it could cause death. "I believe she is our suspect, but we still don't have concrete evidence. Do you want to go ahead with further investigation?"

"I'm undecided. Can I think about it and let you know?"

"Sure. And let me know if either of them contacts you."

"I will."

"I want to hear more detail about this phone call from Reb."

Alison reiterated the story how she tricked Reb into talking about the letters. But only Mac and the sender of the last letter knew the contents. It seemed obvious to Mac that Christine had written it without Reb's knowledge. It seemed to be a pure scare tactic; or did Christine intend something else?

When he had taken Alison safely back home, Mac promised that he would check in with her often.

***

Still fearing that Reb might come looking for her; Alison purposed to give the whole situation to the Father.

Alison prayed and felt a renewed mindset. *"Lord, Reb didn't stay to the end of the church service, but Mr. Hardin said he cried. I'm thinking now that the sermon might have softened his heart. Please work out the details. Thank you. Amen."*

***

The next afternoon, Alison heard a knock on the door, and then a muffled, "Helloooo beautiful one."

"Mac, is that you?" Her bubbly laughter must have encouraged him because he kept calling until she unlocked the door. She peeked around the half-opened door. Her laughter increased when she saw the clown outfit with a red nose and big blue tears painted on white cheeks. Now she knew why his voice had a nasal twang.

"I come bearing gifts to liven up this place." He stepped in, dropped the bag in the middle of the floor, and proceeded to pull out party decorations of balloons, streamers, and noisemakers.

"This is wonderful of you, Mac," Alison exclaimed. "I was just thinking about you."

"That sounds encouraging." Mac said with a smile and raised eyebrows as he gave a little nod. "I came to decorate your apartment with hanging party streamers to cheer you up."

"I like surprises, but what's the occasion?"

"You're the only occasion I need."

In that instant, she chose not to worry about Mac's advances anymore. All she had to do was desire the Saviour's presence.

***

Needing to talk to her pastor, she phoned late that afternoon after Mac left. "Hi, Rev, do you have time to talk?"

"Yes, this is a good time. What's our topic of discussion?"

"Rev, last Sunday Reb was in the church service. I didn't see him, but Mr. Hardin thought he saw him crying. Then Reb hurried out the door."

"Oh! What a surprise that he was in church. I thought he was still in prison. Be careful, Alison. You don't know for sure that he was crying because of a repentant heart."

"You're right. What should I do if he comes to my door?"

"You have a sturdy lock and a friend who is a policeman, don't you?"

"Yes. And I know God watches over me."

"I think you stole the pastor's line." They laughed, prayed, and said goodbye.

***

After Sandy's duties were done she said, "I've edited some of your writing. Do you want to look at it and ask me any questions?" She handed Alison the pages.

Flipping through them Alison asked, "What are the different colours for?"

"The red marks are corrections in spelling and grammar; the green are my suggestions you may or may not follow to increase the story's interest or understanding; and the blue are my comments or encouragements."

"I see a lot of red."

"Don't lose heart; the content is more important than the grammar. This is your first draft. Afterward come rewrites—sometimes it takes many of them."

Alison read the comments first: good choice of action verb; I could really put myself in your shoes. The green ink showed that Alison had left out some of the story, causing ambiguity.

Feeling a little overwhelmed, she still wanted to improve. Some phrases had to be moved, a more appropriate word used, unnecessary words removed, and other words were in the wrong position in a sentence. She kept these colourful pages to review and to use as a learning tool.

Alison had a question. "What does this symbol mean?"

"That means a new paragraph should start."

"I see I'm going to learn a lot. Thank you for doing this for me Sandy."

"You're welcome."

chapter twenty-eight

She answered her phone with a tremble. "Hello?"

"Alison, I'm sorry I'm calling so late. How many pictures do you have—framed and unframed?" asked her father.

"I haven't counted them, Dad. I've been working on them every day since settling in my apartment and have averaged finishing three a week."

He whistled. "Wow. You're an eager beaver. Will you make a list of their titles, size, and the medium you used? We still have the painting of the gristmill you did in Grade twelve."

"I'd forgotten about that one. What's this all about?"

"I don't want to spill the beans in case it doesn't pan out. You'll hear either way tomorrow."

"Okay. Bye, Dad." Her father had already hung up.

Alison, too busy thinking to sleep, got ready for bed anyway. Once she settled on the pillow, she mentally counted every painting. The recent ones came to her mind easily. Each week she seemed to concentrate on one theme. The first week, babies and children occupied her thoughts; the next week she concentrated on wild animals; and this week she was painting landscapes. As she recalled their titles, she counted them on her fingers. Nine creations in less than three weeks. Her university days might total twenty pieces, but only two from high school. She drifted off to sleep.

Full of expectation the next morning, Alison recited, *Seek ye first the kingdom of God and His righteousness and all these things shall be added unto you.* Not sure what "all these things" included, she made herself mentally ready.

After dressing and breakfast, she got out her journal.

Oct. 5, 1977

God spoke to me this morning:

"I will take you as you are; you don't have to perform for Me. I rejoice over you with singing. My thoughts of you are pleasant. Remember this when the enemy wants you to think poorly of yourself. I believed in you the first day you accepted My call on your life. Even in your imperfect state, I loved you. I will continue to care for you for all eternity.

"I have put a spirit in all humans so that I might communicate with them. At some point in life, their spirits may soften to respond to My call. Your desire is for all your loved ones to know Me, and so is Mine. I have made you My ambassador so you will show forth My love.

"If I call you to do something for Me, guard each moment as sacred, so it will not be stolen from you. Continue to be soft before Me and you will always be soft before others. Be gentle, with love expressed in every word you utter and even those thoughts by which you judge yourself. This is a high calling, and I know you will rise to the occasion."

A Gift of Love

Dear God, You know me and have chosen me for a great task that has just been revealed. You see my inner person, and I want to love as You have told me to do. Please cause Your Spirit to rule my heart that I may be Your witness. In Jesus' name. Amen.

Alison positioned herself in front of the keyboard to lift her voice in song as her fingers graced the keys. God's presence felt tangible.

She shivered with excitement as she ate her cereal. *How will I do all the measuring and unpack the art pieces in the closet while in my wheelchair? Maybe all I can do is the paperwork.* Between bites, she jotted numbered lines from one to nine to list the paintings without mats and frames, then listed her works from university. Alison discovered that many of them did not even have titles. Next she looked in the closet and her eyes fell on a box labelled Sculptures. *It is definitely too heavy to lift. Lord, please send some help.* She left the closet door open and looked for a measuring stick in the kitchen.

Several acrylic paintings from her university days hung in the hallway, looking like stained-glass windows with the ceiling lights reflecting on their glossy surfaces. She held up the measuring tape and attempted to reach the top edge. Alison's thoughts kept returning to why her dad needed the dimensions. *He may know of a gallery that takes pieces of art on consignment, but that wouldn't include* The Gristmill *because it isn't for sale.*

A phone call interrupted her thoughts. She answered with a chopped off "Hello."

"I had an urge to call you," Mac said. "Is everything all right? Did Reb call you again?"

"I'm fine, Mac. Reb didn't call, but I'm glad you did, because I need your help."

"I've been concerned for your safety. What a relief. I'd love to help. What kind do you need?"

"I need help with lifting and measuring my art pieces."

"It will probably take me more than an hour before I can get there though."

"Okay, that's good. See you whenever." *Thank you, Lord, for sending Mac. Please help me to guard my heart.*

She turned her wheelchair toward the kitchen. The phone rang again. "Did you forget something, Mac?"

"Who's Mac?"

"Oh, Dad. You remember Mac—the police officer that interviewed us about Reb's case."

"Why would you expect a call from him? There's no hanky panky going on, is there?"

She let out an exasperating breath. "No, Dad, he's a friend. He said he was coming over to help me with the paintings and to unpack the sculptures."

"Please forgive me, Daughter. I'm sorry for jumping to conclusions."

Alison shot up a quick prayer. *Dad's not always the easiest person to deal with, but You say to forgive.* "I forgive you."

Her father continued in a normal tone. "I forgot about your sculptures. They're outstanding. Everything's arranged for my first surprise—with one condition."

"What's the condition?"

"Do you have twenty pieces?"

"I have about thirty-two—more if you count the sculptures. Do I have to wait to find out what the surprise is?"

"I've set up a solo art show for you."

With a whoop, she gave her father a smacking kiss over the phone. When she found out that the date was about a week away, she went into a state of panic.

Her voice, an octave above normal, said, "Dad, that's too soon! How will we get everything done by then?"

"I have my ways and many recruits."

"Okay. I'll trust you to take care of it."

"You just take care of yourself and keep painting."

Alison felt warmed by her dad's affirmation.

She went immediately to ready herself to receive Mac. She made a simple snack of cut vegetables, salmon sandwiches, cookies, and the squares that she and Sandy had made. Mulled apple cider that her mother had brought over yesterday sounded rather special. Alison was surprised at how quickly everything came together.

Wait a minute there, Miss Busy-bee; you haven't even consulted God.

She bowed her head. *Forgive me, Lord.* The main theme of her prayer was: *What direction should my business take in the future? And how much attention should I allow myself to give to Mac?*

After praying a while longer, she quieted her mind to hear from the Lord: "*These times of meditation are of utmost importance. You cannot have Me in your life the way you desire without taking time to hear from Me through the Bible and through journalling. Acknowledge the reality of My presence and believe that I am causing you to write these words. My aim is for you to be in a place of submission to Me, and then you will walk gently with everyone else. Be gentle not just in the actions everyone sees but also gentle in your thoughts about people. You have a natural gentleness about you, and I want to add My glory to it so you will glow.*

"*I don't want you to analyze your motives or assess your performance. I just want you to totally relax and depend on Me. I will do the work, so your efforts will be light. Be open to the moving of My Spirit so that I may put you into motion. As we work together, our accomplishments will have eternal value.*

"*I have been directing your steps throughout your life and I will continue to do so. Be wise and guard your heart as you begin to recognize My call on your life.*"

Thank you, Father. I heard you say that I need to be gentle with those You have put in my life—not just in actions but in my thoughts. Please help me to deal with Mac.

I'm in a place of physical dependence, yet I need to learn to be more dependent on You.

I've seen my work become easier when I've invited You to do it with me. The problem is I don't always remember to ask You to be present. Right now, painting and writing have become my work. I want to do them while being aware that You are doing them with me. I believe that you've called me to be in this place at this time for a special purpose.

Lord, I'll attempt to guard my heart. Will You please help me? In Jesus' name. Amen.

She felt relieved even though there were many more questions.

Alison looked for specific verses and found them in Proverbs 4:20–23: "Listen closely to my words. Do not let them out of your sight; keep them within your heart; for they are life to those who find them and health to a man's whole body. Above all else, guard your heart, for it is the wellspring of life." She believed the Lord was telling her to guard her emotions—especially the romantic ones.

It was almost noon. She put away her books and started to pour the apple cider. The doorknocker sounded out a familiar rhythm—shave and a haircut, two bits.

"Come in, Mac."

Mac brought a bouquet of pink roses from behind his back. "Hi, gorgeous. I've come bearing roses and exotic food from Wendy's." He held the package high on his palm as if on a silver platter.

"Thank you for the roses, but you shouldn't bring romantic gifts. And thanks for the Wendy's items to add to what I've already prepared."

"You're welcome, I think. Where do you want me to put your flowers?"

"There's a vase in the cupboard over the sink."

"You sure are attractive in that blue outfit and with your hair resting on your shoulders like that."

Alison blushed and looked down.

Mac continued. "You were stumbling over your words on the phone. What's all the excitement about?"

"My dad has set up a solo art show for me!"

"What does that mean, exactly?"

"It means that I'm the only artist to be featured. I'll get a chance to show and sell my paintings."

"That's great. I'll be glad to help after I gain my strength. I need food." He feigned a withering look. She chuckled.

During their meal, they spoke about trivial matters. Their chat was mingled with laughter. Everything was going well until Mac said, "Alison, I have something I *must* confess."

"I can't think of anything you've done wrong."

"This confession doesn't involve a mistake." He wanted to hold her hand but refrained. "I'm … I'm attracted to you physically and emotionally." His next sentence shot out with one breath. "Our good friendship has developed into more than a friendship for me."

Alison knew her face must be red; she couldn't escape its heat. A period of silence followed. She had never heard Mac stammer before, and now it was her turn. "M-Mac, I don't really know what to say."

"I've felt this way for some time, so I know it's not infatuation but the real thing."

"Have you prayed about this?"

"Yes, quite a lot. We have many things in common; one of them is having the same values, such as our relationship with Christ. I admire everything about you: your forgiving spirit, your talents, your general upbeat nature. And I see your beauty, not your disability. It's just not an issue for me. Emotionally, I believe we are equals. I don't see the wheelchair as a boundary because I'm in love with the real you. Besides, I'll be able to help you in many ways. I see we both have much to contribute to a relationship. It wouldn't be one sided."

It seemed as if Mac had thought many things through, but not everything.

"Alison, you are very quiet. I've probably shocked you. You said before that I'm capable of finding any woman I want, and you're right—but the one I want is you."

Alison looked down at her shaking hands. "I'm feeling very uncomfortable."

"That's what love is like sometimes."

Instead of being charmed, she exasperatedly let out, "Wait! Will you give me some time to think? I believe the best thing for me is to not respond at all today."

"How much time do you think you'll need?" he asked, not seeming to care if he sounded pushy.

She tried to keep frustration from her voice. "Please don't pressure me."

"I'm sorry. Take as much time as you like, but I'll pray that you'll consider a 'yes'—for a date at least. What could that hurt?"

"It could hurt your heart."

"Don't worry about my heart. Do you remember inviting me to a meal as a thank you for finding this apartment?"

"Oh, Mac, I'm sorry, I forgot all about it with the business of moving in and now all the art show plans."

"I accept your apology. So when is our dinner date?"

"Soon," Alison said curtly, hoping to get off the topic.

Mac seemed partially satisfied. "Let's get to work then. How can I help?"

"I've been trying to arrange my paintings mentally but it's not working. I need to number the paintings in the order in which they need to be hung, so I need to see them side by side. Their colours must be complementary."

"I can give you a compliment."

"Very funny."

Trying to return to a relaxed atmosphere, Alison asked, "Well, what's my compliment?"

"You're the best friend I've had since I was a teenager," said Mac.

The sincerity in his voice touched her. "Thank you, Mac. I believe one good thing has happened from this." She patted her legs. "It's our friendship. You needed to know more about how Jesus could be real in your life, and I needed to get my mind off myself."

"That's true. You do think a lot of yourself," quipped Mac.

A giggle escaped her. She hadn't meant to encourage him. Her reaction to his jokes could make Mac think she cared more than she did. She remembered the lyrics from an old Broadway song: "Don't laugh at my jokes too much. People will say we're in love."

chapter twenty-nine

The next day, Alison rummaged through some art supplies left from university days. A blue paper caught her eye. It would enhance the underlying tone and cold feel of the scene she planned to paint of a mountain range in Yosemite Park. Using soft pastels, she painted craggy mountains that stretched across the page. The foreground presented a river dotted with rounded, snow-covered stones. She could imagine shivers going up her arms when looking at the brilliant white of the icy rocks. Coniferous trees lined the base of the mountains, and diffused clouds swept above the range.

With the art table lamp shining on the paper, she stared at the finished scene for a number of minutes. The blues, mauves, and deep greens created a harmonious effect. She wished she could have it matted and framed it in a fashion worthy of its majestic sense, but all she could afford was to back it with cardboard then cover it with plastic wrap. At the beginning of the week, her father had taken nine paintings to the framers. *This one will have to wait.*

Lord, You say to ask largely, so I believe You'll provide for this painting to be framed, as well. Thank you.

The best way to raise her spirits was to sing, so Alison filled her lungs and sang "How Great Thou Art" to the audience of the One and Only, as she accompanied herself on the keyboard.

Sandy heard the music from the hall, where she stood transfixed. The golden notes moved her to tears. She wiped them away and waited until her emotions were under control before knocking and entering.

As Alison sang the last note, she looked up to see Sandy standing there with an extra soft expression on her face. Sandy hesitated to speak because the music caused a lump in her throat.

"You're early," said Alison pleasantly.

Finding her voice, Sandy said, "I didn't know you could sing like that."

"You heard me through the door?"

"Yes. You sounded great."

"Thank you."

Sandy looked over Alison's shoulder and saw her newest painting. "That's beautiful! It makes me want to go there, even if it makes winter come early."

"Thank you. I'm getting ready for an art show. And this painting is a surprise for my father and mother."

"Tell me about it."

While Sandy carried out her care duties, Alison told her the whole story of her dad's gift. She then ventured to ask Sandy's advice about Mac. "Can we talk about a problem I'm having with a man?"

"This sounds intriguing."

"His name is Mac. He's the policeman who handled the incident when I was injured. He has become my friend, and now he's been showing me a romantic side that I believe should be saved for an able-bodied and younger woman. "

"Can I ask you a question?"

"Yes."

"If he said he was in love with you and wants you just the way you are, would that make any difference in the way you feel?"

"He *has* said he loves me and has implied marriage, but I feel that there is not enough common ground for a lasting relationship. I think of him as a friend, but I don't believe we are marriage material."

"Have you told him how you feel?"

"Yes. Actually in several different ways, but the flowers and gifts keep coming."

"What we have here is a case for ice cubes."

"What are you talking about?"

"It's my saying for giving a cold shoulder. You know how *you* feel, but you haven't been able to get it through. Right?"

Alison nodded.

"He needs to cool down."

"Yes, I agree. So I have to be mean?"

"I wouldn't call it mean, just cool."

"Can you give me an example? asked Alison."

"Before he brings you flowers again, tell him you will not accept any more and that you'll throw them away if he does. That should let him know exactly how you feel."

"That won't hurt his opinion of me will it?"

"It will let him know that you are serious about your decision."

"Yes. I guess you're right. Thank you, Sandy. However, I have to allow him over for one meal to keep a promise. After that I'll try your advice and let you know how things go."

"I'll be waiting to hear the next saga in Alison's broken hearts club."

"You make me laugh. I feel better already."

"Good." Sandy chuckled then raised a different line of conversation. "I wanted to tell you about the phone call to Dr. Shapiro about feeling pain from your bedsores. He said that you must be experiencing the most recovery that he's ever heard of."

"I knew God would answer my prayer!"

"Do you believe that God really exists and answers prayer—like some children believe that Santa Claus knows everything they've done good or bad?"

207

"No-o-o." Alison drew it out unintentionally. "Not like Santa Claus. God is not make-believe. He's the Creator and He loves all of His creation. I asked God to allow my body to recover, and I believe that He's doing just that."

"We'll see." Sandy kept her gaze on the floor.

"Sandy, do you have time to listen to the speech I'll give at the art show?"

"Sure. Go ahead."

Adopting a public speaking voice, Alison began. "Welcome everyone: esteemed guests; former Mayor and Mrs. Copps; my parents, Janette and Bill Palmer; and my sister, Daneen.

"Thank you for arranging this whole evening, Dad. I know it took you weeks of planning. Thank you, Mom and Daneen, for all this delectable food laid out here." She made a motion with her hand toward a make-believe refreshment table. "Final thanks goes to Ed McAlester, our roving musician.

"This solo show is a dream of mine come true.

"The first glimpse of my artistic potential started back in Grade one, when the teacher pointed out my talent to my parents. This teacher said that most children were drawing stick figures while I was drawing people in proper form, doing actions. Although I dabbled in art throughout my school years, I became serious in producing art after the injury that caused my paraplegia.

"In a little more than a month, I've built my inventory to thirty-two pieces. This is my first opportunity to sell my paintings and sculptures.

"I'm prepared to sketch portraits this evening. The first person to sit in the appointed chair receives his or her portrait free. Please enjoy yourself. The show closes at ten o'clock."

Alison looked up at Sandy to receive her comments.

"You have an exceptional and easy way of presenting yourself," Sandy complimented her. "I don't believe I'd change a thing."

"Thank you, Sandy. I'm aiming to deliver it rather than read it."

"That's a good idea. It's more natural that way."

"Don't forget to come early on Friday. Around three o'clock?"

"Right. See you on your big day."

A Gift of Love

After Sandy closed the door, Alison paused to quiet herself and to seek God once more. *Lord, is there anything I'm leaving out? I want this Friday night to be of Your leading and Your plan. Help me to be Your servant and not try to run my own show. You're the one who promotes. Open my spiritual eyes to see who needs Your love.*

***

Before Alison realized, it was five-thirty and quite a bit darker than a few weeks ago. She watched for her "almost acquaintance." A connection existed between them like an invisible line neither of them could touch.

As Alison stared into the dimness, she caught a movement. The tall man was motioning for her to look at a sign. It read, *Hello, Beautiful Lady. Will you phone me?* And in huge script, *555-0870.* He motioned for her to write the telephone number down and held the sign high under the street light. He crossed his affected foot over the normal one and held his fist under his chin. It seemed that he intended not to leave until she complied, so after she had finished writing it, she nodded. He mouthed "tonight," while putting a hand with spread thumb and baby finger up to the side of his face. He pointed at his watch and then held up seven fingers. Her eyebrows lifted as a tingle travelled from her head to her shoulders. She smiled and waved.

chapter thirty

Reuben remembered thinking, *This help group of "has-beens" is going nowhere. All they do is demand—change this, change that.* He remembered thinking that after being away from women for almost seven months, the only thing he had wanted to change was into his party clothes and go find a broad. *How quickly things can change.*

Today, Doug, the group facilitator started the session by pointing out the main problem of abusive men. "Your problems stem from selfishness. Abusers do not like to hear that they care more about themselves than the other members of their family, but only want their own needs satisfied. I'll put it personally to you. The choice is yours: you can overcome your abusiveness, or you can remain the same selfish guys who continue to hurt the ones closest to you."

Thinking back, Reuben knew he was selfish. In the past, he had made excuses for everything he failed at, but he attacked Alison when she made the tiniest mistake. His sister condoned his warped thinking by saying that he was right in putting Alison in her place. His mother always said he was the perfect husband by providing for the family, making sure they had a car, stereo, and other luxuries, such as entertainment and vacations. He remembered thinking that Alison's paralysis wasn't his fault. Now he hung his head in shame.

"Some of you will choose not to change," Doug continued. "In fact, some of you will get even more abusive. When you are heading downhill, the speed picks up unless you put on the brakes and start climbing. Decide today to improve yourself. You can be an over comer."

Reuben shuddered to think what would have happened if he had gotten worse. *Alison could have died as it was.*

"Make a choice today to be one of the guys who will come out of your trouble a better person." This evening Reuben felt like a transformed man with a purpose, and he knew this statement applied to him.

With the casting off of his old nickname, he hoped his old reputation would die as well. Today his goal was to help each member of the group by being cooperative. A renewed joy rose in him.

Reuben approached Doug after the break and asked if there was anything he could do to assist him. "Doug, I want to help with this group as much as possible. Do you think there might be a way for me to encourage the other guys?"

Doug raised his eyebrows and his mouth hung open. "You didn't give me the impression that you were too thrilled last week. Your body language sent me negative vibes."

"Yes, I suppose I did. Well, I believe you're right in thinking that, but you won't see that attitude again."

"What's caused this change?"

"You've probably heard this before, but the truth is that I really have changed. I went to church yesterday and I received hope for a better future. Now, how can I help?"

Doug shook his head. "You could set a good example by being cooperative, participating in the discussions, and by asking questions."

"I can do that. I'm looking forward to the next meeting. What's the topic?"

"Most abusers have repressed anger from their childhood, so we're discussing buried anger."

"Do you mean talk about something that still hurts when I remember it?"

"Exactly. Present anger is usually hooked to events in the past. First, see if you can write about a devastating memory to share. Try to remember your feelings during that time, and then write them as you recall. In next week's discussion, express how that experience still affects you today."

"I'll do my best. How long do you want me to spend on this?"

"Fifteen minutes is the minimum time it takes." Doug handed Reuben a pen and paper. "See if you can do it here; write the first thing that comes into your head. Don't worry about spelling or grammar. Then we'll discuss what you've written.

***

If I phone this man on the dot of seven, Alison thought, *it'll look as though I'm too anxious for male companionship. I didn't really agree to phone at seven—just that I understood.*

She decided to wait until bedtime, so she could talk comfortably while lying down.

Before dialling, Alison noticed the stillness of her apartment. She could hear the hum of the refrigerator and the sound of cars passing on the wet pavement. *I wonder what he's doing right now? Is he sitting in his favourite recliner with his feet up, staring at the phone?* She envisioned his twisted foot at its awkward right angle raised on the footrest. *I won't mention his disability or mine. If I'm going to call, it had better be now. What makes me think that he's even home at nine o'clock?*

She picked up the phone.

"Hello."

"Hello. I'm the lady you see at the window on Maplewood. My name is Alison."

"Oh, yes. I prayed you'd call tonight."

His pleasant voice sounded as if he had a wide smile. "My name is Rolph Vonderland."

"Hello, Rolph, I'm pleased to speak to you. Did I hear right? Did you say you prayed?"

"Yes, I'm a Christian. You must be a Christian, too."

Alison laughed. "You're right; I am."

Laughter bubbled out of him as well. "I'm glad."

How do I continue this conversation? God help, prayed Alison.

"Just talk about him."

Alison thought of a non-intrusive question. "Your name is German, right?"

"Yes, I'm of German descent. Several generations ago my great-great grandparents immigrated to New York City. The whole family lives there, except for my uncle and me."

"Tell me about your uncle."

"Uncle Otto is a fun guy. He lives in the east end of the city. Unfortunately, he hasn't made a decision for Christ, yet."

"Salvation is so important. I know I couldn't live a day without the Lord," responded Alison. She tacked on a question. "Would you be interested in telling me your salvation story—if you feel comfortable?"

"Sure. When I was eight years old, I was sent to my bedroom on a summer evening before the sun had set for being naughty to my younger brother. It was a big punishment because all my siblings would play hide-and-seek each evening with the neighbours. And there was a girl with golden ringlets I wanted to see."

Alison sensed his sincerity.

"As I looked out the window, envying my brothers and sisters and that special neighbour, I felt bad about my meanness to my brother, and I accepted Jesus as my Saviour and asked Him to change me. I said the prayer that I had heard many times in church. I believe I started changing after that unforgettable evening."

Rolph continued on the same line. "Tell me your story."

"You probably remember the year and the month that you accepted Jesus Christ, but I don't. I was brought up in a Christian home and always felt saved. I've always loved my Saviour and accepted His death on the cross for the payment of my sins. I must have been too young to remember the first time I prayed but not too young to understand that I was a sinner."

"That isn't the first time I've heard a similar story," Rolph responded. "The Bible tells us how to remove any doubt: 'By their fruit you shall know them.' But did you have any doubts?"

Alison felt that he had gone beyond a usual response. Maybe he's prophetic like Rev. "I did struggle when others asked when I received Christ. Some said that if I didn't remember a specific time of repentance, I needed to repent and make sure."

Rolph waited a moment. "May I ask you another question?"

"I've a question myself." Alison wanted to keep the attention on him.

"Okay. Go ahead."

"What made you look up at my window, the first time our eyes met?" Did he feel as she did, or was it just a coincidence?

"I don't really know; it was kind of like someone called me."

Alison thought about that for a few seconds.

Rolph continued, "I feel we may have some things in common." There was a brief pause as if he assessed what to say next. "I must tell you that there are a few things I promised myself not to talk about, if you should call."

"What are they?"

"What denomination of church you attend. And your occupation."

She let out a little unexpected laugh. "That's fine with me. But why?"

"First, I didn't want to make any judgments of you because of how you worship. Secondly, I'd like to know you for who you are, not by what you do."

"I agree; so what do we talk about?" asked Alison.

"Tell me why you're always seated at your window when I get off the bus."

"I enjoy painting, and that's the time I've slotted to spend creating. And I also like to look at the people in my neighbourhood without them being aware."

Rolph chuckled. "I'm artistic, as well. I enjoy photography."

"I saw you with a fancy-looking camera."

An uneasy silence lingered before his next question. "Do you live alone?" asked Rolph.

"Yes."

"You're not married then?"

"No. And what about you?"

"No. I'm a widower."

"Tell me about your wife, would you?"

"Do you want to hear the long or the short version?"

"The long one."

"Okay. Remember—you asked for it." He let out his easy laugh again. "For four years, very happy years, I was married to Nora. Four years did not seem long enough; I felt that I was still on my honeymoon.

"Even now, many months after her death, my love for her remains alive. However, wishing her back would make no sense since she's in a far better place. This life of living alone with my thoughts and memories isn't what I plan to do forever."

"Mmmm." Her sympathetic response let him know she was listening.

"Each time I tell someone the events of Nora's death, it brings back the memory of the sights, smells, and sounds in almost every detail."

"Are you sure you want to talk about it?"

"Yes. I feel I need to reminisce."

"Okay, then. Go ahead, I'm listening."

"Nora was late in returning home the third week of last March."

"That's only six and a half months ago. I'm sorry."

He cleared his voice. "My next-door neighbour phoned to say that there had been an accident at the corner and that one of the vehicles was the same make and colour as Nora's. As I ran as fast as I could on the icy sidewalks to where the accident took place, I prayed for mercy and strength while hearing my heart pounding in my ears. The car that was the same as ours was severely bashed in at the front. A red sports car rested along the driver's side of our blue Chevy. I saw Nora from the passenger side. Her head was slumped forward. I couldn't see an open wound, but blood was oozing out of her ear."

A tear escaped Alison's eye.

"I remember thinking, 'Nora must be in heaven already and our unborn baby, too.' I didn't try to feel for her pulse. I couldn't." Rolph let out a big sigh.

Oh! He's suffered a loss of a child as well. God may have planned our meeting just because of this. Alison wiped away a tear.

"The driver of the other car was alive, and one policeman seemed to be trying to assess his injuries while the other officer was searching the car. I guessed that he was looking for liquor.

"When the ambulance arrived, one attendant opened the passenger side of our car and reached to put his fingers on Nora's neck. Then he put a cervical collar on her. He asked if I was related to her. I just nodded. I couldn't speak at that moment, but I thought I must let them know that she was seven months pregnant. When I finally told him, he said he could attend to her as soon as she was removed from the car. The steering wheel had her pinned.

"Then I thought the impossible: maybe she wasn't really dead."

Alison didn't know how long she could keep her sobs from being heard.

Rolph seemed to push himself to continue. "The paramedic said he would attempt resuscitation as soon as possible. Although that sounded hopeful, the word 'attempt' only seemed to say what my spirit had already revealed to me. My beloved would not be with me in this life. And I would never see my baby ... until I go to heaven myself."

He took a deep breath, and then continued more smoothly. "It took a long time to move the sports car to release Nora from the steering wheel and the seat belt. Her skin was pale and bluish."

It seemed to Alison that he was rushing to get the story finished. "Do you want to continue, Rolph?"

"I'm alright. Yes, I want to finish." He took another breath. "The paramedics shocked Nora's heart, and it started to beat. They continued to give oxygen because she was not breathing on her own yet. The other paramedic started an IV, and she regained some colour.

They lifted her into the ambulance.

"When I arrived at the hospital and gave the necessary information, she was already being attended to by numerous medical people. The doctor gave me permission to be in the room, after warning me that I must stay calm and stay off to the side. Electrodes were applied to her chest and even more to her scalp, leading to another machine."

After a pause, Rolph addressed Alison. "Are you okay?"

"Yes. I want to hear the rest." She did well to disguise her shaky voice while she wiped the tears that streamed down.

"Later, a nurse took me into an empty cubicle to speak with a doctor. He told me my wife was what was referred to as 'brain dead,' but she could not be classified as officially dead because her heart was still beating. She still was not breathing on her own. It was my choice alone to unplug the machine and allow her heart to stop on its own. There was nothing more difficult than making that decision.

"I called out to God: Father, help me to make this decision with Nora's best interest in mind, not my own. I know that she is, or will be, with you in paradise and would not want to be here in a body that would be paralyzed. I can't understand why You need her with You more than I need her and our little child, yet Your will be done."

Alison controlled herself not to gasp when Rolph recalled his prayer about Nora not wanting to live in a paralyzed body.

"Although I was unsure at the time, I made what I now believe was the right decision. The nurse turned off the resuscitator machine. It took only a few minutes before Nora's heart stopped beating." He asked, "Are you able to hear all this?"

"Yes, Rolph. Continue." She moved the phone away as she sniffed.

"My next duties were completely foreign to me. I asked myself what was expected of a man at his wife's funeral. Somehow, I managed to give a eulogy and greet those who attended. I seemed to be in a protected sphere, with the hurt in the background.

"Getting through the funeral ordeal was the easy part compared to the time spent in grieving. It takes a different kind of energy. There have been many nights without sleep. My appetite left me almost altogether for six weeks. Now I'm able to eat some."

Alison thought that grieving a death must be worse than divorce, but thought that many would disagree with her.

"Another thing happens regularly: right in the middle of trying to concentrate, my memory triggers something pleasant Nora would say or do. At first, I would push those memories away and force myself to think of something else. It seemed that the recall of these memories was a type of suffering that I must bear. But just recently, the Lord spoke to my mind that He could help me ponder these memories with fondness. I now choose to remember those precious times with my wife while giving thanks to God. Once this new idea took residence in my heart, I was able to go about my days with more ease.

"Thus ends the lonely heart's saga."

"Oh, Rolph, you have suffered a lot." Tired from holding all her emotions inside, Alison felt her heart flutter like a wild bird flapping its wings, trying to escape.

"Alison," he said her name one more time. "I heard you yawn or something. We can have another talk soon. But before you go, may I have your phone number?"

Her voice was almost a whisper. "Certainly. And thank you for sharing your story with me."

Alison was tired, but she wanted to run to God for fellowship and for Him to ease her mind so that she'd sleep without thinking of all that Rolph had suffered. She sang one of her favourite hymns, "Fairest Lord Jesus," before drifting off.

chapter thirty-one

Rolph had stirred Alison's mind as well as her heart, causing her to have active thoughts all night. With the window open to the bright morning rays, she awakened to chirping of songbirds and the harsh call of a blue jay. Autumn was in full colour and some birds had already left to avoid the harsh winter of Ontario.

But this was a day for rejoicing; the art show promised positive unknown horizons to launch a new career. Although a new friend had filled most of her thoughts during the night, an old one lingered, showing signs of being very hopeful of a future with Alison. *What should I do about Mac? I wish he would find a special female friend.*

The week had passed quickly, and the art show was opening tomorrow. *Lord, grant me success, please. I'm so excited, and I'll need Your calm to be able to sleep tonight.*

***

Mac felt he had to work fast to get into Alison's good graces, so he phoned to say he must see her because he was working the graveyard shift and wouldn't be able to go to the opening of her show. *It may take another month before she'll invite me for that thank-you meal.*

When Alison opened the door, he held out his large palm, balancing a silver box with a lacy pink bow. After she unwrapped it carefully, Mac saw her eyes glitter when she picked up the jewelled comb from the cotton fluff. He heard a pleasing sound escape her throat.

"It's made from mother-of-pearl, and the stones are the same colour as your eyes. I couldn't resist buying it for you." Purple-blue amethysts alternating with natural pearls graced the top of an iridescent comb.

"Thank you, Mac. What an elegant gift. I'll wear it to the opening night."

"You're very welcome. And good luck with the show."

"I'm sorry you won't be able to make it, Mac. I'll have Dad take a lot of pictures, and I'll give you the whole story when I have you over for dinner next week."

"That'll be great. I'm off on Wednesday. Will that work for you?"

"I think so, but I'll let you know for sure on Monday."

"Okay. I'll be thinking of you." He winked and blew her a kiss.

***

Alison totally forgot about the advice Sandy had given her. More importantly, she had forgotten her first love. The Lord pricked her conscience: *"Seek Me first."*

I'm sorry, Lord, for not putting You first today. She quickly picked up her Bible along with her journal, taking them to her sanctuary. She read a passage in the Bible, prayed, and then attempted to write in the journal, but today she couldn't settle down. Leaving the alcove, she went to the keyboard in the living room. The instrument beckoned her to worship.

Alison started to play chords and arpeggios in the key of D. A tune emerged as the major chord slid into a minor one. A love song to her Saviour was on her lips before her mind could even plan a tune.

A Gift of Love

I love You, for You are my King.
I love You; You make my heart sing.
My hope is in you alone,
Expressing joy with this song.
Yes, I love You.
I truly love You.

And as if in reply, a song came from her Lord.
Because you came to Me, I will kiss you with the kisses of My mouth.
I'm your true love, and I give you the kiss of life.
This kiss will set you free more than if you could walk or leap.
My kiss is all you need.

Music kept pouring out until every cell of her body filled with life-giving joy. She knew that the words "Let me kiss you with the kisses of My mouth" came from the Song of Solomon.

Moving away from the keyboard to her journal, as if on wings, she wrote the first sentence that had already begun in her spirit:

"Look at all I have done for you. Count all the ways and be grateful. Rely totally on Me in all things large or small, and then I will make sure everything turns out for your best. You have counted the positive things that have just taken place, which at first did not look that way. Therefore, don't look at your circumstances the way the world does, but look through My eyes of love. That changes the whole picture.

"Do you see why it is good to write these things down? You can read them later and remember what I said to you, and you can use them to speak truth to others.

"Keep your eyes open to see the ones I am leading you to share these sayings with. This is not a great spiritual feat; just let Me give you a warm feeling for someone, and then ask if they would like to hear a message you believe is from the Lord to them.

"Be a blessing to My people, My daughter. Let your love and joy overflow."

I must remember to take my journal with me to the art show. I really do want to be a blessing to others.

She opened her Bible to 2 Corinthians 4. Her eyes fell on verse 18 as if it were written in bold print: "So we fix our eyes not on what is seen but what is unseen. For what is seen is temporary, but what is unseen is eternal."

Father God, let me understand this passage and make it practical: I'm not to look at this art show for temporary gratification and accolades from others, but as someone who sees through Your eyes. The important things are not what I see with my natural eyes, such as the money that may come from sales, but what I can't see that will last for eternity.

***

Last week, Janette had bought Alison a pantsuit so she would have something new to wear to the art show. The top, with a straight neckline and a brocade bodice of satiny flowers, was a soft, warm green that complemented her colouring perfectly. Alison took it out of her wardrobe to admire it again.

Sandy arrived to help her shower.

Something's different. Sandy looks very sullen. When Sandy was writing in the agency chart, Alison saw her wipe away a tear. Sandy nervously twirled strands of her hair around her index finger. Several times now she had sneezed with a polite-sounding "achoo," followed by a high-pitched "eeeh" made by a quick in-draw of air. At any other time, this unique sneeze would have made them laugh until their sides ached.

"Sandy, please tell me what's bothering you."

In a flat, even voice she said, "There's nothing to tell."

"Did your parents leave for their vacation?"

"Yes."

This is strange. Sandy verbalizes about everything and usually is full of laughter. "Did you say they were going to Mexico?"

"Yes."

She didn't ask any more about my art show, pester me to deep breathe, or remind me to do my pressure-relieving exercises. "You're still able to come to my art show opening?"

"Yes, I plan to be there at six, in time for your speech." All said without a hint of a smile.

"Great. I'll see you there later and introduce you to Mac." This was a test to see if Sandy was listening, because Alison had already told her that Mac wouldn't be able to come. Sandy didn't even lecture her about accepting the hair comb.

Like a zombie, she replied, "That's nice."

Alison was concerned. Her caregiver helped her dress with perfunctory swiftness in silence, and then said, "Goodbye. See you at six."

***

Rolph worked through the day on this week's human-interest story but had trouble keeping his thoughts on what he was supposed to write. Thoughts of Alison motivated him to get to the end of the day so he could see her at the window. It seemed different now that he knew her name. He hoped to meet her face to face someday. Disappointed that he wouldn't be able to phone her this evening because of a special assignment to see a Mr. William Palmer, Sr., about an artist who was disabled, he planned an extra long wave.

***

The paintings that had been expertly framed at her father's expense were hanging in the rented hall, waiting to be viewed—and bought, Alison hoped. Her father and mother would pick her up any minute now.

Bill's excited voice sounded from the door. "Sweetheart, are you ready to go? The great adventure begins."

"Hi, Dad. You're a bit early, but I have everything ready." On the kitchen table was her bag with her devotional book and other items for personal needs.

"Your mother is in the car, sitting like a nervous cat. But she's been praying for success and believes that this will be a pivotal night for you."

"I believe she's right, Dad. There'll be more happening than meets the eye, but I have no idea what it might involve."

Her father gave her a questioning look, trying to understand what she meant, then smiled as he wheeled her out.

***

Rolph's bus stop was in sight and his heartbeat quickened. He wondered if she waited for him with similar anticipation. His heart was in his throat, making him feel as if he had parachuted out of a plane. *What?* The window was dark!

***

Soon they pulled into the hall's parking lot. Inside, everything was ready for a potentially spectacular show. The food table looked elegant with candles, flowers, decorative fruits, and vegetable displays.

When the former mayor arrived, he greeted Alison. "Hello, Alison. It only takes a glance at these walls to see that you are a talented artist. I'm looking forward to this evening. I understand my wife and I can pose for a quick portrait to take home tonight."

"I do hope you enjoy yourself. If you want a portrait tonight, please allow at least forty minutes for me to complete a sketch, or consider making an appointment to come to my home for a more complete composition."

"I'll talk to the missus to see what she thinks."

Alison looked around the room and saw a considerable crowd gathered. Instead of having a case of the jitters, a thought distracted her. *Dad mentioned a "first surprise" when he told me about the art show; I wonder if there's a second one. Dad always does things in a big way.*

Before starting her speech, Alison glanced at her mother, who encouraged her with a wink and put her palms together in a praying manner. Then her father put his lips close to the microphone and quieted the people with a "ssshh" sound.

"Good evening, ladies and gentlemen. I would like to introduce my daughter, who has produced all of these wonderful paintings—Alison Palmer."

Alison found that she rather enjoyed being in front of a microphone. She looked over the audience. *Hey. Where's Sandy? She's never late.* After

A Gift of Love

getting me ready, I thought she would have come straight here instead of going home. Even with Alison's distractions, the speech kept the audience attentive.

As she concluded, Alison noticed a man at the back of the hall. He seemed to be looking closely at the paintings. After everyone had finished clapping, Bill whispered in her ear. "Alison, do you see the man at the back? He's my second surprise. He's from *The Hamilton Spectator.*"

As she watched him proceed gradually around the room, she thought, *This man has a different walk. There's something very familiar about him.* He walked slowly, examining the paintings as he went. The one titled *Day of Discovery* was of a fascinated toddler who was inspecting her belly button. The next, *Jimmy's Joy*, captured a barefoot two-year-old boy with his white-blond hair flying up as he jumped, holding the handles of a wheelbarrow, and having a grin that could make anyone smile.

At the moment Rolph took the photo, Alison recognized him. He turned his head in her direction and had the same swift insight. "You're my friend at the window—Alison."

"And you're Rolph Vonderland, my father's surprise!"

chapter thirty-two

Alison's beautiful face captivated Rolph. He thought, *This is what it must feel like to be stunned by an "adoration gun."* Instead of focusing on her wheelchair, his attention was arrested by her amethyst eyes. *Her violet eyes only complement her other lovely features—perfectly arched eyebrows and full lips.* It took several seconds before his glance descended to her limp, thin legs, leaning together to one side as if glued.

Oh, yes. This assignment is to interview a disabled *artist! I want to make a difference possible in the life of this woman.* This thought was so animated that he was not sure if he had thought it or said it aloud. He also forgot that it was his turn to voice the next response.

"Rolph?" Alison's voice finally reached his ears as if from a great distance.

When her voice finally registered, his face heated. "Sorry. I was just thinking—now I know why you weren't at the window tonight." He knew that when he smiled the dimple in his left cheek deepened. "I wondered at the whole reason why you sat there every day."

"When we talked on the phone, I purposed not to talk about my paralysis. I guess God wanted you to know about it anyway."

"He always has a different and better idea."

"Yes, I agree. Would you like to see the rest of my paintings? I'd like to give you a personal tour after I mingle for about ten minutes."

"Sure! That sounds fine."

***

She wheeled into the centre of the room to await her well-wishers. Her mother came first to tell her that the speech was "just fine."

Her father seemed more interested in hearing about the newspaper reporter. "Is he interested in interviewing you for an article?"

"I'm not sure, Dad. But I believe that some photos of my paintings will be in the newspaper."

Daneen was next in line. She complimented Alison on how the pictures were arranged, the fluency of her speech, and the arrangement of her hair.

William and Judy had planned to come from Sudbury for Thanksgiving weekend, but they decided to arrive early to take in her event as well. Sandy arrived next and joined the circle. Janette and Bill made Sandy especially welcome and thanked her for taking care of their daughter. Other people started milling around for handshakes, congratulations, and more compliments before returning to view the rest of the pieces.

Alison thought she noticed someone sitting in the portraiture chair. The packed crowd blocked her view. Another disadvantage of being in a wheelchair.

It was Rolph waiting for a free portrait! Her stomach tightened. Alison wheeled in front of him and sent him an inquisitive smile as she raised her eyebrows. "I'm amused by your swiftness to take opportunity of getting something free."

"You've spotted my best German characteristic," he joked.

Amused by her new friend, she mentally listed all the new information about him and his occupation. She wanted to find out if he was only a photographer or a writer as well. But at this moment his expression reminded her of one who delighted in keeping secrets and, without warning, her heart took a leap. He was handsome, with wavy, dark-blond hair having natural highlights. His pale aqua eyes seemed to be smiling. Relaxed in the chair, this fair-skinned man with a well-built body looked as though he were reclining in a lawn chair at a picnic, soaking up sunshine. His relaxed manner gave the impression that he had never known a distressing day in his life, but she had some knowledge of what he had suffered.

"At least someone took me seriously," Alison said.

"I do want a portrait, but I'd like to see all of your paintings first."

"Your personal tour begins after you write your name on that board to let the others know that the free portrait has been claimed."

He got up swiftly and wrote his name with a flair.

"Where would you like to start?" she said as she moved toward the perimeter of the room.

With his camera hanging from his neck, he followed her. "I'm fascinated with wildlife. Let's start with that white tiger. Why the title, *Spring Snow*? I'm also interested in the medium you use and your personal thoughts about each piece. I need information to write an article."

"So you're more than just a photographer; you write articles as well. Do you know something about art?"

"Yes. I've written other articles on the subject."

Alison nodded and continued with the tour. "*Spring Snow* is named for the time of year this snow tiger kitten was born. And the medium is soft pastel."

They moved on.

"This next painting, of a couple of lions, is called *Primitive Affection*. The medium is watercolour."

"Can you tell me how you made that effect in the sky and the grass to have so many colours?"

"For you to understand that it would take several art lessons."

"Oh, do you give lessons?"

"I will once I get at least one student. Might you be interested?"

"I'll consider it." He flashed his smile again. "So, you haven't lived in your apartment for very long then?"

"Just over a month."

As they continued, Rolph said, "These paintings of children are my favourite. I do love children, although I don't have any of my own yet. This girl seems to be looking for some little creature. I see that you have named it "Minnow or Tadpole?" There is quite a bit of detail in the water. I like it. How did you make those sparkles of sunshine on the water's surface?"

Alison's crooked smile and raised eyebrow gave the answer.

"I know. I'd need lessons to understand your explanation. Right?"

"Right. Are you ready to sit for your portrait, now? We can see the rest later."

Before she began his portrait, Rolph asked, "Your mother looks very familiar to me, but at the moment I can't place her."

"Ask her before the night's over."

"Okay."

Alison picked up the charcoal, and then the Lord reminded her of the passage in her journal that He had given her. She remembered that God had said that there were people He would bring along her path this day who needed encouragement, needed someone to listen to them, and needed to be loved. She put the charcoal down.

Lord, are You letting me understand that Rolph is one of those people who need to be encouraged by the reading of one of the passages? Please give me the words with which to start, and then lead me to the passage you want me to read, and anything I'm to say afterward. I love you Lord, and I'll obey.

After a deep breath, Alison ventured, "Rolph, you know of my personal relationship with Jesus Christ, and now I want you to know that I believe that He speaks to those who love Him and take time to listen. I believe that He has just let me know that He has a message for you. Are you willing to hear it?"

Rolph didn't hesitate, but welcomed it. "Please tell me."

Following a quick prayer, she began to read the last entry:

"I am your living water. I am your eternal fountain. You have neglected to drink from it for days. Now that you have returned, I will increase your thirst for My presence. You have been mourning, and you have not looked fully to Me for help. Today, that will all turn around as you deliberately look into My face as you refuse to hide yours.

"Let My light transform your surroundings. All you need is My light. Your problems will fall away as you rejoice in Me. Let joy flood your whole being, which includes your spirit, soul, and body. Be more aware of Me, and how I am able to help you than you are aware of anything you have suffered. Don't allow the enemy to distract you. Keep your eyes steady on Me.

"Go in My strength. Don't look at your weaknesses because I do not see them. I only see you as one of My ministers. And you can minister to Me wherever you go. Ministry is not limited to those with theological schooling. I have promoted you in My ranks!"

After a brief pause, Alison asked, "Although this pertains to my life, does it seem to apply to yours as well?" She picked up the charcoal and started the portrait.

"Yes. Many statements seem applicable."

"Can you tell me what part affected you most?"

"The part that said that I have been mourning, but have not fully gone to God for help. This could be true, but I will have to take some time to ponder it. You know of the tragedy in my life, and I'm beginning to see more of the tragedy in yours. Is there more?"

"Yes."

"I'd like to get to know more about you—and your art. And I need more material for the article."

As Rolph kept his pose, she responded to his request for more information, by saying, "Ladies first."

He had to laugh at the comical way her nose wrinkled. "Okay. Ask away."

"I surmised your father is German because of your last name. Is your mother German as well?"

"My mother's descendants have been Canadians for many generations but originally were from the British Isles." Rolph wanted to learn more about her tragedy. "Now it's my turn. I'm feeling you have suffered a loss yourself. There's more than the loss of the use of your legs, isn't there?"

She answered automatically before there was time for a tear to start. "Yes, my unborn baby died at the time of my injury. We've both suffered a loss of an unborn child."

"I see we do understand each other's pain. Would you please tell me about your injury?"

Alison gave a brief account of her abusive marriage and a semi-detailed version of the last abusive incident. At first, Rolph was angry with Reb but then was moved with compassion for Alison and, without understanding why, for Reb, as well. This woman he had so recently met showed remarkable qualities as she relayed each event without a trace of vindictiveness or animosity.

Warmth blossomed in his chest as she shared. He wanted to be the one in Alison's life who caused her to forget all she had suffered. *She deserved to be loved.*

With glistening eyes, Rolph said, "I see you have experienced mourning in different ways than I."

She just tilted her head and shrugged.

Rolph perceived that Alison was an unusual artist because she continued to perform her art without being distracted. She finished the portrait with a few final strokes and signed it.

"Could I leave it here until I am finished taking all the photos?"

"Yes, certainly." Holding up the sheet for his evaluation, she asked, "What do you think?"

"That didn't take as long as I thought, and it looks exactly like me!"

"Putting modesty aside, that's my aim and claim to fame."

To end a serious talk with a joke might be her trademark, thought Rolph. "It looks like there are others willing to pay for portraits, and I got mine free. I consider myself blessed."

chapter thirty-three

Rolph arose from the portraiture chair and motioned for the next person waiting. As he approached the paintings he hadn't viewed, he began an internal dialogue between photo shots. *Rolph, it's true, you are one blessed individual.* He photographed the rest of the paintings and sculptures while his mind concentrated on Alison. Glancing over his shoulder to get another look at her, he believed his yearning for her would never be satisfied.

Lord, more than a month ago, I asked You to allow me to meet the woman sitting at the window, and here she is in the same room—and what amazing violet eyes. Her shiny, auburn hair is making me stare. Looking up at her from the street, I knew her hair was a dark shade, but I didn't expect such a radiant colour.

Jerking back to the present, he scolded himself, *What's wrong with me? I can't think straight. Oh, Alison, Alison, I could write a poem about you, but I must concentrate on your superb works for now.*

He admitted that he was smitten. No longer trying to keep his mind on his work, he allowed the camera to dangle from his neck as he stood among the sculptures. A poem started to form as he allowed his thoughts to create it.

Alison with those winsome eyes,
You have intrigued me day and night
As the sea entrances a sailor's heart.

It would be pure bliss,
If you'll allow me to love you,
And share the warmth of a first kiss.

When I ask you to be my wife,
Should you reply with a yes,
I'll be happy the rest of my life.

I must truly be lovestruck.

Oh God in heaven above, this angel could be Your choice for me. She has a disability and so do I. I know that she's one of Your special children. She professes her faith so openly with her words and in her paintings. The only problem is having patience. I know I've been a widower for only eight months, but if she's to be my future mate, I believe You'll arrange for us to really know one another. Thanks, God, for everything. Amen.

He put the camera to his eye and photographed the *Two Profiles of Christ* sculptures. They were bookends made out of soapstone. One face showed Jesus with his head tilted back in laughter. The other represented His battered head, wearing a thorny crown. Rolph took photos from every angle to decide the best lighting.

Every ten minutes or so, his gaze returned to Alison's intense face as she sketched. He admired her talent, yet he knew that it would be her inner beauty that would keep his mind intrigued.

Nora had caught his eye ten years ago. He hadn't thought it was possible to have similar feelings again. It had taken months of dating Nora before he felt truly in love. Here he was trying to create a poem about a woman he just met. It didn't make sense. *Maybe true affection isn't supposed to make sense.*

Alison appeared to be finishing the last portrait; no one else was waiting in line. Rolph thought it would be an opportune time to ask about the bookend sculptures he wished to purchase.

As she received the money for the last portrait, he approached her. "Alison, do you have time to tell me about the sculptures of the faces of Jesus?"

She shifted her position, flexed her neck left then right, followed by a rolling of her shoulders, then lifted her bottom up and down several times. "Yes, but how about some refreshments first?"

"Great idea." He pushed her wheelchair toward the food tables. "Was this catered?" He pointed at a rooster made of vegetables.

Alison shook her head.

"Wow." The vegetable sculpture used a large potato for the body, an oddly shaped yam for the head and neck, a carved carrot for comb and beak, overlapped radish slices for feathered wings, cucumber-skins for the tail feathers, celery-stick legs pressed into a block of cheese, and pretzels for claws.

"My sister, Daneen, made the rooster. The rest was a joint effort between my mother, Sandy, and me."

"How interesting! Artistic ability must run in your family." He loaded his plate as any bachelor would. "By the way, who is Sandy?"

"She's my caregiver. I didn't mention her in our phone conversation for the obvious reason of not wanting you to know about my paralysis. I'll introduce her to you in a few minutes."

A variety of food was arranged around the rooster's base: fancy sandwiches, mini pizzas, guacamole and nachos, cut veggies, cheeses, crackers, and pickles of every kind. The desserts looked so tempting that Rolph wanted to try each assortment.

After finishing all they wanted, they returned to the sculpture display.

"My favourite of all your works are the bookends of the *Two Profiles of Christ.* Why did you do one of Jesus laughing and the other wearing thorns?"

"Before Jesus died on the cross, He was mocked, beaten, and a crown of thorns pierced His head. The other one might be contrary to the way the majority of people see Christ. The Bible says, 'The One enthroned in heaven laughs.' If the Father laughs, so must His Son."

"I never thought of it that way. The label says the material is soapstone. Is it a soft type of stone and easily sculpted?"

"It's soft for a stone but it isn't as soft as soap. Soapstone is naturally compressed talc that has a soapy or greasy feel. It takes a fair amount of pressure to carve."

"Are these real thorns?" he asked pointing to the protrusions.

"Yes. They are from a hawthorn tree and glued into the indentations I made."

"I want to buy these bookends, but I don't have the whole amount available tonight."

"If you can write a cheque for half the amount, I'll consider them sold and you can pay the rest when you pick them up after the show ends."

"Great! That will work out just fine. Now, tell me about this driftwood sculpture of the unicorn."

***

Mr. and Mrs. Copps interrupted their conversation to hire Alison to do their portrait. The former mayor and his wife arranged to stop by Alison's apartment in a few days for their first private sitting. Alison was a little nervous at this prospect, but, as in the past when feeling a similar apprehension about creating art, she took her fears to the Lord.

Soon after their conversation ended, it was almost time to close the exhibition for the day. This truly had been an exciting day for the new entrepreneur. She had never dreamed that the evening would procure so many portrait commissions and sales. And everyone had been so friendly and kind to ask about the various paintings. The success of the show had gone beyond her wildest imagination.

Where was Rolph? She wanted to make sure he picked up his portrait before leaving, and they still needed to talk to her mother about Rolph's recollection of her. She spotted him and wheeled over. "Oh, there you are. I was just wondering if you were coming to pick up your portrait and if you wanted to speak to my mother tonight."

Rolph brought a chair to sit beside Alison. "I wouldn't forget this treasure; it's only people I have trouble placing when they are in different settings."

Alison handed him his portrait. He looked at it closely and opened his eyes wide with astonishment when he saw her larger signature. On her paintings, she hid her name well. "Your last name is Palmer?"

"Yes. Didn't you hear my father announce my speech?"

"No." Rolph dipped his head. "I came in late, after your speech began."

"You seem surprised by my last name."

"It's because now I know who your mother is," he said. "I met her in the hospital on two occasions. The first time was the night of Nora's accident."

They moved toward Janette as he revealed to Alison the incredible coincidence.

Alison shook her head slightly. *His wife and baby died the same day as my baby?*

***

After renewing his acquaintance with Janette, Rolph gathered his equipment, rolled up his portrait, and left to catch the bus. Deep in thought, he sought the Lord's guidance. *If this is the girl of my dreams, I ask that this dream never ends.*

Pleased that he owned two of Alison's works, he envisioned his apartment filled with many paintings and sculptures, because he planned to keep on buying her works regularly. Devising a way to see her soon, he remembered that he didn't have all the information he needed to write the article. Monday afternoon seemed like a good time to finish his research. He would make an appointment with her.

Quickly he prayed: *Father, please confirm to me that this woman is to be a definite part of my future. I don't want to jump ahead of You, especially when it concerns something as important as a mate for life.*

Show me what I should do next and when. I want to lean on You for everything.

He felt a new type of peace in his being.

***

As Alison opened the window to let some fresh air rush in, she welcomed this balmy day in mid-October. Now that the art show opening was behind her, Alison planned to continue writing her biography. First, she needed to pray.

I seek you, Lord. I choose to set my mind and spirit on You. I understand since I've started writing my story that I am indeed the author of my life. Today, I can record godly encounters. Show me whom I can bless today with some act of kindness.

Thank you for preserving my life. It's a very good life and I expect good things to happen. Amen.

She wrote in her journal:

> Oct .13, 1977
>
> God gave me another message this morning.
>
> "I have no formulas, no maps, only a way of life for you. Seeking Me takes only a second. I am here even before you ask for My presence to descend. Guidance can come to you immediately.
>
> "Take a portion of your day and devote it to Me, regardless of how you feel about your limitations, or even when you feel pain. Keep coming to Me. I want to take over and dispel every area of discouragement. Relax and let My thoughts run through your mind. I see all and know how to fix what is wrong.
>
> "The relationship that you have with Me, many people would like to have, so be grateful, and then speak My Word to them. Encourage My people; bring life wherever you are. Don't stop gaining ground.
>
> "Keep renewing your good habits, and don't let anything get in the way of the time you spend with Me. This is how you keep your spiritual muscles strong.

A Gift of Love

"I love you and am interested in everything about you. Don't forget I put in you at conception everything that you need for life. Use all your potential.

"Rest in Me today. Don't have any concerns about your life—your health, your finances, or your self-image. I want charge of all these things, so keep on giving them to Me as often as it takes to keep the burdens off of you.

"Sing, and be merry. Lift your voice to Me and celebrate this day. I have made this day with you in mind. I will help you where you are weak and encourage you where you are strong. Let Me help you as you write, read, and worship. All these are spiritual happenings when you do them with Me."

Alison moved from the secret listening place encouraged with a new desire to give her best. She sat at her keyboard to sing a new song to the Lord, her true love.

A thought surfaced after singing her last note. Instinctively she knew that Sandy needed extra compassion today and wondered if she might come to understand how much Jesus loved her. Alison knew very little about Sandy's personal life, yet she felt that Sandy had experienced some kind of distress recently.

Sandy arrived, gave a perfunctory apology for not making it to the art show on time, performed the necessary chores, and sat beside Alison to write her nursing notes. Alison broached the subject of the trouble she perceived in Sandy's life. "Sandy, I'm wondering, since you've read my biography, if you've noticed that I have a close relationship with Jesus? Do you have any thoughts about what you've read so far?"

"Honestly, I've been concentrating on the grammar rather than the content. I don't have the religious upbringing that you've had, if that's what you're getting at." Sandy hung her head instead of giving her usual beaming smile.

"I wouldn't describe my experience as 'religious.' I think of it rather as a relationship with Jesus, who created the earth and the whole universe along with God the Father and the Holy Spirit."

Sandy's head popped up like a jack-in-the-box. "I don't know how

241

you can know that for certain."

"Let me explain: God is a spirit being, and He exists in a totally different realm than this world. Believing is a matter of faith, but once you accept God's existence, you have an inner knowing that He's real. It's Jesus, God the Son, whom you may have heard about. He can make Himself known to you through the ability of the Holy Spirit. He's the other part of God."

"I've heard of Jesus in the programs on TV at Easter and Christmas. I thought He was a fictional character. Are you saying that Jesus is God, a real being, and that He's interested in people?"

"He's very interested and loves you so much that He gave up His life. He suffered horrible persecution by being whipped and then was nailed to a cross. At His death the sins of every person in the world—from the beginning of time to those still to be born—were charged to Him, although He never did anything wrong. If we accept these facts and ask for forgiveness of our sins, we're forgiven, and Jesus' Spirit comes to reside inside us."

"So, you have God's Spirit living inside your body?"

"Yes, exactly—the Holy Spirit. You see, we have three parts to our being: the body, which everyone sees; the soul, which makes up our personality; and the spirit, which can communicate with God in prayer."

"You learned all this in church?"

"Yes. And I read my Bible, pray, and listen for His thoughts."

"That sounds like science fiction."

"I guess it does." Alison chuckled.

"Alison, I've noticed you have a happiness about you. I've wondered how you could be so cheerful in your unfortunate circumstances. Is this why you give off this aura of peace?"

"I'm happy and peaceful most of the time. Jesus is called the Prince of Peace, and I'm learning to look to Him for my needs. Would you consider accepting Him as your Saviour, Sandy?"

"Saviour—what does that mean? I'm not drowning."

"When He died, Jesus saved us from the penalty of sin, which is eternal death."

"I'm beginning to understand. How could I learn more before I decide to be saved?"

"I have a Bible I would like to give to you, from one friend to another." Alison handed her a white leather-covered Bible that she had set out for her.

Sandy took the Bible. "Thank you, Alison. Should I start at the beginning?"

"The best place to start is in the New Testament, the book of John. You may want to read John through a couple of times. Let me know what you think." Alison opened the Bible to the Gospel of John and put in a special bookmark someone had crocheted.

"Thank you." Sandy looked at her with a sad expression.

Alison felt the timing was right to ask the question that she had been rehearsing. "Sandy, you've looked a little down the last few times you've been here. Is there anything you would like to talk about?"

Looking at her hands in her lap, Sandy said, "I'm scared. But I promised not to say anything." She started to cry uncontrollably, covering her face with her hands. Her contorted mouth was still visible; she let the tears drip from her chin. Alison was not sure what to do. She moved as close as her wheelchair would allow and patted Sandy's arm. She stuffed a tissue between Sandy's thumb and finger. After several quick intakes of air, Sandy straightened slowly and wiped her face as the tears started to subside. She lifted her red-rimmed eyes above her hands to focus on Alison.

Sandy croaked out a little of her story intermixed with jerky breaths. "I live at home … with my parents … and younger brother." She let out a big sigh. "I told you … my parents went on holidays?"

"Yes." When Sandy didn't continue, Alison prompted, "I think it would be best if you just tell me the whole difficult situation, but you're the only one who can decide if you should break your promise."

Sandy crumpled soggy tissues in her ever moving hands, and then opened her mouth to speak but nothing came out. Finally, she screamed, "He … he … my brother raped me!"

"Oh, Sandy!" Alison tightened her arm around her shoulders and put her other hand lightly on Sandy's agitated ones. They were trembling

243

as if attached to a vibrating machine. Alison was silent for many seconds because of the shock of Sandy's declaration; she called out to God for wisdom. Sandy's body shuddered with another sob. Alison felt she should listen to the whole account before saying anything. "Tell me as much as you feel you want to."

"I couldn't stop him." Sandy relayed her dark secret between sobs. She said she had never expected anything like this from Donald, who was four years younger. He was the type of kid who spent a lot of time on his own in his room. He never caused their parents an ounce of worry. As she gained some composure, she said, "It happened on the first night my parents were away. As soon as I crawled into bed and turned out the light, I heard heavy breathing near my bedroom door. I was worried that there was something wrong with Donald's health. I called out, 'Donald, are you all right?' In an instant, he crashed into my room and was on top of me in one swift move. I screamed, ripped at his hair and ordered him to get off me. He let all of his weight press down on me. I couldn't breathe. I would never have guessed that he was that heavy."

Crying even harder now, she managed to continue. "He finished, and then threatened that if I call the authorities or tell Mom and Dad it would destroy the family and no one would recover. The trouble is, I'm not able to act as if nothing happened. Often the memory of the smell of sweat and semen and the heaviness of his body causes me to wonder how I'll go on much longer. I was a virgin! He hurt me so badly; it was so painful and humiliating. I've lost my virginity to my stupid kid brother! I didn't sleep a wink that night and very little since. I feel so ashamed and filthy and disgusting."

"Sandy, you're not any of those things." Alison remembered thinking similar words, but it was her husband, not her brother, who had forced himself upon her when he was intoxicated. It was extremely painful, physically and mentally. And how she had cried.

There was a questioning wrinkle on Sandy's brow. "Alison, I can hardly believe that this has really happened. Donald has always been a good brother to me. What could have caused him to do this to me? He never gave any clues."

Alison sent up a quick prayer for guidance as to how she should answer this question. Then the words came. "In the teen years, hormones rage, and if one's mind is fuelled by other sources, such as pornography, evil behaviour can result without anyone's detection of this dangerous addiction."

"I guess that could be the case." Sandy's head was bent low as she slowly shook it back and forth.

"Sandy, can you come here?' Sandy looked up, and Alison motioned her to come into her arms. Sandy got on her knees and allowed Alison to hug her at length. The women's tears mingled as their heads pressed together. At that moment, they seemed to bond as sisters.

With tears still streaming down her face, Sandy told of a happy memory of when she and Donald were young, building an airport with toy blocks. "Every good memory has been spoiled now. And you're the only one I'll ever tell." Sandy dried her face and neck with more tissues.

"Sandy, I've something very important to tell you. I've suffered abuse too—sexually and physically. My experience is that an abuser will repeat his actions unless it's reported."

Unable to speak the word 'rape' again, Sandy said, "Really? My brother might do it again? But he said he was sorry, and he implied that if I didn't tell, there would be no further trouble."

"I believe he told you a lie, hoping your parents wouldn't find out."

"What should I do?"

"I would like to pray before answering your question. Would that be alright?"

"Okay—only because I admire you."

"Dear, Heavenly Father, I bring this whole situation to You. You know all. Sandy is such a strong person, and has held everything in these many days. She doesn't want to hurt her family. But please give her the courage to speak to her mother and father.

"Sandy didn't know until today that Your Son is a real person. Please give her understanding as she begins to read about Jesus' life. Amen."

Alison looked over at Sandy to assess her state of mind. Her breathing was even, and she appeared to be calmer. Alison finished by saying, "You must tell them, Sandy."

Sandy said, "It's strange, but I already have this incredible sense that everything is going to be alright. It's going to be tough, but I'm going to talk to my parents."

"I think you made a correct decision," said Alison, feeling a deep sense of compassion mixed with relief.

chapter thirty-four

Alison dressed for church in the same pantsuit she had worn to the art show, while she hummed her favourite hymns one after another. She tried to arrange her hair like Sandy had done two days ago, adding the special comb from Mac. Her father poked his head in her apartment door after knocking. "Is my girl ready for a most excellent Thanksgiving Sunday?"

***

Many people had already filed into the pews, and Mac entered the church hoping to sit beside Alison. He looked pleased when he saw she was wearing the comb. Daneen, Mark, and their two children were in church together for the first time. Janette had stayed home to prepare the meal. They shifted to make room for Mac.

A short message by Pastor Ed, ending with a salvation invitation, affected several people. They came forward to invite Jesus to come into their lives for the first time, but Mark and the children were not among them. Following the service, everyone met in the rear of the sanctuary, where spiced-pumpkin cookies and juice were served. Mac couldn't join them because he had to work the afternoon shift.

When the family returned to Janette and Bill's home, Bill asked everyone to leave the van except Alison. She had not shown the slightest sign of grasping the reason for the children's excitement. As soon as they entered the house, they called for their grandma to come, and then took her hands, planning to drag her to the front door so they could see their aunt's surprised face. "Come quick, Grandma." The children ran, forcing Janette's steps to quicken.

As Bill unloaded Alison in her wheelchair, her eyes widened. "Dad, you built a ramp! I sense there's going to be other surprises. Am I right?"

"Of course," responded her father as he started to push her up the newly constructed ramp. "Life would be boring without them."

Peter and Victoria, Alison's nephew and niece, jumped around her wheelchair as she ascended the ramp. They decided that Grandpa was pushing too slowly, so they each took an armrest and helped.

After a tour of the wheelchair-accessible bathroom and a second look at the larger entryway, Alison praised her father profusely. Then everyone headed for the dining room. The wonderful aroma of the turkey and the beautifully set table, with a fall-theme centrepiece, earned Janette many compliments. Their Christian tradition was to sing a Thanksgiving hymn, Bill leading with his baritone voice. Janette prayed a blessing of thanks for each individual around the table. Happy chatter criss-crossed the table between bites.

As they waited for the pumpkin pie to be served, Victoria had a question. "Auntie, I want some cousins. Do you think you can get me some girl ones? I asked Mommy for a sister, but she said no. I like to play with anybody but my brother." She wrinkled her nose as she said the last word. Everybody tried not to laugh, and then looked at Alison to see her reaction. Alison could feel her cheeks heat. Victoria was too young to know the whole situation, and only Daneen knew of Alison's secret fear of being unable to conceive another child.

"I can't explain everything to you, Victoria, but I don't have a husband now. You may have cousins yet." After the words were out of her mouth, Alison glanced at William and Judy, hoping this conversation was not causing them any distress. They earnestly wanted children. "Just be happy that you have a brother." Victoria's almond-shaped eyes looked at her aunt, and then she nodded.

I don't have to be healed myself before I pray for someone else. Why not pray for Judy and Will, now? Moved with compassion, and putting aside her own needs and fears, Alison had prayed privately for them to have children. Now she wished to ask aloud for their healing. First she prayed in the Spirit under her breath, as she always did before waiting to hear from the Lord. His go-ahead came immediately.

She asked William and Judy for permission to offer a prayer. They nodded and everyone at the table bowed their heads. "Dear Father, our healing God, I want to thank you for hearing our prayer for my brother and sister-in-law. They have wanted children for a time now, and we're asking together as a family that you will bless them with as many children as You have in Your heart to give them. Thank you. In Jesus' name. Amen." Not many words were needed. Tears ran down Judy's cheeks while William held her hand and leaned his head to touch hers.

Janette got up from the table and walked over to the counter, where she heaped mounds of whipped cream onto pie. William slipped over to the sofa, behind which he had hidden a parcel from the van while others were admiring the renovations.

Alison said, "Mom, remember the painting you couldn't keep from staring at during the show? Well, it's yours and Dad's." William displayed the painting according to the pre-planned cue from Alison.

Two days ago, Alison had put a "Not for Sale" sign on *The Yosemite Mountains* painting without her parents seeing. Mac picked it up after his shift the next night then, with William's help, sneaked it into the van after the service that morning.

"Oh, thank you, Alison! Janette said. "It reminds me of our honeymoon in the Rocky Mountains. I could get lost in the whole scene and feel that I'm right there!" Bill echoed his thanks.

The holiday ended with goodbye kisses. Janette and Bill took their youngest home. Alison, tired from the long day, looked forward to getting into bed. Her mother offered to assist her and Alison gratefully accepted.

Janette ventured a question. "Is there something bothering you, dear? You were awfully quiet on the way home."

"The trouble is that I'm afraid that I may never have children. I think it's possible that I'll be married again someday, but I don't know if I'll be able to have children."

"What has triggered these thoughts?"

"There's a special someone on my mind since the art show. I know it's been only a few days, but I've been thinking about this man for a while." Alison recounted the development of her acquaintance with Rolph. "I sense that he has some feelings for me, too." Her mother nodded but just continued to listen. "I found out that he's a widower and lost his wife and unborn child the same day Kathlynn died."

Janette's expression showed recollection. "Are you talking about Rolph Vonderland?"

"Yes. You remember his name?"

"Yes. I offered a prophetic prayer concerning him the night of your injury. And weeks later, I saw him again in the hospital hallway after I visited you. And again when I answered some questions for that article he wrote."

"What do you think of him? Do you think that he's the kind of man who could deceive me as Reb did?"

"I don't think he's capable of harming anyone. And he seems to be a sincere Christian. He must be lonely. I think you should call him this evening. Just show him some friendship on this holiday, and let your light shine."

"I'm still harbouring fear of any man being in my life in a permanent way. But I don't like to think of being alone for the rest of my life either."

"This man is definitely not like Reb, Alison. Call him tonight. Okay?"

She smiled up at her mother and in a soft voice said, "Okay."

Her mother left as Alison reached for the phone.

He answered on the second ring with, "Hello. Happy Thanksgiving."

"Happy Thanksgiving, Rolph. This is Alison."

"I recognized your voice immediately. I'm so glad you called me. I didn't want to intrude on any of your family's plans. Did you have a good Thanksgiving?"

"Yes, very good. How about you?"

"It was okay. I spent it with Uncle Otto. He's a pretty good chef, but the conversation is limited. He's not a Christian, and that makes our discussions strained at times."

"My sister, Daneen, accepted Christ as her Saviour just this past summer, and this was her first Thanksgiving as a Christian. It was nice to see the difference in her."

"That's good to hear. It gives me hope for my uncle." A short pause ensued before Rolph continued. "We talked some about my background on the phone, but I never got around to telling you about a few famous Palmers in my family. My great-grandmother was Phoebe Sarah Knapp, whose maiden name was Palmer. And my great-great-grandparents were Walter and Phoebe Elizabeth Palmer. Maybe you have heard of them?"

Alison gasped and then giggled with delight as shivers travelled up her arms. She called them God-bumps rather than goose-bumps.

Rolph said, "I hear by your reaction that this news has stunned you in some way."

"Yes. Our pastor told us about a revival that happened in Hamilton in 1857. I asked my father to look up some information about Walter and Phoebe Palmer, and I learned that we are not related, but I did gain facts about them. Maybe you could tell me something that I might not have heard."

"Just a minute! Do you mean that our family made the newspapers way back then? We were famous!" They both laughed.

Alison wished the whole of Hamilton knew about this revival. "Maybe a story about the revival can get into the paper again—through a certain relative." She held the phone tightly to her ear, while she giggled.

Rolph came out with a very different response than she expected. "It seems as if God wanted us to meet."

After seconds of stunned silence, she agreed. "Perhaps you're right."

"My mother told me quite a lot about my Christian heritage," Rolph said. "She remembered her grandparents and relayed many stories to me. Did you know that Phoebe Palmer Knapp was a friend of Fanny Crosby, the blind hymn writer, and they wrote "Blessed Assurance" together?"

"No, I didn't know that!"

"Fanny Crosby wrote the words, and my great grandmother composed the melody."

"I would say you do have a famous heritage in any Christian's estimation. Did you inherit any of your ancestor's musical ability?"

"I like to sing in church and whistle in the great outdoors. But I've never written a tune."

"I've seen you whistle at the bus stop. Maybe I'll get a chance to hear you whistle and sing someday."

"How about this Sunday, if you'll go with me to Lake Gospel Church. We can sit together."

"That's *my* church! When did it become *your* church?"

"I attended for the first time last Sunday, but I didn't notice anyone in a wheelchair."

"I was sitting in a pew. Mac lifts me."

"Oh?" Rolph was silent for a moment. "You're good friends, then?"

"Yes, we're friends. He's the officer who's been working on my case and advises me about potential problems that might arise with Reb."

Rolph changed the subject to some common interests in the arts, and he eventually encouraged Alison to finish her autobiography.

"Have you ever attempted any writing before?"

"No, I have very little confidence. I never did very well in English composition or grammar; I wish I'd paid more attention," said Alison with a nervous laugh.

"Maybe you could call on a friend who has had training in writing to assist you."

"Actually I've asked my caregiver to help me."

"You can always call on me if your caregiver isn't available."

"Thank you. I'll keep that in mind."

Silence reigned in the place of their light chatter, and Rolph noticed that it wasn't uncomfortable. He told Alison that he needed more information to write the human-interest story about her for *The Spectator*. He asked, "Would tomorrow morning or afternoon be better for an interview?"

"Late morning would be the best for me. How about eleven?"

"That's perfect. That way I get to sleep in." Rolph laughed.

She had to respond with a chuckle. "Good for you. See you tomorrow." Alison hung up and looked at the ceiling for a few minutes as her mind skimmed over the past hour. She let out a satisfying sigh and smiled to think that God had indeed brought a new friend her way.

chapter thirty-five

Alison desired to listen to the Lord.

Oct .14, 1977

This is today's message from the Lord:

"There is a place of individual worship that only you and I will share. It will be uniquely yours. Your Father has planned a secret place to share with you alone. I know you want to know of such a place.

"The way to get there will require patience at first, until you know the way well from taking many trips. Only you and your Lover, Jesus, will share this secret place. Each time you come to the secret place, it will become even more exciting.

"The love we will share will have no boundaries. Some have made a choice for a superficial knowledge of Me, but you have chosen the deep things of your God. I am pleased. Now come with Me.

"'Camarada' is your password to enter our secret place. I desire oneness with My true children. If you are one in Me, and because I am in all things, you will never be alone. I say to you, My loved one, I am with you always. My thoughts are continually on you to perform My will in you. You will turn your thoughts toward Me and I will be there with words of wisdom that you will need.

"My heart of compassion will be transferred to you so that the gifts will be brought forth. You will also know when evil is hindering My presence from descending and you will recognize those things that try to soil the anointing. This does not mean that you will never fail, but it means that you will learn to stay tuned into Me for a longer time. Abide in Me as the branch abides in the vine, which John wrote of in the gospel in Chapter fifteen. Study its meaning for you."

"Camarada" was not a word Alison knew, although it did sound similar to another word. *It sounds close to camaraderie.* She had to put off looking it up in the dictionary because the thick book was out of reach.

***

Sandy arrived earlier than usual that morning to assess Alison's skin, assuming she had sat a long time on Sunday. She helped Alison onto the bed to look at her lower back. Sandy announced that her skin looked fine and then helped her back into the wheelchair. Alison noticed Sandy's continuing quietness, although she did not seem quite as distracted. Sandy still twirled her hair frequently and had a faraway look. "Sandy, would you please lift that red-covered dictionary down to me?"

"Are you planning to work on your writing?"

"No. I'm not sure what I'll find, but I'm looking for a word. I think God has a special message for me if I can find this word's meaning."

Alison looked up the word "camaraderie": loyalty and warm, friendly feelings among comrades. She looked up "comrade": [Fr. camarade < Sp. camarada, chamber mate]. *That's it! The word is Spanish and it means chamber mate. My God is inviting me into His chambers. He wants a personal relationship with me, which possibly compares to an extraordinary love relation between a husband and wife.* "Whee!" She offered a brief silent prayer of thanks. *As I go to our secret place, and proclaim my entry word, You'll come and meet with me. Oh, thank you, Lord.* Then she burst forth with a joyful laugh.

"That's a strange reaction to a definition of a word. What could be that exciting and funny?" asked Sandy.

"You know about how I write in my journal every day?"

Sandy nodded.

"Well, this morning was extra special because I felt I should write a foreign word that I heard in my mind. The word was "camarada." Then the Lord let me know that this word is my password to enter an unearthly secret place while I meditate, or commune, with God. I just found out that "camarada" is a real word in Spanish that means chamber mate. I believe it is God's desire that I know Him in an close personal way." *Possibly similar to how a bride enters a room where her groom awaits.*

"That's remarkable. While meditating, you heard a word in a language you don't speak, and you found it is a real Spanish word?"

"Yes, that's right. I'm in awe and excited at the same time. I don't know what it all means right now, but this I know—God really loves his children and wants them to know Him personally. I don't think it will be a chore to get up every morning. In fact, I can hardly wait for tomorrow."

Sandy didn't comment but had an inquisitive look.

After arranging for Sandy to return tomorrow morning to sit for a portrait, they said goodbye. The portrait was to be a thank-you gift for the work Sandy planned to do in editing Alison's autobiography.

***

Shortly after Sandy left, Rolph phoned to let Alison know he was ready to leave to walk to her apartment. "Alison, after the interview, could I show you the photos and get your opinion about which ones you would prefer to appear in the paper?"

"Yes. I'd like to see them. So, you'll be here soon?"

"Yes. It's only a ten-minute walk." After a slight pause and a little laugh, he asked, "Will you do me a favour?"

"What?"

"Will you watch for me at the window?"

She returned a joyous, bubbly laugh. *What a sentimental guy.*

That laugh was enough of an answer for him.

***

Precisely ten minutes later, Alison watched him arrive at the corner and give his usual wave. She buzzed him in and heard his pleasant whistle even before he knocked. "Come in." He entered the hall that held the bookshelves. "I hope you didn't have trouble getting in the front door. It usually sticks, I'm told. When you leave, I'll show you the rear entrance I use."

"It only took a little extra strength," he responded with his usual crooked smile.

I think he's nervous. "Please come in and make yourself comfortable."

"This is a cozy apartment. One can tell you have an eye for colour and also a green thumb." A Christmas cactus hung from a hook on the ceiling. At least a hundred fuchsia-coloured blossoms draped over the pot. It was as luxuriant as if it had been transplanted from Solomon's garden. "Apparently your Christmas cactus doesn't know what time of year it is." They both laughed.

"I guess it is early this year." She brushed a curl from her eye. "The plant gives some colour. Usually there are paintings covering almost every wall."

"Oh, that's right. They're hanging at the art show for the rest of the month." He wasted no time and spread the photos on the kitchen table and counters, except for one, which was sticking partially out of the envelope. "The paintings mentioned in the article are on the table, but not all of them can be included with the article due to limited space."

"How many am I to choose?"

"Three."

She wheeled to the counter to see the other photos, and then pointed out three: the mountainscape, the toddler looking at her belly button, and the tiger kitten.

Rolph removed the remaining photo from the envelope and held it behind his back. "I want to commission you to do a pastel portrait of yourself." He showed Alison a head-and-shoulders close-up of her with a pleasant expression, and held it at arm's length from her nose.

"Why?"

"It's for me."

Alison felt warmth ascending from her neck to her face as she guessed at his reasoning. "I can do that for you Rolph. When would you like it?"

"There's no hurry."

"Would you like to know the price?"

"No, that's okay. I know you'll be fair."

"I'll get started on it as soon as I can."

"Great." He took out a yellow legal pad. "Are you ready for a myriad of questions?"

"Yes, I suppose."

With his pen poised, he began. "First, I'll tell you what I already know and then you can fill me in with anything you would like to add."

Alison nodded.

"Your Grade one teacher recognized that you had potential before your parents did. You took an art course in university to fill in your credit schedule. Did you use that knowledge at all?"

"Yes. I taught art, as well as physical education at a high school."

"You were very athletic, then?"

"Yes. Track and field was my specialty."

"Your paralysis must have come as an awful shock. I've heard it said that more-active people find it harder to accept disability."

"You might think that was the case, but with God in the equation it makes all the difference in the world."

He put his pad down. "At your art show, you said that I would need lessons to understand the explanations of your techniques. Were you serious when you offered art lessons?"

"Yes. And I've wanted to learn more about photography. Do you think you could teach me some of your techniques? We could do the barter system."

"Hmm … that might be possible. Let's talk more about that later." He picked up his pad with a calm that he didn't truly feel, and positioned his pen. "In the article I would like to include a question that people frequently ask. Can you think of one?"

"The most common one is, 'How long did it take you?' My usual answer is that if I timed myself, I think I'd become discouraged because it would work out to such a small amount per hour. And I think timing myself would take away from the pleasure of creating."

"I agree with you. How did you get started in sculpting?"

"I received training in university. The faces of Jesus started with two bars of Ivory soap."

"I'm glad I asked, but I'm no further ahead in understanding."

"Soap is very easily carved, whereas soapstone is not. I first drew what I had in mind for the two faces, and then I traced it onto the bar of soap. I carved it with a paring knife. For the soapstone, I used a machine called a Dremel that scales a small amount of stone away with various bits that have a burred end. It took some time. I enjoyed the diversion from watercolours or pastels immensely."

"How did the sculptures of the unicorn and the eagle come about?"

"I collected pieces of driftwood during high school and university. I can see objects, usually animals, when I look at a shape, then I remove what doesn't fit. The unicorn was practically all formed to begin with so I needed to remove only a little."

"My last question is, what's your favourite subject to paint, and why?"

"That's a difficult question because I enjoy everything." She rolled her eyes upward. "I'd have to say my favourite is wildlife, because I can get close to God's creation without having the creature in my home."

Rolph laughed at the image this statement evoked. "That conjures up a strange picture of live bears and tigers in this apartment." The interview started and ended with laughter.

At the rear entrance, they said their goodbyes and expressed that they were looking forward to future art and photography lessons.

A Gift of Love

***

The doorbell sounded the following morning. Sandy entered. One look at her face and Alison guessed that Sandy had confronted her parents and that today would not be a good day to do her portrait. "I'm sorry I can't sit for a portrait today. What I need is your counsel and a shoulder to cry on."

"What's happened?"

Sandy's shoulders heaved and she could not talk, even after it appeared that her tears had subsided.

Alison broached the suspected matter. "Did you tell your parents about your brother?"

"Yes. I talked to my mother alone while my father was in the basement and Donald was out for the evening."

***

Sandy flashed back to the previous evening, when she had sidled up to her mother.

"Mom, please sit down here with me. I have something very serious to tell you, and I'm afraid to begin."

Her mother sat down slowly, wearing a frown. "Go ahead, I'm listening." Her response was clipped.

"Mom, when you and Dad went away, a crime was committed in this house."

"What crime? What are you talking about? A crime should have been reported right away! Why did you wait this long to tell me?"

"I was afraid that telling you would cause too much stress in the family, but now I believe that if I don't tell, it may be repeated." Sandy focused her gaze at the floor because she could not bear to see her mother's expression. "Mom, this is going to be hard for you to believe … Donald raped me."

"No! No!" her mother screamed. "Not my Donald! Why are you lying? You've always sought attention! This is the wrong way to go about it!"

Now that her courage had taken her this far, Sandy turned her back on her mother and went downstairs to the recreation room to find her father as heaves of emotion were trapped in her chest. "Dad, I have something very serious to tell you. I told Mom, first. She didn't believe me, so I'll try to tell you."

She allowed the dam to break. When he looked at her tearful face and heard her sobs he remained seated, although one would expect a father to give some physical comfort. Sandy took a heaving breath and repeated a short version of what she told her mother: "When you and Mom were away on your trip, Donald raped me."

The emotional blow appeared to hit him deeply because his face crumpled. Then he jumped up to wrap his arms around her.

Sandy relaxed with relief and let her tears fall on her dad's shoulder. With a muffled voice, talking into his shoulder, she said, "I've kept quiet about it because Don said that it would ruin our family life. A friend told me that if I don't disclose this information, he may do it again."

Her father seemed to be in a daze. "You said it happened when we were on vacation?" Her father cried openly as the truth sank in. "How could he do such a thing? What *did* your mother say?"

"She doesn't believe me. She called me a liar and said I was just trying to get attention."

"I don't think you would fabricate a story like this. How dare she! I'm not sure what to do!" he said with his voice breaking. "First, tell me all the facts."

After ten minutes of listening, Sandy's father said that charges must be laid. He told Sandy that she should go to bed and he would handle her mother. He would also wait up for Donald. Sandy crept up the stairs to her room, carrying her raw nerves like a sack of rocks. She wouldn't try to sleep; rather she opened the Bible that Alison had given her and turned to the book of St. John, where Alison had put a bookmark. She found the part where Jesus was teaching the disciples about heaven, in Chapter 14. The subject changed part way through the chapter to talk about the Holy Spirit. The Bible portrayed the Holy Spirit as being a friend who was sent to earth to take Jesus' place. He was also called the Spirit of Truth. The word *truth* seemed to stand out.

What captured her attention was verse 27: "Peace I leave with you; My peace I give you. I do not give to you as the world gives. Do not let your hearts be troubled and do not be afraid."

Sandy thought over the sordid situation. Her feelings had not become more settled as she had hoped. Nightmares still harassed her. Hatred for Donald grew. She became fearful of what could happen if her father did not take care of everything as he said he would. She didn't know if she could disclose all that transpired to the authorities, to strangers.

Sandy read the Bible until three in the morning to finish the book of John. She heard Donald come in the front door. The sound of heated words leapt up the stairs from the front hall. It seemed her father had kept his promise and did not waste any time confronting his son. After only a few minutes, she heard the front door slam and assumed that Donald had left again. Sandy wondered if her father actually phoned the police. She finally turned off the lamp and lay awake in a trance-like state, staring at the moonlight filtering through the curtains for what seemed like hours until her heavy eyelids gave in.

***

Sandy tried to calm herself by taking deep breaths after telling the story. "I came here after only a couple of hours of sleep."

No wonder her eyes are blood-shot. Alison needed to pray for wisdom before she continued. *Speak to me Father; I need Your direction.* She dipped her head slightly and listened for His voice. She wondered if she'd be able to hear in this stressful moment.

"Present the gospel to her again. Start with Joshua one verse nine. 'Have I not commanded you? Be strong and courageous. Do not be terrified; do not be discouraged, for the Lord your God will be with you wherever you go.'"

Alison reached for her Bible and located this verse, although she knew it from memory. She read it aloud to Sandy. "I believe that God, in the form of the Holy Spirit, resides in those who ask Jesus to forgive their sins. That is when one becomes 'born again.' Do you remember reading about the ruler who came to Jesus by night?"

"Yes. It was early in the book."

"That's right. Tell me what you generally understand about this book."

"I understand the facts of Jesus' death and resurrection."

"Good. I'm glad you understand what happened to Him, but there is more. Jesus gave up his life to make amends for our sins. Those who accept Him have the right to address God as Father, and are assured of a home in heaven after this life is over. A simple prayer is all you need to do this." She allowed a few moments for these words to register. "Would you be willing to follow me in a prayer?"

"Will that be enough to become a Christian?"

"If you believe what you read in John, it's enough."

Sandy confessed that she did believe what Jesus had done. "Yes, I believe. Let's say the prayer."

Sandy repeated the prayer after Alison and then smiled. "I feel a peace that is often evident on *your* face, Alison. I'm not afraid of facing the authorities now. In fact, I've decided to go to the police today. I don't feel free of the shame. Are you sure my sins are forgiven?"

"Yes, and I'm rejoicing with you, Sandy, and so are the angels."

"The angels?"

"In the Bible it says that the angels in heaven rejoice over just one sinner who is repentant. I'll look it up to see where the verse is and tell you about it the next time you come."

They bowed their heads and Alison prayed. "Dear Lord and Saviour, thank you for the blood You shed on the cross that paid the penalty for all our sins, and thank you for making this real to Sandy. Help her to speak with courage to the police. The Bible says that You know what we need even before we ask, so thank you before we know what will happen. Amen."

Sandy looked up and asked, "Is that true? God knows what we need even before we ask for help?"

"Yes."

"Then why is it necessary for us to ask?"

"I'm not trained to give you a biblical answer, but I believe it's good for us to voice our concerns and needs, and then when the answer comes we remember that the Lord accomplished exactly what we've asked."

"That makes sense. Thank you, Alison."

"Will you read a story in the Old Testament of the Bible and tell me what you think about it the next time you come?"

"Sure. Tell me about it."

"It's the story of Joseph. Start to read in Genesis—that's the first book of the Bible—in Chapter thirty-seven, skip Chapter thirty-eight, and then read thirty-nine to fifty. It's about a teenager who was mistreated by his brothers."

Sandy nodded and may have guessed at Alison's line of thinking.

Alison felt now was a good time to start Sandy's portrait while the newly born-again glow was on her face. In fifty-five minutes, the pastel portrait was completed. Alison sprayed it with a fixative then handed it to her caregiver.

"I'll always cherish this treasure, and it will be a reminder of the day of my salvation."

"I'd like to pray again before you leave."

Sandy nodded.

"Dear Father in heaven, Sandy is in a difficult situation. Please guide her and give her direction. Speak peace to her heart and let her know, without a doubt, that she's doing what is right. Bless her newfound faith and give her confidence that You have the answers. In Jesus' name, I pray. Amen."

Sandy knew what she had to do.

chapter thirty-six

Doug started the rehabilitation group session. "Anger is the wrong way to express feelings in order to make yourself feel powerful. Deep down you all know that this is true. I would like you to try to recall a recent situation that triggered intense anger.

"I'll give you an example. Someone criticized you in front of another person and you responded with shouting. Instead of feeling belittled by their words, your anger makes you feel on top of the heap.

"Write about the last time you were angry; record what happened before the situation that contributed to feelings of violence. This may reveal one of your triggers. Go back to the first time those feelings led to anger. I know it isn't going to be easy, so I'll give you plenty of time."

Reuben remembered the last time anger overtook him; it was just yesterday. One of the guys at the halfway house asked him a question and then prevented him from turning away by holding his shoulder. Reuben lifted a hand to smack the guy's arm but at the last moment refrained. Now that he had tuned into looking for a cause, he remembered the first time that being grabbed had turned into anger. At six years old, he accompanied his father to the field. When little Reuben either asked too many questions or got in the way again, his father grabbed him and tied him to a fence. He screamed for his father to let him go, but it didn't help. Reuben's anger reached an extreme high that day. The feeling of being frantic to be released never left him; nor did he ever forgive his father. Reuben figured that every time he was physically held back in any manner, the same rage overtook him.

The men finished their writing and the lecture continued. "The second part to this teaching is 'time tripping.' You may have just written about a dreadful experience when you were helpless to vindicate yourself. Most likely, you wrote about a time when you were quite young and didn't have the ability to defend yourself.

"Time-tripping helps your 'younger self' to be rescued by your 'wiser self.' When you return to this hurtful memory, I want you to become the wiser self and tell the person who hurt you how you feel. Then let the wiser self give soothing, loving words to the younger self. We can never go back in time, but we can go back to the feelings. Let's give it a try. Fold your paper in half; on the left side put the heading 'wiser self confronts;' on the other half write 'wiser self soothes.'"

The men began to write again. The role of being a wiser self was more difficult for Reuben than he had expected. He wrote calmly, but in his mind he was shouting at his father. The wiser self confronted: "Reuben was just being a normal kid with normal questions. You could have handled a six-year-old with some understanding. You could have taken him back to the house to his mother."

The wiser self now soothed: "Reuben, are you all right? I'll take those ropes off and let you run home. I'll stay with you until you feel safe."

When Reuben returned to his room at the halfway house, exhausted from the stirred-up emotions, he had an idea of what might assuage this disturbing memory. He wanted to plan something amazing for Alison so that she would see him again. *I sense that Christine wants me, but she's of the past. I'm a new creation, now. Who knows? Alison may even remarry me.*

A Gift of Love

I know, I'll buy her a hand-operated vehicle. But how can I do that without a job? He thought for a while. *I'm the best truck driver I know. I bet I can get a job. Tomorrow I'll check in with Bodine.*

***

Reuben needed to pay Christine a visit; he hadn't spoken to her since he had been released from prison. He owed her at least that much. Besides, he wanted to look over the used vans on the lot. *Will Christine notice any difference in me? I sure feel different, even though I probably have a long way to go.*

A changed, thinner Christine walked briskly toward him. *I didn't know she could look so good.*

"I'm surprised to see you, Reb! When did you get out?"

He felt he needed a little fun, so he feigned a confusion of identity. Taking on a deeper voice and an aristocratic air, being careful not to use contractions, he said, "You must have mistaken me for someone else, madam. In this part of the city, people mistake me for another man frequently."

Christine had a comical, confused look on her face. Reuben couldn't hold back the laughter.

"Reb, it *is* you!" She swatted him on the arm, and then a soft look came into her eyes. "Hi, hon. You clean up real good."

"You're looking pretty good yourself."

"Thanks. I've been going to Weight Watchers."

His old flirtatious ways came back. "Oh. I thought you were pining away for me." Reuben winked.

Christine looked down, laughing.

"I got out for good behaviour."

"Oh, sure. And I'm Little Goody Two-Shoes." She laughed again. "So, why are you really here?"

"I'm interested in a van, about two years old, or even older is okay."

They spent a half hour looking at vans. "Now I know the amount I'll have to save, "Reuben said. "It may take some time, but I'm determined.

269

"Christine, I have something special to tell you; I rededicated my life to Christ."

"What do you mean, rededicated your life? Was it ever dedicated?"

"I guess I never told you about how I got the name Reb. It was because people saw me as a rebel for Jesus. I used to go on downtown streets and try to talk to heroin addicts about Jesus. In those days many people were talking about Him. You heard of Jesus People?"

Christine nodded.

"I was one."

"So you're saying that you're a Jesus Person again?"

"Something like that. I went to church last Sunday intending to harass Alison, and I ended up listening to the preacher. He really made sense. I got sort of mushy and asked Jesus to forgive me. I feel different now."

Christine challenged him. "If you're so mushy now, why didn't you ask about Samantha? All she says these days is, 'I want Daddy.'"

"I'm sorry, Christine. How is Samantha?"

"Wow, you are different! I've never heard you say you're sorry before. She's growing like a weed. She misses you. When are you coming to see her? Her third birthday is this Saturday."

"I'll see what I can do. I'm sure to start a new job soon, which may include weekends. I'll let you know."

"So now you're going straight, getting a job, and a van?"

Reuben couldn't hold back the laughter. "Yeah. You got it."

***

Gathering every last vestige of courage, Sandy entered the busy main police station on King William Street. At the main desk sat a female officer. Sandy lowered her head, unable to look the officer in the eye, and quietly stated, "I want to charge my brother with rape."

The officer asked her name. "Please take a seat. I'll get someone to help you immediately." The officer picked up the phone as she sent a half-smile toward Sandy, who sneezed several times and fiddled with her ponytail.

Sandy's hands were sweating as she twirled her hair. She prayed, *Jesus, I'm your follower now, and I believe I can call on You whenever I need You. I need You now. Comfort me, and cause my heart to be calm.*

A Gift of Love

***

Mac's shift was just beginning, and he moaned that it would have to start by dealing with a breakdown in family harmony. He gathered his report materials and glanced though the window to see his first case, standing with her back to him. A shapely woman wound strands of her light-coloured hair around her index finger. When she turned halfway, he whispered, "What a knockout!"

Mac proceeded to the information desk then approached the young lady. "Hello. I'm Corporal Ron Mackenzie." He shook the slender, velvety hand. "I understand that you wish to lay charges."

"Are we going to discuss it here? I've had a difficult time deciding to come here. I'd hoped that a private room was available."

Glancing down at her name again, Mac said, "Come this way, Miss Dailey." They entered an uncluttered room with three chairs and a desk. "Constable Hannah Schmidt will be joining us."

Sandy let out an audible sigh.

They waited briefly for Hannah to arrive. After introductions, Sandy was encouraged to tell her story from the beginning. The officers were not surprised that the incident had happened some time ago. They knew it took courage to report a crime like this.

The facts were scribbled on paper while Mac listened compassionately. Sandy waited while Constable Schmidt swiftly typed out her statement. Mac read the statement then handed it to Sandy to read and then sign.

"What will happen to my brother, now?"

"We'll go to your home and arrest Donald. After questioning at the station, we will charge him, and your family will decide whether to pay bail or not. If not, he will remain in custody. Since you still live at home, I would suggest that you stay with a friend. Is that possible?"

"Yes, it's possible. I have one friend I think will gladly take me in."

"That's the kind of friend you need right now. I'll wait until you've had a chance to go home to pack some things before I send an officer to your house. Will two hours be sufficient?"

"I'll try."

"Good enough. Try to relax. Bye for now." *This sweet woman has touched my heart.*

271

Ron Mackenzie seemed to be a very practical, yet sympathetic officer in Sandy's estimation. He was the proverbial perfect man: tall, dark, and handsome. She added good at his job to the list of his attributes. Sandy left the police station relieved and thankful to God for providing kind officers.

When Sandy returned home, she phoned Alison immediately to ask if she could stay overnight.

"Oh, yes, Sandy. I have Mac coming over for that promised dinner, and you can arrive at eight o'clock. That will give me the perfect reason to make the evening short. Is there something you can do in the meantime?"

"Yes. I think everything will work out. Thank you so much, as long as I'm not intruding?"

"Like I said, it'll be perfect. We'll have time to talk then, and you can have the bed that I used before my hospital stay. I'll have Mac set it up in my bedroom. There's plenty of room beside my hospital bed. Then you can tell me all about what happened at the police station. I'll try to make you giggle to relieve your troubles, at least for tonight, although you're welcome to stay as long as you like."

"Thanks, Alison."

"It won't be a problem. I'll tell Mac that he has to leave earlier than eight."

"Okay then. I'll make sure and come after eight."

"I'm glad to have a live-in caregiver. I'm joking. I won't put you to work. It'll be nice to just have you around."

"Maybe I'll be able to earn my lodging by doing some extras. I'll assist you with as many showers as you like."

"Great."

Alison hung up and thought of what it would be like to have Sandy as a house guest. Quickly she switched her thoughts. *Now to cook a hearty meal for a hard-working policeman.*

***

Mac arrived on the dot of six with a bouquet of flowers as Alison had expected. Everything seemed to be fine, but Mac's comments and mannerisms seemed different; he was less attentive and flirtatious. She saw this as a sign from the Lord. After devouring the special meal, giving many compliments, Mac willingly helped Alison arrange her bedroom to accommodate a girlfriend. He left early with a simple, "See you in church."

chapter thirty-seven

Early the next morning, Reuben went to see a friend who had served time in prison with him in '69. Bodine, nicknamed after Jethro Bodine, one of the Clampetts from the TV series *The Beverly Hillbillies*, had developed a trucking company after his release, in spite of others' low expectations. Reuben left the house with optimism that Bodine would have a job for him. Within the hour, Reuben indeed had a job, along with a hope to save enough to buy a van and convert it into one with hand-controlled acceleration and braking. He planned to save as much as he could by spending a minimal amount of his wages on his own needs. After a time of courting, he hoped to rekindle Alison's affections. Reuben encouraged himself with the quote, *With God, all things are possible.*

***

Janette ran up the steps to Alison's apartment with haste, radiating excitement. Her daughter's beauty depicted on the front page encouraged this mother's pride. Saturday's feature section told the story of a handicapped artist making it big at her first art show.

Janette knocked and entered. "Alison, look! Isn't this a beautiful photo of you?"

Alison recognized it at a glance; it was the same photo from which Rolph wanted her to do a self-portrait. Alison asked, "Will you read it to me?"

Janette read: 'An Artist with a Difference: She chooses to support herself.' The article on the second page told briefly about Alison's past as a high school teacher, the incident that took away her career and independence, the long hospital stay, and finally, her decision to support herself instead of living off the system. Some of Alison's paintings were arranged around the border of the piece. When Janette finished reading, they both let out a satisfying sigh.

Alison took many minutes to look at the pages and smiled that Rolph had described many paintings in the article, not just three. "Well, Mom, I guess I'd better get to work now that it's publicized that I'm a self-supporter." They laughed. Janette left after sharing a meal with Alison.

***

Reuben arrived early for the next anger management help group and asked if he could help. Doug described the agenda and asked Reuben to do a writing exercise before the other guys arrived. He wrote for a solid fifteen minutes without making corrections. He had no trouble in picking the most traumatic memory of his youth. The feelings he had experienced over ten years ago were intense, and he wondered if he had the ability to label them.

He began to write:

> When I was sixteen years old my dad tried to kill my mother. I hated him then and that hasn't changed. It was a hot day in July. Mom had been up before dawn made a large breakfast of eggs bacon toast with homemade jam. Mom was the best cook

in the world. I loved her more than most kids. She worked so hard. After breakfast she would go into the fields and work like the hired guys while my father would sit under a tree and drink his homemade wine. My lazy father had too much to drink and took it out on mom. I wasn't going to stand by and see my mother beaten. I wasn't going to stand by this time. He beat my mother as he beat me many times. My mother always took everything he dished out. I'm so angry I didn't do more. I hate myself for this more than I hate my father. I think about that day almost every day. I screamed at Mom to go hide when I saw him go for the gun. She didn't listen. He aimed it at my mother. I was going to wrench that gun from his hands. If I got in the way he was going to kill me too. I was sweating and crying even if I was almost a man. My father said to stop acting like a girl. The gun was now aimed at me I was so scared of dieing and leaving my mom. I don't like to see anyone crying to this day. Why do I have to be like him? He aimed the gun at me and mom jumped in between and she got the riffle slug in the stomach. I thought she was dead on the spot. I charged at him and wrenched that gun from his hands and knocked him unconscious. I emptied the bullets. When the ambulance and police came I was holding a towel on my mothers stomach to try to stop the bleeding. She couldn't talk her eyes were closed and I thought she was dead. The police took my father and I stayed with Mom in the ambulance. Mom made it but her spunk was gone. She loved me but something happened to her brain. She was never the same. We went to live with my aunt and I got a job in Hamilton. Mom never really recovered and I guess neither did I.

The sweat was pouring down Reuben's back, making a dark streak in his shirt. *God, if this will help, I'm willing to share this story. Please help me to do it without crying in front of the guys.*

Reuben hoped to read what he had written and not expound on any of it because he didn't trust his voice to be steady. The other men had arrived by the time he took the end chair. *God, help me, please.*

Doug started the group by welcoming them back. "Today we are going to be talking about a topic called confiding. All of you have a problem with anger, and usually no one wants to talk about it.

"The format of our meetings will be similar to AA meetings, where individuals give their name and then admit they have a problem with anger. I see this as the first step to recovery. I understand that it isn't easy. Who'll be the first one to give your name then admit that you have a problem with managing your anger?"

The room became silent. God was speaking to Reuben, compelling him to be first. The chair scraped the linoleum floor as Reuben stood and reached his full height of five foot eleven. "My name is Reuben Steele and I have a problem with anger."

"Thank you, Reuben. Who will be next?"

Each one did the same.

Doug continued. "Each of you has been living with unresolved emotional baggage. Bad things have happened to you at some point in your life. They have caused feelings that were upsetting and possibly scary. In general, men do not like to talk about their feelings. But the more you talk about them, the less potent they become. When you talk to someone about such things, you are confiding in that person; therefore, we call this practice confiding. What makes this practice valuable is that as you verbalize the facts and label your feelings, you lessen the power of the painful event—you lessen its ability to wound you.

"Writing is preferred over just speaking because it slows down your thought processes. The pain that you stuffed and kept inside will finally be expressed. Write for fifteen minutes about your most upsetting experience without stopping to think about what you are writing. Write about your feelings, not just the facts. If you run out of words before the time is up, just repeat what you've already written. Go find a place now and I'll tell you when the time is up."

Fifteen minutes later, everyone reconvened in the semicircle. "Avoiding verbalizing your feelings leaves them untreated, and therefore not healed. It takes a great deal of energy to suppress distressing emotions. We naturally avoid anything that hurts us. Some of you were taught—probably by your fathers—that it is weak to cry. But crying is the basic way we express strong emotions, from birth and on.

"My puppy died when I was seven. My dad told me that men don't cry, and if I cried I was a girl. I have told this story so many times that it doesn't hurt to tell it anymore, but that was not the case three years ago when I started this program. As I related this story, my eyes were tearing up. Now I understand my father. His father told him the same thing. You see, it wasn't really his fault.

"After talking about my puppy several times, I realized that it didn't make me cry to talk about it, so I don't try to avoid this story any more. You may have moist eyes today as you tell your experience. And that's okay. Someday in the future you will find that it no longer hurts so much. You each have secret wounds that are not going to be kept secret any longer, if you are willing to share. Which one of you is going to be the first to share his story?"

Reuben knew what he had to do. No natural inner strength could withhold his feelings from showing while reading his paper, he knew, so he called on his renewed relationship with his heavenly Father for support. He read what he wrote without embellishments and found that it was not as embarrassing to be tearful in front of others as he had anticipated. Each of the men followed Reuben's example and shared their stories openly and with emotion.

***

Alison looked forward to the promised surprise from Rolph after the article was published. It felt like waiting for Christmas. In an hour he planned to arrive for her first photography lesson. The phone rang.

"Hello, Alison. It's Rolph. Did you see it?"

"Hi, Rolph. I certainly did. You did a fine job. My mother was so excited."

"Thank you. I must say it was a pleasure to write it—not like work at all. About the lesson this afternoon, I would like to take photos outside. It's a sunny fall day."

"What did you have in mind?"

"Gage Park is close to our homes, so I can push you there, and then have the bus for the handicapped take us to a restaurant after."

"Oh, that's perfect."

It wasn't the surprise he had planned but he would let her think it was.

***

They made their way leisurely along a path lined with crunchy leaves. With the traffic noise fading in the distance, the park's natural sounds of birds and squirrels surrounded them.

Rolph planned to spend an hour in instruction before their appetites would peak. "Once you like what you see in the view finder, zoom in even closer, then focus," he instructed. "Find how little you can include in your picture and still make your statement. Ask yourself if the background surroundings add to your statement or distract."

Rolph had a teaching talent in addition to his ability to take photos. "This may be surprising to you, but light areas carry more weight in a picture than darks. The emptier part of the frame must balance with the weight of the main subject. There must also be a balance between vertical and horizontal lines.

"I want you to look for your first effective subject. When you think you have found it, see if any objects in the foreground or the background may detract or look out of place before snapping the picture. For example, if you were taking a picture of me in front of this tree, see if there is a branch that lines up with my ear that makes it seems that I'm growing it with earwax." This brought gales of laughter from Alison.

They proceeded to shoot one scene after another until their stomachs were rumbling.

After taking the bus to a nearby family restaurant, they settled in a booth and ordered chicken. With their meals in front of them and a prayer offered, it was time for Rolph to reveal Alison's actual surprise. "*The Hamilton Spectator* is looking for a human-interest story. I was thinking about your autobiography that you're writing about your troubled marriage and your hospital experience. I think it would be perfect for the kind of story they're looking for. You would have to weave it together and shorten it into a series of segments." Rolph straightened and took a deep breath. "I think you'd do a good job."

"Oh, Rolph. Do you really think it's possible?"

"Entirely. And I know the guy who is in charge of it—Jordon Kind. He's my work buddy."

Alison's tone raised a notch. "This is so exciting! I'll have new energy in completing it now. Is there a deadline?"

"It's for mid-December and I'll help in any way you wish."

The laughter and the adventure of the day bound them in what seemed a transforming closeness for Alison. Rolph returned her to her apartment door and said goodnight. He wanted to kiss her, but felt instinctively that it was too soon.

chapter thirty-eight

In a daze of semi-wakefulness, Alison sensed that her Chambermate, the Lord, was summoning her companionship. Occasionally her first thoughts took her down the questioning alley: *How long before You send me into my ministry? What if I get distracted with art and miss my calling?* However, this morning she felt that God had something exciting to reveal to her. After arising, getting dressed and sitting at the art table, she took out her journal from its usual place, and with her pen poised, she concentrated on hearing what the Lord might say.

    Oct. 20, 1977

    "You do not need to evaluate your life's performance; while being conscious of My presence you need to live just one hour at a time only. Pay attention to Me—nothing else. Everything will fall into place for I am the One who guides you.

"All your prayers are valuable because they accomplish much. The prayer of thanksgiving is the most effective because it sets your sight beyond the problem. If you can see it done, it will be done. Only you hold yourself from going forward.

"Give Me all your shame from everything you wish had never happened. I have made you pure and have replaced your thoughts of regret with songs of praise. Tell everyone you can that I am able to give them a gift of a clean slate."

Alison knew that God was referring to the guilt she felt about her failed marriage, and her reticence to become devoted to any man. She felt vulnerable to the possibility of entering into another failure.

Lord, I give you everything I am and everything I'm not. You know what is best. I'll be seeing Mac and Rolph at church today and I'm wondering what might transpire. Don't let either of them become discouraged because of me.

I want to live in peace and rejoice before You. I will thank You and look beyond my problems and expect positive outcomes in everything that I've placed in Your hands—Mac's friendship, everything concerning Rolph, the loss of Kathlynn, and the trial of keeping discouragement behind me because of the paralysis. In Jesus' name. Amen.

Alison spent the next half-hour reading the Bible. Isaiah 49:13 spoke to her: "Shout for joy, O heavens; rejoice, O earth; burst into song, O mountains! For the Lord comforts his people and will have compassion on his afflicted ones." *I'm thankful for Your comfort, Lord, and that you chose me to be an ambassador of love. I will keep singing on the days the paralysis continues, and I'll also thank You that You have heard my prayers. I see myself walking again. Amen.*

***

Rolph met Alison in the foyer of the church, where the autumn sun filtered through the stained glass. Half of her face was golden and the other half rosy. She looked like a two-toned angel. His heart leapt when he thought that she might be the Lord's choice for a lifelong partner for him.

A Gift of Love

Lord, she has suffered much, but I want to change the memory of her trials into joyous praise. Please help.

Rolph suggested a different pew from her usual one. Alison agreed and positioned her chair at the end of the second row. When Rolph twisted halfway to see whether she was comfortable, he noticed Mac enter the sanctuary, focus on them, and then sit in the back pew.

Pastor Ed's first statement was, "Give them a gift they don't deserve—forgiveness!" Rolph was caught by surprise. *How did this pastor know his deepest trial?* The sermon was going to be about bestowing forgiveness, and Rolph felt that God was speaking directly to him.

The pastor asked the congregation if anyone came to mind when they thought about resentment. "We should consider relinquishing those persons from the hold of our bitterness."

Immediately Rolph knew there was a man he thought he had the perfect right not to forgive—the drunken man who had caused his wife's death.

Pastor Ed talked about the blood of Jesus Christ shed for *all* humankind.

When the sermon ended, he invited those who needed to forgive someone to come forward and kneel at the altar. Rolph stood up immediately and went to the front of his new church, lowered himself to his knees, carefully positioning his foot, and prayed: *Father, the man responsible for Nora's death doesn't deserve my forgiveness, but I'm willing to forgive because I don't want to hang on to this resentment. I've decided to give him a gift he doesn't deserve. Amen.*

Then he carried out the act of forgiveness: *I release you, Hector, from my judgment and forgive you.*

Rolph opened his eyes and saw a wheelchair beside him. Alison raised her head a second after Rolph's prayer ended and they found themselves gazing into each other's eyes.

For the first time Alison recognized these eyes as the same ones she saw in a recurring dream about a kind stranger who took her hands and helped her to stand. In the dream they walked arm in arm down a country lane in autumn. *Those are the same aqua-coloured eyes. How did I miss this?* She realized at that moment that Rolph could play an important part in her future. He might even be responsible in assisting her to walk again. *The dream could have been prophetic!*

After they returned from the altar, Rolph waited for Alison to look at him. "Alison, I would like to invite you to Poland for lunch." He snickered.

"That could be expensive," said Alison, returning the humour.

"It's my birthday and I want to spend it with you."

"Oh. Happy birthday. You should have said something last week. I could have been prepared."

"That's exactly why I didn't tell you. So, may I take you out for lunch?"

"Certainly, if it doesn't take too long to get to Poland."

He laughed.

"I'll let my parents know that I have a way home."

***

Rolph didn't have a vehicle, so he had arranged the bus for the handicapped to take them home from the restaurant. Walking there was fine as long as it didn't rain. Rolph prayed to the maker of the weather. *Lord, the clouds look dark, but I'm asking You to hold them back from dumping while we're walking. Thank you, Father.*

The chef at Karolina's Restaurant served superb European food. The atmosphere and food reminded Rolph of a restaurant he had enjoyed in Warsaw. Karolina knew Rolph by name. He was one of her favourites because he always made a point of asking about her arthritic symptoms and offered to pray. When Alison whispered to Karolina that it was his birthday, she promised to bring a piece of cake with a candle to the table at the end of their meal.

After a savoury meal of cabbage rolls and schnitzel, Rolph looked into Alison's eyes and thanked her for being with him on his birthday. When she blushed, he asked, "Do you like guessing games?"

"Yes. I suppose so."

"Okay, how old would you say that I am?"

"Let's see. You graduated from university just before you started as a reporter/photographer, and you worked there for five years before you married. You were married for four years, and then have been a widower for almost seven months—that would make you about thirty."

"You're very good at guessing games. I am thirty. It's my turn to guess. You were married for five years; you were married before you graduated; you taught for a year; and your injury happened almost seven months ago. You look like you are in your early twenties. Let's see—you were a child prodigy and graduated from university when you were eighteen, which would make you twenty-two."

She bent forward with laughter. "How kind of you. I'll leave it at that."

"That's right—a woman never tells her age."

They continued talking until the handicap transport arrived. Alison learned a lot about Rolph and admired him even more. She was amazed at how easily they conversed.

Rolph wanted to see her again. "Alison, would you go with me to the movies on Friday?"

"Maybe. Which one are you considering?"

"There's a science fiction movie by the producer Steven Spielberg called *Close Encounters of the Third Kind*, with Richard Dreyfuss and Teri Garr. Or there's a kids' movie, called *The Bad News Bears*, with Tatum O'Neal, Walter Matthau, and Michael Ritchie."

"Can I decide later?"

"Sure. There's no hurry."

They finally said goodnight at her apartment door and reiterated what a good time they had had. Rolph walked home to his empty apartment with a light, uneven step, whistling all the way.

***

Alison thought, *There must be a perfect match for Mac. Maybe that young woman who has been coming to the church for the past three Sundays. Natalie is a vivacious, good-looking blonde with grey eyes the colour of an autumn sky. If their personalities clicked, the rest could be history.*

Alison had an idea. She could give a harvest party on Halloween.

chapter thirty-nine

Sandy moved into Alison's apartment temporarily until she could rent one of her own. Her parents bailed out Donald, who returned home to await trial.

Sandy had never felt as relaxed in her life as she did living with Alison. They had long talks, worked on her autobiography and had TV nights while munching on popcorn. No secret was too sacred to share. Many times Rolph's name came up in Alison's conversation. Sandy pointed this out, making Alison blush. The two young ladies had fun conversations and serious ones about passages in the Bible. The two women became close in a sisterly companionship.

Alison generally woke earlier than Sandy by an hour at least. This morning, Sandy had risen earlier than usual and was bustling around the kitchen when she heard Alison call from the bathroom. *She hasn't asked for assistance before. I wonder what's up.*

When Sandy dashed into the bathroom with a dishrag in her hand, Alison said, "Sandy, I feel a sensation of pressure in my lower abdomen."

Sandy checked the catheter and saw that the drainage bag was empty. "Your drainage tube must be blocked. I'll get my equipment." She hurried away.

In a short time Sandy had the problem solved, and Alison reported that the pressure was relieved. When Sandy looked up after emptying the bag into the toilet, Alison had a smile as wide as a muppet from *Sesame Street*.

"I've never seen you smile like that before."

"Don't you see? I felt pressure! Isn't that a good sign that I'm regaining feeling?"

"Oh! I was too absorbed with the problem to think about what that sensation might mean."

"What does it mean exactly?"

"It means that you have deep core sensation in your pelvis."

"Deep core? What's that?"

"Deep core sensation is what gives you feeling from things like a full bowel, menstrual pain, discomfort due to a bladder infection, or orgasm."

Alison didn't acknowledge the full implications until seconds later then let out a whoop. "Oh! You mean I could have sexual pleasure and live happily ever after?"

Sandy couldn't help but smile at the excited expression on Alison's face. "Only if you marry Mr. Right."

Alison laughed. *Sandy was getting her old sense of humour back.* Alison couldn't stop singing for the rest of the morning, filling each room she entered with a godly atmosphere.

***

Oct. 21, 1977

"My thoughts are constantly with you. You can never escape from My love. I dwell with you and you are conscious of Me when you seek My presence. Practise this seeking time more often until you bubble up with joy, until no more negative thoughts plague you.

"Because I have made everything, it is natural for you to consult Me about any concern. It is true that everything is in My control and I am working out My perfect will in you. Never forget or leave out the Comforter, your Helper. Call on Me at any time, in fact, all the time.

"My thoughts are not your thoughts, so let Me change them. I want you to be lifted up and excited about each day. Live in My joy. Continue to sing and rejoice. This day was made with you in mind. "

Thank you, Lord. I'm very excited about what you did for me this morning. You must have a special purpose for me in regaining sensations. I could live in this joy alone. And I'll heed Your warning. She looked up the word "plague" in the dictionary, which now sat on a small table in the alcove, where she could reach it easily. Plague was defined as anything that afflicts or troubles—a nuisance, an annoyance. *Help me, God, to keep negative thoughts under control, and if possible, away altogether. I know I must rely on the Holy Spirit's wisdom.*

***

"Sandy, I'm wondering if you ever had a desire to see two people get to know one another." Alison noted a questioning lift of Sandy's eyebrows as she tucked in her chin. "Don't look at me like that. I'm a romantic. Can I talk to you about it?"

"I think I know who one of the two is, but go ahead and tell me your idea."

Alison grinned. "Yes, you've heard a lot about Mac, the ice cube case." Sandy couldn't hold back the laughter. "Well, there's this fantastic woman who started coming to our church a few weeks ago, and I would like to see them become acquainted.

"I was thinking about throwing a harvest party on Halloween. I thought it would be a good way to invite the young people from church and some personal friends, as well. You may even want to come to the church and check it out this Sunday."

"I'll seriously consider it sometime, but I'm working this weekend."

"Do you think that the party's a good idea?" Alison sought reassurance.

"Yes, I do. I'll help you plan and prepare for it. We can make invitations."

"Great. Thank you, Sandy. By the way, I almost forgot to ask you, did you read the story of Joseph, from the book of Genesis?"

"Yes. It was helpful."

"Do you have any comments about it?"

Sandy paused. "I didn't know the Bible had such interesting stories. I noticed that Joseph was mistreated by his brothers, but eventually showed love toward them. Can we read that verse in the last chapter again that says that God meant good to come from the evil that Joseph received?"

Alison got her Bible out and found the verse, Genesis 50:20: "You intended to harm me, but God intended it for good to accomplish what is now being done, the saving of many lives."

"That's the one. Does anyone know how long Joseph was in prison?"

"The Bible said he was seventeen when he was sent to take food to his brothers. And one chapter says he was thirty years old when he had his audience with Pharaoh. So, it must have been many years," said Alison.

"How could he just forgive his brothers without harbouring resentment?"

"Joseph knew that God was in charge even during his suffering. He couldn't have seen the good of being in prison at the beginning of this trying situation, yet he kept a noble attitude. And I have a feeling that good is going to come out of the evil you have suffered, too."

"Do you really think so?"

Alison nodded. "Yes. I can see at least one similarity between your story and Joseph's: he needed to forgive his family." A serious expression clouded Sandy's face. "Suppose your brother accepts the Lord as his

Saviour someday. It may happen that he will be truly sorry, not just to remove the guilt but to please his new Master. God was willing to forgive us for the sins that caused Jesus to be put to death even before our existence. Shouldn't we forgive those who hurt us in advance of their apology?"

"I guess I've had trouble doing that because to me it seems I'm saying that what he did wasn't serious."

"Let me explain. It doesn't excuse your brother, but it releases your spirit from anger. It gives God a chance to deal with him while your life progresses."

"I'll have to think about that." After several minutes of silence, frowning and fiddling with her hands, Sandy said, "I've decided to forgive Donald. I don't feel forgiving, but I'll do it for peace of mind." She released a shuddering sigh.

Alison took Sandy's damp hand. "I'm proud of you. You have taken a noble step. I believe that the release will come later. Do you want to pray after me for God's help?"

"Yes. I do need His help."

Alison was not trying to control Sandy but simply stated the words that she heard in her spirit, much like when she wrote in her journal. Alison started and Sandy repeated it phrase by phrase. "Dear Heavenly Father, I am finding it difficult to forgive Donald. I feel violated because of his sin, but I have come to know that if I don't release him my life will be held back from healing, and Donald's spirit will be held back from accepting You. Will You please give me the ability to have the correct thoughts and release me from any anger? And I want to feel that I've forgiven him. Thank you. Amen."

***

Later the phone rang and Judy greeted her excitedly. "Alison, I have terrific news. I'm pregnant!"

"Congratulations to you and William. I'm truly thankful to the Lord for this blessing. Is your mom excited?"

"I haven't told her yet; you're the first."

"Thank you. I feel very privileged."

They chatted about morning sickness and doctor's appointments and laughed at how husbands tend to get the same symptoms as their wives. They promised to talk again after the whole family was informed.

Alison thanked the Father for this tremendous miracle and realized that He had used her to pray with confidence for this child to be conceived.

Sandy and Alison rejoiced together. Then Alison said, "Rolph is coming over this afternoon for an art lesson, and then we're going to dinner and a movie."

"That's great. It sounds like things are progressing between you two," said Sandy.

Alison held up the party invitation she had finished designing.

"You sure work fast."

Alison tilted her head and wrinkled her brow. She was confused, thinking Sandy was commenting on the date.

"I'm not talking about your friendship with Rolph." Sandy read Alison's expression correctly.

Alison giggled at her mistake.

"Have a good time. I'm leaving for work soon. I'm sorry I won't get to meet him this time."

"Oh, Sandy, I almost forgot. Remember when I told you last week that I would look up the verse about the angels rejoicing?"

Sandy nodded.

"It took a little while to find because the actual words are 'rejoicing in heaven,' not the 'angels rejoice.' In Luke 15:7 it says, 'I tell you that in the same way there will be more rejoicing in heaven over one sinner who repents than over ninety-nine righteous persons who do not need to repent.' You caused quite a party in heaven the day you accepted the Lord as your Saviour." Alison took Sandy's hand and looked up at her with a radiant face, hoping that Sandy would respond in the same manner. The smile was catching.

"Thank you, Alison. I promise to think about the day of my salvation and less about that horrible night. But it's not easy."

"I can truly say I know how you feel."

chapter forty

After spending hours at a car lot several Saturdays ago, Rolph looked forward to getting into his new vehicle and going on his first real date with Alison. He wanted to express his feelings for her in a poem, as he had done privately the night he met her at the art show. *It's time to declare my feelings, even though it's only a short time ago since I met her face to face.*

In a Hallmark store, his eyes fell on a romantic card in the religious section. It had a lacy heart with a backdrop of roses and golden writing that said, 'God Gave Me a Treasure In You.' When he read the poem inside by Emily Matthews called 'A Gift of Love,' it seemed perfect:

God answered my heart's deepest prayer the day He gave me you.
God gave me a great treasure of immense and untold worth,
And brought a touch of heaven to my lifetime here on earth,

For he sent me someone wonderful, an angel from above,
When He blessed me with the gift of you—my friend, my joy, my love.

He felt it was just the right one to buy and wrote his own rhyming couplets on the blank middle page of the card:

> Who could have dreamt of a love like this,
> Except the Father who arranged this timely bliss?
> So, my love, to experience God's plan,
> We must admit it's an adventure that in heaven began.
> With future years that will be filled with love's emotion,
> I'll give you the gift of my pure devotion.

Only You know, God, if this declaration of love will be received. I admit I'm terrified.

He planned to give her the card at a dessert café after the movie. Later, he would voice his feelings in the privacy of his new vehicle—a burgundy Chevy van that could be equipped with a hydraulic lift for raising an occupied wheelchair.

He hid the card in the inner pocket of his jacket, ready for tomorrow.

***

Rolph arrived on time, dressed in a dark blue suit and turtle-neck sweater. He greeted Alison with a warm smile and sparkling eyes. "Hello, Alison. I hope I'm not too early." He heard his heart beating wildly in his ears.

"No, you're just in time for a cup of tea or coffee."

"I'll have tea, thank you."

"You may want to remove your suit jacket. Painting can get messy."

He smiled to think she was taking care of him already. "You're right." He hung his jacket on the back of a chair. Alison poured his tea and placed cookies on the saucer and passed it to him when he was seated. Rolph nodded and simply said, "Thanks," and then poured the milk into his cup.

Alison joined him at the table and asked, "Now that you know all about my disability, can we talk about yours?"

He took a sip of tea. "Okay. What would you like to know?"

"What is your condition called?"

"It's a birth defect called a clubfoot, or a non-traumatic congenital foot deviation."

"That sounds like a dictionary definition."

"Exactly; and it says that it didn't happen accidentally. I was born that way."

"Has it caused you trauma even if it didn't happen accidentally?"

"As early as I can remember, I had a great fear of being separated from my family—Mom, Dad, two brothers, and three sisters. I spent many weeks in the hospital almost every year as I grew. The surgeons tried to correct the deformity but it made little difference.

"When it came time to begin school, a different kind of pain started. The other kids called me limpy-gimpy."

"You seem well adjusted. I admire your joy of life and your positive attitude."

"Thank you, Alison." He said her name with a gentle lilt. "I've learned to accept my lot in life."

He finished his tea and cookies. Alison asked, "Are you ready for your first art lesson?"

Rolph took the lead. "May I suggest that we begin with prayer? I think I'm going to need it." He chuckled.

Alison let a small, nervous laugh escape. "That's the reason I truly admire you, Rolph—you put God first."

Rolph smiled wider than before and said a simple prayer.

Alison began the instruction. "Rolph, this is all that you'll need to complete your first painting. It's important to not be too concerned if it doesn't turn out as you'd like."

"Yeah." He put his fingers to his mouth as if he were biting his nails, which caused more laughter.

297

"But you must keep it for all time as a fond memory of your beginning."

Rolph's face became serious at his private response: *Only if you will be there to make sure that I do.* He was aware that his cheeks heated.

Alison carried on undisturbed. "You may even produce a painting you'll want to frame."

Rolph put aside his embarrassment and raised his eyebrows at this encouraging statement.

"We're going to do a landscape with sky, water, and mountains."

"Can all the colours be a mixture from just three primary colours?" He looked down at the sparse palate.

"Yes, basically. You'll get on to it."

"What is this brush used for?" Rolph pointed at the fan brush that looked like its name.

"It's used mostly for making tree leaves or plants. It takes a free movement of the arm, which you'll learn."

"You make it sound easy. Let's get started."

Two hours later, two almost identical paintings were propped up on the counter.

After praising his efforts, Alison asked, "What movie have you decided on?"

"Because I'm a baseball fan and I enjoy a movie with a general rating, I picked *The Bad News Bears*."

"That suits me, too. Let's try out that restaurant you were raving about. I'm starving."

Rolph helped with her coat, and then pushed her wheelchair out into the night breeze. He stopped alongside a shiny van. It wasn't until he opened the passenger door that Alison realized that it was his vehicle.

"This is yours?"

"Yes. I've been saving for many years by staying close to home and taking transit. I'll lift you into the front seat, and then put the wheelchair in the back. Are you ready? Hang on."

The film at the Westdale Theatre was enjoyable and funny. Their next destination took them to *Main Desserts* at Locke and Main. As Alison swallowed the last forkful of apple pie and sip of tea, Rolph removed the card from his jacket pocket with a perspiring hand.

"I have a card that expresses what I've been feeling."

"Thank you." Her reply was barely audible. She read the card with her head down.

Is that a teardrop forming at the corner of her eye? Rolph's stomach tightened.

Alison thought, *This poem says he loves me and that it's God who has directed him to express these feelings.*

When she slowly raised her head she looked into large blue-green irises that were concentrating intently on her face.

Rolph's mind raced. *We've known each other for such a short time, but I'm sure she's the one for me. I've never been disturbed by her paralysis, and I'm able to look after her. I hope I haven't shocked her completely.* His thoughts didn't ease his jitters. He needed to rehearse the words he'd use to tell of his love once they were settled in the van.

Alison, you are very special to me. I have been in love before.

"Make her feel as if she is the only one you're thinking about, My son."

Okay, starting over: Alison, you are very special to me. I'm in love with you. I've asked the Lord to allow me to fall in love only with the one who is to be permanently in my life.

But what if she's not ready to respond in the same way?

"Be patient with her."

***

Seated comfortably in the van, Rolph took a deep breath and began. "Alison, I have something very important to say to you." He wanted to hold her hand but felt restrained.

"Let's talk at my apartment." She paused briefly. "Thank you for the dinner, movie, and dessert."

"You're very welcome." He decided to discuss the contents of the card when God let him know that the timing was right.

"I'm planning a party for October thirty-first at seven p.m. I hope you can come, Rolph."

"Certainly, I'll come. A costume isn't required, I hope."

"No. I'm calling it a harvest party. Just a get-together with the young adults of our church. I'll have the announcement made this Sunday."

When they entered Alison's apartment Rolph helped her remove her coat, and then she went to take care of her personal needs. When she returned, Rolph was sitting on the sofa.

"Rolph, I appreciate everything you did tonight. I want to tell you that you are very dear to me and I enjoy being around you and look forward to every photo and art lesson. I also believe that God has brought us together, but I'm not ready to say that four-letter word. Can you understand that?"

Rolph swallowed then answered, "Yes. I believe I understand more than you know. I'm happy to hear of your feelings and I'm content to carry on as we are while I learn more about you. I want to hear about your marriage when you feel free to tell me more. I want to know everything about you, your family, about your hopes and dreams. Everything!" An old Broadway song, "Getting to Know You" from the musical *The King and I*, came into his head So, he sang it.

Alison was surprised at the quality of his voice. It was the first time she'd heard him sing a cappella, without instruments or other voices interfering. Each note seemed in perfect pitch, even the high ones. It ended with "day by daaaay." He held the last note as long as a virtuoso, and then took her hand and gave it a gentle squeeze and said goodnight.

chapter forty-one

Father, I feel so vulnerable today. Rolph's visit yesterday turned very serious. I'm troubled by his feelings for me that I can't return right now. I'm lonesome for a husband-and-wife relationship, but I'm afraid of another failure. And I miss my little Kathlynn and the life I could have had with her. I know You have a plan in all this. Please lead me through these dark thoughts. Speak to me, Lord.

Alison took out her journal and poised a shaky pen, waiting to hear the first words.

Oct. 23, 1977

"There is a journey you have been on, and it will continue throughout your life on earth. No one else can walk the way I have called you to walk; you alone are in charge of that. Be released from trying to please others; only please Me. I am your Director. Trust that I am doing a good job.

"Today, don't speak a negative word, only express everything in a positive light. I am the Light Bearer. I am directing you away from this time of darkness and pain. Watch Me work out the details you can't see, for you are not accustomed to the light as I am. I will bring you out of the darkness with My glory evident on your face. So start rejoicing now.

"As you become perfected in hearing My voice, you will know when a 'word' you receive from others is right for you now or in the future. Today, you are in the process of learning, so don't get down on yourself when you miss My input, but praise Me for the learning experience. Love to learn. Rejoice always and praise Me exceedingly.

"These are special days that I have planned for you. See each day as a gift from Me. Be conscious of the people I put on your mind for whom you are to pray, then take it one step further and ask what it is that I am asking you to do for them. Don't lose sight of the uniqueness of individuals while you keep My words flowing from Me to them. Encourage everyone you meet.

"Touch through Me; speak through Me. Let every action have a purpose, and then you will be My true disciple. It is easy to show love if you are able to put yourself in another's place. If you have trouble imagining any aspect of people's lives, ask me to open your eyes to see them as I see them.

"Trust Me that this day has much potential for you. I will see you through any and every difficulty, for nothing is too difficult for Me. Seek Me every moment, and then you will find I have been there all the time."

Lord, I've been hindered because my mind repeats hurtful memories. Set me free from the pain and negative aspects of my past. Change me so that everyone who sees me will know of the joy that You can give. Help me do everything as if I am doing it for You, and let me perceive the positive lessons You have for me.

A Gift of Love

***

After the heaviness lifted, Alison hummed "Getting to Know You" for the next hour, on and off. It seemed that she couldn't get rid of it. Sandy heard a complete account of their date and knew the reason for Alison's humming.

It had taken weeks for Sandy to become familiar with Alison's routine. After rising, Alison pulled on a terry-lined housecoat, wrapped a plaid throw around her feet, then wheeled herself into the alcove. After an hour, sometimes more, she would emerge with a peaceful look.

A few days ago Sandy had followed Alison's advice to attend her church by trying the young adults' weekly meeting. She soon became involved by volunteering for the position of secretary/treasurer. That's how she became familiar with Lake Gospel Church without even attending a Sunday service so far.

***

Oct. 24, 1977

"I am your Father, today, and always. I am rich in mercy, and abundant in possessions. In fact, I own everything. I have all knowledge of today and all the days to come. Is anything too difficult for Me? Then trust Me to look after My own, which includes you and all those who are dear to you.

"Lean on Me, for My shoulders are wide. You can tell Me anything. Although I know everything, you still need to voice your desires. This is important for your spiritual and mental health.

"I want to give you a special gift today. Watch for it and see what I have for you. By the end of the day you will see glimpses of many gifts that can be yours.

"I do have your life planned, while you get to choose what path you take: A or B. Stop and meditate about these two choices for a while. Both paths are righteous: one is excellent and the other is good. Give time for thought, and you will see what I mean.

"I love you and am watching over you. Don't worry; you will make the right choice.

Then she read from her Bible:
My son, do not forget my teaching, but keep my commands in your heart, for they will prolong your life many years and bring you prosperity.

Let love and faithfulness never leave you; bind them around your neck, write them on the tablet of your heart. Then you will win favour and a good name in the sight of God and man.

Trust in the Lord with all your heart and lean not on your own understanding; in all your ways acknowledge him, and he will make your paths straight.

Do not be wise in your own eyes; fear the Lord and shun evil. This will bring health to your body and nourishment to your bones.
(Proverbs 3:1–8)

For the first time, she recorded the essence of her prayer because she felt that it would be important to remember.

Lord, I know you are with me wherever I go. I think You were talking about my relationship with Rolph, whether to go ahead and enter this relationship or wait until my fears are gone.

I must know for certain that Rolph is Your choice of a husband for me. Deep down I know that he would never hurt me, but what if we don't get along? What if we fight and wish that we had remained only friends?

Thank you for the special gift you promised to give me later today and all the potential gifts that will be coming my way. Open my eyes that I may see Your wonderful spiritual gifts.

Let me recognize the qualities I need to see in Rolph. I didn't choose well the first time. If there is to be a next time, I need to hear from You. I need confirmation. I'll wait on You. Amen.

In silent contemplation, she thought that God was saying that a "fleece test" was in order. In Judges 6, Gideon, chosen to lead the Israelite army against the Midianites who greatly outnumbered them, wanted a sign that God was really talking to him. He set out a fleece of wool and asked God to make the fleece wet with dew but to keep the ground dry. The second time he reversed it: keep the wool dry and make the ground wet. It happened just as he asked. So Alison asked God to lead Rolph to bring her one white rose, which stands for the purity of the Holy Spirit, one red rose for the blood of Jesus, and a pink rose as a gift from Father God to his girl.

That's too easy.

The test must be difficult to ensure that nothing happens by chance. She decided that Rolph must say why he decided on those colours of roses and the symbolism must match hers. She knew that it was too difficult for a man to come up with the same answers by his own intellect.

***

Rolph planned to ask for another date. He also had news for Alison, so he phoned. After the preliminaries, he jumped right to his announcement.

"I have some good news for you. *The Spectator* has been swamped with requests from the public to see more of your paintings to buy, and the paper wants to do a follow-up article about your life. May I come over and discuss this, and then take you out? I can be there by six-thirty."

It was all arranged.

When Alison opened the door, Rolph was holding something. He said, "I felt an urge to get these for you."

"You're so kind."

Rolph eyes twinkled as Alison took the package.

The gift reminded her of what the Lord had told her this morning—that she was to receive a special gift, but she had assumed God was referring to a spiritual gift. She gingerly pulled open the paper then stopped as she beheld three long-stemmed roses along with greenery and baby's breath. There before her eye was the test for which she had asked. Alison's face turned pale and her eyes misted.

"Is something wrong?"

"No, nothing. I'm just surprised."

"At first I was going to buy a dozen pink roses as I pictured Father God, telling His daughter that she was precious. Then I changed my mind and chose red roses as if from Jesus—red representing his shed blood. And again I changed my mind and chose white roses to signify the purity of the Holy Spirit. As I consulted God for a moment, I decided to buy just one of each."

Alison took a deep breath and held it.

Rolph heard her gasp, and for the second time asked, "What's wrong?"

Alison let out her breath, but didn't answer.

"Are you going to tell me what this is all about?"

"I need some time alone, Rolph. There's nothing wrong, but I need to consult the Lord in prayer for a few minutes. Will you excuse me, please?"

"Yes, of course. I'll say a prayer of my own."

Alison went into her bedroom and closed the door. *Dear Lord, You are moving so fast that I can hardly catch my breath. Please be patient with me, I must make sure Rolph is the one.*

"How should his proposal sound?" This question came from deep within her spirit and she knew it was the Lord's voice, but she needed to clarify His meaning. *God, do You mean, what words should Rolph actually say?*

"Expect him to voice your heart's desire."

She didn't hear the words audibly, only the impression and the Presence that accompanied them. She knew immediately what she wanted to hear—expectation of a future ministry. Her dream was to have a home for battered women and possibly a help group that assisted people with disabilities to gain employment.

Lord, will You have Rolph propose marriage and a ministry?

She left her bedroom, hoping Rolph had not thought that she was having a serious problem. Rolph appeared to be in prayer as he sat at the table with his chin resting on his intertwined fingers. He heard her wheelchair return with its usual creak. He looked at her and smiled.

"Rolph, I have something to share with you that happened during my devotional time this morning."

"Tell me about it."

She swallowed and prayed for the right words. "I told the Lord about what I wanted in a future husband and that I needed help because I made a poor choice the first time. I remembered the story of Gideon and the fleece, and I asked God for a fleece-type test. Are you familiar with the story?"

Rolph's imagination caused him to jump ahead in his thoughts. His stomach tightened but he managed to answer, "Yes, since I was a child. Go on."

"I asked God that if you were to be in my life, you were to present me with one white, one red, and one pink rose."

"Wow!" His surprise made him take an awkward step backwards. "You mean, you believe I'm to be a part of your life, as in … husband?"

"It all depends on what happens next."

***

Rolph asked God silently, *What does she mean?*
"A proposal."
"Do you mean it all depends in how I propose to you?"
"Exactly."
"Oh, God. Oh, God." Rolph's urgent prayer was audible.

***

She looked into Rolph's eyes and felt his anticipation. Wondering what his next words might be, she knew that it must include his desire to give her love.

Rolph got on one knee. "Alison, you are the dearest woman. I love you with everything that is within me. But before I ask you the ultimate question, I want to tell you of a dream of mine. I desire someone to help me run a ministry that will give hope to lonely women, as well as their children. To help widows without a home, and the same for aimless men. My dearest wish is that you become my wife and share a lifetime of serving the Lord with me."

"Oh, my dear Rolph, I'm ready to say that four-letter word, now. I love you and I will be pleased to marry you and join you in serving the Lord."

Rolph got on both knees and gave Alison a pure kiss.

She wanted to remember its sweetness forever.

"I promise to demonstrate my love for you each day for the rest of our lives. You truly are a gift to me, beautiful Alison, and I will purpose to give you my love, always."

Instead of taking Alison out as he planned, Rolph stayed at her apartment, and they talked for hours. He was amazed at the unusual way God had made it known to Alison that they should be married. They marvelled at their common desire to have a ministry to bring healing to those who suffer. And to Alison's surprise, it was Rolph who wanted to talk about wedding plans.

chapter forty-two

"Go ahead and consult your calendar concerning a wedding date," said Rolph.

Alison went to her bedroom for the second time. When she came out, she was beaming. What do you think of a Christmassy wedding?"

"Sounds wonderful!"

"How about Saturday, December second? Will five weeks be enough time to make plans for our honeymoon?"

Rolph lifted his head to heaven and almost shouted, "Thank you, Father God." To Alison he said, "If you can be ready, so can I." With only a breath between, he announced, "Let's have our first prayer meeting."

"Since you are the future head of the home, I'll pray after you."

"You're my kind of girl." *She's perfect for me, Lord*. "Dear Heavenly Matchmaker, I approve of your choice for me. Alison is the most amazing woman. Thank you for the love you have given us. We are thinking of being married December second and we ask for Your blessings on that day.

"I also pray that I will be granted sufficient time off from work. Thank you. Amen."

Alison's choked-up voice continued. "I want to thank you as well, Father. You propelled me from not knowing if I would ever marry again, to setting the date. Help us with the plans so that this ceremony will be a witness to everyone who attends. We both want a life of serving You. It is obvious to us now that You brought us together. Thank you. Amen."

Rolph was the first one to speak after the prayer ended. "That felt so good to pray together. Kiss me goodnight."

"Good … mmmmmmmmm … night," was Alison's reply as Rolph kissed her in mid-sentence.

"Good-bye, until tomorrow."

***

"Reb, thanks for calling. It was so good of you to make it to Samantha's birthday. She hasn't stopped jabbering about it," said Christine. "And I'm the only one that can understand her."

"That's the least I could do. I owe her so much more."

"How's the job going?" asked Christine.

"Good, but I haven't saved enough for that van I was looking at."

"I have news for you. At Samantha's party, you mentioned that you wanted to transform a van into one with hand controls. Yesterday, a hand-controlled van came on the lot. I might be able to get you a deal."

"Yes! God is really on my side."

Christine had guessed why he wanted a hand-controlled vehicle. She pushed away the jealousy. Seeing the transformation in him made her glad. *The change must be because of his religion. Maybe I should look into this for myself.*

***

Oct. 31, 1977

"My name, the Most Holy One, who has brought you two together, is over you. This is not a small thing that I am doing.

My plans for you are great indeed.

"Be careful to remain holy. Rely totally on Me, for I will be your strength. All you have to do is to follow Me, and I will definitely show you the way.

"I have called both of you to the lonely and the brokenhearted. You will not have to be concerned with what you need to say, for as you open your mouth the Holy Spirit will descend on you with great power. My words will be your words. Get ready to hear the Holy Spirit speak to you during many different circumstances. Let the wave of My presence come over you.

"I will provide for everything that concerns you as long as you put Me first. Let worry be far removed from you.

"Come learn about Me. I give no thought of My own well-being because I know who I am. In the same way, know who you are in Me and that you are joined to Me. Let no one, nor anything, come between you and Me. Keep My words and I will make sure of your success. I say again, follow Me in all your ways.

"My plan for you in a ministry with Rolph is to bring the lost into the kingdom and to bring help to those who think they know who I am but have not been intimate with Me.

"Study to equip yourselves for this task. Remember, My yoke is easy and My burden is light. If you find the task is becoming heavy, know that you have fallen off course. Seek out My wisdom and I will direct you back where you should be.

"All these things are awesome for you to contemplate, but don't you realize that this was My plan for you and Rolph before you were born? I have put in you all the talents, desires, and capabilities to do this 'light' work. Keep our communication lines open and you will never veer off the course.

"How I love you both and am pleased with your desire to do My bidding. Excitement is in Me as well, as I see My plan unfolding. I rejoice over you with singing. You have come to know that I have orchestrated everything. I accept your thanks.

Oh, Lord, how I rejoice in what You are doing. I am so full of love for You and for Rolph. I'm thinking about the ministry You will have for us. Help us to lean on You and not to rush ahead, trying to make it happen on our own.

Help me to do all my tasks with peace and wisdom. Thank you again for this most wonderful man. Help me now as I finish writing the article for The Spectator. *Jesus, I love You.*

A week earlier Rolph had helped Alison formulate a human-interest story for Jordon Kind's department of the paper. He needed one that would hold people's interest.

"I believe you need a story that shows the challenges facing paraplegics. Something they'll remember. Something that has humour. Does anything come to mind?"

"The best would be my home-simulation practice with Rachelle. She was my rehab/occupational therapist. She has an excellent sense of humour. A phrase she used often was, 'Don't worry, there's still time before you're ready to leave the nest, but each chick must learn how to fly.' How do you like this title: 'Learning to Fly'?"

In a kidding manner he said, "I don't know. A reader may pass it by unless they're interested in aviation."

Alison laughed and gave him a playful slap on the arm.

***

Pleased with the story his fiancé had written, Rolph corrected a few misplaced words and some punctuation. Overall, he was impressed with her ability to express herself. Next, he found Alison in the kitchen with Sandy, whom he had met earlier when he helped hang decorations. The apartment was decorated with streamers and fall arrangements of red, orange, and gold. The table held a harvest centrepiece of painted oak leaves around a wide candle—a gift from Rolph. The aroma of pizza buns filled every room.

***

While guests were arriving at Alison's, Mac busily worked at the station, labelling the items removed from a suspect's home—a blond wig, a scrub uniform, theatrical makeup, a hospital employees' housekeeping uniform, and a female fat-suit. When he finally finished, he passed some orders to a subordinate and donned his party clothes.

***

Mac arrived to the aroma of spicy buns. "What's that smell?"

"It's Alison's favourite party food, pizza buns," responded Rolph.

"Hello, Rolph. Are they as good as they smell?"

"Time will tell. I haven't had one yet." Rolph shook Mac's hand. He thought Mac was showing signs of accepting his and Alison's new relationship. Mac seemed to want the best for Alison.

"You have a great gal there, Rolph. I'll never stop admiring Alison as long as I live. I've never known such a capable, godly girl." Mac slapped Rolph on the back. "To keep Alison's friendship, I'd better get to know you."

"I'd like that. Would you mind helping me with these chairs?" said Rolph.

Waves of titters reached the men's ears as Alison and Sandy continued to work in the kitchen. Mac knew that Alison had a roommate. He didn't know her name, but expected she'd be introduced tonight.

Once the living room was set up, the two men approached the kitchen to beg for some early handouts. As they entered, Alison heard them whispering and wheeled around to say, "I know what you guys are up to. Stay out of my kitchen!"

Mac took a long look at Alison's roommate's back. "Is that you, Miss Dailey?"

Sandy turned around to stand motionless a few inches from Mac's grinning face. Trying not to stutter, she said, "So you're Mac—Ron *Mac*kenzie."

Noticing her heated cheeks, he responded. "Have I been the object of some of your late-night conversations?"

The two women smiled at each other.

"We'll leave you ladies to do what you do best," Mac said as he and Rolph left with a pizza bun each.

Alison said to Sandy, "I think Mac likes my good friend." Sandy looked down at Alison and grinned.

***

Mac spoke to Alison privately. "Mr. Johnson, the head of physio, is invited, right?"

"Yes. Why do you want to know?"

"When he arrives, I'll have to leave for awhile."

"How long will you be gone?"

"Not long. Just go ahead with your plans and I'll join you later."

"Okay." Alison wondered what this was all about.

Every few minutes the doorbell rang. More young people from the church arrived, mostly in pairs, some by themselves. Alison had also invited everyone from the hospital who had played a major part in her recovery. Skeeter Johnson arrived with Rachelle, followed shortly by Sharon and Dr. Shapiro, and Nancy and her husband.

Mac took Skeeter aside, and then they both left without anyone noticing.

***

In the cruiser, Mac recited, "Mr. Hubert Johnson, I'm placing you under arrest for sabotages leading to aggravated assault in the acute trauma unit of the Hamilton General Hospital." Mac read him his rights and then asked him if he understood the charges.

Skeeter hung his head and nodded.

In the interrogation room, Mac found out that Skeeter had lived his childhood in the shadow of his quadriplegic brother. Skeeter's twisted mind had determined to put all "helpless geeks" out of their misery. In adulthood he pursued a job in physiotherapy, where he'd find many opportunities.

***

Mac returned before the main course was cleared.

While Alison focused on Rolph's conversation, Sandy removed the centrepiece and brought out a surprise engagement cake she'd ordered. It said Congratulations to the Couple in an arch above interlocking hearts with the initials A.P. on one heart and R.W. on the other. Wedding bells and rings decorated each corner.

Alison motioned for Sandy to bend down. She whispered, "It's wonderful, but you have the wrong initials on the one heart. It should be R.V. Rolph's last name is Vonderland."

"At the young adult group, he's registered as Rolph Wonderland."

Rolph's ears perked up as he overhead the conversation. He hadn't realized until now that he had never discussed this seeming discrepancy with Alison. "The correct spelling of my last name is 'W-o-n-d-e-r-l-a-n-d.'"

"Why do you pronounce it Vonderland if it's Wonderland?"

"That's the German pronunciation."

"So your last name is actually Wonderland?"

"Yes."

Alison started to laugh.

Rolph wanted to know, "What's so funny about Wonderland?"

"Say my name first and then your last name." She waited for his reaction.

He laughed even louder. This brought the crowd gathering around.

Rolph put his arm around Alison's shoulder and bent to whisper, "We'd better make an official announcement." Alison nodded and gave Rolph a wink.

"Ladies and gentlemen, may I have your attention." Rolph's raised voice brought a hush to the room. "This is a momentous occasion for Alison and me. I have asked Alison to marry me, and she has accepted." Cheers erupted.

Everyone expressed their congratulations as they enjoyed the cake and coffee. As the party wound down to a close, the couples left together while some singles found new soulmates. Rachelle and Jordon left together. Mac accompanied Sandy to a coffee shop, leaving Rolph and Alison alone in the apartment.

Rolph took Alison's left hand with his own and got down on one knee. "I'm glad we're alone." He removed a small, royal blue velvet box from his pocket.

Alison gasped.

"I hope you'll like what I've chosen." Rolph opened the box to reveal a pear-shaped diamond larger than Alison thought he could afford. The centre diamond was raised higher than the smaller diamonds set on each side.

"Oh, Rolph. I love it, but not as much as I love you."

"I love you, my Alison Wonderland. Look at the engraving."

She read, "U R my Gift of Love."

Rolph got up from his knees, picked up Alison from the wheelchair, and set her beside him on the sofa. "When you came into my life, I received the greatest gift. God has given you to me to love every day for the rest of my life, and eternity too."

She beheld the soft wonderment on his face as his lips left hers. "Oh, I love you." This came not just from her voice but from deep within. A small tear came to each eye as a pleasant sensation tingled her nose. No more words were needed. They had a lifetime to express all their hopes and dreams.

Watch for Kathleen's biography called, *I Knew Your Heart*, that will also have study questions concerning marital abuse.

To contact the author for speaking engagements, email her at: kreichert@cogeco.ca .